WANT YOU

JEN FREDERICK

ALSO BY JEN FREDERICK

Sacked (Knox & Ellie)

Jockblocked (Matty & Lucy)

Downed (Ace & Bryant)

Undeclared (Woodlands #1)

Undressed (Woodlands #1.5)

Unspoken (Woodlands #2)

Unraveled (Woodlands #3)

Unrequited (Woodlands #4)

Unwritten (Woodlands #5)

Losing Control (Kerr Chronicles #1)

Taking Control (Kerr Chronicles #2)

Revealed to Him

Last Hit (Hitman #1)

Last Breath (Hitman #2)

Last Hit: Reloaded (Hitman #2.5)

Last Kiss (Hitman #3)

Last Hope (Hitman #4)

ISBN: 978-1722116361

Copyright © 2018 by Jen Frederick

Cover Photo © Thomas Mathew Photography

Cover Design by Meljean Brook

ACKNOWLEDGMENTS

Not gonna lie. Writing can be tough and I wouldn't have made it through this past year without my friends. I needed every bit of encouragement they gave to me.

Eagle aka Aquila Editing: You were so patient with me and all my editing mistakes. Thank you for helping me polish this manuscript into a better finished product. All errors that exist are mine.

Anne Sowards and Christina Hobbs: Stanning BTS with you has been the best mental health medicine in the world.

Claire Contreras: Why did it take so long for us to meet? This book wouldn't have been published without your daily encouragement. Let's keep pushing each other up that publishing hill.

Jessica Clare: A day without an email from you is a dark one.

Jeanette Mancine: Your willingness to read this book in chapters was invaluable, but I treasure your friendship even more.

Lea Robinson: Thanks for understanding even the things that I can't bring myself to say.

Mel King: Your existence is precious.

Meljean Brook: Your creativity and skill in writing never ceases to awe me. The critique of my first draft made this a better book. I don't understand why you are so good at everything. Thanks for my cover. It's awesome.

Nicole: I don't know how I functioned before you. Thank you for helping me take care of business.

To Claire,
we're on this path together

PART I

1

LEKA

Scritch.

Scratch.

A rat, I think. I glance to my left to make sure. My job depends on silence and swiftness.

Instead of a small animal, I see a small human crouched in the corner, just beyond the doorway of a crumbling brick apartment building I'm using as cover. Behind her, a big wooden fence blocking off the end of the alley looms upward. Her big eyes glisten with fear.

She draws her feet closer to her, making that scratching noise. Her dirty, threadbare tennis shoes are rubbing gravel against pavement.

We both hold our breath and stare at each for a long moment. I don't know what she's thinking, but I finger the blade in my sock. Could I? I run my thumb around the hilt, imagine lifting it to the girl's chest. My hand falls away.

No.

I don't have the balls to do it.

Instead, I press a finger to my mouth. *Shhhh,* I warn silently.

I need her to be quiet. She covers her mouth with a grimy hand and nods. It's risky to trust her. She could ruin this for me unintentionally. Or she could scream and out me on purpose. I give her one last hard look before peering around the corner again.

Officer Dumbfuck has his back to me. He's feeling up a prostie. From my position, I can't tell if she's willing or just suffering through it. Most of the beat cops that work this section of the city dip their dicks in the community wells without paying. They tell the girls that payment is not getting dragged down to booking.

I feel sorry for the working girls. They get it from both ends—the pimps and the cops. And if the pimps find out that their stable is giving it away for free to the boys in blue, there's hell to pay. For those on the street, the whores have it the worst.

Nah. Strike that. Rent boys are somewhere below the girls. It's the worst sort of contest. With Stinky Steve's gang, you either serve a purpose on your feet or on your back and the only way out is a bullet in the head. I flip the silver disc between my fingers. Good thing I've got some skills, or my callouses would be on my knees, not my hands.

A clink of metal against metal provides me the signal. It's go time. Officer DF loosens his duty belt and pushes down his pants. They sag under his white, hairy ass. His fat fingers fumble with the hem of the girl's skirt. I dart forward, clinging to the shadows. He's inside of her when I reach him. Or, at least, he's busy thrusting into *something* and doesn't notice the loss of the police radio from his belt.

The prostie doesn't notice either. Her eyes are closed. Probably focusing on something pretty to get her through this bad fuck.

Because I practiced, it takes me less than thirty seconds to bust open the radio, insert the bug and then return the radio to its holster. Another thirty seconds has me back into my hiding place behind a dumpster. Good thing, too, because Officer DF is a three-pump chump. His loud groan of satisfaction fills the alleyway.

I check on the girl, whose face is filled with confusion. She mouths something to me. I can't read her lips, so I back up until my body brushes hers. I dip my head low and point to my ear.

She bends forward, whispering so lightly that I can't even feel her breath on my skin. "Is man hurt?"

I shake my head no. She slumps backward, her small brow bunched together.

There's the sound of a hand slapping flesh. I poke my head out to see that it's just him tapping the whore's ass and not her face.

"Dammit, Patty, you made me come too fast," he complains as he hauls his pants upright. "Next time you're gonna be on your knees, sucking me good. You hear me?"

Patty replies, but her voice is too quiet for me to make out the words.

It must be a yes, or something close to it, because Officer DF slaps her ass again before zipping up.

"Good girl. Now, we're going to have a probie working next week. Don't come on to him until I give you the okay. Got it?"

This time she nods.

"We don't know if he's into this or not. If he's not, he's probably a fucking twinkie, but your guy sells boys, too, right?"

Patty shrugs. "Don't know what you're talking about. I work for myself," she says.

Officer DF pinches her chin. "You lie to me and it won't be good for you."

Patty twists her head out of his grip—which I think is a bad idea. She's thin and small. A bundle of toothpicks held together by stretchy fabric. The cop agrees. He punches her in the gut. She folds in half, her cry of pain filling the alleyway. My fist clenches at my side, and my gut churns at my own helplessness, but I'm no hero. If I go out and help Patty, I'm gonna get nailed.

There's a tug on the back of my T-shirt. I turn to see the little girl twisting the cloth into her fist. She's trembling like a leaf in a windstorm. I peel her fingers away and give her a rough shake of my head. I can't have her hanging on me or distracting me. She retreats into the shadows, a tiny ball of misery.

I'd feel bad, but I don't have the luxury of pity—haven't had it. Ever.

I direct my attention back to the cop. He's our biggest danger. The cop hauls Patty upright by her hair. Black streaks down from her eyes, and the red on her lips she used to attract the cop's attention is smeared, clown-like, around her mouth.

"You going to treat my probie right next week?" he asks.

Patty nods obediently.

"Good." He yanks hard on her hair once more before releasing her. She stumbles but manages to right herself. "And brush your goddamned teeth next time. You taste like a fucking ashtray."

He wipes his hand across his mouth. Creep had his dick in Patty's pussy and he's mad about the taste of her mouth. That shit is stupid and wrong. He adjusts his gear belt, gives her a brief nod and walks off. His boot heels make a crunching noise as he stomps out of the alley.

Patty waits until he's cleared the opening of the alley before scurrying out.

I give her a minute head start before creeping forward. A squeak of anxiety escapes the little girl behind me.

"I'm checking to make sure it's all clear. I'll be back. Promise."

Her big dark eyes have tears in them. Whatever her age is, she knows one important thing. Most promises aren't worth shit.

I reach under the hem of my jeans and tug the wad of money out of my sock. I hand it to her. "This is all the cash I got in the world. If you don't believe I'll come back for you, believe I'll come back for that."

She doesn't make a move to take it, so I stuff it into her lap, my hand brushing against her bony ribcage. My own stomach clenches sympathetically. I haven't had a crumb today either.

"After I check out Officer Dickhead, we'll eat. Keep my loot safe. 'Kay?"

That earns me a tiny nod. Good enough.

I spring to my feet and hug the shadows as I make my way to the sidewalk. Patty is a block down, getting shoulder pats from the other girls in the stable. The cop is in his patrol car, head down, doing fuck knows what. I flip my hood up and continue in the opposite direction until I reach a black, ten-year-old El Camino. The window rolls down just far enough so I can see a fist and a thumb pointing upward.

I don't stop or nod or give a hand signal in return. I just keep walking. The listening device has been planted, and from the sign of approval, it's working. From what I gathered this morning, the bug I planted allows my boss to listen in to a private police channel on the radio. He thinks the cops he bought might be working against him—either with a rival gang or a plant from the feds.

I walk two more blocks down, in case the eyes in the El Camino are watching me. Then I hang a right. Hunching low, sticking to the dark spaces, I make my way through backyards and alleys until I reach the wooden fence. I run up the brick wall and use the angle to propel myself high enough to grab the top of the fence. Effortlessly, the momentum carries me over. I drop to the ground, tucking myself into a ball and rolling to a stop not far from the girl, who hasn't moved an inch.

I find the wad of money tucked exactly where I left it.

"You hungry?" I ask, dusting myself off.

She nods.

"Come on, then." I jerk my head toward the side door of the apartment building. It opens after a sharp kick.

She follows behind me, moving lightly and quietly. Her tennies don't make any noise. *Quick learning*, I think. I lead her up the stairs, looking for the right apartment. The third one down, left side with small tennis shoes on the mat next to a larger pair of work boots, fits the bill. Slipping my knife out of my sock, I make quick work with the lock.

The apartment is dark. I position the girl by the front door and motion for her to stay. Silently, I move down the hall. The living room is empty. There are two bedroom doors, one is slightly ajar. The junk inside tells me it's the mom's room.

I twist the knob of the other room. Jackpot. There's a doll on the floor and a stuffed animal on the bed. Inside a small dresser, I find what I need. I jam the stuff under my own shirt and then leave two twenties on the dresser. I take the girl to the stairwell.

I hand her everything. "Can you dress yourself?"

She stares at the pile of stuff in her arms and then at me. Sighing, I take the clothes and drop them on the floor. Holding up the jeans, I say, "Legs in."

She places a tiny thin hand on my shoulder for balance and steps into the clothes. They're way too big for her, but shit, too big is better than the ripped, dirty thing she's got on. I motion for her to pull the nightgown up over her head and then turn around. I can hear her struggling but keep my eyes down. At the small tap in the middle of my back, I twist around to see her dressed, with the sweatshirt on backwards. It's good enough.

I roll up the sleeves three times before the tips of her fingers peek out. The socks, which I think are ankle ones, go up to her shins.

Resting on my haunches, I take a look at her. She's a drowned rat in this stuff. I pull the last piece off the floor. It's a knit cap. I fit it over her head, tucking her long hair up until there's not a strand hanging down.

"I'm hungry," I tell her, getting to my feet. "Let's eat."

She follows me down the three flights of stairs. We exit out the back of the building—away from the cop, Patty, and the El Camino. I'm a fast learner, too. You have to be to survive on the streets. Information is key. The more you know about a person, the more you can control them.

So I keep all my shit locked down tight. Not that I have a lot of shit right now. Other than the cash that's back in my sock and a few other pieces I've managed to squirrel away, I don't own anything. But I will. Someday.

2

LEKA

Right now, I'm living in a solid two-bedroom off the blue line train in Midtown. Most of Stinky Steve's gang lives in a house on the north end of Jackson Heights, shoved together like sardines in a can. They call it the Pie House because that's where they do all their fucking. It smells like rancid spunk and shit-streaked underwear.

I spent two nights there dodging piss buckets the older guys balance on the top of doors in hopes that the victim gets a yellow shower. Maybe I would've taken that, but when they started trying to shove crap up my ass so I could prove to them I was a man, I lit out. I'd rather sleep on the street.

I did that for a couple months until I stumbled onto this particular setup. Two years ago, I was trailing a realtor, Mike, who was dating the boss's sister. Stinky Steve runs a crew of about a dozen who deal mostly in stolen electronics. He rose to power after pulling off a robbery of a thousand iPhones. Sure, that was eight years ago and it was a single job, but that's all it takes in our world. Plus, Stinky Steve's got good instincts.

He knows things about people, like how the delivery employee in charge of all those phones would be easy to flip with the promise of new wheels, or how tying his boat to the Big Boss would protect him from the Tong gang that is cutting into everyone's profits, or how cutting off the thumb of his second-in-command for leaving a partial fingerprint at a scene would make everyone in the crew fall in line forever

Stinky Steve thought the mark was cheating on his sister. He was right. The realtor fucked a lot of his clients, usually in the condos and town homes that he was listing. These places had lockboxes, a little metal box that hung on the door handle. Inside the metal box was a key. Sometimes the metal boxes had a key code, but other times, Mike, the realtor, would just use this magical thing called a master key.

One day while he was busy fucking a client in somebody's bedroom, I copied the master key. Since then, I've surfed from one nice apartment to another. In a city this big, there's always an apartment for sale.

My current digs have been empty for months. I heard it's because someone died here and whoever owns it doesn't want to come off the "fucking ridiculously high" asking price, as Mike had screamed into the phone the other day. I hope it never sells. It's the perfect place for me—close to the subway with a street side entrance that's supposed to be for staff and deliveries. There's a drugstore and grocery a block away. There's even a library that's big enough to hide in. In this place, I can pretend I'm not a twelve-year-old thug who'd rather keep all his fingers than interfere with a prostie getting beaten by a cop.

This is where I take the girl. I don't know why I'm making all these risky decisions. Jerkoff Jon, the head of the Pie House, would've snuffed her out, but not before violating her. He's that sick of a dude. One day I wouldn't mind sticking a railroad pike through his forehead.

"You need to use the bathroom?" I ask the girl, closing the door behind us.

She's stunned silent as she takes in the tall ceilings and white walls. It's the cleanest place she's probably ever seen.

"Bathroom?" I ask again.

She nods slowly.

"You think this is the shit, you should see some of the other places Mike has for sale. There's this place uptown that has three bedrooms and a view of the park. You been to the park?" That place is amazing—a green island in the middle of this grimy, sick city. There are places, deep in the heart, where you can't hear anything but your own quiet breath.

She doesn't answer. Other than asking me if the prostie was hurt, the only sounds I've ever heard her make were squeaks. It don't matter much to me one way or another. I like the quiet.

I flip on the lights to the bathroom. "Here. I've got one towel, but that's it. I hope you don't mind." I pause. "Do you know how to wash yourself?"

She stares at me and then the shower and then back at me.

I crouch down to her level. "How old are you?"

She lifts her hand, unfurling her tiny fingers one by one until they are splayed like a starfish.

"Five, huh?"

There's a hesitation followed by a small nod. I get it. She's not sure. I'm not either. When you're born on the street, the days and months and years all blur together.

"Okay. Do you shower? Cuz I can't remember if I knew how to shower when I was five."

Her shoulders lift.

"Bath?"

After a second of hesitation, her head bobs. I reach behind her and plug the tub drain. I wonder how much water she needs.

"You like a lot of water?"

She looks uncertain but still won't talk.

"Do you know how to talk?"

Another tiny nod and then, "yeah," comes out in a whisper.

"So shower or bath."

"Bath," she says.

"Got a name?"

She rubs the tip of her toe into the tile. A word swooshes out of her mouth, but I don't catch it. Not fully. *New chance? Noosance.* Oh hell no. Nuisance? I'm not calling her that.

"Yeah, I can't pronounce that," I lie. "You got a nickname?"

"Noosance," she repeats.

I rub a hand across my forehead. We'll have to think of another name because I'm sure as hell not calling her a nuisance.

"My name is Leka, but everyone calls me Monkey."

This time she shakes her head.

"No? You don't like that?"

"No," she says.

"You don't like that?"

She shakes her head more vigorously. "It's not nice. You're nice."

I rock back on my heels. She doesn't like Monkey? "I don't love it either, but you're called what you're called. It's not a fight I want to take on."

She presses her lips together as if she wants to say something but is afraid to.

"What?" I prod.

We stare at each other, but she doesn't utter another peep. I shut off the water.

"Hop in. And don't drown."

I run into my bedroom and pull out a towel that I pilfered two apartments ago. That one was all furnished with towels and shit. No clothes, though. The towels were just for show. Afterward, I heard the mark complain on the phone that a prospective buyer must've lifted those.

I've taken a few other things. Food, if I could find it. Towels, a couple of pans, plates, forks and spoons. I can't have too many belongings because I'm carting this shit from place to place, but enough so it's not like I'm living on the street. I hate that feeling.

When I return to the bathroom, the little bit is in the tub. The too-big clothes I stole for her in a neat pile on the floor. She can't really fold, but she's tidy. I like that.

I place the towel and a bar of soap on the toilet. "Sorry. I don't have shampoo and shit. I just use the soap."

"Is okay," she says, like I need reassuring.

"Great." I head out. At the door, I call over my shoulder. "I'm going to make some soup." Cans of tomato soup and a couple of pieces of bread is all I've got here. I can't keep much around in case someone wants to come and see the place. "Wash up and when you're done come out."

I've barely got the can of soup dumped into the pot before she appears behind me wearing the oversized sweatshirt. Water drips down behind her.

"Shit, girl, you scared me." I peer down at the top of her dark hair, lying in little waves around her head. "You wash already?"

She nods vigorously and points to the stove. I don't have to ask what she wants. Her belly grumbles loudly. She claps her hands around her waist and folds over, embarrassed by the sound. Eating is more important to her than being clean.

I rub my forehead. This poor girl is fucked up. The brief image I glimpsed of her scrawny body in the tub is seared into my head. I could count each individual rib. She needs more than me taking care of her. What do I know about little girls?

I pour the half-heated soup into a mug and pull out a loaf of bread. I break the loaf in half and place both the bread and the soup on the floor in front of her.

"Sorry I don't have a table."

Surprisingly, she doesn't fall on her food right away. Instead, she sits down cross-legged and gives me an expectant look.

"Don't worry about me," I reassure her. "I'm eating the same thing." I grab a spoon and the remainder of the bread and join her on the floor.

I don't waste my breath talking to her. Even if she was a talker, she wouldn't be able to say a word. She's too busy shoving food into her mouth.

As I eat, I run through the few options I have for her. Beefer is the guy I report to. He's got two little ones and is probably the best suited to taking care of this girl. But Beefer's not happy with the two he has. He's always complaining about how they're greedy animals who'd bite off his hand if it didn't hold the checkbook. That's why he always has to fuck one of the girls from the stable.

He still has to pay for the girls. It's just at a discount. Everyone in the organization has to pay for their use of the girls except for the big guy. At least, that's what the birds chirp about when they get together.

I've never spoken to the boss. I don't know that he knows I work for him. I'm too far down on the food chain. For now, that's a good thing. But I know if I am going to stick around, I need to be good at something. I have to offer the big guy value. From what I've seen, if you want to wear the suit and eat at the table with the boss, you need to be good with money or good with a gun.

I'm not good with money. I don't have much, and at the rate I'm saving it up, I doubt I'll ever have enough to buy my way to the table. But I can be good with the gun. I can be violent and cruel and harsh. It's the only way to stay alive in this world.

I consider the girl. She's so fragile that a strong breeze would tear her apart. She's not going to survive with Beefer. Stinky Steve's kids are older than me. None of the other families that work for Steve would want to take her in either. They'd see her as baggage. Another expensive mouth to feed.

Sensing my attention, she pauses, a piece of bread in her mouth. Haltingly, she pulls the uneaten portion out of her mouth and offers it to me. Yeah, there's no way I can give her to Beefer.

Besides, why does she need to go anywhere? I've kept myself alive since I was her age. I was on the streets since I was barely older than she is. If there's anything I know how to do, it's survive. I can teach that to her, right?

She offers me the bread again.

"Nah, I'm good." I hold up my end of the loaf. "I got half, remember. And there's more where that came from." I swallow the rest of my soup and pick up her empty cup. After washing the dishes, I stick them in the drawer under the stove. It's the one place most people don't pull open.

"Look, I've got to go and meet someone and get us more food."

She stands immediately. A bunch of crumbs tumble out of her sweatshirt onto the floor, crunching under her feet as she turns to run. I catch her frail, matchstick-thin arm. "Wait. You can't come with me."

Her eyes widen and pool with water.

Oh shit.

"I'm coming back," I declare. Her upper lip trembles. I crouch down. "I'm going to leave all my shit here with you, and I need you to protect it for me. Can you do that?"

The trembling lip gets sucked in and she gives me a brave jerk of her head.

With a sigh of relief, I stand. "I'm going to make a bed for you. Try to sleep while I'm gone." I doubt she will, though.

I lead her into a small bedroom—the one Mike says is for guests. I've got all my shit stuffed into a closet. The blanket will make a nice bed for her. I rearrange a few things and pat the bed of clothes with my hand. "Climb in. I'll be back as soon as I can. Stay here and be quiet."

She gives me another of those tiny nods before settling in. I close one of the closet doors, leaving the other one slightly ajar. Before I leave, I make a sweep of the apartment, cleaning up all signs that we were here— just in case there's a surprise showing. I doubt there will be. This place hasn't had any takers for a while. She should be safe.

IT TAKES ME TWENTY MINUTES TO GET OVER TO MARJORY'S Cafe where Beefer is. He's sitting in a back booth with a girl who doesn't look much older than me tucked under his arm. Her hands are under the table and Beefer's face is flushed red. Could be the booze but could be the girl's hands on his dick. Could be both.

"Hey there, Monkey. You did good." He slides a few bills across the table with one hand. The other is busy under the girl's halter, fondling her tit. Close up, I now see that the girl is a little older, wearing a fuckton of makeup to disguise the marks of her drug use.

I count out the twenties. There are five of them. I stuff the bills in my back pocket. Not much money, but I didn't do much work either. Just standing around watching and then planting the listening device. That said, there's no way I'm supporting myself, the girl, and putting any green away for the future doing these small jobs. Complaining about how much he's paying me won't get me a raise. He'll slap me across my face and then withhold work until I come crawling back.

He did that to a kid a month ago.

"How do I make more?"

"More what?" He pauses his fondling.

"More money."

"A hundred isn't good enough for you?" He pinches the girl's nipple. "You keep working," he tells her before turning his attention back to me. "I'll have another job for you. Come back next week."

I pretend to think it over. "Okay. Maybe Rod has work."

Beefer sits upright, jolting the girl next to him. "You're my kid," he protests. Rod is Stinky Steve's idiot cousin. The guy couldn't hit a target five feet in front of him, bolted to the floor. Still, Beefer worries that Rod's going to be promoted and then it'll be Rod in this booth at Marjory's getting hand jobs from drug-addled girls too young to know better.

I remain silent. Better to look disinterested. Out of the corner of my eye, I see the girl lean over the table and take a snort. I hadn't even seen the drugs when I walked in.

With an internal sigh, I realize I could deal. There are kids my age that are trafficking in pills and meth. The turnover rate is high. In the past, it seemed like a good way to get shivved in some back alley, but I'm bigger now and the product doesn't tempt me. I know it's good money.

"You." He taps the girl on the shoulder. "Get gone."

She swoops down for another snort and then hustles off. I keep standing.

Beefer waves a hand at the left-over drugs. "Want some?"

"No thanks."

"Good kid. Keeping your nose clean is half the battle." He laughs a little at his own joke. He jerks his head toward the seat opposite him. "Sit down."

I do as I'm told.

"How old are you?"

I try to recall whether I told him how old I was before. I don't think I did. Still, best to hedge here. "Old enough."

He snorts. "That's a politician's answer. I'm guessing you aren't more than twelve because you don't sound like your balls have dropped yet, but Christ, you're big for your age."

I remain silent.

"Fine. If you don't want to tell me, you don't have to." He motions for me to lean in which I do. "Here's the deal. We listened to the cop, and the boss doesn't like what he heard. He wants the cop gone. You get rid of him and I'll pay you five large."

My heart thumps madly and I'm glad my shaking hands are on my lap under the table where Beefer can't see them. As coolly as possible, I say, "Is the boss hurting for money?"

"No. Fuck no," Beefer exclaims. "We're the biggest operation on this coast. We're rolling in it."

Then why the fuck are you offering me five Gs? Of course, I don't hit him with that. Instead, I go for the ego again. "I heard the Tong gang pays a half million for one hit."

"A half mil—" He cuts himself off. "Look, kid, you want this job, the most I can pay is fifteen."

Fifteen thousand? I dig my nails into my palms to keep the surprise off my face. "I guess. If that's all the boss can afford. How should it be done?" I ask, as if I've done this a thousand times before.

"Execution-style."

I clench my back teeth to keep the dismay off my face. "When?"

"Tonight." He leans back, spreading his arm across the back of the bench. His expression says he thinks I'm going to fail.

I slide out of my chair. "I'll see you later."

3

LEKA

"You're wet," she says when I creep into the spare room.

I'm too tired to be shocked that she's decided to talk.

"Yeah, I took a shower." Shooting someone in the face is surprisingly messy. I wasn't prepared for the splatter. I will be next time. My stomach clenches. *Next time.*

I rub a hand across my forehead and toss the sleeping bags I picked up onto the floor.

"Hey, come on out. I got us some different shi—stuff to sleep on." I'm too weary to wait for her to come out of the closet. Instead, I unroll the bags and place a couple towels under hers. Tomorrow I'll get a pillow.

I drop to my ass and wriggle down into the tube of nylon. The minute my head hits the floor, my eyes float shut.

A few moments later, I feel the weight of her stare. I twist around and find her standing inches from my head.

"What's up?"

"Do you—" She points toward my body. "Should I—" She wrings her small hands together. It's weird hearing her talk. She must really need something.

I prop myself up on an elbow. "You need to go to the bathroom? Hungry?"

When she doesn't say anything, I drop back to the bag. Little people are kinda freaky, I decide. My eyes drift shut again. I'm so fucking worn out. Pulling that trigger wasn't easy tonight. I thought it would be. Don't know why. It's not like I thought it was going to be movie-like, but I didn't think I'd still be tasting the copper of the man's blood on my tongue hours later. I shudder a little and pull the corner of the bag up higher so the kid can't see me. I don't like looking weak in front of anyone. Not even a five-year-old.

I sense, more than hear, her shuffle near. Out of the corner of my eye, I spot her little ankles. Then her knees as she bends down. Then her— I lunge forward, grab her arms and jerk her into a sitting position. Bile shoots up my throat.

"What the fuck?" I yell.

She jerks back, stumbling and tripping over the sleeping bag I'd laid out for her. She draws her knees up, close to her chest, until all I can see is her little peanut head sticking out the top of the large sweatshirt, like a round jack-in-the box. Her body starts shaking.

I crawl over to her, unsure of what to do. I run a light hand down her back.

"Shit. I didn't mean to shout at you," I say. She trembles even harder, so I shift away. "I'm not mad. You just caught me off-guard." Still nothing. "Can I get you something? Like a water?"

I run a hand over my face. What in the hell do I do now? I probably scared the shit out of her. But to be fair, she scared the shit out of me. If this is the shit she was doing, no wonder she ran away.

"Do you want me to leave?" I ask. Maybe I make her uncomfortable. She's obviously been abused in ways that I don't even want to think about.

I'm about to take off when she turns and throws herself at me. Just launches herself like a rocket and all I can do is catch her. I stagger and then drop to my knees. She clings to me like a scared kitten I just saved from drowning.

I pat her lightly on the back, getting angrier and angrier with each passing moment. Yeah, a lot of kids out there are abused. Most of the girls that walk the streets probably were raped or assaulted or beaten at some point. I've got a couple scars on my back, but holding this tiny human as she sobs, part from fear and part from relief, makes me want to fish the gun I tossed into the river and put a bullet into every dick that I see.

"It's going to be okay," I assure her.

I'm not sure she hears me, but her head digs into my chin as she nestles close. I don't know how long we sit there, but eventually her heaves turn to sniffles and then to snores. My legs are numb by then. I lift her up and stretch out. I try to lay her onto the sleeping bag, but she's velcroed herself tight against me, even in sleep. I give up trying to separate us.

Since she doesn't weigh more than a bag of flour, it's easy enough to hold her with one arm and unzip the two bags. I lie down on one and throw the other on top of us. She remains asleep the entire time.

I'm out of my element. I haven't had to care for someone other than myself for years. I don't remember my parents. I assume I had a mom, but I don't remember her. Some of the other kids that work for Steve talk about their shitty parents—often with a confusing hint of longing. Take Gerry Lester, for example. One minute the ginger is moaning about how he misses his ma and the next he's whining about how she'd burn his arm with her cigs if he didn't move fast enough to get her a beer.

I drift off to sleep. I'd gotten sick after the cop killing, and as I was coming home, I wondered how I'd get the stomach to make my second kill, but I'm thinking it won't be hard if I imagine it's the person that hurt this girl. She's a pure and innocent thing. No one should be hurting her. No one.

"HEARD YOU OFFED A PIG LAST NIGHT." GERRY WAGGLES HIS thick, peach-colored eyebrows at me. He looks like he's got two caterpillars attached to his forehead and he tends to move them around a lot. It gives me the willies, but Gerry's a decent guy, so I hide my response.

As part of my day job, I work at Marjory's. Who the hell Marjory is, I have no clue. It belongs to the Big Boss—the one that turns Stinky Steve into a slavering fool. There aren't many customers here other than the ones that work for Steve. As I understand it, cash businesses like this one wash the under-the-table money clean. Marjory could lose money every year and Stinky Steve and his boss would still be smiling.

"Don't know what you're talking about." I heft another flour bag off the truck. The girl is definitely lighter than one of these. I'll have to take some food home for her tonight. She's not going to fatten up on the bread and soup in the apartment. I toss the bag to Gerry, who catches it and stacks it inside the door.

"What was it like?" he asks.

"What was what like?" I'm not admitting to loose-lipped Gerry I killed a cop. I might as well hang a neon sign around my neck that says *arrest me and make me your prison bitch*. I toss another sack to Gerry and then throw the last two onto my shoulder before hopping off the truck.

After dropping the bags off, I turn to the two guys slurping down a plate of noodles and gravy. "Truck's unloaded and you're good to go."

I wonder what these guys do for the Big Boss. One's got a belly that hangs at least two inches over his belt and the other is whip-thin. I don't see muscle or enforcer in their build. Not like Beefer, who's all muscle and neck.

The curly-haired one with the high forehead and flat nose looks at his phone. "That was quick."

I shrug. No sense in wasting time. Maybe these guys *just* do deliveries. That can be a difficult job, especially when you're moving illegal product. I recall the hollow sound as I traipsed across the metal floor of the truck. I open my mouth to say something and then snap it shut.

I don't know these guys, and they don't know me. If I mention the false floor, they could decide I'm a liability. I save my observation for Beefer. He's the guy who recruited me, and he's who I report to. I give the two guys a brief nod and return to the stockroom. Gerry's got the door propped open and a cigarette in his mouth.

"You want to do the dry goods or the fresh ones?" I jerk a thumb toward the crates of tomatoes.

Gerry makes a face. "Dry."

Of course he'd say that. Fresh stuff takes more effort and care, and Gerry's a lazy motherfucker with a big mouth. He runs it all morning as we unpack the stock. The meat and cheeses were delivered earlier. Now, we're dealing with dry goods and produce.

"I was two blocks over when Mort got offed. Remember him?" Gerry says. It's not really a question. Gerry can talk for hours without any prompting. "He was the dealer on 90th and E street. I once saw him snort his product off the back of his hand. How bad of a druggy do you gotta be that you gotta have a hit while you're working?"

He rips open a bag of flour and dumps it into the holding bin while I stack the tomato crates in the corner.

"Anyway, it was pow pow pow. Three shots." Gerry holds up his middle fingers. "I ran over and there was blood and brains and guts everywhere."

"Guts, too?" I say. Blood and brain, I could see. Guts, not so much.

That would require a shot in the belly, and if you're doing a headshot, what's the point?

"Yeah, all of it. Gore everywhere. It was like everyone who ever ate at Marjory's barfed it all up in one place."

"Nice."

The parsley and other herbs go into the walk-in cooler. In here, Gerry's blather is muted. I can barely make out the sounds—just that he's talking.

"—He was staring straight up to the sky. It was freaky, man. You ever see a dead person?"

Last night. I make a sound in the back of my throat. It's enough to set my co-worker off again.

"Right. Anyway, whoever shot him was long gone, so we did a field strip. Took his belt, shoes, glasses. I sold those glasses on the street for 10 bucks. Pretty great, eh?"

"Like you found a lottery ticket," I say. It occurs to me that if anyone would know about where the girl came from, it'd be Gerry.

"You hear anything about a runaway? A kid?" I ask him, helping him finish with the flour and sugar.

His brows beetle together. "Like a new recruit for Beefer?"

"No. Like a...street kid."

Gerry continues to appear puzzled. "Don't know of anyone new. There are some funny talkers"—that's what Gerry calls foreigners—"but they're always in and out."

Is that what she is? A refugee? A foreigner? Nah, she doesn't talk with any kind of accent. And she understands me just fine.

"You see something?"

I place the last of the lemons into the bin and then bend down to gather up the empty cardboard boxes. I gesture for Gerry to open the door for me.

"Did you?" he presses.

"I thought I saw someone the other day who I didn't recognize, but when I went back the kid was gone."

"Where was it?"

"Over on M."

"By the Stop and Shop?"

"Yup," I lie.

"Probably some rat from the subway. There're kids who live down there. They got the weird eyes and everything." He shudders. "They freak me out. So you going to do wet work from now on?"

"Does it look like it?" I ask, punching the boxes flat.

Gerry picks up a rock and chucks it down the alley. "I guess not. If I was doing wet work, I wouldn't be hauling trash at Marjory's. I'd be sitting in the front of the house, eating linguini and getting prime pussy."

"Ger, you wouldn't know what to do with a pussy if it came up and sat itself on your mouth." I dust my hands off on my jeans. If Gerry has been within sniffing distance of a real live girl's snatch, I'll eat the boxes I just tossed into the recycler.

He flushes "Fuck you, Monkey. Like you've punched that V-card. I've had plenty of pussy. I'm getting pussy every weekend. I have to beat the bitches off."

I shrug and walk away. Where Ger sticks his dick doesn't interest me.

I've been gone for three hours. The girl was sleeping when I left, but I placed a bowl of cereal on the floor with a note that there was milk in the refrigerator. I figure if she can clean herself, she can pour milk into a bowl. I was doing it at five, wasn't I? Still, I need to get back to her.

Keeping her safe is becoming important to me. More important than most things.

I don't know why, but I'm not sure the *why* matters.

4

LEKA

"Speaking of prime pussy, look who's coming our way," Ger exclaims.

I glance up to see Mary Shaughnessy saunter into the stockroom with a half-full pitcher of coffee in one hand and a carry out container in the other. Mary, tall and curvy, is one of the prettiest girls I've ever seen in real life. According to the other birds, all those pretty things are courtesy of Beefer's wallet. Her nose, chest, lips and ass have all been under the needle or knife. Whatever. It looks good.

"Hey, sweetheart, Carl wanted me to give this to you." She flashes me a smile as she hands me the white styrofoam container. She's also one of the few that call Beefer by his first name.

"What is it?" Ger asks, crowding over my shoulder.

She bends down to tap Ger on the nose. He flushes the same red shade as her lipstick. "Now, if Carl wanted you to know, he wouldn't have put it in a box, would he?"

Ger's eyes fall to the ground. "Guess not."

"Carl needs a coffee refill. Could you do that for me?" She hands him the coffee pot.

He dawdles for a moment, clearly not wanting to leave and miss out on whatever Mary wants to tell me without Ger hearing.

"Ger," I say tersely. You don't keep Beefer waiting for anything. The last time one of us rats made him wait, Beefer beat the shit out of the kid. The kid, Loose-lipped Lou, couldn't see straight for a week after.

Ger gives me the stink-eye but takes the pot and skedaddles out front.

"That was nice and commanding of you," Mary coos. She doesn't need to bend down to tap me on the nose. I realize I'm almost as tall as she is. Too bad. I kinda liked it when I was boob high.

"Beefer doesn't like to be kept waiting," I say.

"So true." Her painted lips come together. "Honey, I heard you're taking on more, ah…" She pauses as she tries to find the right word.

I don't help her.

She scrunches her nose. "Responsibilities. That's as good of a word as any. Anyway, you're taking on more responsibilities. You sure you want to go down this road?"

I take a step back and cross my arms, the styrofoam cracking in my grasp. I don't like that Mary knows I killed the cop. Is Beefer whispering shit across his pillow to her? I decide to deny it. "Don't know what you're talking about."

She places her hands on my shoulders. "You're a sweet boy, Monkey. You could do so many other things with your life."

It takes effort not to flinch away. I'm not a fan of being close to others. "Like what?"

She steps closer. The lack of space between us makes the hairs of my neck rise. She's so close that if she takes a deep breath, the tits that are nearly pouring out of her low-cut waitress top would brush against my chest. I glance past her. If Beefer would come through the stainless steel doors separating the stockroom from the kitchen, I doubt he'd like our positions. Is Mary really so dumb she'd try something with Beefer less than fifty feet behind her? Is this some kind of fucked up test? An initiation? Kill someone for the boss and you get your willie sucked by the prettiest waitress in the hood?

Her hand comes up to sweep my hair out of my face, reminding me that I need a haircut and have needed one for the last six, or has it been eight, months. "You could drive a taxi or do construction. There's honest work out there."

For a twelve-year-old? "How old do you think I am, Mary?"

"Old enough that you should know better than to get involved with these guys. It's a bad business and you're such a handsome kid. Too handsome to be here working for Carl. You stay in the game and you'll get hard, scarred and dried up." The last is said in a whisper as her lips brush the top of my ear. "I'd hate to see that for you."

That's too much closeness for me. Stiffly, I move away. "I need to get home." If this is a test, I'm okay with failing it.

She tugs on the neckline of her dress. "All by yourself? I'll see if Carl wants me to walk you home."

"No. I'm good. When does Beefer need me back?"

"You know what I'm offering, right?" She reaches around and taps the top of my styrofoam box. "For a little of what you got in there, you can have some of this." She spreads her hand across her chest and down lower.

"When does Beefer need me back?" I repeat.

Her mouth turns down and her eyes narrow and suddenly, she doesn't seem as pretty as she was when she first walked in. "At seven," she says tersely.

"Thanks, Mary."

"I'm not making this offer again," she snipes, but she says it to my back because I'm out of the door.

I don't look in the container until I'm at the apartment complex. I didn't want anyone catching a glimpse of it on the street. Folks around here have been killed for a ten-dollar bill or a pair of tennis shoes. A stack of green this big could've sent a gang after me.

In the quiet of the stairwell, I finally give in to my curiosity. A white envelope lies inside the container and inside the envelope, a stack of green. Despite the urge to count it, I stuff the envelope into the back of my jeans and take the rest of the stairs two at a time.

I knock on the door so I don't scare the girl. "It's me," I call out. I press an ear to the door but don't hear a thing. When I peek inside, the apartment looks the same—empty and sterile. I make a lot of noise, again so I don't scare her.

I find her huddled in the closet.

"Anyone come here while I was gone?"

"No."

"Good. You hungry?"

She shakes her head, but her stomach growls.

I can't help but grin. "Me, too. Let's go get some real food."

She starts to rise when I hear a sound. I press my finger to my lips in a totally unnecessary move and then hustle to the door. The sound comes again, and I realize it's a key in the door. *Fuck.* The realtor is here, and from the sounds of it, there are people outside.

I run to the closet and grab everything. With the two sleeping bags, it's almost too much for me to handle, but I manage to stuff half of one in my backpack. I can't do much about the milk in the fridge or the pans under the sink, but I've got money to replace those. With a hand on her back, I urge her toward the window and the fire escape.

"You're going to love this place," I hear the realtor's voice announce. "It has two bedrooms, which, you know, is impossible to get in the city at this price."

I push open the window. Cool morning air blasts us. The girl climbs through, and I shove all the shit out onto the fire escape. "Up," I mouth. She climbs up the stairs like the monkey I'm nicknamed after.

"How long has it been for let?" a male voice asks.

"A month, give or take," comes the smarmy response.

Bullshit. The place has been empty for at least three. I toss the bags up and then scramble up the stairs.

"The window," the girl urges.

"Oh, fuck." I heave off the backpack and swing down the side of the fire escape, dropping as lightly as possible. I grab the window sash and start to press it down when the realtor and his two clients enter the spare room. I drop to the bottom of the landing and roll myself flat against the side of the wall.

"This room's closet is small," the woman says.

"It's the city. You're not going to get big closets and two bedrooms in the city at this price," Mike advises.

"It's cold in here. Are the utilities included?" the woman asks.

"It's covered by the maintenance fee," he answers. "Feel free to crank it up as high as you want. Ladies—they always like to keep things hot, don't they?"

I don't hear an answer, which means the clients have moved on. I glance up. The master bedroom shares the same fire escape. The open iron work of the landing digs into my shoulder. The girl is curled into a ball behind the sleeping bags. She's good at hiding. I don't like thinking about how she picked that skill up.

My hiding skills are well-honed, too. Last night, I broke into the cop's apartment and sat in his closet until he came home. He changed, shat, brushed his teeth and then climbed into bed—all without figuring out another human was sharing the same space as him.

I plugged him while he was watching a porno. It might've been safer to kill him while he was sleeping, but that didn't sit right with me. I kinda regret the decision. I'll be seeing his wide-eyed shock in my dreams for a long time.

It takes fucking forever for the realtor and his clients to leave. I make the girl wait out on the fire escape until the realtor gets into his car and drives away. Finally, I go retrieve her.

Her legs are wet and she smells like urine. Poor kid.

I carry her into the bathroom and turn on the bathtub, making sure the water is only lukewarm. "Wash up real quick. We're going to find a new place."

"This not yours?" she asks quietly.

"No. I'm squatting, but I have some money, so we'll go and stay in a hotel tonight."

Her face is blank when I say that. She doesn't know what a hotel is, but, hell, at her age, I probably didn't either.

I shut the door and hurry into the kitchen. The refrigerator is empty and the milk is gone. The realtor must have dumped it. He knows something is wrong, then. My instincts are right. We can't stay here another night. The biggest problem I have is that I don't have an ID. I can't rent an apartment. Shit, I don't even know if I can get a hotel room.

I scrub my hair back. What'd Mary say? That I looked old enough? I straighten my shoulders. Okay, then. Step one. Get an ID. On the streets, you can buy anything. I just need to find a place to stash the girl until I can get the ID.

I pack up everything, attaching the two sleeping bags to the backpack —one on top and one underneath. I tug the pack over my shoulders and knock on the bathroom door. "You ready?"

The door opens and she comes out, carrying the towel all carefully folded as best as her little hands could do.

"We're going to find someplace new."

She nods and walks straight to the front door. Man, the little kid's got a lot of courage. I don't bother to lock the apartment behind me. Mike the realtor will be back as soon as he dumps his clients.

We take the stairs and exit out back in the alley. It's quiet back here. Most everyone's working. It's a pretty nice neighborhood, all things considered, but in order for the money I made to last, we're going to have to go to a place where it's not so nice.

Something brushes my hand. I look down to see that she has slipped her fingers into my palm. As I watch, my own fingers close reflexively around hers.

"Thank you."

"For what?"

"Helping me."

"You got a mom somewhere?" I should take her to her family.

Her eyelashes flick down, but not before I see the pain in her eyes. "Not now."

"What do you mean? She...die?"

She gives a fierce shake of her head and curls her fingers against my skin. "She's not my mom anymore." She gives me a worried look. "You're not going to send me away, are you? I can help. You wait and see."

"No. I'm not sending you away, but if you want to go home"—the notion makes my stomach churn, but I bat that anxious feeling away—"I'll help you get there."

"You're my home now." She presses her head into my arm.

I gulp, a big rock lodging itself in my throat. Before her, I didn't have a purpose beyond surviving. I do now.

5

BITSY

Leka doesn't like the lady behind the desk. He's smiling, but his leg is rigid, like the floor boards. I press a hand against his knee to let him know I don't care if we stay here. I liked the last place. It was quiet and warm. The closet felt safe.

But the stranger came and poisoned the place. I know we weren't supposed to be there. My heart beat super fast, like when I got caught under Mommy's bed that one time. I was playing there with my toy. One stranger gave Mommy a pair of bunny slippers. I stole one and made a nest for it under the bed.

When Mommy had strangers over, I'd slide under the bed frame and hug my bunny. The squeaky springs above me weren't a bother. The noise told me Mommy was home. It was always better when she was around, even when her eyes were all black after she sniffed the white stuff that the strangers brought.

Then she started to leave me with strangers. I didn't like that. I didn't like it at all. I dig my face into the side of Leka's legs. Those are bad memories.

"How much do you need to overlook the ID issue?"

"Four hundred," the lady says. She's not happy either. I can tell because her lips disappear when she frowns. That's not a face of a happy person. A happy person looks like my bunny slipper—both sides of the mouth curve up and the eyes smile.

"Four hun—" Leka cuts himself off. "Fine." He flings something at her. "One night. One key. Second floor"

The lady hums to herself as she does something behind the desk. "Room 212. Be quiet and no pets." She leans over the counter as if to double-check that I'm not a dog.

I scuttle close to the desk, trying to make myself invisible.

"Thanks," Leka mutters. He peels my hand away from his leg and curves his fingers around mine. I squeeze him back as best I can.

The lady stares at my savior's back as we walk away. I don't think she trusts us, but I wait until we're up on the second floor before I tell him that.

"She shouldn't trust us," he says as he fits a plastic thing into the door. I hear a click and then a tiny dot of light above the door handle turns from red to green. "I'm supposed to give her an ID card, but I don't have one."

I don't know what that is, so I keep my mouth shut.

The room is smelly, and the little dust clouds poof around my shoes as I walk on the carpet, but as soon as the door closes, I feel safe again. I stare up at Leka in amazement. It's not the room or the place that makes me feel safe. It's him.

He pulls the backpack off his shoulders and drops all the stuff onto the bed. "This place is a shithole, but it's got a lock. This is a keychain. I'll put a chair by the door so you can reach it after I leave." I tremble at the thought of being alone but try to hide it. I can't be a nuisance to Leka. I don't want him to send me away. He doesn't seem to notice and continues, "If you put it on, not even the creepy lady downstairs can get in."

I watch carefully as he slides a metal button into a dull metal channel attached to the door. When he twists the knob, the chain prevents the door from opening all the way.

"Got it? Don't take that chain off for any reason, okay?"

"What about you?" If no one can get in, then does that mean he's locked out? I twist my fingers together. That sounds terrible.

"I'm not going to use the door." He shuts it and then drags a chair over. He jams it up against the doorknob. "That should keep anyone out."

He crouches down so we're eye level. "I need to go get shit. I mean, stuff. I need to get stuff. I need to get us some food and I need some paperwork so that I can find us a better place to live."

My heart is beating fast again. I think he means him and me, but I have to ask. "Us?"

The side of his mouth quirks up. Not a full smile like the bunny, but a half one. I'll take it. "Yeah, both of us. We're a team now." He holds out his hand, palm up.

I lay my own hand on his and he closes his big fingers around me. It's like a hug for my hand. I love it. I love *him*. I throw myself at him, remembering how safe and good and warm it felt when he held me last night. He catches me, this time not even rocking backward an inch—like he expects me to hug him, like he wants me to.

He drags his chin over the top of my head. I love that pressure. I close my eyes and inhale. This is where I want to be forever. I let myself sit for a minute before wriggling off his lap. He needs to go and get us shit, err, stuff. I don't want to be a hassle.

My mommy called me a clingy brat. I think that's why she left me alone with the strangers. I won't be clingy with Leka. Or a noosance.

"We need to decide on names for the ID. You got a favorite name?"

He doesn't like *noosance*. It must be bad. I thought it might be. Mommy's boyfriends made a funny face whenever she called me that. But a new name? I don't know what.

"How about Bitsy? Because you're a little thing?"

I nod because I don't care what Leka calls me. He could call me a brat and I'd be happy.

"No. That's not a good name if you get a job." He taps his fingers against his knee and then snaps. "Elizabeth. How do you like that?"

I nod again, but this time I really do like it. It sounds important. Powerful. I saw an old lady with the same name on television once with a crown and big robes and everyone was kneeling in front of her. It's a perfect name.

He straightens and then digs around in his backpack. I didn't look in it once when he was gone even though I wanted to. He hands me a rectangle, the plastic wrapping making a crinkling sound. "Here's a candy bar. It's a crappy meal, but I'm going to get you a better one. I don't know how long I'll be gone, but it might be a while. Do you know how to use this?" He waves a black oblong-shaped thing with buttons.

"It's the remote." I know how to use this.

"*Weemote*, huh?" This brings a bigger smile. "You're cute."

His words warm me like a beam of sunshine. No bunny slipper ever made me feel this good. I show him that I know how to use it. The red button is off and the green button is on. He gives me another half-smile and then walks to the window.

"Don't watch anything bad," he says.

I'm not sure what he thinks is bad, but I nod eagerly.

He shoves the window open and straddles the opening. I watch wide-eyed as he swings his legs out of the room and into the air. I jump off the bed and race to the window in time to see him slide down a metal pole all the way to the ground.

Leka is a magician. He can lift a cop's radio, run up walls, and slide down poles. Most of all, he can save little girls.

There won't be anyone I meet in my entire life that is better than him. Not even the old lady with the crown.

6

LEKA

It takes me three days and half my stash to get a credit card and fake ID that says I'm nineteen. I was advised not to use the credit card as it was stolen and it'd only be good for using a couple of times before the credit card company would shut it down, which means I'm going to need a legit one at some point. I'll deal with that issue later.

The guy who made my ID up said I could get a real one from the state if I could get my hands on a birth certificate. I don't know where in the hell I'd get my hands on that.

I guess at some point, I'll need to break into a hospital or wherever they store those things and get one for Bitsy—she's too small now to be an Elizabeth—and myself. Maybe I'll snatch a couple, just to be on the safe side. For now, though, I've got what I need. Except I'm rapidly running out of cash what with the way that the New Inn and Motel is robbing me. Every night, the bitch adds another hundred to my bill. I know she's pocketing the money, but since I've got no alternatives, she has me over a barrel.

At least Bitsy is safe. That's what matters.

I find a studio apartment on the fourth floor one metro stop away from Marjory's. It's a rundown neighborhood, but there are signs of improvement. There are dumpsters in front of a building down the street filled with old toilets and drywall—a sign that they're gutting it for renos. The sidewalks are fairly clean, like someone's spending time picking up the litter. The apartment building that I leased has working lights at the front door and the back, but there's no elevator. That's why the five-story walk-up is cheap enough for me to afford.

"What do you think?" I ask Bitsy as I lead her into the apartment.

"It's really nice." She spins around, taking the small space in. Near the window, I have our two sleeping bags set close to each other. I bought us air mattresses, too, so that we're not sleeping on the floor.

"This one is yours." I point to the sleeping bag next to two pink crates. "And this is mine. We don't have a TV, but I did get you this." I pull out a computer tablet. The guy who sold me the fake IDs threw this in for fifty bucks. It's got a crack on the upper right corner, but it works. I figured Bitsy wouldn't care.

By the size of her big eyes as she cradles the tablet in her hands, I guessed right. A strange feeling of pride fills me, and I start showing off all the other sh—stuff I bought.

"I got you a pair of shoes, socks, other stuff." The weird feeling I had picking out these little girl items in the thrift store leaves me as she excit-edly digs through everything.

"This? All mine?" she asks, as she examines the contents of the crates.

"Yup." I sit down on my air mattress.

She flings herself at me, as I expected. Tears wet my neck as she rubs her face against my shoulder. I'm assuming that she's crying because she's happy. This time when I pat her, it's not so awkward. I'm getting used to her throwing herself into my arms. Her thin frame is starting to fill out. I'm going to have to start lifting more flour bags at Marjory's if she gets much bigger.

Speaking of food, I push to my feet and carry her over to the refrigera-tor. Gently, I set her by my side. "Got some food, too."

She shakes her head in wonder. "I won't eat much."

"Eat whatever you want. I bought it for both of us. Should we have a sandwich?"

She nods enthusiastically.

"Grab the bread." I nod toward the loaf on the counter. "What do you want on your sandwich? Cheese? Mayo? Mustard?"

She taps her chin. "I like butter?" Her voice ends in a question, as if she's not sure.

I unscrew the top of the mustard. "Stick your finger in."

Tentatively, she does as I say and then dabs a tiny bit of the yellow stuff onto the tip of her tongue.

"Eww." She screws up her face and makes little spitting noises.

I laugh my head off. "No mustard, then."

In the end, she gets butter, ham and cheese. I layer mine with mustard, mayo, ham, cheese and butter. She watches me carefully, as if she thinks she's going to be tested later on how one of these suckers gets made. I add extra ham for both of us. The sandwiches are so thick we can barely get our hands or mouths around them. After dinner, we wash the dishes, dry them, and stack them away. I show her how the locks work and then give her a phone.

"This is for you to contact me in case of an emergency. Press this button." The device only has four buttons. I programmed all four to ring me.

"Okay." She tucks it carefully by her pillow and picks up her tablet. "Will you watch a cartoon with me?"

I check the time. Beefer wants to see me at eight and it's six now. "Sure. I've got some time."

We lie on her mattress and watch *The Powerpuff Girls* on YouTube. Bitsy seems to love it. As for me...well, I don't hate it. After three episodes, though, the alarm on my phone goes off.

"Time for me to go," I tell her. "I've got to go to work. Can you tell me the safety rules?"

"No strangers. Don't open the door. Stay away from the windows." She ticks them off on her small fingers.

"Good. I'll be gone until late. Don't watch too much on the tablet. The internet is full of sh—stuff that's bad for you."

"I won't. I'll be good."

"I know you will."

"Be safe, Leka," she says as the door closes.

I wait outside, listening as she drags a folding chair over to the door, slips the chain lock into place. I knock twice, and she returns it, telling me I can leave.

I force my feet to move. As much as I'd like to spend the night in my new place, snug in my sleeping bag with Bitsy next to me, Beefer's got a job for me. Those jobs are going to keep us fed and safe, so no matter what he asks of me, I'll do them.

7

LEKA

"You handling this shit okay, kid?" Beefer asks. I glance over my shoulder. He's at a folding table behind me, counting out bills.

"Yup." I turn back to the faucet and scrub under my nails again.

The big enforcer comes up behind me. "Your hands are clean. I think they were clean five minutes ago. Wash them again and you're going to run out of skin."

I eye the clear water that streams over my knuckles to spill down into the drain. "Just making sure."

Beefer reaches around and turns the faucet off. I shake my hands briskly and accept the towel he's holding out.

He leans a hip against the metal sink and taps his chin with a stack of bills.

"Whaddya need all this cash for? You doing drugs?"

"No. I don't touch that stuff." First thing Beefer ever said to me when he recruited me off the street was to stay away from the product. Using any of the product gets you killed and usually in a nasty way. Sometimes a finger gets cut off. Sometimes it's the whole hand. Sometimes you get electrocuted until you piss and shit yourself and then you get chopped into a dozen pieces. I resist the urge to look over at the black garbage bag leaning against the stairs.

Instead, I focus on the scratch on Beefer's cheek.

"Good, cuz otherwise, you'll end up in the chair down here and that would seriously bum me out."

"I'm saving up." I decide to give him a tiny bit of truth so he gets off my back.

"For what?"

"Better digs."

He huffs out a laugh and slaps the money against my palm. "You sound like my fucking wife. Always wanting some new place. You watching home and garden shit in your spare time?"

"Nah. Need a safe place to store all this." I hold up the stack. It feels substantial. The cash I have is piling up, which is both good and bad. I'm getting worried about leaving both Bitsy and the cash in the apartment that's got all of two locks on the door. I don't know what I'm supposed to do, though. I can't go into a bank and deposit it. As for Bitsy, she's safer in the apartment than on the street.

"You keeping that at home?" he says in astonishment. "Hope you've got a strongbox. Bolt that shit to the floor or someone will just carry out the safe."

Shit. A safe. That's what I should get. I wonder if the thrift store has those. I wonder how I'm supposed to "bolt the shit to the floor." I didn't read the papers that I was forced to sign before I could get the keys to the apartment, but I'm guessing one of the many clauses says no bolting anything to anything.

I'm too lost in my thoughts to catch Beefer's expression change from cheerful to concerned, but I hear it in his voice when he says, "This type of work is rough." He jerks a thumb over his shoulder. "You sure this is the path you want to go down?"

As if I have so many options. "You got other ideas?"

"There's school," he suggests.

"School?" I'm startled.

"Right. That thing with the pencils and chalkboards and books and shit?" He twists his wrist so his watch is face up. "The place you should be today."

Holy fuck. Bitsy is probably missing school. I haven't gone to classes regularly for years. I went in the past if I couldn't escape the truant officer, but every minute you spend with your butt in a chair is a minute you're not making money.

Beefer sighs. "Okay, I know I'm the last person to give anyone lectures, but this sort of shit can take the strongest of us down. If you're going to do more of it, you need to find something to hang on to. Family, pussy, something. You got anything like that?"

I zero in on the one thing that's important in the mess of words he just spewed out. "You've got more of this kind of work for me?"

He sighs. "Did you hear a thing I said?"

"Yeah." This is the longest and weirdest conversation I've ever had with Beefer. Do I have something to hang on to? I have myself. What more do I need?

"Fine. Don't say I didn't warn you. Come back tonight. I've got another job for you."

Already? My stomach tightens. "All right."

"It's not like tonight. It's a delivery, but since you know how to handle a piece, you can ride along."

I try not to let my relief show, but I'm not ready for another one of these torture sessions. I check my fingernails again to make sure they really are clean. I don't want to touch Bitsy with someone's blood on them. "Great. I'll be there."

I walk toward the stairs, pausing at the garbage bag. I swallow down the acid that's creeping up my throat. "You want me to take the trash out?"

Beefer nods and takes a seat back at the table, shoving the cash back into his green cashbox that he keeps in the basement refrigerator. He doesn't have a strongbox bolted to the floor. Then again, who's going willingly climb down into this claustrophobic concrete box and expect to leave Marjory's with Beefer's money? No one. That's who. An idea pops into my head.

"Hey, Beefer, think I could store my cash here?"

He pushes out his bottom lip and considers it. "Yeah, I suppose. Why not? Bring your cashbox over the next time and we'll store it underneath mine. A man'd have to have a death wish to come down here and steal from us. Ain't that right?"

"That's right."

The side of his mouth curls up. "I like this idea. You'll watch my back and I'll watch yours."

His words make the load in the trash bag a helluva lot lighter.

8

BITSY

"You have to wear your tennis shoes," Leka insists. He holds one up to my feet.

I shake my head furiously. I've never had white tennis shoes before. If I wear them outside, they'll get all dirty. I want to keep them white and new like I kept my bunny slipper. I miss Bunny.

"We can't go to the park unless you wear them," he warns.

I peek out the window. It's real sunny outside. I bet it feels good. "But my shoes."

"Don't they fit?" He picks one up and looks at it. "The person at the store measured your feet and everything."

He sounds mad, but not in a *frightening, I should go hide under the blankets way* mad. Just mad. Still, I don't want to make Leka mad.

"I'm afraid I'll get them dirty," I mumble.

The clouds in his blue eyes clear right up. He sets the shoe down by my foot. "We'll clean them off when we get home, and if we can't get them clean, we'll get another pair. How's that sound?"

I drop my butt to the floor and scramble to tug the shoes on. "I don't need another pair. I love these."

I don't want Leka to think I'm ungrateful. I've heard that lots before. *You ungrateful little shit. Get the fuck out of here.*

Mommy didn't care about saying *shit* in front of me, but it must be a bad word because Leka tries to use *stuff* instead. It doesn't bother me what words he uses. He could call me *brat* if he wanted to because I know he's not going to hurt me. And I don't want to give him a reason to.

I jump up. "I'm ready."

The corners of his lips turn down. I've made him unhappy, which is worse than mad. I squeeze my hands together. How do I make him smile? The shoes! I say nice things about the shoes. I stick out my feet. "These are pretty."

"Yeah, they are." His big hand curves around the back of my head. "You don't need to be afraid of me."

I lean into his touch. All the fear that was stirred up inside of me just disappears. "I'm not."

The unhappy look fades some. He nods to the door. "Ready to go?"

"Yup." I rock onto my tiptoes.

I follow him into the hallway and watch as he checks the locks twice. He jiggles the door handle a little before turning toward the stairs. I jog behind him. It's hard to keep up with Leka's long legs. He doesn't know it, but he walks fast. I bet if I had a cape, it'd be a big help. I share this tidbit with him.

"A cape?" he asks. "Why do you need that?"

"Blossom, Buttercup, and Bubbles have one."

He halts abruptly. "Who are they?"

I skip the last step. "They're the Powerpuff Girls!" I lift my arm and knee as if I'm about to launch myself in the air. "They fly. Well, not all the time, but lots."

His face grows confused. "The Powerpuff— Oh, you mean the cartoon?"

"Mmmhm. What park are we going to? Does it have a name?"

He doesn't answer right away, but when we reach the sidewalk, he admits, "It's a park attached to Middleton Elementary School."

I wrinkle my nose. He's tricked me.

"School?"

"You have something against school?"

"Do you go?" I ask.

"I can't because I'm working."

"I work, too."

"Oh, yeah? At what?" There's a smile in his words.

I beam at him. "Protecting our stuff. You told me my job was to make sure all our stuff is taken care of."

"Is that why you fold everything? I wondered about that." He scrapes a hand through his hair. It falls right back over his eyes. "I'm going to buy an extra lock for the door and that lock will keep all of our sh—stuff safe."

I wonder if I should tell him it's okay to say *shit*. He seems to struggle with that.

"Your job," he continues, "is to go to school. Don't those Powder girls go to school?"

Glumly, I kick my toe against the cement. "They do," I mumble.

"Then you should go, too. Maybe they have capes there."

That cheers me up a whole bunch. "Really?"

He hesitates and then shakes his head. "Nah, probably not. But we can make one when you get home."

He's a little ahead of me, so he doesn't see my mouth fall open at the discovery I've just made. Leka isn't going to lie to me. Not ever. I race forward until I'm even with his legs and slip my fingers into his again for my hand hug. His rough palm closes around me.

"I'll be the best at school," I declare. "You'll see."

"I've no doubt that's true."

And then he smiles. Suddenly, I don't miss that stupid bunny slipper at all. Leka's better than a thousand bunny slippers.

9

LEKA

Two years later

"Thank you for coming, Mr. Moore. Please have a seat." Bitsy's principal, Ms. "Call Me Annette" Swanson, gestures toward one of the two plastic chairs facing her desk.

"What's the problem?" The question might've come out harsh, but I'd rather be back in Marjory's basement pulling someone's fingernails out than be sitting in a principal's office. Under my borrowed suit coat, I'm sweating like a punk who's just gotten collared by the cops.

She tries to charm me with a smile. "Please, won't you sit down?"

I'm unmoved. "Is Bitsy sick? Is she hurt?" My heart's racing.

"No. Not at all. *She's* perfectly fine." The principal puts an odd emphasis on *she*.

"I'd like to see her. You said it was urgent."

"Did I? Well, she's in art right now and we don't want to take her from that, do we?" She flutters her hand again. "I can't sit until you do. It's one of the rules of my office."

I want to suggest stepping outside then, but this is Bitsy's school and I don't want to make waves. Besides, the sooner I hear her out, the sooner I can get out of this place. It smells like day-old milk and cereal in here, which makes me feel mildly queasy. I was busy this morning chasing down a dealer who Beefer says is skimming product. What an idiot. I was washing away the blood when my cellphone rang and some lady, not the one wearing the pearls in front of me but some other one, was telling me I was needed right away.

I paid for a fucking cab to bring me here. I never do that. It's public transportation or my feet.

"Why'd you say it was urgent if Bitsy's not hurt?"

Call Me Annette's smile becomes strained. "Because we had an incident that we needed to discuss and it was important we do it right away. Now, if you sit, we can take care of business."

I suppose I can't threaten this woman like I did the dealer earlier. Blood's hard to get out of light fabrics, for one, and her sweater is off-white. For another, she probably has family that would notice she was missing. I plop my ass down.

Surprisingly, she takes the seat next to me instead of the big-ass leather one behind the desk. A wave of sweet perfume assaults my nose. I start breathing through my mouth. Someone oughta tell the woman she's spraying it on a tad thick. She crosses her legs, her nylons making that swishing noise as her thighs rub together.

"Mr. Moore," she begins. The fake last name sounds weird out loud. I wonder if I should've chosen something different, but Bitsy liked it. "I take it your parents are gone and that it's just you and your sister at home?"

"Sister?"

"Elizabeth," she clarifies.

"Oh, yeah." When she said sister, I blanked. What did I put on Bitsy's school admission records? It takes a moment, but the name comes to me: Elizabeth Jean Moore. I try to remember what questions they asked and how I answered. The key to not tripping on your own lies is to make sure you don't tell any, which is generally why I let everyone else do the talking. When I enrolled Bitsy, a bird-faced lady out front stuck a few papers in front of me and told me to sign. I did, gave my sad girl's hand a squeeze, and forced myself to walk out before I picked her up and ran back to the apartment.

I go for vague. "It's just me and Bitsy, err, Elizabeth."

"I thought so given that you look so young—"

"I'm twenty-one, ma'am," I interject with a lie.

"Still young." She smiles, but it's a fake one. "I have to say, you and your sister don't look much alike. Different fathers?"

"Something like that." I glance at the clock above her head. Class will be out in a couple of hours. I wonder why I had to come over right away. "You said it was some kind of emergency?"

She's been in school for a couple years now. It's easier, but she still gives me that accusatory stare when I drop her off in the morning. The one that says, *I can't believe you're leaving me with these snot-nosed brats. I belong with you.* But, like the trouper she is, she marches into the school. I loiter outside until I can't see her anymore before going over to Marjory's to find out what grim task Beefer wants done before noon.

She leans closer and lays her hand on my arm. "It's Leka, right? You don't mind if I call you that, one adult to another."

I look pointedly at her hand. I might not mind that she uses my first name, but I do care she's touching me. I draw away. "I'm here about Bitsy. I don't give a—" I self-correct. "I don't care what you call me."

Annette doesn't like my tone. She purses her lips tight. All signs of her smile have disappeared. I'm too much of an asshole to be charming. "Fine. Your sister, Bitsy, as you call her, struck another child. We are a zero-tolerance school, so she will be suspended for a day. I recommend that you get some counseling for her."

Bitsy hit another kid? "That doesn't sound like her." She winces whenever one of the Powerpuff girls so much as bump their animated elbows.

"Unfortunately, it's true. Brandon—"

"Brandon? She hit a boy?"

The teacher's already thin lips disappear at my interruption. "Yes, a nine-year-old. Now, Leka—"

"You called me here because a seven-year-old hit a nine-year-old?" I ask incredulously. I start laughing.

Call Me Annette is not amused. "Mr. Moore," she snaps, "this is no laughing matter. It's entirely inappropriate for her to be getting into fights."

I struggle to get myself under control. "Bitsy's no bigger than a peanut. Her fists aren't going to hurt anyone." I get up. "Thanks for calling me, but as long as she's okay, then you don't need me here and I gotta get to work."

"I actually do need you here because after today, Elizabeth will not be allowed back to school tomorrow. And she'll need to apologize to the boy she hit. We do not advocate violence in the classroom or outside of it, regardless of the provocation. So, if you will wait here, I will have Elizabeth brought to the office so you may escort her out of here." Call Me

Annette rises from her chair and stalks over to the door. She flings it open and addresses the old lady behind the desk. "Ring up Mrs. Donner's classroom and have her send Elizabeth to the office. Mr. Moore is taking her home for the day."

Confused, I step into the front room. This all seems fucking ridiculous. I don't give a damn that she hit someone. She's so small that it probably felt like a bug bite, if her tiny fist even made contact. Not a minute later, Bitsy trudges into the office, her usually bright face looking glum. I curl my fists in my pants pocket and remind myself I'm dealing with little kids, not street goons.

She lets out a happy yelp and throws herself at my legs. "Leka! Are you coming to school, too?"

"No, Bitsy, I'm taking you home." I grab her hand and start for the door.

"We'll expect her back day after tomorrow, Mr. Moore," Annette calls after me.

We'll see about that. I leave without saying another word. The hallways are empty and my boots clunk heavily against the tile floor. Bitsy's sneakers make no sound because she doesn't weigh more than a flat of tomatoes. Besides, if she punched someone, he deserved it.

She breaks the silence. "Am I in trouble?" Her voice is a mite wobbly.

"Nope, but I hear you hit someone today. Want to tell me about it?"

"No."

I'm glad I'm taller than her so she can't see me grin, but that's a funny-ass response.

"Let me try again. Tell me why you hit that boy today." I shove open the door to the school.

She shrugs as she hops down the stairs. "He was being mean."

"How so?"

"Just saying stupid stuff. He was stupid," she repeats.

"So you hit him because he was dumb? Maybe he can't help being dumb."

"He's not dumb. He's stupid," she declares.

"Is there a difference?"

"Yeah. Dumb is when a person's born that way. Stupid is when they're mean."

I stop on the sidewalk. "What'd that ass—dic—boy say to you?"

She stares at the ground. "Nothing."

I crouch down and tilt her chin up, forcing her to look me in the eye. "You tell me what that boy said to you."

"I don't wanna." Her lower lip quivers. I brace myself for her tears. They're my kryptonite. I can't stand seeing her cry, mostly because I know she hates it, too. Her mom or someone must've told her she shouldn't cry, so Bitsy always tries to hold it in. The big silent sobs that shake her body are worse than if she was wailing loud enough to wake the neighbors.

"Why not?" I wonder how bad of a person I am to want to beat a nine-year-old into a bloody pulp.

"Because."

This is getting us nowhere.

"All right. You don't have to tell me. You're going to stay home tomorrow." I spin around and point to my back. "Climb on. We'll get some lunch."

She scrambles onto my back. "I can teach myself," she says. "I don't need school. I can learn from Dora and the Girls and Sid the Science Kid." She prattles on about all the TV that she can watch.

I tap on her shoe to get her to stop talking for a second. "Other than the boy whose nose you punched, you like that school okay?"

"It's okay," she concedes.

"The other kids are nice?"

"I guess. They're not bad."

"You sure you don't want to tell me what the boy said?"

She rubs her nose across one shoulder blade.

I keep quiet, thinking she'll spill eventually. In the two years that we've lived together, there's not one thing she's ever kept a secret from me. She's always confessing, even to little shit that doesn't matter like copping an extra cookie before bedtime.

I hitch her a little higher and pick up the pace. "I'm hungry for meatballs. Should we eat at Luigi's tonight?"

"I guess." Her hands twist under my chin.

Man, she must really be feeling blue. The kid loves meatballs. I guess I gotta wrangle the intel out of her. "Look, Bitsy, if you don't tell me what happened it's gonna fester like an untreated wound. It'll build inside of you until you're sick. Best you spit out what he said and we'll deal with it together."

She heaves a big sigh. "He said you looked like you hurt kids."

"What?" I swing her around so I can see her face. "Why'd he say that?"

Tears pool in her eyes. "I don't know. I swear I didn't say anything. I told him you were the best. That you were the only one who ever took care of me. He said you took care of me cuz you wanted to diddle me. What's that mean?"

I set her down carefully and wipe her tears away with my thumbs. How bad would it be if I hit a nine-year-old boy? "It's a stupid thing. Is that when you punched him?"

She ducks her head and says quietly. "No. Not until the other boys started in, too. It's bad, isn't it?"

"Yeah, it's bad." How the hell am I explaining this to her? "Then what?"

"And then he said that you're stinky and that I'm stinky, too. So I punched him."

"Show me how."

She lifts her tiny hand and folds her fingers into a fist, the thumb lying on top. I tuck the thumb lower and across her fingers. "Gotta keep your thumb down when you punch. Did you hurt him?"

"Yeah. He cried like a baby," she says scornfully. Then she ducks her head, as if remembering she wasn't supposed to be happy she punched a kid. "I'm sorry."

"For what?"

"For getting in trouble."

I start to say I don't care, but I realize that I have to pretend like I do. I don't know much about school, but I know enough that watching TV isn't going to cut it. I don't want Bitsy having to spread her legs for someone like Beefer, which means I'm either going to have to swallow my pride and beg for Annette to take her back or find some other way to get my girl an education.

"Remember how I said that school's your job?" Her head bobs up and down. "Part of your job is not hitting kids."

She sighs heavily. "Why?"

"So you can grow up and be better than the Powerpuff girls and Dora and Sid put together."

"Like you?"

A vision of my fist caving in a dealer's face over on the south side flashes in my mind. "Better than me."

Her hair whips from side to side as she shakes her head. "No one's better than you."

I bend down and flip her onto my back again. This time, though, it's so she can't see me struggling with the wave of emotion that her words brought about. There are thousands of folks better than me. Guys that don't kill, maim, threaten, and mete out violence for money. But if she wants to believe I'm good for her, I'm going to do everything I can to keep that fantasy alive.

10

LEKA

"Should've been a banker, then I wouldn't be here," Beefer says right before he drives the butt of his gun across the client's nose. Blood sprays Beefer's black shirt. He's in a bad mood. "I'd be in bed getting my dick wet instead of teaching some motherfucking cokehead who thinks that his fat wallet gives him the right to mess with our property."

"Isn't he a banker?" I ask, pointing my own Glock to the row of suits hanging to my left. The closet we are in is bigger than my entire apartment, but I'm the one with the gun, and the owner of all those clothes is on his knees getting a beat down from two thugs without a high school diploma between them.

"You got a point there, kid." He pauses to swipe an arm across his face, the blood spatter messing with his vision. "Still, the hours are good. Nine to five. After-dinner drinks at a swank bar. Enough money to order up your favorite snatch." He taps the client's forehead. "You like your job?"

The client throws a panicked look in my direction.

I lean back against the marble countertop that covers a big island full of drawers. None of the places Mike listed looked like this. I didn't even know kitchen counters went in closets. "You should answer him. Beefer's pissed that he had to get out of bed for this."

He bitched for twenty blocks about how Mary's wet pussy was going to be dry as a bone and did I know how much effort she required these days? *Too much,* he grunted. *Too damn much. She's not my fucking wife,* he'd ranted. *Side pieces are supposed to have open legs and closed mouths. If I wanted to jack off, I would've done it at home with the old lady.*

So...he's in a bad mood.

"I-I-I like my job," he gasps.

I sympathize. It's got to be hard to talk with Beefer choking you with your own tie.

"See, he likes his job." Beefer jerks on the tie. The client wriggles, but we secured his hands behind his back, so he looks like a fish flopping on the beach. "And I like mine, just not after about ten. I wanted to fuck tonight, but I had to leave my warm bed to come here to teach you some manners. The next time you get a hankering to choke the shit out of a girl, you do it with someone you pick up at the bar. Not a girl from our stable or you're going to get more than a pistol-whipping. You hear."

That last bit doesn't require a response, but the client nods anyway.

"Good. Glad we had this talk." The enforcer yanks the john to his feet and then thrusts him toward the bedroom. I get busy cleaning up, bundling up the two black trash bags we laid down to catch most of the blood splatter. Then we haul our butts back to Marjory's, burn the plastic, and wash up. By the time I get home, it's around four in the morning.

Bit's sleeping like an angel, so I fall onto my own mattress and am dead the minute my head hits the pillow.

When I wake up, she's still sleeping. I check the clock. It's nearly noon. Even on the weekends, she's up with the sun. She likes to watch the birds in the morning, she told me.

I debate going back to sleep or getting something to eat. My stomach grumbles, making the decision for me. I take a detour to piss and shower. When I get out, the peanut is *still* sleeping. I decide to make us sandwiches. No point in getting her up only to have her sit around until I can throw some grub together.

In the kitchen, I make plenty of noise, though, tossing plates onto the island. Slamming the fridge door shut. With the sandwiches made and the milk poured, I go over to roust her.

"It's lunchtime, Bitsy."

She doesn't stir.

I raise my voice. "Come and eat a sandwich. It's your favorite. Ham and cheese."

She still is motionless.

I walk over and bend down next to her mattress. I give her shoulder a little shake. "Bitsy, it's—" I break off. Her head lolls to the side. Her face is all flushed.

I press a hand against her cheek. She's flaming hot.

I shake her again, a little harder this time. "Bitsy, Bitsy," I say loudly. Maybe I'm shouting. I'm definitely feeling panic. I jump to my feet and run to the kitchen to pour a glass of cold water.

I hurry back, lift her head up and tip the glass against her lips, which I notice for the first time are dried and cracking in the corners. Her lips part, but the water dribbles out of the glass, down the sides of her cheeks. I call her name again and again, but she doesn't respond. I dump the entire contents over her face.

This time her eyelids flutter. I lift her off the now soaked mattress and shift her over to mine.

"Bitsy, you okay?"

She blinks listlessly at me. Fuck me, of course she's not okay.

I rub a shaky hand across my forehead. What the hell do I do? I've never been sick in my life. And I've never taken care of a sick person.

I grab my phone. I could call Beefer. He's got kids. I can't really take this girl to the hospital, can I? Any scratches or cuts I've ever had were taken care of by a doc Beefer called. We're supposed to stay away from hospitals. They report things.

My heart thuds violently. If I call Beefer, though, and reveal her to him, I'm placing Bitsy in danger. She's only seven, maybe six. As a girl, she's real vulnerable. The whole reason we beat up the banker wasn't because he'd killed the call girl, but because he'd done it and refused to pay for it. I haven't seen a girl in this organization do anything but wait on the men, either serving them food or their bodies. That includes Mary, who pretends like she runs Marjory's.

I don't want that life for Bitsy, but what are my choices?

I can't do nothing. I press a hand against her cheek. It's still too fucking hot, and despite the water I threw on her face, she's still barely conscious.

I take a breath and call Beefer.

He answers on the third ring. His voice is rough and gravelly, as if he just woke up, too.

"My...sister's sick."

There's a beat of silence and then, "You got a sister?"

"Yeah."

"Shit, kid, since when?"

Since, fuck, how long has it been? I look down at Bit's still frame. The time before she came into my life was dull and lonely. Now, it's filled with white tennis shoes, pink ribbons, Powerpuff Girls and Hispanic girl explorers. "Forever," I tell him, and it's the truth. My life started when I met Bitsy.

11

LEKA

"What's her temp?" Beefer asks.

I press my hand to her forehead again. She moans. "She's hot. Real hot."

"What's the thermometer say?"

Thermometer? "Fuck, I don't have one of those."

There's a rustling sound. Beefer must be climbing out of bed. "How long have you been on your own?"

"A long time. What should I do?" I grow impatient.

"Get a thermometer. Try to get some fluids down her. I'll send Mary over. Where're you living?"

Reluctantly, I give him the address.

"Way over there? You should move closer to Marjory's."

"It's only one metro stop away." I tuck the phone against my shoulder and walk to the sink to get more water. I grab a can of soup and grab the wicked knife Beefer gave me a while back. I stab it down into the lid in two spots and then pour the liquid into a bowl.

"Wish you told me you had a kid sister before."

"Why?" I pop the soup into the microwave.

"Because."

Because it'd be leverage. That's why.

"She's seven, Beefer. She's just a little girl."

"Yeah, I hear ya. I'm sending Mary over. She'll take care of the girl for you."

The microwave dings, but I make no move to take the soup. I need for Beefer to assure me that he's not going to use Bitsy in any way.

"Whatever you need from me, I'm up for it."

"Just leave your sister out of it," Beefer finishes for me.

"Yeah," I manage to push out past the fear clogging my throat.

"We're not monsters. The girls in the business are there because they need the money. No one's pushing them on the street."

"Right. Well, Bit's not gonna need anything." I'll provide for her. No matter how many heads I have to bash in, it'll be worth it. I grab the soup bowl.

"I hear ya. It's why I get out of bed every day, too." I nearly drop the bowl in surprise. Beefer chuckles. "I mean, sure, I don't mind beating the shit out of someone, but like I told you before, the only way you survive our kind of work is to make sure you got something to anchor you. I'm glad to hear you got family. I feel like I can trust you more."

The bowl tips again. I decide I better hang up before I end up with no soup. "I gotta run, Beefer."

"All right, kid. Mary'll be over soon."

I hang up and sit down by Bit. "Got some soup for you."

She tries to roll her head to the side, but it takes too much effort for her. A whimper escapes her lips. The sound tears at my insides. I grab a sweatshirt off the floor and roll it up. Tucking it behind her back, I prop her upright, but she falls over, too weak to sit on her own.

Frustrated, I pull her into my lap and cradle her head against my chest. I try tipping the bowl against her lips, but, like the water, it just dribbles down the side. I set the bowl down and dart to the kitchen for a spoon. Then I hustle back. The spoon works better. I'm able to get her to swallow some soup by sticking the spoon into her mouth and then tipping her backward. The process is messy as hell and we're both covered with the sticky liquid by the bottom of the bowl.

"You're scaring the hell out of me," I tell her.

The last time I felt this helpless was when I woke up to find a dead woman in the living room of the foster home I'd been living in. The woman who'd been cashing the state check and using it on meth had OD'd. I thought the police might blame it on me, so I took off. I ended up living on the street, sleeping in the metro like one of the rat kids, and stealing food and money where I could.

Kinda like Bitsy, I guess.

I lift her up and carry her to the bathroom. She moans when I lay her on the floor.

"I'm just cleaning you up," I tell her. I don't have washcloths, so I use the end of a towel to wipe over her face and throat. She seems to enjoy that. I decide to soak the entire towel and lay it on her. But it's not too long before she starts shivering. Whether it's because she's too cold or too wet, I have no clue. I whip off the towel and her jammies and carry her frail body back to my bed. I fit one of my T-shirts over her head.

"You're going to be okay, Bitsy. You're going to be okay." I keep repeating myself. If I say the words enough, they'll come true.

12

LEKA

Mary shows up with a grocery bag full of drugs, crackers, and, thank fuck, a thermometer.

"How come you never told us you had a sister?" she exclaims as she bustles in.

I lock the door behind her. "Didn't think it was necessary."

I take the bag from her and dump the contents on the counter. "What do we give her first?"

"Oooh, she feels hot," the waitress says.

No shit. I look up from the contents to see her sitting beside the mattress with her hand on Bit's forehead. The urge to go over and yank Mary away fills my gut. It doesn't seem right, anyone else touching my girl.

"You got something over here that's going to make her better?" I wave my hand to the mess of stuff Mary brought over.

The woman looks over at me and then back at Bitsy. "Let's take her temperature first."

I rifle through the shit until I come up with the right package. I throw it to Mary.

"I can't believe you don't have a thermometer." She rips open the package, shakes her wrist and then shoves the glass into Bitsy's mouth. She glances down at her watch and then around the room. Her eyes grow judgmental as she takes in the small space. Even with Bitsy in my life, we don't have much. There are some clothes, a couple pairs of tennis shoes, the two air mattresses and Bit's tablet. Before, I didn't feel like we needed anything more, but seeing our place through Mary's eyes makes me stiffen defensively.

"You don't even have a bed. This girl is going to need her own room. You two can't share." Mary shakes her head. "What are you doing with all the money that you're making?"

None of your business. Stiffly, I explain, "Saving it."

"You men can be so tight with your money. Getting Beefer to part with even one dime of his is more difficult than serving tables during the dinner rush. And it's frustrating. Because I know you guys are pulling in some real good coin. Why you can't spend even a little of it to make the women in your life comfortable, I will never know. I mean, I do so much for Beefer. So much," she emphasizes with raised eyebrows. "You know?"

I give her a short nod hoping that will cut her off. I don't need a play-by-play. "The thermometer thing done yet?"

Mary gives a little yelp of surprise as if she totally forgot why she was here. She pulls the thermometer out and looks at it, reading something in the markings. "Looks like she's a little around 103."

"That doesn't sound good."

Mary shakes her wrist. "No, it's not real good. Let's get some Tylenol in her and see if that brings down the temperature. If it gets any higher, though, we might have to take her in."

"In where? Can Doc Read see her?" I dig through the pile again and find a bottle of thick pink liquid. Read is the man who stitched up my wounds before.

Mary flicks her hand down in disgust. "No. We are not taking this little girl to that quack. She needs to go to a pediatrician. That's a children's doctor," she says, her nose sticking a little in the air.

She thinks I'm a dense motherfucker. Maybe I am, but even I know what the hell a kid's doctor is called. I squeeze the bottle tight so I don't strangle her. "How much of this?"

"It should say on the bottle."

The bottle instructions say a "tsp and a half" for kids six and under. I don't know exactly how old Bitsy is. She said she was five when I found her, but I know that was a guess. I could be overdosing her. Fuck. I go for the higher dosage. Despite not knowing what the hell a tsp is, I use the little plastic lines to measure out the appropriate dose.

Mary props Bitsy up and holds her hand out for the medicine. "How long have you and your sister been alone?"

"A while?" A little of the pink fluid dribbles out of the corner of Bit's mouth. Mary ignores it and tries to pour the rest of the medicine down, but Bit's not swallowing.

Her sick eyes blink suspiciously at Mary.

"Ugh," Mary grimaces. "Can you get me a towel."

I kneel down next to the bed and softly shove Mary out of the way. "Let me." I lift Bit's head up and wipe the sticky medicine off her cheek with the bottom of my T-shirt. Her neck feels limp as a noodle. Panic beats inside my chest like a herd of bat wings.

She moans. "Leka?"

"I'm here. I've got something that you need to swallow. Can you do that for me?"

Her little head bobs once. Something in my chest squeezes tight. This time it's me holding out my hand to Mary for the medicine. When she hands me the plastic cup, I double-check the dosage line.

"I filled it right," Mary says irritably.

I don't say a word, but this isn't her girl. Bit's mine, and I'm going to be damned careful with her. I tuck her against my chest and hold the plastic cup to her mouth. "Small sip," I say.

Bit's mouth opens to do as I ask. I watch as she takes a difficult swallow, her throat working overtime.

"Again," I say, and this time I force myself to be stern. "All of it."

Her eyes flick open, and when her lips part, I dump the rest of the meds in her mouth. I rock her back and then sit her upright, and somehow, she gulps it down, coughing a bit. I grab the glass of water near the mattress and hold that to her lips. She's able to keep a little fluid down, too.

"Was that necessary?" Mary gripes behind me.

"It worked," I say.

"She's a homely thing, isn't she?"

"Who?"

"Your sister. I mean, it's too bad God gave you all the looks. Girls need them more."

Bit's homely? What does that even mean? Bit's the prettiest thing God ever made in this stupid world. Since I don't care about Mary's opinion, I don't answer. I lay Bitsy back on the bed and check the time. "How long should I wait?"

"A few hours." She leans against the counter.

I notice for the first time her shoes are off and the dress she's wearing is sliding off her shoulder. I shake my head. I guess I gotta give her some credit. She never stops working.

"Thanks for coming, Mary. What do I owe you for the meds and shit?"

Her face, the one I once thought was nice, takes on a sly expression. "Let's have some fun. You and me. Beefer doesn't have to know. I'm not asking for money. Just a good time. You are clearly packing some power down in your shorts" She pushes her arms together and the sleeve falls farther down her arm, the fabric around her tits barely hanging on.

I reach into my front pocket and grab my stash. Peeling off a few bills, I leave Bitsy to walk over to Mary. Careful not to stand too close, I extend my hand. "Thanks for coming over and bringing all the stuff. This should cover it and your cab back."

She runs her tongue along her teeth, but not in any sexy way. No, it's more thoughtful and calculating. "You're missing out," she tells me.

"I suppose I am," I concede. Arguing with her isn't going to get her out of my place any sooner.

She sighs and grabs the money. "At least you're not cheap like Beefer."

I bite my tongue and walk over to the door. She toes on her shoes and rearranges her dress. As she walks out, I give her a low warning. "You should be careful who you run down Beefer to. Not everyone's going to keep their mouth shut."

I close the door on her surprised face.

Mary's smart. She's lasted longer than any of Beefer's other steady side pieces. I try to think back to Beefer's last chick, but I can't remember her. She didn't last long. Before Mary, none of them did. I don't know why, though. Maybe it was loose lips. Maybe he got tired of them. Or maybe they got tired of him. Mary's different, though, and I can't puzzle out the why.

I shrug. Women seem like they're a lot of money and hassle. Even if Mary wasn't Beefer's girl, I wouldn't touch her. Something's off about her. That said, who the fuck cares? What she and Beefer do is none of my business. My only concern is the little girl lying on the bed.

I take an inventory of the shit Mary brought. There's another bottle of drugs. Three cans of soup and a box of crackers. Under the cracker box is a receipt. The total is $23.99. I curse under my breath. I gave Mary two hundred bucks. That bitch fleeced me. Oh well. Live and learn.

I go and heat up another can of soup and then go sit beside Bitsy.

"I don't know what the fuck I'm doing, so you're going to have to help me out." I grab her tablet and start typing stuff in. Since I can't spell for shit, it's a good thing the words are magically correcting themselves. At least, I assume that's what's going on. I manage to read some of the stuff on the internet. After I conclude that all the diagnoses lead to death, I toss the tablet aside. "Mary didn't think much of our place, Bitsy. Think we should move? I'm making good money. These jobs I've been doing for Beefer pay real well. Besides the rent here, we're not spending much." I nudge her lightly. "You don't eat more than a bird. And you never ask for sh—stuff."

I lace my fingers behind my head. "I could get you a real bed. Like a princess thing. Would you like that? It'd be white with flowers. Or hell, we could get you a race car bed. I saw one of those once. I was boosting a car out in the burbs—I did that for a while before Beefer found me—and when I was driving it away, I saw a set of headlights coming out of a bedroom window. Inside, the bed was a fucking car. Like it had real tires on the sides and a chrome bumper. This thing was tricked out." I lapse into silence, remembering how long I watched and how I almost got caught by the cops, drooling like a dumbass over some burb kid's furniture. "We should buy you a bed like that. A car or a castle or whatever. You're never gonna be the girl who's on the outside looking in. Not while I'm around."

She shifts on the bed. I reach over and touch her forehead. Is it still hot? I can't tell. I grab the thermometer and study it a bit. There's a blob in the middle. That must be what tells me how hot her mouth is. Seems like a stupid-ass way to tell if someone's sick, but it's a helluva lot better than using the back of my hand. I stick the glass rod in her mouth and hold her jaw shut. She moves a little, like a normal person would in response to something weird being shoved in between their lips while they're sleeping.

While I wait, I keep talking. "I don't think I wanna be on the outside looking in, either. If I'm going to be doing this shit for Beefer then I might as well live right. Not that I think we should have steaks every night, but we don't need to sleep on the floor, eh?"

She doesn't answer. I pull out the thermometer and squint. These things are hard as hell to read. I tap the camera flashlight app and hold it over the instrument. It reads a hundred and two. That seems good. Temp's going down. I get up and check the medicine box again and am disappointed to see I'm not supposed to give her any more meds for a couple more hours.

My knowledge of little kids is so shallow it wouldn't fit the medicine cup. I shouldn't keep her. I know this, but she's mine now and I can't seem to give her up. I'm going to keep her for as long as I can.

I stretch out on the floor and reach up to tuck her hand in mine. She likes holding my hand, and maybe I imagine it, but it seems like her fingers curl up inside my palm, like she knows I'm with her.

13

LEKA

Two days later, I'm back to work. Bit's fever broke after the first day, but I couldn't leave her. We watched videos, lots and lots of videos about Dora and the puff girls and bunnies. Bitsy really likes bunnies.

After the videos were done, she asked me to read her a story. I looked up a couple on the internet, but I had the same problem with the words as I always did. They were jumbled around and I couldn't make sense of the letters. I felt embarrassed that I couldn't do the one thing she asked of me, but in the end, Bitsy was thrilled that she got to read to me. I actually fell asleep, listening to her soft, sing-song voice tell me about the friendship of a frog and a toad.

"Mary says you live in a shithole," Beefer mentions. He rests his shoulder against the delivery van door, a toothpick hanging out of the corner of his mouth, watching me do an inventory of a gun shipment we're shepherding through the territory.

"Mary's got a big mouth," I say. There's enough ammunition here to blow up a city block. I don't know who's buying this shit or why, but, then, it's not my place to ask.

"That's why I like her," Beefer jokes. "Big mouth, big tits, tight pussy."

I nod, like I understand what he's talking about, but I wouldn't stick my dick in Mary for all the money that the dozen crates of guns and ammo represent. There's something off about her. I don't share this with

Beefer, though. If he wanted my opinion about her, he'd ask. Until that time came, my mouth was shut.

"You got a babysitter for your sister?" he asks. "Who takes care of her when you're doing shit like this?"

I gnaw on the inside of my cheek. Leaving Bitsy alone scares the shit out of me, but I don't like letting a stranger into our place. I give him a non-answer. "It's safe."

He shakes his head. "That's not good, kid. Not good at all."

I grind my back teeth together. I don't have many choices. Besides, being alone in our apartment is better than where she was when I found her. I make the last tick mark on the notepad and hand it over to Beefer. "Looks like it all matches up."

He straightens up, becoming all business. His eyes run down the marks I made on the sheet, and then he leans forward to do a quick tally of my calculations. When it comes to his work, he's real careful, so why he keeps plowing Mary when there are other big mouths, big tits and tight pussies out there, I don't know.

Done counting, he clicks the talk button on his comm device. "We're good to go here. The money all there?"

"Roger. The money checks out." That's Cotton's voice. He's in another location. That's how we run these deals. Money and goods are never in the same place. It's harder for people to get ripped off that way.

Beefer jerks his head. I jump down and palm my piece. I don't sense any trouble here, but there's no harm in being prepared.

The enforcer raises his hand, first to the dark car to the left and then to the dark car on the right. Every criminal in the city drives a black car. You'd think they'd mix it up now and then to keep the coppers and feds on their toes.

From the car on the right, a guy steps out of the passenger side. He's about six inches shorter than Beefer. Both hands of his are jammed into his coat's pockets. One or both of those pockets have guns in them. At least, that's how I'd do it.

His boots crunch heavily on the gravel as he makes his way toward the van.

"Money exchange is happening," Cotton announces over the radio.

"Product exchange is happening," Beefer responds.

"All there?" the man says, both hands still concealed. I clench my piece tighter, the metal reassuringly heavy in my grip.

"You heard the man on the comm, it's all here." Beefer steps away. "Feel free to see for yourself."

"Nah, we trust you."

The hair on the back of my neck prickles. I slide my finger into the trigger.

Beefer tosses the keys to the guy. When the buyer doesn't pull his hand out of his pocket, I know. Beefer does, too, but he's closer to the buyer. I jump, shooting as I do, my body flying in front of Beefer's.

The buyer falls back. I pull the trigger twice more. The buyer's body jerks and falls back. My shoulder hits the ground first and then my hip. Motherfucker.

"You hit, Leka?" Beefer yells.

"No." I have no idea if I am. "You?"

"Nope."

Adrenaline's got me by the balls. I duck around the side of the van, using the wheel well as protection. Beefer's inside the van. He tosses an AK on the ground like a gift. The wheels of a car squeal, and I jerk my head around to see the sellers' car backing up.

The buyers are shooting at us. And so are the sellers.

Dust flies up as bullets hit the ground near the van. I army crawl and grab the gun.

"Take out the buyers' first," Beefer commands.

"Got it." I mean both the gun and the order and use the dead buyer's body as cover. I rest the rifle's barrel on the guy's stomach and set the butt against my shoulder.

I pull the trigger. Nothing.

"How the fuck does this work?" I yell.

Beefer sticks a barrel out from behind the van's door, pointing it toward the sellers' car. He doesn't want them to get away. More bullets rain down near us.

"Pull the rod back."

I do as he says and hear the first bullet slide into the chamber. I press down on the trigger and the bullets start flying out. They spray the ground halfway between us and the buyers.

"Aim higher!" Beefer screams.

I shift the barrel up and fire again, this time I hear the *ping ping ping* as my bullets hit metal. I keep shooting, the sound of the gunpowder igniting exploding in my ears. It's why I can't hear Beefer get out of the van or his shouting to tell me to stop shooting. It's why I keep my finger on the trigger until all is left is empty clicks.

I jerk upright at the tap on my shoulder. "You scared the shit out of me," I say.

Beefer mouths something back to me. I can't make it out. I clap a hand to my ear a couple of times. Guess the noise from the AK has made me temporarily deaf.

He points to the car and then slices his fingers in front of his neck. I nod in understanding. No more shooting. He's going to check out to see if anyone is still alive. He hands me another magazine. I figure out how to release the empty one and install the full one.

And, then, like a good soldier, I walk forward with the barrel up and scan for signs of life. There are none. We killed them all.

Beefer drags the bodies out and lays them—all five of them—in a row. He takes out his Glock and fires a bullet into the forehead of each one. Then we loot the car. We find cash, some small jewels and more guns. There are also IDs, cell phones, two tablets and some comm equipment. We load it into the van and head for Marjory's.

My hearing is clearing up, so I catch part of Beefer's conversation over the radio. "We're heading out. No casualties here."

A different man's voice comes on. I don't recognize him and I can't make out all the words, but the feeling is obvious. It's grief. "Cotton... make it. Wife...tell her."

"The boss will do it," Beefer says abruptly and then cuts the comms off. He rakes a hand through his hair. "Fuck. Cotton, can you believe that?"

I shake my head because that's the response Beefer wants, but, in truth, yeah, I do believe it. The fact we're still alive is more incredible than that Cotton got plugged.

"The one goddamned good thing about this business is that ninety-five percent of these goons can't shoot worth shit. They spend zero time with their pieces, thinking that pointing is the only aim they need," Beefer rants. He makes a hard right. I hang on to the granny handle so I don't end up in the enforcer's lap. "You practice with your piece, kid, or you'll end up like Cotton and then who the hell is going to watch after your sister?"

I freeze. In the firefight, I hadn't thought of Bitsy at all, or my own death.

"Didn't think of that, didya? Next time, don't throw yourself in front of me. I had a gun, you dumbshit." But he takes any sting out of it by reaching over and rubbing a hand through my hair.

"What's going to happen to Cotton's family?" He just had his first kid. They'd closed Marjory's in celebration. I picked up baby shower crap for two days afterward.

"The boss will take care of them," Beefer says. And for a slim moment, I give the boss props for decency, but Beefer goes and ruins it. "It's not good for business for someone like Cotton's old lady and kid to be dangling out there. Someone who's not happy with the boss can shake her down for info. Not that she should have much because Cotton shouldn't be talking about the boss's business to anyone, not even the wife." He slides a glance in my direction.

It's a warning, to keep my mouth shut around Bitsy. Like I want her to know what I do. Like I want her to know that the same hand she thinks is so safe holds a gun half the time. But I want her to be taken care of when I bite it. Because running around with Beefer isn't going to get less dangerous over time.

"My money goes to Bitsy. Whatever I have, you'll make sure she gets it, right?" I tack on the last word so it doesn't sound like a command.

Beefer tosses me an amused look. "You don't got much in there. It might seem like a lot, but it's a drop in the bucket of what you're going to need if you want her out of this life."

I remain silent.

He continues, "Which I know is what you want because you've hid the girl from us. She must've been an infant when you started running errands for me. I'm kind of pissed you didn't tell me before, but impressed you kept her alive."

A knot forms in my stomach. I didn't do shit to keep her alive as a baby. She tumbled into my life and all I've done is give her a mattress on the floor and a few bottles of kid's Tylenol.

"I didn't do nothing," I inform him.

"Sure you didn't. Look, you want the deal that the boss is going to give Cotton's family, you gotta bring the kid around. If you'd have died the other night, no one would've even known she existed. So bring her around and let us get to know her. We don't got cooties, you know."

"Didn't want to cause trouble," I mumble. I didn't realize that my motives would be so easy to see through. Beefer never seemed to be that insightful of a guy. I need to remember this for the future.

"Family's not trouble. Well, except for my old lady. She can be a pain in the ass, but she's my pain in the ass," he chuckles. "Woo-eee. That was some kind of fight." He reaches for his phone. "I gotta burn some energy off in Mary's pussy tonight." He thumbs down the screen and presses a number. As it rings, he says, "Should I have her bring a girl over?"

"Nah. I'm good. I'm going to go home and wash up." I smell of gunpowder and blood, but, mostly, the only thing I need right now to feel good is to see Bitsy.

Beefer's disappointed. "See, if you bring your little girl to Marjory's, we can help take care of her. That way, you can let loose. I'd even give you the family discount on one of the girls in the stable if you don't want to spend the cash on your own."

"Thanks." It all makes sense, but there's something inside of me that rebels at sharing Bitsy with the world. Even having Mary over to help care for Bitsy while she was sick felt like a strange and uncomfortable invasion.

Beefer pulls into the lot behind Marjory's. I start to get out, but Beefer grabs me. His face is serious. "You think you can do this on your own and you're going to fuck up. Better to ask for help now. No one's going to think less of you. You're a valuable asset. The boss is going to want to reward that. The reward extends to your family. There's no reason to hide her from us. It makes me think you don't trust us."

He doesn't mean to threaten me, I don't think, but I hear one anyway. I rub the back of my hand against my mouth, not enjoying the feeling of being cornered.

"I'll bring her over in the morning."

He breaks out in a smile. "Good call. We'll see you tomorrow then."

14

The letters over the door are M-A-C-Y. I sound that out. "Maky."
"Macy's," Leka corrects.

The circular door spits out another person. I eye it with suspicion. What's wrong with the flat doors? This round one looks like it'll squash you if you aren't fast enough.

"Are you getting new shoes?" I ask, looking to see if there's another way inside.

"Not today. We're buying you a new outfit."

"Bummer. What's wrong with what I got on?"

I've a Hello Kitty T-shirt on and black jeans. "This is my favorite shirt." I pull it away from my chest so he can get a good look at Ms. Kitty. She's cute.

"Yup. Ms. Kitty's the bomb, but you probably need a dress."

He picks me up and steps into the moving door before I can stop him. I open my mouth to complain but then realize the door moves by itself. It's like a ride! I wriggle in his arms to let me go.

He sets me down but not until we're clear of the door. I dart around his leg, but my feet leave the ground before I can make it back into the circle doors.

"Oh no, you don't." Leka carries me, football like, into the store. "We have a meeting after this."

I perk up. "What's a meeting?"

This sounds important. Maybe I do need something new. "I think I should have new shoes for the meeting."

His side shakes a bit. He's laughing! I clap excitedly. Leka never laughs. He's always very serious.

"You and your shoes."

New shoes are my favorite. I like white the best, but Leka doesn't own white shoes. He has two pairs of black boots. They're big, heavy things with zippers and laces. Mine have velcro. I like mine the best.

He sets me down and snags the attention of a tall lady wearing shoes with really thin spikes. I look up, but it seems like her legs never end.

"Hey, can you tell me where the kids' department is?"

"Of course. What is it that you're looking for today?" The lady's got a nice voice. I can tell she's smiling without even seeing her face. I crane my neck to see her face. She's got lovely dark hair that falls in waves around her face. Her lips are red, like the boots Dora's monkey wears. She can't seem to take her eyes off of Leka's face.

I sigh and step in between the two. I've seen that look before. She likes Leka, but this sort of attention makes Leka feel awkward. He gets stiff and irritable. I don't want her ruining our day because she stares at Leka's face too long.

"We're gonna get a dress," I tell her.

She peers down at me. "Aren't you..." She presses her lips together, some of that bright smile dimming as she examines my face. "Aren't you interesting?" she says finally. "Is this your..."

She has a hard time finishing her sentences.

Leka helps her out. "Sister." He takes my hand. "This is my sister."

The smile comes roaring back. "Of course. Let me show you a few selections. My name is Nina, by the way."

She gets silence in return.

"He's Leka and I'm Bitsy. Or, actually, Elithabeth, but Leka calls me Bit or Bitsy, don't you?"

He nods slowly. "Yeah, I do."

"You can call me Bitsy," I tell her because the longer name is hard to say and I wanna be nice.

We ride up an elevator that looks like it's all gold but that Nina says is brass because a gold elevator would be ob-nock-sushlee expensive. I file that away. Gold, silver, brass. Brass is nice. Obnocksush, even.

At the very top floor we get out and Nina takes us all the way into the back, her spikes making clickety-clack noises on the floor. Unlike Leka's boots that, despite being heavy, make no sound at all. My tennies squeak if I twist them just right against the floor.

I do that a few times until Nina shoots me an angry look, one that changes to a smile when she gazes at Leka again.

"What were you thinking?" she asks.

"How about that?" He points to a white statute with hands but no head wearing a black dress. The skirt is poufy and the lace around the bottom looks like I could tear it just by blowing on it.

"I don't know," Nina and I say at the same time. We share equal expressions of surprise.

"Okay, how about that?" He shifts his finger, and this time, I see a dress that looks like a long T-shirt, but instead of having a kitty or bunny on the front, it's got lots of stripes.

"I like that one," I say.

Nina grabs one and holds it up to me. "Looks like a four will work."

"I'm seven," I correct her.

"It's the dress size, not your age, dear," she says.

"We'll take it." Leka reaches inside his front pocket where he keeps his money.

"Let's go over to the register." Her long fingernails point to a desk.

"Can she put this on?"

"You mean try it on?"

"No, um, wear it out."

"Of course." Nina directs us to a small hallway with little stalls that have a curtain closure. She plucks a pair of scissors off a shelf, clips a white tag off my dress and then hangs it in the first room. "Go ahead and change. I'll ring this up."

Leka gives me a nod and I scuttle inside. As the two move away, I hear Nina say, "Your sister doesn't look like you."

Leka doesn't reply. He never does when people say that. It doesn't matter what we look like on the outside, he says. Our insides match.

AFTER MACY'S, WE HOP ON THE SUBWAY. WE GET OFF AT A stop called Farfield. Leka is tense. One hand is curled tight around the shopping bag holding my T-shirt and jeans, and the other grips my left hand.

My right is busy holding my new toy against my chest. He saw the white bunny before I did and had the money for it slapped on the counter before Nina was done wrapping up my old clothes.

I can't stop petting her. She's soft and so cute. I drop a kiss on her nose. When Leka is gone at night, I can sleep in his bed with my bunny. It'll be almost perfect.

"I'm going to name her Carrots," I announce.

"I like it," he says, but he doesn't sound happy. We stop at the top of the moving stairs and he pulls me out of the way.

Crouching down, he puts both hands around my shoulders and gives me a serious look. "We're going to Marjory's."

I recognize that name. "Where you work," I supply.

"Yeah, that's right. Where I work. These folks don't know about us. No one does."

I nod solemnly. When Leka took me to school, he said we had to pretend we were a family or they wouldn't let him sign all my papers. It wasn't hard because that's what we are. I remind him of that. "It's you and me."

"Right. But I didn't find you on a street or—"

I cut him off. "I knooooow," I say. "We've been together always." I place my own hand—the one not holding Carrots—on his shoulder. "Just you and me."

He takes a deep breath and then blows it out before pushing to his feet. "We're going to be okay. This is the right thing to do."

The way he says it, though, it seems like he's talking to himself rather than to me.

We don't walk long. Six and a half blocks at the most. Two blocks left of the stop and then four blocks straight. We stop in front a brick storefront with a green door and a green and white striped shade pulled out over the sidewalk. There are chairs and tables under the shade. Marjory's is a restaurant. Leka works at a good place. That makes me happy for some reason—probably because I like food.

"This is it," he says, and again, it seems like he's telling himself something important. But I pay attention.

Inside, the smells of spaghetti sauce and cooked meat fill my nose. My stomach grumbles in appreciation.

Leka gives my hand a squeeze. "We'll get you something to eat, but first, let me introduce you to—oh shit." He stops walking and talking.

I peek around his leg to see the place is empty but for one table in the middle of the wall. There is a man sitting in the booth. His eyebrows are dark and look like wings at the end. His hair is slicked back and his shirt is open. I see a glint of something—gold or maybe brass—at his neck.

It's darker in Marjory's. None of the sunlight from outside can be seen and the green lamps are all low, but I still make out that the man at the table is someone important.

I think it's because of how everyone around him is acting. A really big guy with no neck stands arrow straight on the right. There's a pretty woman, prettier than even Nina, sitting next to the seated man. She has a hand on his shoulder and her boobies are pressed into his arm.

There are two other men wearing dark clothes, their hands hanging at their sides, their feet shoulder-width apart. The seated man gestures for us to come forward.

Leka does another one of those inhale and exhales before walking slowly toward the table. I follow behind, clutching the bunny for reassurance.

"Leka, come in. Beefer was giving me a report on your heroics last night. Apparently, without you, we would have lost the shipment. Now who is this?" the seated man says. He curls his fingers, gesturing for me to come closer.

I look up at Leka for permission. He gives me a short nod. I creep forward. The man frowns. "You don't look much alike. Different mothers or different fathers?"

"Yes," Leka replies.

Yes, what? I wonder, but the man grunts as if Leka fully answered the question. "She's not much to look at, is she?"

I glance around. Is he talking about me? I'm a fully-grown girl. I draw myself up and take another step forward. Maybe it's the light. He can't see me because of the light.

The pretty lady scratches her nails against the man's shoulder. "I told you. God gave all the good looks in the family to your soldier. What a shame."

"What's your sister's name?"

"Elizabeth."

He doesn't share my nickname. I decide then and there that I won't either. Bit and Bitsy are for just Leka and me. It's too bad I told Nina. If I see her again, I'll have to give her the news that she can't use Leka's nickname.

"Grand name for someone like her."

Leka doesn't like these comments. I don't really understand what they all mean, but I get the feel of it. The man doesn't think I'm worthy of being Leka's family. I hug my bunny close as I press myself tight against his leg.

The man gives me another once-over before turning to Leka. "Beefer says you're doing a good job for him."

"I hope so. I'm trying."

"That's all we can ask for. Now that we've lost Cotton, we'll need you to step up."

"Whatever you need." Leka's stiff as a board.

"Good. I like that attitude. Beefer says you want the family to take care of Elizabeth here if something happens to you."

"Yessir."

"As long as you keep doing the kind of work you've been doing, that won't be a problem," the man says. "We take care of our own here at the business. Right, Beefer?"

The tall man with no neck nods stiffly.

"All right. Why don't you take the girl into the kitchen while I get to know this young woman better. Mary, isn't it?"

The pretty lady flips a hank of her hair over her shoulder. "It's whatever you want to call me," she purrs like a kitty.

The man's eyes grow dark. "Another good attitude." He flicks his hand, waving us toward the back.

Leka grabs my hand and starts walking quickly in that direction. I can't resist a peek behind me, but all I see is the man's head. The pretty lady has disappeared.

"Where'd she go?" I ask.

"On her knees," the no-neck man mutters as he slaps the door open.

Leka closes the door and leans against it. "What's going on, Beefer? I didn't know the boss knew Mary."

"He didn't. Walked in and Mary couldn't get her underwear off fast enough," the one called Beefer replies.

"Damn, I'm sorry, man."

There's a cry in the outer room followed by a smack. Then I hear Mary's voice. "Yes, God, yes."

Leka claps his palms over my ears. Sadness briefly flashes across Beefer's face before it hardens into one of those masks like the big dolls at Macy's. I've heard these sounds before. Mommy used to make them in the bed above me where I hid with the bunny slipper. The mattress would squeak squeak squeak as she bounced on top of it with some man. Or men.

Even with Leka's hands over my ears, I can still make out Beefer's words.

"It is what it is. Whores like Mary are only interested in how fat your wallet is, and let's face it, the boss's wallet is a helluva lot fatter than mine."

"Loyalty should count for something," Leka insists.

"She's loyal to the green. It's something for you to remember."

"How am I supposed to trust the business to take care of Bitsy if we're all just loyal to the money?" Leka's voice is as harsh and angry as I've ever heard it.

"We're all brothers here, Leka. The boss said he'd take care of your girl and he will. He won't go back on his word. Not to you, at least. Not to any one of his soldiers. Pussy, on the other hand? That's expendable." Beefer points toward the main room where Mary's cries are mixed with the chairs and tables scraping against the floor.

"I don't know, Beefer. I'd be careful around her," Leka warns, dropping his hands away.

"She was never anything more than a warm hole," Beefer declares. End of story. He doesn't want to talk about it anymore. He jerks his head toward a door behind him. "Take your sister to the back and let's get some grub in her."

That sounds like a good plan to me. Bunny and I aren't big fans of the sounds going on out in the main room.

In the back, there's a small table. Beefer brings out a bowl of noodles and sauce. Leka follows with three bowls and three glasses of milk. Once the door is closed, I realize that the other two men stayed in the main room with the one they call the boss and Mary.

I find that weird, but I keep all my observations to myself. Leka warned me to be careful. I don't think I'll come to Marjory's again, if I can help it. Even though the food is real good, Leka doesn't like me here. And I'm not doing anything to make Leka unhappy.

15

BITSY

Three years later

"Who's going to be there?" I ask, watching as Leka dips his head under the faucet. He came home from "work" about ten minutes ago and has been rushing around since, muttering that he has to get to Marjory's for some event tonight.

"Not sure. Beefer said I should go, though."

Beefer. That man runs Leka's life. "I thought we were going to watch *Lord of the Rings* tonight." I try to keep my whining to a minimum, but it still leaks out.

"I know, Bitsy. We'll do it tomorrow night."

He slicks his hair back with one hand and shoves the other in front of me. I slap the towel in his waiting hand.

"This sucks."

He pauses in mid-scrub. "Don't say *suck*."

I roll my eyes, but he catches me. In the mirror, our eyes meet. His are so blue; mine are so blah brown. His hair is golden brown, a thousand different shades of yellow and caramel and wheat and wood. Mine is one color—black and coarse. I run a hand over it. It takes a lot of effort to smooth the curls down. I wish I had straight hair. The most popular girl in the fifth grade is Emma Wilson and *she* has the straightest, blondest hair of any girl I've ever seen. All the boys love her. Hell, I love her.

I sigh. "Do you think I'm ugly, Leka?"

He scowls, his perfect features scrunch up and his eyes narrow to mean slits. "No. Who called you that?"

"No one." No one has to say it. I can see the difference. My skin's slightly darker than everyone else. In second grade, Tommy McKenna asked me if I showered enough. In third, Wesley Holt said I reminded him of Pig-Pen. I told him he reminded me of Babe, the pig, only not as cute and that if he spoke to me again, I'd make him into bacon and eat him for breakfast.

I got detention for that. Worth it.

"First, looks don't mean sh—sugar and second, you're not ugly. You're beautiful."

"You have to say that," I proclaim and jump off the vanity. I'm done with mirrors.

"I don't have to say it," he yells after me. "I say it because it's true."

"Whatever," I mumble. I hate that he's going out. I decide to eat my feelings away with a pint of ice cream. I'm pulling the lid off when the intercom rings.

"Will you get that?" he yells.

It's the doorman announcing my babysitter. Funny how in the first years of my life when we were living in the studio apartment over on K Avenue, I stayed at home by myself. A year ago, Leka came home and announced we were moving.

Up here on 74th Street, far away from Avenue K, I have more stuff—a bed rather than a mattress and a sleeping bag, a closet full of clothes versus a milk crate and a backpack. I also have a huge assortment of bunny rabbit stuffed animals. Along with all of that good stuff are the unnecessary extras: a babysitter and a school uniform.

Life, I've learned at the age of ten, is half full of good shit, as Leka tries not say, and half full of actual shit.

"I'm ten. I can take care of myself."

"Good thing you don't have to. Now get the da—darned door," he yells from his bedroom.

I get into my boxing stance, tucking my thumbs across my index and middle fingers like Leka taught me so long ago and stare at myself in the mirror in the front hall. I look tough and capable. Like I could take down anyone who tried to come after me.

That skinny white kid did it in *Home Alone*. No question that I could defend myself. Unlike that kid, I have access to real guns. Leka has a couple that he keeps in his bedroom. I'm not sure if he knows that I know he has them. I suppose he does. There's not much he misses.

The doorbell rings and I drop my fists. Straightening, I go to the front door and throw it open.

"Hi, Mrs. Michaelson."

The older lady leans down and gives me a peck on the cheek. Her lavender perfume assaults my nose and I rub it to keep from sneezing.

"Don't sound so excited to see me," she mocks. "I might get my feelings hurt."

"Sorry." I try to keep my pouting to a minimum, but I hate it when Leka is gone. And lately he's been gone a lot. "It's not you."

"I know, dear. You miss your brother, but he's only going to be gone for a few hours." She bustles inside. A big bag knocks against her leg. I reach over to take it. A familiar excitement stirs at the sight of its contents.

"Is this the new *Cat Girl?*"

Mrs. Michaelson's cheeks glow with pride. "It certainly is. I brought you one of the very first copies."

"Oh my God!" I clap my hands together and then race to my bedroom to get my tackle box full of art supplies. Mrs. Michaelson's daughter is a comic book illustrator and she sends me uncolored proofs so that I can see the art strokes and copy them. I intend to draw for a living when I get older, even though, as Mrs. Michaelson tells me, it doesn't pay more than peanuts. Her daughter works as a barista in her full-time capacity and does the art work on the side.

I'd be cool with that. I don't mind serving coffee in order to pursue my dreams. After all, Leka works at a restaurant. There's absolutely nothing shameful about serving people. If it's good enough for him, it's good enough for me.

"You look happy," Leka remarks as he meets me in the hall.

"Mrs. M brought a new proof from her daughter."

"Cool. So does that mean you're done being mad at me."

I shake my head. "No. I can do two things at once. So when will you be back?"

The light in his eyes dims. "Not sure, Bitsy. You know I don't stay away unless I have to."

Immediately, I feel guilty. I drop my eyes at the floor instead of his face so I don't have to see that I disappointed him. "I know. I'm sorry." He's so good to me. I throw my arms around his waist, the tackle box banging against the back of his legs. "It's only that I'll miss you."

He returns my hug. "I'll be home soon. Besides, five minutes after I'm gone, you'll be knee deep in Wonder Woman and Batman and the Green Lantern and will have forgotten that I'm not here."

"Whatever," I mumble again, soaking in the pleasure of his arms around me.

He always makes me feel good. He peels me off of him and goes to greet Mrs. M.

"You look nice, Leka."

"Thanks, Mrs. M. You look fine yourself."

She blushes, as all the ladies do around him. He doesn't even smile at them, but they love him anyway.

I've noticed this ever since I was a kid. Women's eyes soften, their voices get huskier. They will tug on their clothes or flip their hair. They smile and touch him. I kinda hate it that even Mrs. M, who I like, gets all flustered and girly around him.

He's mine, I want to shout at all of them. He's mine.

The only thing that keeps me in check is that he doesn't pay attention to any of them.

"I'll be back in a few." He stops and corrects himself. "I'll be back as soon as I can. Be good for Mrs. M, Bitsy."

"I will." This time I force myself to smile so that he doesn't worry.

"Thanks again, Mrs. M."

"No problem, dear. You take your time. Elizabeth and I will be fine tonight."

And then he's gone.

"Leka needs to find a nice young woman," Mrs. M declares as she walks into the kitchen.

"Why?"

She turns to me. "Because he does. Doesn't he seem lonely to you?"

"No."

She lets loose a gusty sigh. "Of course you'd think that. But that's a child's way of thinking, Bitsy. A man needs a woman."

"He has me."

She pats me on the head. "No, sweetheart, he needs a *love* love, not a fraternal love."

A fraternal love? I don't even know what that means. "I love Leka." There's no one that loves him more.

Mrs. M gives me another of her pitying glances, the kind that she tosses in my direction whenever she thinks I'm too young to understand. I don't think I'm too young. I think she doesn't make sense.

"Do you want me to make you a shake for while you draw and color?" she asks.

I nod, but the whole thing bothers me. I press her. "What kind of girl do you think he needs?"

"Someone sweet. Real pretty because your brother isn't going to want to be seen with a girl who isn't pretty." She bends over to grab the ice cream. Alarm bells go off in my head. Is she thinking of shipping Leka and her daughter together, because that's not going to work. Her daughter is too soft for Leka.

"Looks aren't everything," I say, echoing Leka's earlier words.

"Like attracts to like." She sets the ice cream on the counter. "Men like your brother have something special, and that means the best-looking girls are going to flock to him."

I hate that she calls him my brother because he's not. We're not related at all, but I can't tell her that. I can't tell anyone that.

I lay out the proof and pick up my Micron pen. "He's not like that."

She makes Leka sound so...fake, but he's real. He took me off the street and has cared for me for the last five years without wanting anything in return. Not that I have anything to give him.

I draw a few quick lines.

"Oh, of course, I don't mean to say he's shallow. He's not. He loves you dearly and that's another mark in his favor." She scoops the ice cream into the blender and pours in the shake mix that she brings with her. "He's the whole package. I'm surprised some enterprising young woman hasn't already snatched him up. Maybe he's going to meet her tonight, though."

My pen skitters across the paper. Crap. I crumple it up and grab a new one from my stack. "He doesn't need a girl," I maintain.

Mrs. M hears me and turns. With hands on her hips, she scolds, "Now, Elizabeth, you can't stand in the way of your brother finding true love. That'd be selfish, and I know you're not that kind of girl."

I stare mulishly back at her.

"You're not," she insists. "You're full of love in your heart for your brother, and because of that you'll welcome any girl that he loves. Besides, he's not going to choose anyone that doesn't love you, too. You two shouldn't be this little island. It's not healthy. You could both do with a little feminine influence here." She waves a hand. "It's starker than a museum in here. No pillows. No decorations on the wall. And you—" She wags a finger at me. "You need a mother. Someone to show you how to do your hair, how to dress, make the best of those features." She draws a circle in the air.

My cheeks grow hot. Mrs. M must think I'm ugly, too. Make the best of my *features?* Like, what? Somehow my nose and eyes and mouth are all wrong. I duck my head and pretend to be immersed in the drawing.

Over at the counter, Mrs. M sighs. I think she says something like, "I try. I try." And then flicks the blender on.

What the hell do I care what Mrs. M thinks of me. It's not like I'm marrying her. Under the cover of the noisy appliance, I mutter the one thing that really matters. "He's not my brother."

16

LEKA

When I arrive at Marjory's, Beefer is leaning against a tricked-out Escalade. Two other men are already in the SUV. One I recognize. Tam O'Reilly is the distributor for our section of the city. He doesn't deal drugs, he sells the product to the dealers. The other guy, with a slim arm resting on the rolled-down passenger side window, is new to me.

My hand slides close to the butt of my Glock resting in the inside pocket of my windbreaker. I don't do well around strangers. The only time I'm around them is when I'm shaking them down for nonpayment to the business or killing them.

Maybe we're killing the new guy tonight.

"Beefer. Tam" I give him and Tam a chin nod of acknowledgment to keep my hands free.

Beefer doesn't miss this. He shoots me a warning glance and then taps the arm of the new guy. "Cesaro, this is Leka. Leka, Cesaro. He is Arturo's nephew."

"On his mother's side." Cesaro flashes a line of perfect white teeth in my direction.

I blank for a moment—on both Arturo's name and this supposed relative. Cesaro catches it.

"He doesn't even know who Arturo is?" he scoffs. He whips his head around, sweeping a hank of hair off his face. "Did you just pick this guy off the street?"

Beefer opens his mouth to defend me, but I give him an abrupt shake of my head before opening the rear car door. I like my low profile. If Arturo's nephew thinks I'm nothing more than a scrub, what do I care?

The only disappointment here is that we're not killing him, because I can already tell he's a guy that at least needs a good pistol-whipping. I buckle up and ask, "What's the plan?"

It's Cesaro that answers rather than Beefer. "We're going to the Underground, bro. I hear that's where the hottest pussy is these days. Actresses, models, socialites."

"The Underground?"

Tam playfully punches me in the shoulder. "Leka takes care of his little sister. He doesn't get out much. It's a club, dude. Think dance floor, skinny dresses, fuck-me shoes, lots of booze."

"Isn't that over in the Red's territory?" Never mind the women or the booze, the Underground isn't owned by the business, which means the guns inside won't be in the hands of friendlies. "What's wrong with the place on Oak Street?"

Arturo liked to go to that one when he wanted to go to a club at all. There was a VIP section behind bulletproof glass. He'd sit up there with a few women and be entertained—both by the women on their knees around him or grinding against each other on the floor. There were a surprising number of chicks who didn't mind exchanging fluids with Arturo in exchange for free drinks and the so-called honor of sitting in the VIP lounge for one night.

Whatever was good enough for Arturo should be good enough for his nephew.

"Cesaro wants to go to the Underground, so that's where we're going," Beefer says flatly. Translation: he doesn't like it either, but there's not much we can do about it.

"Are we expecting trouble?" I ask. "Not that I care, but I like to be prepared." I dip my head forward to the dark SUV ahead of us. I'm certain Beefer's spotted that one and the one behind us. Three cars full of muscle to take a single guy that I could probably break in half with my left hand seems overkill, but what do I know?

"Nah, but we can't let anything happen to the boss's nephew. Looks bad." Beefer and I make eye contact in the rearview. So Arturo delivered the message himself, and if Cesaro comes home without having had the time of his life, then we're the problem.

"What's wrong with our girls, Cesaro? Didn't you get a good look at them? We've got some hot ones. I like that redhead. What's her name?" Tam nudges me.

"No clue." I look out the window. The girls come and go. I don't keep track of them.

"Claire," Beefer offers. "And, yeah, C-man, you lay eyes on Claire? She's got more curves than Bugatti."

Cesaro shrugs his shoulders and then lights a cigarette. Beefer's jaw tightens. This is his ride and it's fucked that Cesaro didn't ask.

"Some of the girls Uncle Art has collected aren't bad, but they're all used. I don't want some pussy that's been destroyed by everyone else's dick. Like that chick I got last night. I never felt a pussy so loose. It was like she stuck the entire contents of a clown car up her snatch." He laughs. "You guys had that Mary chick?"

Tam and I both stare at the back of Beefer's head. By now his jaw is so tight, I worry it's going to crack. Mary still works at Marjory's, although that's putting a shine on it. She sits in a booth while the rest of the crew work their tails off, but because she's on Arturo's dick regularly, she gets away with it.

I'm fairly sure that Beefer still has feelings for her. I know he's slept with her on occasion when she's bored and Arturo is busy with other women. No one's allowed to talk smack about her, not in his presence.

It's gotta be killing him not to say anything to Cesaro, who's going on about "her saggy tits. Dude, and her snatch smelled like fish. She wanted me to go down on her, which is fucked up." He pauses to take a drag.

I jump in so Beefer doesn't fuck up his relationship with Arturo over some faithless shit like Mary. "That sucks, man."

Cesaro twists in his seat. "Yeah, so you know what I'm talking about. There was no friction. It was like I was fucking air. The old Rosie Palm gives better than that bitch." He holds up his hand and waves it at me.

"Leka wouldn't know," Tam unwisely offers. "He's never boned Mary."

"Don't blame you, bro. So who do you like?"

"He's not interested in any of them. The guys call him Priest. He hears all the girls' confessions but doesn't fuck any of them. And it's not because he's gay either, cuz we got that covered, you know? We're equal opportunity pi—"

"That's enough," I say quietly. Tam knows when he's gone too far. He shrinks back into the seat, but Cesaro is like a bloodhound, scenting out weaknesses and weirdness.

"Don't like the whores, do you?" He guesses wrong. I give a bare nod of my head. If he wants to run with that thread, let him. "Me, too." He offers me a hit off his smoke. I shake my head. "I'm tired of all these whores. I want a virgin. Someone who'll take some goddamn suggestion."

Someone he can train.

"You'd have a better chance at church," Tam declares. "I go to mass with my momma every Saturday, and the girls there have their knees locked so tight together, you'd think Father Mike puts superglue on the kneeler."

Cesaro doesn't agree. "Here's the problem with church virgins. They're too fucking demanding. They want you to go to mass with them. Dress a certain way. They don't want it up the ass. They talk too much when they should be on their knees with their pie holes open and ready."

"Some of these chicks are picky as hell," Tam agrees. I've seen him get shot down several times. He probably knows what he's talking about.

Cesaro is shaking his head again. "You're going about it all wrong. You don't aim for the alpha woman. She's gonna be shitty in bed anyway. You go for the shy ones that the alphas bring along to make themselves look better. Those side chicks are vulnerable. You give them a compliment, throw a few drinks their way, and then invite them to the VIP room. Pretty soon you've got both the ugly chick and her hot friend fighting over you."

Beefer slides to a stop in front of the Underground. Before Cesaro jumps out, he jerks his head toward the front of the club. "Come on and learn. You, too, pretty boy. You'll be a good lure."

"I'll watch the front door," I say. "You go on in with Beefer and Tam."

"Nope. Like I said, you're going to help lure the pussies in."

I grind my teeth together and glance toward Beefer. He's my boss. He's who I report to.

Cesaro snaps his fingers in my face. My hand whips up and grabs them, twisting his arm to the side. Beefer's there in a nanosecond, drawing me away.

"Sorry," I drawl, but no one, not even Cesaro, believes me for a second.

He gives me a grim smile. "You serve at my pleasure, you dumbass."

"Your uncle's," I correct.

"Which means me, tonight." He snaps his fingers again like I'm some fucking mongrel he can order around.

I start forward, baring my teeth. Beefer holds me back. With a nod, he tells Tam to take Cesaro inside. He draws me to the end of the SUV.

"Look, put aside the guard dog that you do so well and enjoy yourself. Cesaro's an asshole, but if you play his game, you can move up in the business. Find him a chick. Grab one for yourself. Take them both home and fuck them until you guys are friends."

"Is that what you'd do?" I ask with real surprise. Is he that lax with his security that he'd bring a stranger into his place where his wife and kids slept? I stalked Mrs. Michaelson for two months and researched her background thoroughly before I offered her the babysitting job. "I'm not bringing that dickhead or any woman into my home."

Beefer sighs impatiently, his fingers digging into my biceps. "I'm not telling you to bend the girl over the kitchen table as Elizabeth's eating her mac and cheese, but I am telling you that you're way too intense. And you don't have to be. Not tonight. Tonight, Cesaro wants you to play wingman. Draw in some babes and let him choose. You don't got to do nothing. If he's happy, Arturo's happy. Fucking next to some guy is one way to create a real bond. It'll help build trust between you and Arturo."

"If I do an orgy with Cesaro in my home, the boss is going to trust me more?" I can't believe what I'm hearing.

"Christ, you're hardheaded. Then don't bring her home. Do her in the VIP lounge. Or out in the parking lot. Shit, we'll take a whole passel of them back to Marjory's."

This shit is going nowhere. I clap a hand on Beefer's shoulder. "Let's see what Cesaro wants," I say.

Beefer visibly brightens. Making this pencil dick happy is clearly top priority.

Inside, I'm forced to give over my gun and my jacket. My only consolation is that Beefer is as miserable as I am about being disarmed. We make our way to a table that Cesaro has claimed.

"What'll you have?" he asks. "I ordered shots for the table."

"That's fine."

I slide into the booth. Beefer stands guard at the end where I would rather be.

Cesaro lights up another smoke and surveys the crowd. "What do you think of her over there? The girl in blue?"

"Hot," I lie. I can't even see the girl in blue. The bar's dark and the strobe lights discolor everyone.

"Yeah, but not as fine as the blonde over there in the corner. Look at that ass. I'd like her to twerk all over my dick."

I find that Cesaro doesn't need any more from me than a few grunts of pretend agreement.

I sag against the booth's leather and stare out at the dance floor. This is my world, but I can't let it be Bitsy's. Whatever I do in the future, I have to make sure she's never prey for men like Cesaro.

"YOU MIND IF I USE YOUR TABLE FOR A SEC?" A THIN GIRL SETS a plastic cup on the table.

"Go ahead."

"Hot in here, isn't it?" She waves a hand in front of her face.

"Yup." Sweat is making my T-shirt stick to my back. The girls wearing their tiny dresses have the right idea. If you're going to be jammed into a giant room with hundreds of other people, there's no point in wearing lots of clothes. I eye the dance floor where Cesaro is sandwiched between two women. "What's the capacity of this place?"

Beefer's too busy downing another beer to answer. At this rate, I'll be driving us back to Marjory's. I turn to the girl. "What do you think?"

She smiles and bats her eyelashes. "About what? About how hot it is in here?" Her hand runs over the bare shoulder closest to me.

I shift to the side to avoid her fingers and tilt my head toward Beefer. "How much longer?"

"A while, brother."

I clench my jaw. We've been here at least two hours. In that time, Cesaro has racked up a five-figure bar tab; tried to storm the DJ booth to play "some real fucking music"; and had me stand outside the men's room while he fucked a club girl who looked like she'd made this trek more than once tonight. After having the coke bitch, as he referred to her, he started hunting the club for the perfect girl to take home. He's come up empty-handed so far. Like I told him, not too many virgins hanging around a nightclub known to cater to the criminal element of the city.

I survey the crowd. Maybe if I find him a girl, we can all leave. I'm not a fan of clubs in general. I don't like being around unfriendlies without my piece. And I haven't spent any time with Bitsy today. I worked all day at Marjory's sorting shit with Beefer, and then I had to come back out to ride herd over Cesaro's dumb, horny ass.

"So you want to dance?"

"She's talking to you." Beefer nudges me.

"Huh?" There's a table of six girls about twenty feet away. Odds are that there's one shy girl in the group willing to get down with Cesaro's cheap brand of seduction.

"She wants to know if you want to dance?" Beefer leans in front of me. "Don't be offended by clueless Joe here. He doesn't get out much. Leka, the girl's talking to you."

I twist to face the girl, who's drawn back, one hand on her hip, looking at me like my elevator doesn't go all the way to the top floor. What we were talking about? Oh, right. The temp in this shithole. "Yeah, it's hot in here," I say, ignoring the dancing shit.

"She asked if you wanted to dance," Beefer unhelpfully points out.

"No. How shy are you?"

"Shy?" Her confusion deepens at the same rate as my irritation.

"Yeah, you see that guy over there between the two blondes? That's Cesaro. He's got a shit ton of money and wants to get laid tonight. How about it?"

"Jesus. Are you a pimp or something?" She grabs her drink. "Your friend is fucking weird."

That last bit is directed toward Beefer before she stomps off.

He looks at me with suspicion. "Did you just do that on purpose?"

I pick up my water and take a long draw, letting my silence talk for me.

"Fuck you, you stupid bastard." He laughs as he says it, but I get the sense that part of him believes it. "You coulda banged that chick. She was eye fucking you so hard I was getting a woody."

"Then you should've dived in." I catch an ice cube in between my back teeth and set my plastic cup down.

"She didn't want me."

"She wanted to get chased and then laid. I didn't feel like doing either."

"You're going to hurt yourself, playing possum like you are."

"It's my choice." I shake the cup and watch the ice cubes clink against the side of the cup.

"But why? Give me one good reason why you're not out there on the dance floor, rubbing your dick against some girl's pussy. Why you're not taking her to the bathroom and having her suck you dry. Why you're not in pound town every night when quality snatch is always trying to ride your dick!" Beefer slams his fist on the table.

He's worked up about something and it's not my lack of fucking around.

"Well?" he asks. There's sweat on his forehead. He's feeling stress from Arturo, I guess. And babysitting Cesaro is a shit job.

For all of those reasons and because Beefer saved me, I give him an explanation he isn't owed. "One time you told me to find an anchor. I did, and I'm not going to cut that chain for a quick lay with some random woman."

I stay in my lane because Bitsy would know. She's insightful like that. She can read every mood of mine. And if I did any of those things that Beefer suggested, Bitsy would see that something had changed. And there is no one, not a casual encounter that lasts five minutes, ten minutes or even a full day, that would be worth marring the perfect oasis that is my home with Bitsy.

Beefer's jaw flaps open, wanting to argue with me, but Cesaro struts up to the table. It's the first time since I laid eyes on the asshole that I'm even marginally glad to see him.

"These two ladies have a hankering for a little VIP action." He squeezes the two girls tight against him.

"Best take them to Oak Street," I say, and for once Beefer agrees with me.

"Yeah, let's roll."

IT'S FIVE IN THE MORNING WHEN I LET MYSELF IN. MRS. M IS asleep on the sofa.

Since she likes to make breakfast for her husband, I give her a small shake on the shoulder.

"That you, Leka?"

"Yes." It wouldn't be anyone else. "I got you a car. It's downstairs. How's Bitsy?"

"She was a doll as always. Such a sweet girl." She rubs her eyes and then rolls to her feet. "And you're a good brother, Leka."

I give her a nod and help gather up her things. I can't walk her downstairs because I'm not going to leave Bitsy alone, but I do stand in the doorway and watch until the elevator doors open.

She gives me a wave. I go to my laptop and fire up the building security cameras I've tapped into. Mrs. M makes an uninterrupted trip down the elevator to the lobby. The doorman waves to her and makes a note in his book. The outside camera shows her getting into the car I called for her.

Once she is safely away, I go check on my girl.

I give a passing glance to her bedroom, noting that her bed is empty. I'm not worried, though, and as I stop in the doorway of my room, my suspicions are confirmed by the small lump on the left side.

Lightly, I cross the room. She's lying on her side, her hands tucked under her face. In the circle of her arms is her bunny that I bought so many years ago at Macy's. I've given her others since, but this is the one she loves the most.

I grab my sleep clothes off the top of the dresser and walk to the bathroom. In the shower, I realize that I ran out of bar soap this morning. I'm stuck with Bitsy's stuff. I unscrew the strawberry-shaped cap and give the contents a whiff. Shrugging, I squirt pink stuff onto my palm. So I smell like strawberries. There are worse things. After the shower, I towel off and throw on a pair of sweatpants and a T-shirt.

I make my way back to my room and lower myself onto the other side of the mattress. Cesaro is going to be a problem if he sticks around. One of the girls balked when it came to taking off her clothes and Cesaro punched her. It took a shit ton of money and a well-worded threat to buy her silence.

What bothered me the most was that Cesaro wasn't high or drunk. He got off on being cruel. He liked it when the girl resisted and liked it even more when she cried.

Beefer drove the girl and her friend home while I watched Cesaro grow angrier and angrier as he struck out with the girls at his uncle's club. When the club began to close, he called his uncle demanding a fresh whore. Mary showed up fifteen minutes later. Cesaro wasn't pleased at first. He called her every name in the book and asked her why she thought he'd wanted to fuck her loose meat sandwich again.

Mary didn't even flinch. She closed the door and a half hour later, Cesaro came out, somewhat subdued. Mary followed behind. Her hair was fucked up. Her red lipstick was smeared all over her face, and there was a cut on her cheek she didn't have when she arrived. But she wore a satisfied expression.

Maybe she liked the force. Some girls did. Whatever the case, she didn't complain.

"Need a ride?" I asked her. "Beefer'll be back soon."

She shook her head and tucked her hand into the crook of Cesaro's arm. "No. I'm going with Cesaro."

"You sure? I could run you home." I'd never offered that before, but giving her over to Cesaro didn't feel right.

"She told you she's coming home with me. Get your own bitch, Priest." He said the word with a sneer.

I dismissed him. "Let me give Arturo a call so he knows where you both are."

"He knows and approves. He's happy that I'm with a man who can please me." Mary turned her face into Cesaro's biceps and laid a kiss against it.

I had no choice but to let them go.

I waited in the darkened restaurant until Beefer came back. I debated not telling him, but if it were me, I'd want to know.

In the end, I didn't have to say a word. He'd walked into the restaurant, saw me sitting alone at the table in the stockroom and knew immediately.

"Mary came, didn't she?"

I nodded.

He cursed. "I can smell her. She still wears that damn Gucci perfume I gave her all those fucking years ago."

I didn't know if I should apologize or sympathize or what, so I kept my mouth shut. Beefer closed his eyes, squeezed the bridge of his nose between two fingers, and let out a string of curse words. When his outburst was over, he gave me a sheepish look and asked me to drink a beer with him.

I tried not to look impatiently at the clock, but it wasn't easy. He finally called it a day when the morning staff showed up to do the food prep. I ran home. Literally sprinted all the way home.

Next to me, Bitsy tenses and mumbles something in her sleep. Something like, "I'm not fuzzy" followed by "yours sticks up."

"Shh, shh," I whisper, giving her shoulder a reassuring squeeze. She feels fragile under my palm.

She rolls toward me, her small fingers curving around my forearm. The tension of the night fades with her light touch. No, not for anyone would I trade my life with Bitsy. I place a hand over the top of her head and fall asleep.

17

BITSY

Three years later

"Isn't school in twenty minutes?" Leka yells.

I stare at my reflection and dab a little more concealer over the zits on my forehead. I hate zits. Sister Ruth at St. Vincent's Academy for Girls tells me that it's just hormones and I'll grow out of it. I pointed out that most of the other girls in my grade have perfectly clear complexions and Sister Ruth's suggestion was to pray about it. Given that half of my classmates spend more time on their knees blowing boys than praying, I highly doubt that a few Hail Marys are going to clear up my face.

This is not a tidbit that I share with Leka. He'd have an absolute cow. No, he'd have a herd of them.

After applying the makeup, I give myself another once-over. Blech. Now my bumps look like they have a tan. I toss the concealer into my drawer and head for the kitchen.

It doesn't matter what I look like. Today, I'm going to mete out the first prong of my revenge. Mrs. M's advice to be creative in my problem-solving sprouted an idea. I might be smaller than rat-faced Felix, but I could be craftier.

He is going to regret ever harassing me. I reach under the sink and find the plastic baggy I put together last night while Mrs. M was taking a bathroom break. Carefully, I open one end of it. Tears sting my eyes. The combined stink of the day-old fish and egg nearly knocks me over. Quickly, I zip the bag shut.

I tuck it into the side of my backpack. I'm in the process of swinging the pack onto my shoulder when a voice behind me says, "Hold up there."

I yelp and jump straight up. A big hand reaches out to steady me.

"Jesus Chri—stopherson," I exclaim, revising the swear words at the last second. "You scared the stuffing out of me."

Leka's free hand comes up to cover a huge yawn. "Sorry. What time is it?"

I give him a once-over, taking in his rumpled hair and the hooded lids. "You look like you got an hour's sleep after a night at a rave."

Or bonking some girl's brains out. He did come home super late last night and took a shower before he collapsed on the bed. You only shower when you don't want people to smell your sins. That's what Sister Ruth says, at least. Which, if you think about it, is a total contradiction to the whole "cleanliness is next to Godliness" thing they all preach.

"What do you know about raves?" He glowers.

"Not as much as you," I counter and push the strap of the backpack higher up my shoulder. "I'll see you after school. Try to get some sleep."

"Wait a sec. I'll walk you to school." He starts toward his bedroom.

"What?" I balk. He can't come with. It'll mess with all my plans. "No. I can walk three blocks by myself."

"I know you can." He calls over his shoulder. "But today you don't have to. I'm gonna grab a jacket."

He won't admit it to me, but I know, also from past experience, that it's because he always carries a gun.

I think I was eight or nine before I realized that wasn't normal. I thought everyone just carried them around. Everyone associated with Leka does, but at Catholic school, the biggest weapons are a nun's rulers and a girl's words.

I briefly entertain the image of Leka knocking Felix over with the butt of the gun. Felix would probably piss his pants at the sight of a gun. He'd also report both of us, and since Felix's dad is a lawyer, that wouldn't go well for Leka and me.

At least, that's the threat Felix threw in my face a few weeks ago when I told him that if he threw one more apple core at my face, I was going to call the cops on him.

Do it, pizza face. My dad's a lawyer. You're the one who'd end up in jail for being a health hazard.

We'll see who's the health hazard after this. I smile evilly to myself. All of this is contingent on getting rid of Leka, though.

I eye the front door of our apartment and then the bedroom door that Leka just disappeared through. How mad would he be if I just left?

Pretty mad.

I sigh.

Walking to school with Leka is both wonderful and awful. It's wonderful because I get to spend more time with him, and lately, it feels like Marjory's is sucking up all his time. It's awful because the older girls at St. Vincent are in love with him.

After the last time, I had to listen to a week's worth of "Is that your brother?" "Holy park"—(crap backwards)—"he's so hot" and "Which saint do I say thanks to for having an ass like that?" and "I'm ready to sacrifice myself on his altar."

But I'd still suffer through all that to have his company—only not today.

He re-appears. A baseball cap covers his bedhead. There's scruff around his chin, which I know from past experience is pleasantly scratchy. His feet are shoved into one of his three pairs of black boots. Jeans, a navy T-shirt and a bomber coat make up the rest of his outfit.

"Ready?" he asks, lifting the backpack strap away from my shoulder.

I pull back. "I really need to walk by myself. Sister Katherine says that independence is the sign of an elevated mind, and girls that don't get to school by themselves have to meditate on the concept of individualism."

The lie rolls off easily. Leka looks skeptical at first, but when I stare back unflinchingly, he backs off.

"I don't want to be responsible for you having to meditate more," he says. There's a slightly wounded tone to his voice, which makes me feel bad.

"I'm sorry," I say quietly, ducking my head.

He pats me on the shoulder. "No. Don't be. You were right the first time. I'm tired." He flips off his ball cap. "I'll rest up on the couch, and when you're out of school, we'll go do something."

Chin up, I beam at him. "Awesome." I give him a brief hug and then race out the door.

Felix is stationed three blocks away from the apartment, waiting for the bus to pick him up. He's always there early, as if he can't wait to get out of the house and be in position to torment me.

"Pizza face. I was hoping you'd died so I didn't have to see your ugly face again."

"Fuck you, Felix," I give him the finger.

He glowers. "I wouldn't fuck you if you paid me. Bet you're a virgin, aren't you?"

"I'm thirteen, dickhole. Of course, I'm a virgin. Just like you."

His friend Will snorts. This makes Felix only angrier. He steps toward me, a hand down on his crotch. "Wanna bet? Girls are begging to get on my jock."

"The only girl who begs you is the one in your dreams, loser."

Will's snickers grow louder. Felix turns toward his friend. "Shut up, asshole." He twists back to me. "And in your dreams, you beg for someone to love you, but they only vomit when they lay eyes on you. No one wants you, bitch."

The thing about Felix is that he knows exactly where to punch you to make it hurt the most.

"Come on, Felix. The bus is almost here," Will tugs at Felix's sleeve. Felix shrugs out of his friend's grasp.

"Good. I have time to teach this bitch a lesson." He lunges for me.

What I lack in size, I make up for in quickness. I sidestep him and then pretend to trip. I pitch forward, grabbing onto his backpack for stability. I slip the baggy inside the outer pocket. Felix shoves me.

"Get off me, you fucking hag." He shoves me hard.

I fall to the ground, catching myself on the pavement. The cement digs into my hands. I push myself up, but before I can get to my feet, a kick in my side catches me unaware. I bend forward, gasping for breath.

"Come on, dude. Not cool," Will says above me.

I curl into a ball and wait for another kick, but nothing comes. The sound of a bus stopping and the door opening fills the space. I struggle to my feet, still holding my midsection.

I manage to gather up the strength to flip Felix off and yell, "Smell you later, loser."

He leans out the window and is about to shout something when his face pales and he drops down into his seat.

A long shadow appears, superimposing itself over my shorter one. Slowly, I twist around to see Leka's face, which is focused on the retreating bus. A thunderous expression colors his features.

"You forgot your phone." He lifts up my mobile.

"Whoops," I murmur and reach for it. I twist to tuck it into my backpack, but the motion hurts and I let out an involuntary squeak of pain.

Leka's face grows even darker, his eyes still fixed in the direction of the bus. "I'm going to kill that punk."

"No." I grab Leka's arm. "You can't. His dad's a lawyer. We'll get in trouble."

"His dad could be the motherfucking pope, and I'd still carve up that little pencil dick's face and deliver it to his dad during mass."

This is really bad. Fear starts spreading through my veins. Oh, what did I start here? I should've kept my mouth shut and endured. It's not like Felix ever hurt me before. Not really. So he said stupid things and my stupid feelings were bruised, but this is the first time he's ever kicked me.

"Leka." I tug on his arm. "Leka, please." He finally looks down at me. I tip my forehead against his chest. "Please, don't do anything. I already got him back."

He rubs his hand up and down my arm. "How so?"

"I filled a baggie with fish and eggs and then dropped it into his backpack. I gave it a good slap before I let go."

His hand stops. A finger bumps my chin up. I see a reluctant smile tip the corner of his lips. "Smell you later?"

I give a tiny shrug. "Seemed appropriate."

He pulls my phone from my hand and does something to the screen before dropping it into my backpack. "Come on."

"School's the other way," I tell him as he turns and leads me down the street.

"You're sick today," he announces.

"I am?" I raise my eyebrows.

"Yes. Sudden flu. High temperatures. I need to get some fluids in you."

He turns down another street. My heart rate picks up. "Are we getting ice cream fluids?" I ask. This is the way toward my favorite diner where they make awesome chocolate chip pancakes and the best shakes ever.

"I hear that's the best way to bring a fever down."

HE WAITS UNTIL I'VE STUFFED MYSELF FULL OF PANCAKES AND I'm working on sucking the very last of my shake out of my glass to pounce.

"How long has that been going on?" He jerks his head in the general direction of the street corner where Felix and I had it out.

"You're ruining my breakfast."

Leka gives me a dark look. With an exaggerated sigh, I push away my plate.

"Since September."

"It's October."

I resist the urge to say something smart, like *I know. I learned the months in kindergarten.*

"He's only there on Mondays and Thursdays. The rest of the time he gets a ride, I think."

"So twice a week for the last six, this little punk has been assaulting you and you never said one word?"

It's the hurt in his voice that finally penetrates and casts all my good intentions into the gutter.

"I thought I could handle it myself. I didn't want to bug you. You're always doing stuff for me, Leka. You pay my tuition. You buy my clothes. You put the roof over my head and food on the table and what do you get in return?" Heat pricks the back of my eyes. I blink furiously to keep the tears from falling.

"I get you, Bitsy. That's what I get. Right?"

His hand reaches across the table. I stare at it.

No one wants you, I hear Felix saying.

"How can that be enough?" A couple tears slip out anyway. I swipe them away. "Mrs. M says that you need a wife. Am I holding you back? I mean, you never bring any women home. Are you afraid to? Am I doing something wrong?"

Had I been selfish like Mrs. M implied a few years ago? I can't hold on to Leka forever, but the idea of sharing him with someone else makes my heart want to shrivel up into a lump of coal.

Leka gets up and slides into my side of the booth. He pulls me close, and at the first touch of his hand on my back, I start sobbing like a baby.

"I don't need a wife. I don't want a wife." He rubs my back. "You're enough for me, Bitsy."

I snake my arms around his neck and cling like a monkey. "If you want a girlfriend, you should have one. I'm okay with that." That's another lie.

"I promise that if I find some girl that I like enough to call her my girl-friend, I won't let anyone stand in my way, okay? Not even you."

That's exactly what I asked for him to say, but it doesn't feel good to hear it. Still, this is about what Leka needs. I take a few breaths, rub my eyes against his jacket and then pull away.

"Okay," I say, my eyes fixed on the sleeve of his dark jacket where my tears have left a shiny mark. I pick up a napkin and wipe the moisture away.

"Do you—do you need a mom, Bitsy?" he asks carefully.

I jerk my head up. "No. You're all I need. I swear it."

A smile appears at the corners again. His hand comes up to cup my skull. "I believe you. So, we are in agreement. It's you and me, Bitsy."

I turn my face into his hand and press a kiss there. "You and me, Leka. Always."

I swear I feel him tremble.

.

18

BITSY

One year later

"You looking at the clock isn't going to make him come home any sooner," Mrs. M says.

I set my phone down. "I was seeing if anyone from school texted me," I lie.

"And did they?"

"No." That much is true. I've only one good friend at St. Vincent's and she has a no texting after nine p.m. rule.

Mrs. M clucks her tongue against the roof of her mouth, the sound blending in with the tapping of her knitting needles against each other. "You should make more friends. It'd be good for you to get out of this apartment."

"Why?" I look around. "I like it here." It's my favorite place. It's where Leka and I've made our marks for the last four years. There's the gouge in the wood floor in the entryway where Leka had dropped the coat rack we'd bought down in the Village and the dent in the wall right outside my bedroom made from the big globe I insisted on buying. Under the sofa is the nail polish stain I'd made when I was ten. I'd thought Leka would be so mad, but he just smiled and rubbed his hand across the top of my head. The kitchen table has scrapes and paint stains and a burn mark from the glue gun that we've used on so many school projects.

"You should be in a building with more kids or maybe a house outside the city with a yard and a dog." Clickety-clack go her needles.

"A yard and a dog sounds like a lot of work." I pull up my knees and lay my head on them, wishing that Leka was back already.

"Out of the city, you'd get more sunshine," she goes on as if I hadn't spoken. "And there'd be more parks, more people, more fresh air."

It sounded like Mrs. M wanted to get out of the city. I like the busyness and the fact I can get anywhere by myself just using the subway. I'm only a single stop from Marjory's, although I never go there unless Leka is with me. But knowing I'm only a ten-minute train ride from him makes me feel better.

"I heard that Assumption is hosting the sweetheart dance this year. Have you figured out who you're going to ask?"

"Nope."

"There's no one that you don't have a crush on? I hear the boys at Assumption are very handsome. And from good families, too."

The smell from the strawberry lotion on my legs mixes with the lemon polish of the floor wax I used earlier when I draw a breath. Underneath those tones, I swear I can smell Leka's earthy, male scent. I inhale deeply, trying to concentrate on it instead of the stuff Mrs. M keeps nattering on about. Stuff I don't care about. I close my eyes and I inhale again. There it is. I hold my breath and fill myself with him.

Why would I want a boy when I have Leka? No one compares to him. No one at Assumption is as tall or broad-shouldered. No one's hair falls just the right way over his forehead. No one's hands send shivers down my spine. No one's deep voice soothes me when I'm anxious. No one but Leka. I think I've always known it was going to be him, even before I realized that the connection we had was more than just brother and sister. So no, there are no boys at Assumption that I have a crush on. There would be no boys for me, ever. Only Leka.

"Mrs. Michaelson asked you a question."

I jerk upright. "Leka, you're home," I say. I pat my face, wondering if my feelings are written all over my face.

He cocks his head and looks at me curiously. "I am. What's this about a dance?"

"Nothing." Damn Mrs. M and her big mouth. I throw my babysitter a glare. She ignores me, much as I ignored her all night.

"Assumption is hosting a sweetheart dance for all the junior high kids. That's the one where the girl asks the boy to dance." She tucks her knitting gear away. "Elizabeth missed it last year because she forgot to sign the conduct agreement."

I didn't forget. I threw the piece of paper in the trash because I wasn't interested in any school dance. I'm still not.

Leka draws a hand across his chin. There's a rough stubble there. "I didn't know about this. Aren't you a little young for dancing with boys?"

I don't pay attention to his question because I'm too caught up in the state of his hair. It's wet and slicked against his perfect skull. My stomach tightens. That means whatever work he did was messy.

"Of course, she's not. She's a teenager. Many girls start dating at this age. It's perfectly natural." She clucks her tongue again. "Leka, don't be so strict or she'll rebel." I shake my head at him, but Leka's frowning now. Mrs. M is a damn busybody. "You'll need to sign the conduct contract and get it in soon or you won't be able to attend," she continues.

I grab her knitting bag and carry it to the front door so she gets the hint. "I'm not going, so it doesn't matter."

"You can go if you want," Leka says.

"I don't want." I know it's not the time to tell Leka about how I feel. He'll say I'm too young. Or worse, that my feelings aren't real. No, the worse would be for him to pat my head and say that he's my brother and that's all he'll ever be.

"She should go," Mrs. M pipes up. "It'd be good for her. I'll take her dress shopping this weekend if you're not available."

"I'm not going," I insist.

"I'll let you know, Mrs. Michaelson," Leka says and holds the door open. He grabs the bag from my grasp and walks Mrs. M down the hall.

She keeps on chattering about the dance. "You do that, dear. It would be good for Elizabeth. She doesn't have enough friends. It's not healthy for her to be by herself."

I can't make out Leka's words. He's murmuring too low—intentionally, I think.

"Yes, fourteen's a perfect age for this. It's definitely not too young."

I decide I don't need to hear more of this and go inside. I make my way to the kitchen and pull out the makings for a sandwich. Leka's often hungry when he gets home from work. He doesn't eat at Marjory's. I used to pretend it was because Mary turned his stomach, but now I think it's more that he doesn't much like the work he does there.

"So, you have a school dance," Leka says as he enters the kitchen. "What else haven't you shared with me?"

Oh, the usual. The fact that I have stirrings inside of me that'd make him cringe and blush and run away. "Nothing." At his look of disbelief, I sigh. "Hold on."

I fetch my backpack and pull out a sheaf of papers and toss them on the table. Leka takes a seat, and with a sandwich in one hand, he starts leafing through the pile of parental forms. One for a field trip to a gum factory. Another for a visit to the National Museum of History. There were a couple of school mixers: one for Assumption's homecoming last fall and another for the end of the term.

He reads each one and then lays them down until there's a stack of about ten of them. He looks at his sandwich and sets that down, too. "Take a seat, Bitsy."

Heart heavy, I drop into the chair with a thud.

"Why didn't you tell me about this stuff?"

"Because none of it matters."

His fingers curl and his jaw tightens in a sure sign that he's frustrated and trying to control it. "This is the fun school shit and you're missing it. Why?"

"It's not fun, Leka. That's the thing. This stuff is either boring or terrifying." I pull out the museum form. "I looked it up. This place is full of animals that are dead and stuffed, but they're behind glass. You can get as good of a picture of them on the internet, and there's more information there, too." I grab the mixer for homecoming. "This one is for Assumption's football game during which four students got caught smoking a joint in the bathroom and after the game, Misty Price was found on the bus giving consolation prizes with her mouth."

Poor Leka's mind is blown. The once tight jaw is slack. His eyes are slightly widened. "You go to a Catholic school," he says, like the scripture verses from the nuns serve as some kind of holy chastity belt.

"Right, but as long as we go to confession, it's all good." Besides, some of those priests probably get off on the girls kneeling next to them whispering about all the dirty stuff they got up to during the week.

He sits silently as he processes the information. His hand comes up to stroke the bottom half of his face, probably to hide whatever strong emotion he's feeling, but I can always tell what's going on in his mind. Not precise, exact thoughts, but general emotions. Right now, he's upset —likely over the fact that the safe place he stashed me at is a hotbed of vice—drugs and sex mostly.

"And, you, Bitsy? What are you confessing to?"

"I tripped Jillian Murkowski about three weeks ago," I say candidly.

He tries to hide a grin behind that hand, but I can see his eyes light up. "What for?"

"Just being a general bitch. She's in tenth grade and has a boyfriend in high school. She seems to think that gives her an increased status at school and goes around telling the other girls what she doesn't like about their looks. Leila is so tiny that her parents must be munchkins. Is she sure she's an eighth grader? Camryn is heavy. Do you really think that you should have that dinner roll with your lunch?" I mimic Jillian's nasally voice. "That sort of thing."

"What does she say about you?"

"Nothing. This isn't the first time I've tripped her." Last year, I accidentally, on purpose, stepped on her hand during PE as she was leaning on a riser in the gym.

Leka snorts. "Fine. So your school's a mess. Why haven't you told me before? You could've gone somewhere else."

"There are going to be jerks everywhere. What's the point in starting over? At least here, I know who the jerks are and can stay out of the way of the really dangerous ones."

"I don't think that's how school's supposed to be," he chides gently, but he's done lecturing me. He's also done being upset, because he's picked up his sandwich again.

"If you say so." But I think that's how school is everywhere. You just endure it and once it's over, then you start living. At least that's my theory. Once school is over, once I'm eighteen, then Leka will see me as a woman and we'll live happy ever after.

Not that we aren't happy now, but I feel like we could be closer. Or maybe I fear that Mrs. M is right and that some woman is going to snatch him up before I'm ready to claim him. Or, rather, he's ready for me to claim him, because I'd announce to the world right now that it's going to be Leka and me forever and not in that brother/sister shit that everyone is trying to press on me.

"I still think you should go to this dance. These things are supposed to be fun."

"I'd rather have every tooth pulled without Novocaine."

"That's real painful. I'd go for the dancing over the teeth pulling."

"I have a better idea of what to do with my time," I propose.

"What's that?" he asks.

I wait until his mouth is full before springing my brilliance on him. "I should get a job."

He starts shaking his head before I can even get my last word out. Since his mouth is full, though, I press my advantage. "Yeah. Remember how I told you how Mandy's dad owns that frozen yoghurt joint over on Beecher and 2nd?"

"No." But I can tell by the shift in his gaze that he does recall it. Leka's not great with reading, but his memory is near perfect.

"Mandy's working there a few hours a day and said that I could help her out. He pays $7 an hour and I could work like ten hours a week. Maybe more on the weekend. That'd be like a $100 a week."

"What do you need? I'll buy it for you."

I tip my head back in frustration. He can be so dense sometimes. "I know, but I want to earn my own money. Every gift I've gotten for you, you've paid for, so it's like you buying yourself a present, which is dumb." He opens his mouth to interrupt, but I barrel on. "And, if you really feel like I'm missing out on something, then this is the perfect way for me to fit in better. Lots of St. Vincent and Assumption kids come to the place and hang out."

"Then you should go and hang out," he says. Abruptly, he shoves away from the table and takes his plate to the dishwasher. For anyone else, I suppose his flat voice and closed face would put them off. Not me.

"How about this? I'll go to the dance if you let me work at Froyo."

"No."

"How about Marjory's?"

He shudders and slams the dishwasher shut. "No."

Turning, he braces his arms behind him. The muscles in his biceps bulge slightly and the blue T-shirt with the faded Adidas logo pulls up slightly from his jeans. A tiny sliver of skin peeks through. I take a heavy breath, not fully understanding why my heart rate is speeding up or my hands feel slightly sweaty. I rub my palms against my own jeans and play my trump card. "I'll enter a piece of my art in the Junior League Art show in the spring."

Silence hangs between us. I know how much he wants this. He's been hounding me to do it for a year now, ever since a visit to the Met when he discovered that it was a thing students could do.

I press. "Froyo, where I'm working with people you don't know, hanging around that bad element of teens who smoke weed and have sex, or Marjory's, where you can keep an eye on me."

"One hour a week and only when I'm there." I jump up in the air and let out a yelp of victory. "And I want to see the application to the art show filled out in the morning."

"You got it."

I throw myself at him, like I wanted to do when he first came home but I was afraid to. Afraid he'd somehow read my inappropriate thoughts about him and push me away. He catches me—as he always does. His big arms pull me up against his frame. I bury my face in his neck and inhale his special scent straight from the source. I have this overwhelming urge to stick out my tongue and see what he tastes like. Wonderful, I imagine.

I wriggle out of his grasp before I can do something stupid.

THE NEXT DAY I SHOW UP AT MARJORY'S RIGHT AFTER SCHOOL. The place isn't very full, and Mary is sitting at one of the back tables, her feet up on a chair, reading a magazine.

She lowers it slightly as I approach. "What do you want?"

"Hi, Mary." I hesitate, because Mary's like Felix. She knows where to strike to hurt you. I'm careful not to get too close. "Is Leka here?"

She raises the magazine again so I can't see her face and so she doesn't have to look at me. "No."

That's it. No, he's out or he'll be back soon. Just a no, like I'm some stranger off the street. Still, if I'm going to work here, I need to be able to hold my own with her, so I take a deep breath and say, "I'm here for a job."

The magazine falls out of her hands. She laughs, a full-on belly laugh, and I stand there like an idiot watching her. Finally, she dabs a napkin at the corners of her eyes. "God, kid. I needed that. How hilarious."

"I'm not kidding. Leka said I could work here an hour every day."

"You ever look in the mirror, honey?" she asks. "Because it's a fright. No one's going to eat if you're out here taking orders and delivering food. They'll take one look at your mug and lose their appetite." She places a hand on the top of her big tits. "You've got to have good looks to work in the front of the restaurant." She picks up her magazine and starts reading it again. The silence is punctuated by a few giggles.

"I'll work in the back then. I can wash dishes, cut stuff."

"No. We don't need help."

"But Leka said—"

She slams her hand down. Her pretty face screws up tight, making her look like Felix the rat. "Leka doesn't run Marjory's. I run Marjory's, and what I say goes. You don't belong here. Now get out."

A bell tinkles and we both twist to see the door from the kitchen swing open. Through it walks Leka and Beefer.

"Hi, Beefer." I wave a limp hand in his direction.

He comes over and gives me a big hug. "How're you doing, Lizzie?"

I grimace into his chest both because I have to endure this hug and because he calls me by that hideous nickname. "Good."

"I hear you're going to work for us after school."

I glance toward Mary, who glares at Beefer.

"I thought I was in charge of the staffing decisions here," she snipes.

"You are," he says, giving me another squeeze before releasing me.

"Then no, she's not working here."

Leka steps up between Beefer and me and places a hand at the base of my neck. "Why not, Mary?"

His voice is low, calm, and even, but there's a terrifying quality to it. And Mary senses it, too. The unstated warning in his quiet words is that whatever answer she gives better be one that he likes.

"Sh-she has no experience."

I have to hand it to the woman. She's persistent.

Still keeping his hand on my neck, Leka bends down until he's close enough to feel Mary's breath on his cheek. "Then you'll teach her."

He straightens and gently directs me toward the bar where Beefer's pouring himself a drink. We've all turned our backs on Mary, which, I think, is a very big mistake.

19

One year later

Bells chime as I push open the tall glass door. A blue-suited man wearing a stern expression gives me a sharp nod and Leka a wary glance.

"Are you sure this is the right place?" I mutter to Leka under my breath. The small store isn't like any I've ever been in. I'm used to racks full of clothing. Maybe a few mannequins dotting the floor. This cream and gold wedding cake of a store has about ten dresses on display.

He flips over his phone. "Divine Dresses," he recites. "Mrs. Michaelson said you should get your dress here."

He gives me a gentle shove to move farther into the store.

"What's wrong with Macy's?" That's where I would've bought last year's dress if I'd been forced to go. Lucky for me, I turned my ankle working at Marjory's and convinced Mrs. M that I was too hurt to dance. Believing that I was super disappointed, Leka took me to see *Deadpool* and then spent half the time covering my eyes—as if I hadn't ever seen a guy's ass before. Okay, so it was the first time I'd seen a naked ass, but it wasn't as if the sight of Ryan Reynolds' naked butt cheeks inspired an intense desire to pull down the pants of every guy that walked by me.

After the movie, I did spend more time surreptitiously staring at Leka's butt and wondering what it might look like without his usual jeans or sleep pants covering him, but I don't lie awake at night thinking about it. At least not often. Like, not every night or anything.

"Mrs. Michaelson said to bring you here."

Mrs. Michaelson is the female oracle in our lives. If she says that I should do something, Leka immediately obeys, which is why we are at a store I don't care about to buy a dress I don't need for a dance I don't want to attend.

"I think *Deadpool 2* is coming out."

Leka grunts, which could either mean maybe or no way. But I don't get the opportunity for a clarification because a saleslady clad in cream pants and a cream blouse with a big bow at her neck appears in front of us. "Hello. What can I help you find today?"

I open my mouth to say "nothing," but Leka speaks first.

"She needs a dress for a high school dance."

I wait for her to fawn all over Leka, like every woman between the age of six and eighty-six does, but to my enormous surprise, she barely glances at him. Instead, she addresses me. "Do you have a style or color in mind?"

"Black. Funereal."

Leka rolls his eyes at me. "She's fifteen, so make sure it's age appropriate."

The lady gives a slight nod of acknowledgment but doesn't take her focus from me. "I'm sure I can find something both you and your daughter will like."

"Oh, he's not—" I start to say and then let it go. I need to get over this compulsion to straighten everyone out about my connection with Leka. Besides, I think it hurts Leka's feelings, but he's not ready to hear that I'm in love with him and want to do all the naughty things the senior girls talk about doing with their boyfriends during gym. He'd die. I seriously think he'd have a heart attack. Then I'd have to give him mouth-to-mouth. Hmmm. This might have possibilities.

Before I can chase this fantasy down, the saleslady takes me by the elbow and draws me deeper into the store. "Sir, you're welcome to sit here. I'm going to take—" She pauses, indicating with an arched eyebrow that I should fill in my name.

"Elizabeth," I say.

"—I'm going to take Elizabeth to a dressing room." Leka drops into a chair as the lady leads me away. "If you're open to some suggestions, your skin coloring would look gorgeous with a jewel tone. Perhaps something in green or royal blue?"

"I like blue," I admit.

She casts a look over her shoulder. "I'm not surprised."

Hmm. She must've given Leka a longer look than I suspected. Yeah, he's got the bluest of blue eyes and yeah, it's my favorite color.

"I'm Catherine." She sweeps aside a heavy curtain and gestures for me to step inside. "Let me go find a few dresses for you."

"I don't want anything—"

"I think I know just the style you need. You have a marvelous figure." She gives me another smile. "Take off your clothes. All of them."

"All? Like, as in, my underwear?"

"Yes, all." She lets the curtain fall.

I peek out to see if she flirts with Leka, but she doesn't. She walks straight toward another door and disappears, leaving Leka sprawled out on the cream upholstered chair. He stretches out his legs, his jeans and dark boots an exotic contrast to the airiness of the room. While Catherine was focused on me, she's the aberration. Most of the time, he draws looks from every female within shouting distance. A group of three women sitting in chairs in front of a different dressing room keep sneaking peeks at him.

Leka is oblivious. I haven't been able to figure out if he knows he's being constantly checked out and ignores it or really doesn't understand the waves of interest that are set off the minute he steps into a room. And I don't know exactly what it is about him that's so attractive to everyone else. Objectively, he's hot, but there are hot guys everywhere. There's something different about him that speaks to women, and I don't know what it is.

Maybe they sense his protective nature in the way he opens the door or is always keeping a watchful eye out. There's a sense of wildness about him, too, as if he's the predatory jungle animal let loose in a petting zoo. You know he's dangerous, but you can't help wanting to reach out and pet him. Or maybe it's the way he holds himself. As he sits in the chair, you'd think he owned the place. He has that much confidence. Or perhaps it's something else, something that my fifteen years of living haven't allowed me to precisely define.

All I know is that if I set Leka down in the middle of a football field full of guys, every eye would gravitate toward him. I keep waiting for him to fall for someone, like Mrs. M said he would, but so far, he's been stubbornly, wonderfully single. That doesn't mean he's in love with me. Nope. I'm still the little girl that he picked up in the alley.

With a sigh, I tug the velvet curtain closed. I take off my jeans and hang them by the belt loop on a hook. My I-love-tacos T-shirt comes off next. I stare at myself in the mirror. I have a marvelous figure? Is Catherine blowing smoke up my ass, or does she really believe it? I give myself a good once-over. I'm more hippy than I'd like. Jeans are hard to find. They are either too tight around the ass and too loose around the waist or vice versa.

My boobs are so-so. I'm not flat-chested, but I could easily get away with no bra except for the whole nip thing. A few weeks ago, Leka pointed out in a tight, unhappy voice that my headlights were showing. I didn't immediately understand what he was saying until he awkwardly pointed a finger at my chest while staring at the ceiling. Looking down, I saw my nipples poking out against one of his borrowed T-shirts.

It made me feel strange that he noticed that. At first, I was embarrassed, but later that night when he was gone and I was alone, I thought about what it might feel like if it were his hand cupping the curve of my breast instead of mine. I felt my inner muscles tighten and an unfamiliar ache grow between my legs.

It made me think of when the girls at school talk about sex. How they touch themselves. There are lots of fans of the showerhead. Shelby Mayhew has a vibrator her older sister bought her. She brought it to school and let some of the other girls play with it over their clothes. There was a lot of lip-biting and butt shifting in the bathroom that day. I wondered what it felt like. I wondered what it would be like if it weren't a plastic or silicone penis but a real one, attached to a real person. Attached to someone like Leka.

I drop my hand to my panties. A couple of weeks ago, during gym class, I overheard Allison whisper to her best friend, Rachel, that Allison's boyfriend had gone down on her. That he'd licked her clit and that she thought she was going to die from the pleasure. Rachel couldn't believe it. Neither could I. But I think of that now. I imagine that it's Leka in front of me, sitting in the cream lacquered chair in the corner. That he's the one drawing my white panties over my butt, down my thighs and dropping them to the floor. That it's his fingers that reach behind my back and unhook my bra, releasing my suddenly sensitive breasts from the confines of the lace and wire.

He'd draw me close, his breath heating my stomach, making me clench all over. I wonder what that'd feel like? Would I want to die from the pleasure? My fingers curl against my skin.

A choked sound interrupts my fantasy. Panicked, I jerk around.

"Are you okay, sir? Do you need some water?" a soft voice sounds just outside the curtain.

Blushing, I kick my underwear in the back corner. What the hell was I doing? Leka doesn't care about my body. I'm a girl to him. He'd be the one dying of embarrassment if he knew the contents of my head.

"No, I'm fine," says Leka in a husky voice.

There's more soft murmuring, and then Catherine's voice is outside my curtain. "I have some dresses for you. Are you ready?"

"I guess."

Without warning, Catherine sweeps in. I duck back, covering myself.

"Don't worry, dear. I've seen it all before." She hangs up a few dresses and then sticks out her hand. In it is a contraption made of lace and satin. "This is a special corset that will help all these dresses fit just a bit better. We want to make the most of your assets."

"She's fifteen," Leka interjects loudly beyond the curtain.

Catherine winks at me. "Of course, she is."

She gestures for me to take the corset. I step into it, and Catherine pulls the lace ties tight, tying them in a bow at the base of my spine. Once that's on, she helps me into the first dress. It's a deep red and has tiny sleeves that sit just below the shoulder. There are tiny sparkling crystals that run along the upper border of the neckline.

"This is a modified sweetheart bodice," she says, zipping me up.

I stare in wide-eyed amazement as two swells appear above the crystals. "Wow, I have cleavage," I say in awe. I run my hand over my mounded breasts.

"Yes, good undergarments are the key. What do you think?"

I give a twirl. The diaphanous fabric of the skirt swirls around me. "I feel like a princess," I admit. At least from the neck down. I scrunch up my nose. My face is never going to stop traffic. My heavy brows still look like caterpillars across my forehead, and my hair would rival Medusa. Too bad there's not a corset for my head.

"Why would you need that?" Catherine asks.

"Need what?" I say in surprise. I'd lost the train of our conversation.

"Why would you need a corset for your head?"

"Oh, I said that out loud, huh?"

She cocks her head and looks at me in the mirror. "Honey, you're gorgeous. I hope you realize that. You have eyelashes most women would kill for. Your cheekbones are amazing, and I'm guessing that your lips are all natural."

Self-consciously, I press my fat lips together. "Um, you're nice to say that, but—"

She doesn't let me finish. She places a hand in the middle of my back and pushes me forward. "Take a good look at yourself. What do you see?"

Homely thing, isn't she?

Pizza face!

No one's going to eat if you're out here taking orders and delivering food.

"I see me."

"No, you don't." Catherine shakes her head. "You see some version of yourself, but it's not the real one. I see this all the time with girls. You don't know what to make of the gifts you've got." Her hand reaches up to pat my head. "I bet you've never been to a real salon, have you?"

"Um, no."

She pulls a pen out of her pocket and writes down a phone number. "You call this number and ask for Louis. Tell him Catherine from Divine Dresses sent you. He's hard to get in to, but for me, he'll make time. Ask him to do a keratin treatment, a brow wax, and a curl for those eyelashes. Now, let's get you into the blue dress. I think you're really going to like that one.

The moment that the wispy blue material settles around my legs, I fall in love. The dress creates an illusion of prettiness that I never felt before. I pinch a bit of fabric in each hand and twirl to the right and left. The light catches on the tiny crystals sewn into the skirt. Tiny puff sleeves and a neckline that shows off my collarbones

"I love this," the saleslady declares. She fusses with one of the tiny puff sleeves. "It's classy and wholesome but still adult. Do you want to show this to your..." She stops and looks for guidance.

"Leka," I supply.

"Do you want to show Leka your dress?" she finishes smoothly.

It's the most beautiful thing I've ever worn. I think it's the first time I've ever felt beautiful, even with my beetle brows, wild hair, and uneven complexion. In this dress, I feel like a princess.

"Yes," I say, my voice barely above a whisper. I'm afraid that if I breathe wrong, the image will blow away like a sand sketch on the boulevard.

"Go." She pushes me toward the curtain. "Show your friend."

Without even hesitating, I sweep the curtain aside. Leka's sprawled in the upholstered chair with one ankle resting on his knee.

"What do you think?" I ask, spinning in a wide circle. The silk slithers against my skin, like the caress of a hand. I don't plan on taking this dress off ever. I'll scrub the toilets at Marjory's with a toothbrush for the next decade if I have to. I wait for Leka's smiling response. For once, his declarations that I'm beautiful may actually be true. "Well?" I prompt. I hold out the sides and sway from side to side. "It's gorgeous, isn't it?"

Leka says nothing. He raises a hand to cover his mouth. Is that to disguise a frown? I search his eyes, looking for approval or disdain, but find nothing. His eyes are blank. The silence grows prolonged. Even Catherine, who couldn't seem to stop talking before, can't find anything to say.

My smile wilts. "Do you...do you not like it?" I croak out.

"It's fine," he says, and without another word, gets up and leaves.

Catherine clicks her tongue against the roof of her mouth and pushes me into the dressing room. "It's a lovely dress."

"Okay," I say, but at this point, Anna Wintour could waltz in and say that it's more beautiful than any gown worn at the Met Gala and I wouldn't believe her. Leka hates this dress and so do I.

20

"I'm sorry." I stare down at the large dress box on my lap. I wonder if Leka's pissed because of the cost. The total amount for the shoes, the rhinestone jewelry, and the dress had me gasping. I tried to leave without purchasing it, but Leka was having none of it.

"For what?" Leka asks as the cab driver pulls away from the curb. He takes the dress bag from me.

The wide boulevards and glass storefronts give way to narrow alleys and graffitied buildings before I answer because I don't know what's wrong. I don't know if it's the dress. I don't know if it's because of the cost. I don't know if it's because I'm not doing the right things at school. I don't know anything other than the fact that Leka's unhappy, and if he's unhappy, I'm miserable.

The cab stops in front of the restaurant. "I'm sorry about everything."

He won't look in my eyes. "You're not the one who needs to apologize."

"That'll be ten fifty," the cabby says.

Leka peels off a twenty. "Keep the change."

I scramble out of the cab after him. "Is it the dress? Because I can return the dress."

He shoots me a lopsided smile that is full of emotion I can't read. He's changing on me. I used to be able to understand every single twitch of his brow. Now there are secrets in his eyes.

"The dress is beautiful. You're beautiful. I guess I didn't realize you're growing up." He shuts the cab door behind me and hustles me inside the restaurant.

He *just* realized I'm growing up? And the blue dress did it? That's it. I'm wearing that blue dress every day until I die. "I'm fifteen, not five, Leka."

"Don't remind me," he mutters.

There's no time to respond, because as soon as we clear the doors, Mary grabs Leka, whipping the bag out of his hand.

"Arturo is coming." She points to me. "Get an apron on and go clean table ten. And make sure you get the floor. We don't want his feet sticking to the floor. You—" The finger moves to Gerry, the overly loud, can't-stop-talking goon, who pales. He half loves Mary and is half afraid of her. "He'll want spicy sausage, peas, and orecchiette pasta. Don't forget. He likes it hot."

And, then, as quickly as she appeared, she disappears inside the staff bathroom. Gerry and I exchange apprehensive looks. It's not that we fear Arturo, but it's Mary that we have to worry about. After a meeting with the boss, Mary has only two moods: smug satisfaction and torrential anger. It really depends on whether she gets what she asks for. Most of the time, it's positive.

"Keep your head down," Leka cautions.

I give him a nod of understanding. In the back, I grab a couple of rubber gloves, fill a bucket of water, and head for the corner booth where Arturo conducts his business while in town. While I'm scrubbing down Arturo's table, Leka is watching the door. One of his hands is resting on his belt loop not far from the gun that's holstered inside his blazer.

Arturo is the head of the crime syndicate that Leka works for. I don't know exactly what duties Leka carries out for Arturo, but all I know is that it has to do with guns and blood and that it's not legal. I can't really pinpoint the exact moment I figured that out.

Maybe it was when he first took me home with him and we had to hide on the fire escape while the realtor showed the apartment to prospective renters. Or maybe it was the time I found the gun in his room, tucked under the mattress. Or maybe it was when I figured out that no stock boy at a steakhouse can earn enough money to afford a two-bedroom apartment in this city.

But we don't talk about this. There are a number of things we never discuss, like how he takes multiple showers when he comes home. How his hours of work coincide with times that Marjory's is closed. How I sometimes still crawl into bed with him when I have the odd nightmare. Or how he never, ever has brought a girl home.

"He's here," Leka says.

Mary comes over. She runs a finger over the table, toes the ground. It's clean. I lift my chin. I do good work.

"Go," she orders.

I heft the bucket up and walk to the backroom. As I'm leaving, the front door opens and in walks Arturo's entourage. My feet stop moving as I take in the spectacle. Four dark-suited, sunglasses-wearing, gun-toting goons precede the man who controls half the east coast and six of them trail behind. All he's missing is the tricorn hat and the double-breasted suit coat and he'd be a ringer for Napoleon Bonaparte. Arturo can't be taller than me. He looks like he needs a booster seat to see over the table. I guess he likes Mary because he's at eye level with her chest.

She runs over, darting between the guards to press those titties up against Napoleon's arm. "Arturo, you handsome devil. Why have you stayed away so long? Come over. We have your table all set, and Gerry is making your special dish."

She rattles on, but the doors swing closed behind me. Gerry is stirring his pasta, a couple plates set up behind him under a warming lamp.

"Grab the raspberry dressing, will ya?" he hollers at me.

"No problem." I drop the water bucket near the sink, wash my hands and open the walk-in cooler. When I emerge, I find the kitchen filled up with Mary and a couple of guards.

"Why isn't the food done yet?" she huffs.

"Because genius takes time," Gerry replies, not bothering to look up from the ingredients he's stirring.

"I don't see any genius. I see a smartass who wants to get the side of his head beaten by a crowbar," Mary snipes. "He's hungry, so finish up."

"Yes, ma'am," Gerry salutes.

She looks like she's going to mete out that beating before Ger can even plate the food.

I rush over and hold out the dressing. "Here it is."

"Thanks," he grumbles and points his spatula at the stainless steel prep counter with two plates of salad. "Set it there and don't pour it on. You'll add too much."

This is the way of the world, I think. Mary punches at Gerry, who punches at me because he can't hit back at the one he really wants. I sigh and set the dressing down and back away. This is one of those times where it's best to stay out of the fray.

"This doesn't look like the extra-spicy sausage." Mary peers over Gerry's shoulder.

"It is."

"Where's the red pepper? I don't see any of it."

"It's there," he huffs.

She bumps his arm. "Where? I don't see it."

"It's there!" Gerry explodes. "Are you blind? It's there and there." He jabs his finger down into the pan.

Mary jostles him again, I guess to get a better look. "It's on your head if he doesn't like the dish." She straightens, dusts off her hands against the front of her pretty yellow dress and then flounces away.

"For Christ's sake, I've made this every time he's come and he fucking loves it," Gerry says. "It's better than the sex she's giving him."

I'm glad he waited until Mary left to add that part or she'd probably have one of Arturo's guards pistol-whip him for the after-dinner entertainment.

I turn to dump out the bucket of water when I feel a hand at my elbow. I look up to see one of the guards breathing down my neck, a look of interest in his eye.

He rakes me from head to toe. "Who are you?" he asks, the tone slightly insolent.

"Eh, you might want to take a step back. She's Leka's kid," Gerry calls over. He's finished cooking and is now plating all the food.

The guard releases my elbow and does shuffle back a bit. I try hard to keep the surprise off my face, but I'm not sure I entirely succeed when Gerry winks at me.

"Leka's well known."

I don't ask for what. Instead, I say to the guard, "You need something?"

"Just making conversation," he lies. The interest in his eyes is still there, but it's a lot more respectful.

"She's also fifteen. If you want to hang on to your dick for longer than a day, I'd suggest you lay off. Leka wouldn't be happy," Ger advises. "Come over here and help me carry the food out."

I slip past the guard, who doesn't lose the gleam in his eyes. The only attention I've garnered from males in the past has always been in the form of mockery, so this guard's light flirtation should be flattering. Instead, it makes me uneasy. Like Ger said, I'm Leka's girl. No one should be looking at me like this guard but Leka.

Gerry directs me to bring the block of parmesan and grater while he carries out the pasta dishes. Steam rises from the plate, and the smells of fresh noodles, spicy sausage and butter make my stomach rumble in appreciation.

"Finally," Mary says. "Arturo is so hungry, aren't you?"

"Smells good. Bring it over."

Gerry picks up the pace and slides the plates in front of the two of them. Mary picks up her fork, her eyes bright, and waits for me to grate the fresh cheese onto the dish. Arturo doesn't stop me until there's a veritable snowfall covering the food.

I fall back, unsure of whether I should stand by the side for more grating or leave. Mary doesn't give any instruction. She can't take her eyes off of Arturo.

He takes a big bite and then another. "This is good," he says.

Gerry's chest puffs out. "Made the noodles fresh this morning just for you. The peas are from this farm upstate. I got the sausage—"

Ger's explanation is cut off by a massive coughing fit from Arturo. Mary whips into motion, holding a glass of water up to Arturo's mouth and pounding him on the back at the same time.

Arturo falls backward, a hand over his chest. His eyes roll back.

"Oh my God!" Mary screams. "Arturo! Arturo! He's having a heart attack"

The guards are shoving people out of the way. Leka appears from the front. There's so much commotion with people yelling and shoving. Mary's high-pitched screams are killing my ears, but all I can think of is how right before Mary started screaming, Arturo looked like a mad dog, with his teeth bared and white speckles at the corner of his mouth.

"He's been poisoned," I say to myself. I run to the back room and grab a bottle of charcoal from above the sink.

I muscle my way through the guards and slam the bottle onto the table. "He's been poisoned," I say. "Get this in him."

Mary rears back, nearly knocking me over, but Leka is there and whips me out of the way.

"What'd you say?"

"I think he's been poisoned. We had this thing in health class about suicides, and this one girl swallowed a bottle of pills—"

Leka doesn't let me finish. He springs forward, grabbing the bottle and then forcibly opening Arturo's mouth. A couple of guards reach for him, but Beefer battles them back.

There's a scuffle and a couple of fists thrown, but everyone backs off when Arturo starts vomiting.

"Call 9-1-1," Leka orders.

A guard pulls out a phone and makes the call.

Mary points a quivering finger at Gerry. "You made this."

"Of course. I make all the meals and you—"

Before he can say anything more, Mary's hand whips out and a knife blade cuts him across the neck. Blood spurts everywhere.

Cursing fills the air. I stumble, the backs of my knees striking a chair. Guards jump forward. Someone takes the knife from Mary's hand. Gerry crumples to the floor with a thud. A pool of blood starts to form under his head, spreading outward like a malignant disease. I raise my knees to my chin.

Leka disappears and then returns with a big black tarp. He and Beefer heave Ger's body onto the tarp, and I watch in detached horror as the body of the loud-mouthed chef is wrapped up and carried out. As Leka passes me, our eyes meet. His are full of worry and apology. I try to give him a smile of encouragement, but I'm too shaken. I'm barely holding myself together.

He doesn't have time to say anything. The two have to get rid of the body before the emergency services arrive. I stare at the pool of blood left behind.

We need to get rid of that. The bucket of water I used to clean the tables before Arturo arrived flashes in front of my eyes. I hurry to the back, find the bucket and then return. The blood is still there, congealing on the wood floor. This is Ger's blood. I dip my rag into the fluid. It wipes up so easy—as if it was a spilled drink. *Blood should be hard to remove*, I think as I scrub. *It should require special cleaners that require an ID and are kept behind the counter like the cough syrup. It shouldn't disappear with one pass of a dishrag.*

The bucket of water turns from gray to rust and then to brown.

"Finish up, girl," urges a guard.

In the distance, I hear the faint sounds of a siren. The police are coming. I wring my rag out and reapply myself, finishing the cleaning job right before the front doors open to reveal EMTs charging through with a stretcher behind them.

I hide the bucket behind my legs as I shuffle out of the way.

"Where's the girl?" I hear a faint voice say.

A hand pulls me forward until I'm at the side of the stretcher, Arturo's slim body appearing even tinier now that he's lying down, an oxygen mask over his mouth.

His hand reaches out and grabs my wrist. I still have the rag between my fingers.

He pulls down his mask. "You saved me. What's your name?"

"E-E-Elizabeth," I stammer out.

"You saved me," he repeats. "I'm gonna repay this. You can have a favor—anything you want."

"Okay." Stop me from hearing Gerry's last gasp.

"Tell him. He'll deliver on my word." Arturo nods toward a thick-necked, dark-browed guard who is hovering across from me.

"Okay." Erase this day from my memory.

"No time limit," Arturo says.

"Okay." Don't come here again.

The guard reaches over and shoves the mask back on Arturo's mouth.

"He means it," the guard says.

"Okay," I answer because I don't know what it all means and nor do I care. My mind is stuck on the knife slicing through the air, the gurgling sound as Gerry gasped for air, the ease with which the blood came off the floor.

What does a boon from Arturo matter? He can't bring Gerry back to life.

21

LEKA

Arturo never fulfills the favor he owes to Bitsy. He dies at the hospital from poisoning. In punishment for allowing harm to come to the head of this family, Stinky Steve is killed. He's not directly responsible, but someone has to be held up as an example.

"This is why it's never good to be in charge," Beefer tells me as we burn what's left of Stinky Steve.

Arturo's men, led by a scary man called Sterno, cut Steve up, kept the heart, and left the rest of the parts for us to dispose of. I think we're supposed to be shocked and awed, but Stinky Steve hasn't done anything but pork his stable and drink his bourbon for the last ten years. Beefer's really been running this group. Him and Mary...and me.

"They sending us a new boss?" I ask.

"Don't know. Cesaro's coming down, though, to check things out."

"When?" I want to make sure that Bitsy's not around.

"Probably in a month. He's shoring up his position."

Meaning, he's busy killing anyone who might pose a threat. When he comes down, he'll expect a loyalty pledge. I didn't like Arturo, but I understood him. If you were good to him, he'd be good to you. As long as we were pulling our weight down here, he didn't care who was in charge. Cesaro is a puzzle for me. I don't know what motivates him, so I don't know exactly what he'll expect us to do to prove ourselves. The night out at the club rises to the top of my memory.

"You should send Camella away," I suggest.

Beefer's oldest daughter, Camella, started working at Marjory's a couple of months ago. She's pretty in an ordinary way, but she has a freshness that would appeal to Cesaro.

"Eh, we've got plenty of women to keep Cesaro occupied. Besides, Mary will be riding his dick most of the time anyway." Beefer's still bitter about that.

Someday he's going to appreciate that he got out of Mary's clutches, but it's not today, I guess. I swallow a sigh. I don't know why men are so caught up in Mary or any other woman just because she's good in the sack. Mary's got no loyalty. She doesn't care for anyone but herself and all she wants is power. She's dangerous and I wouldn't turn my back on her, let alone allow her to have her mouth around my dick.

"Still, just to be on the safe side, it wouldn't hurt. You could send her to some spa or some shit like that."

"You sending Bitsy away?" Beefer asks.

"She's working over at the Shake Shoppe now," I remind him. After the Arturo incident, Bitsy and I came to an unspoken agreement that she'd better off far away from Marjory's.

"Cammie's trying to save money for a girls' vacation to Cancún. Boss's crew always tips good. She'd give me the silent treatment for a month if I made her miss out."

"I'll float her a loan," I offer. I don't like our girls being here when Cesaro's around. There's something about that snake that makes my skin crawl. I trust my gut. It's always served me right.

Beefer hits me on the back. "It's not like I can't swing it, kid. Cammie's got to learn some responsibility. It'll be all right. Trust me, Cesaro's not going to be interested in my daughter."

He's wrong, but I'm not gonna convince him of that today.

"You okay?" I ask Bitsy, who is fiddling with a tube of lip balm.

She's been quiet since the Arturo thing. I know it's scarred her in some way, but she won't talk about it. Last Friday was the dance. She skipped it. The blue dress got blood stains all over it and she refused to go shopping for another outfit. I didn't push her because, well, shit, I wasn't thrilled about her going to the damn dance either.

"I was just thinking about my science test tomorrow," she says.

It's a lie, but I don't call her on it. I'm afraid to. I'm afraid to poke and prod at whatever mess is inside her head because she might tell me what I've been scared to hear—that she doesn't think I'm good enough for her. That she should leave me.

It's going to happen soon anyway. She'll go to college. I've been saving up for that. She'll get a real job, not one that involves her blending smoothies for the locals. She'll find a man.

My stomach clenches at that. The idea of another male laying hands on her spins me up in a bad way. It's because I raised her, I tell myself. No parent is excited about their girl getting it on with some punk. My feelings of possessiveness are normal. Or normal for how we've lived.

For so many years, I've had her to myself. While the outside world burned down around us, while I bloodied my hands and traded all my humanity for a few greenbacks, I've been able to escape to the bubble that is Bitsy.

She's growing up, though, and I can't hold her forever. I realized that the other day when she tried on that dress. She looked like a woman and it scared the shit out of me. I glance over at her head bent over her science notes. The sunlight streaming through the windows paints parts of the curly black hair red. My gaze treks along her smooth forehead and down the small slope of her nose. On either side of her cheeks there's a tiny smattering of freckles that she hates and I love.

I drink in her beauty, stopping at the shoulders. Since she started getting boobs, I've refused to look from the neck down—until she tried on that damned dress. Now I can't get the image of her figure out of my head. She reaches for the lip balm and spreads the cherry gloss all over her lips.

I push away from the table and stalk to the fridge.

"You hungry?" She jumps up.

"Nah." I open the freezer and stick my head in. "Not for real food. I thought I'd get a snack."

She pushes me aside. "I'll make you something. Go sit down."

"I'm not hungry," I protest, but my words are ignored.

Bitsy thinks I'm hungry, and in this house that means she's cooking me something. I don't tell her I ate at Marjory's while Mary and Beefer were entertaining Cesaro. I plant my ass in the chair and try not to watch her every move.

"The Shake Shoppe job going okay?" Seeing Cesaro makes me doubly glad Bitsy's nowhere near Marjory's.

"Yeah. Customers are awful, but the money's good."

She's making under ten dollars an hour. Kids her age on the street are making ten times that an hour, delivering drugs or pickpocketing or selling themselves. Yeah, her money is good.

"I think half the reason I want to draw for a living is because I won't have to interact with people." She cracks a couple eggs in one pan and heats up another. Looks like we're having toast and egg sandwiches.

"You'd have to meet with clients," I point out.

"But it's not like a regular stream of people bothering me and asking me to make weird concoctions like almond milk and orange juice and then complaining it tastes awful. And, if I drew for a living, I'd be surrounded by my pens and paints, so that would make up for any forced interactions with other people."

"Okay." Mentally, I run down a list of nearby art galleries. I'll have to see who runs those and what their vices are so I can be sure that Bitsy lands her dream job.

As if she reads my mind, she spins around and shakes her spatula at me. "And I don't want any help from you."

"Why not?"

"Because I'm a grown-up. I can do this sh—stuff all on my own." She dismisses me and returns to frying up the eggs.

"Okay." It's easier to appear agreeable than tell her the truth—as long as I'm alive, she's never going to be alone. "Movie tonight?" I suggest.

Bitsy brings over my snack. I admire the fluffy egg filling and the golden-brown bread, evenly toasted on both sides. She's turning out to be a good cook.

"Sure. How about that anime? The one with the two kids who swap bodies?"

"Sounds good to me." I can't read the captions for shit, but I like the music and the imagery. I take a bite of the sandwich and let the white bread melt on my tongue. Yeah, she's growing up to be a real good cook.

"Let me finish going through these notes and then we can watch it."

She re-applies herself to the schoolwork and I finish the food. After I'm done eating, I tidy the kitchen. She only messed up two pans and a spatula, so it doesn't take much time. With a sigh, I force myself to go sit in my bedroom so I'm not bothering Bitsy while she studies.

I lie on my bed and tap my fingers against my abdomen while my thoughts drift back to the dress shop, or, more specifically, Bitsy in the dress shop. Beefer would tell me I need a woman. Maybe he's right. The only satisfaction I've ever known has been from my own hand. Maybe if I took a woman to bed. Maybe if I had one that would put cherry-colored lips around my—

"You ready?" Bitsy pops her head in.

My head jerks up. "You done already?" I ask, trying not to appear guilty.

"Yep." She gives me an odd look. "Were the eggs bad? You look like something isn't settling right in your stomach."

I force out a laugh. "No. It's all good."

But the night's awkward for us. I sit in the chair instead of on the sofa. Bitsy gives me a wounded look and then wraps herself up in the blanket like a human burrito.

The captions swim in front of my eyes, interspersed with images of plump, glossy lips, long legs, and a high, spankable ass. I end up getting a blanket for myself and covering my lap. Maybe I do need a woman.

A CALL AT THREE IN THE MORNING WAKES ME UP. THE CALLER ID says it's Beefer. "Leka here."

"You—I—" Beefer stops talking.

I sit up and shove my feet into the boots beside my bed. "Where are you?"

"Marjory's."

"You in danger?"

There's a long pause and then, "Not yet."

"I'll be there in twenty." I disconnect and stick the phone in my pocket. A peek inside my girl's room confirms she's still sleeping. I leave a note on the kitchen table in case she wakes up and I'm not back.

I tuck my gun into the shoulder holster and tug on a coat for conceal-ment. At Marjory's, it's dark except for a tiny light from the kitchen sneaking through the glass. The front door's unlocked when I try it.

Gun out, I go in low. The front room is clear, but I hear faint sobs coming from the back. My gut tightens. I straighten and walk toward the sounds.

The scene in the kitchen hits me harder than I thought it would, but I'm not surprised. Beefer's oldest daughter is laid out on the stainless steel table. Her sparkly nightclub dress is torn. There's an ugly bruise forming on the right side of her face. She's crying, softly, almost as if she can't breathe without a sob coming out.

Mary's applying salve to the bruises and cuts and murmuring nonsense like, "it's going to be okay."

I holster my gun. "Where's Beefer?"

Mary jerks her head to the back door. "Outside. Calm him down, will you? We can't handle a fight."

I find Beefer standing against the fence in the alley. He's taking drags on his cigarette as if the stick holds the only oxygen in the world. Around his feet are a half-dozen butts. Beefer hardly ever smokes.

"What do you want to do?" Mary's not going to be the one to dictate what we should do in this case. If we can't handle a fight now, we're never going to be able to hold this territory, and I don't know about Beefer or Mary, but I'm tired of being bossed around.

"Nothing."

"Nothing?"

He flicks the butt on the ground and lights up another, the flame shaking heavily in his hand. "Nothing. Cesaro said it was his right. Right of the king," Beefer sneers. "He's going to be here for three more nights. Clancy's wife is taking her girls to Florida to see his mom."

Clancy's girls are eleven and twelve. I nearly vomit.

"Beefer, this isn't right. Let's do something."

"What do you suggest? Killing Cesaro? The entire organization will come down on our heads. This is his loyalty test. I took it and passed." The hand holding the cigarette shakes violently. "I took it and passed," he repeats before folding in half and puking his guts out.

I take off.

I arrive home in minutes, but it feels like hours. The apartment is exactly how I left it. Bitsy's still in her bed, her lips parted, a tiny snore wuffling between them.

I rush over to the closet and pull out her suitcase. I've got half of her dresser packed before I run out of room.

Bitsy struggles into a seated position. "Leka. What is it? Did I over-sleep? Is it time for school?"

"We're going on a trip," I tell her, stuffing my old duffel full of clothes. I zip it shut and toss her a pair of jeans. "Get dressed."

She blinks in confusion. "Now? I have a science exam."

"Yeah. Now."

"But—"

"Now!" I scream and slam my fist on the empty dresser.

She lurches to her feet, clutching the jeans to the front of her Powerpuff Girls sleep shirt. Tears glint in her eyes. I never yell at Bitsy. Never.

I rub a trembling hand across my mouth. "I'm sorry. I'm sorry, but we've got to go."

I should've never taken her in. I should've left her on the street. Someone else would've found her and given her a good home. Someone else who didn't have to shower three times before he came home so the stink of dead people wouldn't pollute her air. Someone else who didn't have connections that would strip her of her innocence and violate her in ways that shouldn't be possible.

"We have to go," I say hoarsely.

She nods and shoves her legs into the jeans, the sleep shirt riding up to reveal untouched skin and a scrap of lace. I shut my eyes and leave, slamming the door behind me.

She starts crying the minute the door is closed. I lean against the wall and bang my head against it until I can't hear anything but the ringing of my own ears.

"I'm ready," she says. Her eyes are red and her cheeks are flushed and she's so damned beautiful.

I nearly want to cry myself. Instead, I grab her suitcase, shoulder the duffel. "Let's go," I say gruffly.

She doesn't speak to me for the first two hours of our drive. But when dawn breaks through, she can't hold it in anymore.

"Where are we going?"

"There's a boarding school in Vermont. You'll be finishing school there."

"What? No!" she yells. She grabs at the door handle.

I slam on the brake, sending the car fishtailing wildly. "What the fuck are you doing, Bitsy?"

"I'm not going to any fucking boarding school!" she yells back.

"Stop cursing and yes you are." I reach across her and slam the door shut.

"No. I'm staying with you. You said I'd always be with you." Tears are filling her eyes.

Another time, I'd turn the car around, but the image of Beefer's daughter on that table, staring up at the ceiling wishing for death, has me pressing the gas.

"It's school, Bitsy."

"It's boarding school! We never even talked about this. Where did it come from? Did I do something wrong? Is it the dress? I never wanted to buy that expensive dress. We can take it back. I'll get the blood stains out."

I force myself to breathe through my nose until I gain enough composure to answer her. "I've been thinking about it for a while now. Time seems right."

"It's the middle of the semester!"

"It's October."

"Exactly. I have two months left until the end of the semester."

"And you'll spend those two months in Vermont." Along with every other month until Cesaro is out of power. Until the danger is gone. Until...fuck. Until forever because my life is full of danger.

"If you make me leave, I'm not coming back. Do you hear me? Do you?"

"I hear you."

"Take me back, Leka. I promise whatever I did wrong, I won't do it again. I promise." She clutches my arm. Her anguish stabs at my heart, but I knew this day was coming—that at some point, I'd have to give her up.

"It doesn't matter what you do or don't do, Bitsy. You're going." I punch the gas and watch the speedometer creep past ninety. We can't get to the boarding school fast enough. I'm afraid I'm going to give in and turn around.

"Is it because of that night at Marjory's?" she asks quietly.

Bitsy's never been slow. I hate that she saw that. I should've moved her, should've kept her away.

"It's because you'll be safer," is all I allow.

"Beefer has kids and so do a couple of other people you work with."

Yeah, and Beefer's daughter is never going to be the same again after tonight. I clamp my jaw shut and drive.

She finally gets the hint and slumps back in her seat. The rest of the trip is made in terrible silence. At some point, her tears and exhaustion overtake her and she falls asleep.

I make a few phone calls and then, because suddenly the trip is going by too quick, I slow down. My time with her is ending too soon. I take a thousand mental pictures of her perfect, beautiful face, storing them away in the back of my head. I should've taken a real photo.

I fish my phone out of my pocket, and at the stoplight in the small, sleepy town that the Boone School for Girls calls home, I snap a picture. Then another. Then five more.

It's not enough.

I start up the car again and navigate to the five-hundred-acre farm that is the campus of the Boone School. I park in front of a large yellow house with a wraparound porch and climb out as quietly as possible.

The school administrator, Janet Beatrice, is waiting. I'd texted her a couple of hours ago.

"Mr. Moore, it's nice to meet such an unexpected but generous bene-factor." The calluses on her hands scrape against my flesh as she wraps her fingers around one of my hands.

"I'm sorry for the short notice," I tell her. "Elizabeth's not happy about coming here, but she needs this place."

"We'll take good care of her. It's hard for them to adjust at first, but in the end, they love it. I know Elizabeth will, too."

"I hope so." I hand over the keys. "For when Bit—I mean, when Eliza-beth can drive."

"Won't you need this to get back home?"

"No. I've got a car picking me up. I'll be flying back. All of Elizabeth's stuff is in the trunk." I pull an envelope out of my back pocket. "Please make sure she's taken care of."

Excitement flashes in Ms. Beatrice's eyes as she carefully sets the envelope onto the desk behind her. "Why don't you say your goodbyes and then I'll show her around."

"I already did." I give Ms. Beatrice a short nod and walk out. Outside, I climb into the waiting car I arranged to meet me here.

We reach the end of the farm drive when I reach over the seat and grab the driver's shoulder. "Stop," I tell him.

I almost turn around. I almost look over my shoulder. I almost go back.

"Sir?" the driver says.

I let go of his shoulder, straighten the crumpled fabric of his shirt, and slide back into my seat. "Sorry. Keep driving."

Everything I've done since I met Bitsy is to find a way for her to be safe and happy. She'll be both those things here.

PART II

22

BITSY

Four years later

"Are you sure you want to do this?" Ms. Blair asks. She folds her hands over my file and shoots me a concerned look. "It's not that I oppose gap years, but the great majority of students who do not attend college after graduation from high school will not return to complete any post-secondary education. Missing college would be a shame for someone as bright as you."

I knew this would come up. Confidently, I pull out my next weapon, the deferred acceptance form, and lay it on Ms. B's two-hundred-year-old desk she claims was once used by Benjamin Franklin. "I'm definitely going, just not this fall. I plan to major in graphic design and minor in art history with the aim to go into animation and comics."

I also plan to wait tables, make coffee, and sweep floors since the pay for either of those two career options are very low, but this is the Boone School for Girls, where art is still considered valuable. I sometimes wonder if Leka knew this when he dumped me here or if it was a happy accident.

She pushes her glasses higher on her nose and proceeds to scan the contents of my letter. "This is encouraging, but still, a deferred acceptance does not mean you'll attend, only that you have the option." She peers at me over the round spectacles, her dark eyes searching for an answer beyond that which I've given her.

"That would be true for any student, no matter if they graduate early or in the spring to attend college three months later," I point out, trying to appear calm and collected. Any early release is approved by the Dean of Students aka Ms. Kennedy Blair, and so I have to appear as adult as possible, which means no sighs, no temper tantrums, and no vaulting over the desk and shaking Ms. B until she signs the paper.

"And what do you intend to do during these extra months?"

The truth would shock her, so I trot out my prepared answer. "I don't know exactly what field I want to study, so I want to spend as much time as I can volunteering for museums and publishers and artists to see what I like the best. That way my time in college is spent pursuing something I'm super passionate about instead of wasting several years trying to figure out what my major should be."

As Ms. B studies me, the silence stretches out in the small office and the collar of my white cotton button-down grows tight. I start to sweat under the school-mandated blazer, sweater vest and heavy polyester and wool pants. Are my answers too pat? Too practiced? I did spend several days role playing this with my roommate, much to her dismay.

Why do you have to do this, Liz? You are going to miss out on so much fun.

Because I do.

"Have we treated you so poorly here at Boone?" she finally asks. "We have many fantastic events planned for you fourth-year girls. Most of the Boone girls cite their last semester as their best."

"I appreciate your concern and I will miss my friends here, but I want to go home. I miss my family."

"Your file says you live with your guardian." She cocks her head. "Is that the family you miss?"

"Yes." I brace myself for the pity that's about to be thrown in my face. In the four years I've been here, Leka hasn't visited me once. From the outside, it looks like he dropped me off and conveniently forgot about me. Hell, sometimes I feel the same way.

"Is it possible that the memories you have of your home life have been colored by your absence, because when I look at your record—"

"—my guardian's never visited and I've spent every summer and every break except the winter one here at Boone. Is that what you were going to say?"

"Yes." Ms. B pins me with a concerned stare. "I must be truthful with you, Elizabeth, in hopes that you can be honest with me. I view each one of the students here at the Boone School for Girls like my own child and I come to care for each of you, no matter if you spend four years here or one. I've watched you grow from a child to a woman in these past four years and it's brought me immeasurable pleasure. What I fear for you now is not that you will refuse to pursue a post-secondary education but that you will return to an environment that is not good for you emotionally. It hasn't escaped my notice, nor that of the others in the administration, that your guardian has not visited you once in the past four years. Are you certain that home is what you remember it to be?"

"Home is exactly how I remember it," I tell her. "But even if it wasn't, I'd still want to go."

Part of the reason I'm going home is to find out the truth. Did Leka leave me here because he was tired of having to take care of some street kid who he wasn't even related to? Or did he stash me here out of concern for my safety?

But that's a question only I deserve an answer to. Not anyone else.

"He is fairly young. It appears he is only fourteen years older than you. When was it that he became your guardian?"

I have no idea what it says in the file, so I've always hedged this part of the story. "Shortly before I came here for school."

"Is he the only family you have?"

"Yes."

"Hmmm." She wants to ask more. They always do. "His job isn't listed here." She taps the folder. "Neither is his educational background. What exactly is it that he does?"

My preferred response here would be *none of your business,* but because I need Ms. B on my side, I smile sweetly and say, "It's a family business. Food and beverage."

"Ahh." The information doesn't thrill her. She adjusts her glasses. "The only reason I even bring this up is that children of families who do not have a history of college education often do not see the benefit of college as their parents or guardians appear to have succeeded without it."

"Not just appear to succeed, Ms. B. Did succeed." I can't help correcting her. "I wouldn't be able attend this private school "—with all of its very rich kids—"if Leka wasn't successful."

No one gets to bad-mouth Leka. Except me.

And, then, because I need Ms. B on my side, I continue in a more conciliatory tone. "I plan to attend college when the time is right, but for now, like I said, I miss home and want to spend some time with my family"—meaning Leka—"before I go off for another four years of school."

Ms. B brings her fingers up to her lips. The corners of her mouth turn down and a furrow appears in her forehead. She taps her fingers against her closed lips for a couple of beats, appearing to be thinking hard about something.

I fight back the urge to wriggle in my seat like a small child.

Leka's connection to me has always been the source of speculation amongst the teachers and faculty. I've endured random but sly questions over the years from people who think that they need to know the truth. But I've known since forever—maybe since I was seven or so when that punk at elementary school accused Leka of being a child molester—that no one would understand. At least no one who wasn't abandoned as a child, left on the street to die or be taken.

Leka saved me and that's all that matters. Our relationship is not fodder for anyone's lunchroom or textbook, but I have to endure these questions because part of the evaluation is my mental fitness—whatever that is.

Ms. B still hesitates.

"Haven't I been a good student?" I ask, trying to keep the frustration out of my voice. "I've gotten perfect grades. I have a clean record. I can't remember doing anything I wasn't supposed to do. I busted my as—butt to get four years of classes in three and a half. I even have nearly a full year's worth of college credit under my belt from all the AP courses I took. With all due respect, I'm an adult, Ms. B, and I'm done here. There's nothing more for me here in Boone." Not that there ever was. My home has always been with Leka. The question is whether there's still room for me there.

"I'm just concerned that this isn't the right path for you," she says, but she picks up her pen and slides my early graduation form in front of her.

"It is. I know it is." Boone was the detour. Going home—going back to Leka is my course correction.

"SHE SIGNED IT, DIDN'T SHE?" AUDIE, MY ROOMMATE, exclaims when I walk into our shared room.

I wave the paper wildly in the air. "How did you know?"

"Because you have that stupid grin on your face." My roommate tries to muster up a smile, but she fails because she hates this idea of me graduating early so I can go back to "the Deserter" as she calls Leka.

It's hard to blame her, because from her perspective, Leka brought me here when I was fifteen and has never returned. The only thing she's ever seen of him is his handwriting on the label of the packages he has shipped here every month. Guilt gifts, she calls them.

I received a particularly extravagant one a month ago for my nineteenth birthday. Four estheticians and five licensed massage therapists drove a couple hundred miles to give me and all the fourth-year girls in my dorm a spa day. I was very popular after that event. We wrote Leka nice notes which he acknowledged with a terse two word text. *You're welcome.*

Audie knows all about guilt-induced presents. She receives plenty when she goes home. Her mother, a narcissistic hypochondriac, makes Audie feel guilty for being alive while her stepdad actively ignores her. The one person that is decent to Audie is her grandmother, who Audie stays with over the winter break. After finding out that I spent my first Boone Christmas here at the school with the cows, goats and Ms. Blair, Audie made me go to Connecticut with her. I got a first-hand look at how intact families can be as messed up as ones that are stitched together by grit and determination.

"Liz."

"Audie." I pull out my suitcase and throw it onto my cream bedspread with the dark blue flowers.

My roommate comes over and slaps a hand on the top of the case. The dark fringe of her bangs hangs low over her eyebrows, giving her usually round face a fiercer expression. She needs a haircut but refuses to get any work done here in *Hicksville*. Boone is a sweet, quiet town with a decent coffee shop and not much more. Main Street's biggest store is a pharmacy full of walkers, motorized carts, and more shoe inserts than any geriatric truly needs. I've never been able to get that keratin treatment and eyebrow shaping the lady at the dress shop recommended. It's on my list of things to do once I get home, along with eating a decent piece of pizza.

"Don't go. Stay here until May and then come to the Hamptons with me. My grandma would love that. She thinks you're fun."

"I have to go." While I've been alone, so has Leka. For years, it was only the two of us. He misses me. I refuse to believe otherwise. "But don't worry. We'll stay in touch." I reach up and pinch her cheekbone. "Otherwise, I'll miss your face too much when I'm gone."

"Then stay!" She shakes the suitcase so hard that the wooden head-board rattles against the wall. "He's not worth it."

"Audie."

"He's a jerk!" she exclaims. She swings away in disgust. "He left you here when you were a kid and has visited you all of zero times. Worse, he's not like my mom, who is so self-absorbed she doesn't see how she's fucking me over. He *knows*. That's why he keeps sending you shit all the time as if boxes from Saks could be a replacement for someone who actually gives a shit about you."

"If he didn't leave me here, we wouldn't be friends," I point out.

No matter how many times I try to tell Audie that Leka did this so that I'd have a better life, she doesn't believe it. My hands are tied to some extent. Leka won't come here because he doesn't want anyone back home to know where I am. He explained that to me in a text after he'd left me. And while he never explicitly said I shouldn't tell people how we connected, I could tell by the careful way he always introduced me, how he gave the barest details, that private information should never be shared.

"Right, and if you leave now you're going to miss out on Friday movie nights and Saturday morning runs. Who else will watch *Queer Eye* with you and cry at the end when the dude's life is totally transformed by a little hair gel and throw pillows? And what about my period? I can't ever keep track of that without you. Our cycles are the same!" She throws her hands up dramatically. Audie says she's going to be a teacher, but I think she's better suited for the theatre. "Plus, track season is coming up. We all love track season. Why would you go away before you get to see Calvin Kellogg run the 400 meters in those tiny little shorts?"

Calvin Kellogg is a distance sprinter for the Boone Bombardiers, the local public high school. Their outdoor track route and basketball facility can be seen from our third-floor lounge. A certain segment of the Boone girls has been, well, spying on him for years. He's tall and lean with longish hair that he wears tied back when he runs. While a chance encounter on the streets of Boone will feed the fantasies of some of my classmates for weeks, he doesn't move me.

"You can Skype me during track season. I'll sign you up for a monthly subscription box of tampons and pads. Jeanette and Kira" —I jerk my thumb toward the suite next door—"will still be here for Friday movie nights, and the running club has fifty girls in it." I pull the smaller girl in for a tight hug. I would've never survived these past four years at the

Boone School for Girls if it wasn't for her. "I know you think this is a mistake and that Leka is the worst person in the world and that I'm violating every feminist tenet in the book by going back home, but this is what I want. What I've always wanted."

"Then you're dumb," she mumbles into my breastbone.

I release her and set to packing up the last of my things. Most of my stuff is already in boxes sitting at the end of my bed in hopeful anticipation. Or maybe, subconsciously, I'd been planning to leave regardless of the outcome with the Dean of Students.

Audie folds my nightshirt and places it in the suitcase, but she's not done questioning my decision. "I don't say this to be mean, but have you considered he doesn't want you home, Liz? He's a grown man and maybe he doesn't want you complicating things. That's why I got dumped here, remember?"

"Yeah, and that sucks, but Leka had different reasons." Audie ended up here when her mom was dating the current stepdad. He didn't like kids, and so Mrs. Duetermeyer conveniently got rid of Audie.

"And those are?"

I saw a man get his throat sliced through with a steak knife and blood got all over the expensive dress Leka bought me to attend my first middle school dance. "He just felt it was for the best."

Audie hands me the planner and my pen cup from off the top of my desk. "Listen, darling, you're sweet and innocent and I've never brought this up, but have you considered that at thirty plus—"

"He's not old." Leka intentionally aged himself up on his identification papers so he could claim he was my guardian. I don't know exactly how old he is, but I think it's only an eight-year difference. Not that it matters to me.

"—or however the hell old he is," Audie continues as if I hadn't interrupted, "that he's busy getting his freak on with one or two or ten different girls? A young girl at home is going to cramp his style."

Innocent? One of my first memories is my mom humping some stranger for money. Before I could count, I was being forced to do things that adult women would be traumatized by. The only reason I got over that bad past was because of Leka. There was never a time that he didn't catch me when I threw myself at him. I believe that will still be true. I'll drive back to the city, go up to the apartment, and see him inside. I'll drop my bag to the floor and run into his open, welcoming arms. Then, because I'm older, he'll carry me into his bedroom and I'll finally be fully his.

I believe this because in all the years we lived together before I got sent to Boone, the only female that mattered to Leka was me. "He's not like that. He never, ever brought a woman home."

"And he was there every night and every morning when you woke up?"

I want to say yes, but Leka was often gone until the wee hours of the morning. But that was because, well, he was doing stuff that wasn't entirely legal, and most of those things are carried out at night. At least...that's what I've always presumed. The thought of Leka having sex with someone other than me makes me want to barf. *He's mine*, my inner voice howls.

At my silence, Audie clicks her tongue. "Oh, Liz. Sweet, virginal Liz who doesn't even use our showerhead like she should."

"Kira wore it out." We watched *Secretary* a month ago and directly after the credits, our suite mate Kira got up and went into the bathroom. The shower ran for a solid thirty minutes, and ever since then we can't get the jet feature to work.

I don't blame the girl. I had lurid dreams of Leka that night. I hadn't thought I was into that kind of sex, but the idea of Leka bending me over the desk and taking me forcefully from behind turned me into a hot, sweaty mess. I woke up shivering with my hand between my legs for a week straight.

With a scowl, I retort. "You're a virgin, too. Just last week you were moaning about how you were going to die a virgin."

"I was exaggerating. Once I'm out of Boone and in college, I'm going to find myself a bevy of nice young men to experiment with and that's what I want for you. At least go out with a guy your age before committing to an old man."

"Leka is not an old man," I'm starting to feel testy.

Audie ignores me. "You have never even had a taste of guys our age, and that's a problem. It's like sushi. Remember how you swore you were never going to eat it because it's raw and gross and then you went on that trip and ate a bunch of it and said it's the best thing ever? Boys are like sushi!"

"Raw and gross?"

"And the best thing ever after you try it."

"How would you know? Life isn't like"—I tap the back of my phone —"the fiction we read."

"Exactly my point. We don't know if it's raw and gross or the greatest thing ever. We won't know until we try it."

I scrunch up my nose. "Eating sushi is not the same thing as sticking someone's penis in your body. I'm not going to have random sex with a stranger."

The only one I want to touch me is Leka.

"I'm not saying you should have sex with anyone. Just go and see what happens. Maybe you make out. Maybe he sticks his hand up your shirt. Maybe you get excited and decide to do other stuff. The possibilities are endless." Audie rubs her hands together.

"None of this sounds appealing."

"Look at this." Audie shoves her phone in my face. On the screen is a picture of Calvin Kellogg, shirtless and sweaty, getting interviewed by the *Boone Daily*. "Tell me this doesn't make you want to do dirty things in the shower."

"Negative." I move the phone out of my face.

Exasperated, she tosses the phone onto her bed. She stomps over to my closet and grabs my two coats. Under her breath, she mutters, "Bet that Leka of yours doesn't have a body like Calvin."

I smile to myself. Wouldn't she be surprised. Leka took care to always cover up around me, but when you live with someone you can't help but catch glimpses of their bare skin. Leka has an eight-pack that would render my classmates speechless.

Hell, everything about him would silence them immediately. He's tall, golden, with a jawline so sharp I could cut myself against it. His nose is straight and long but fits in with his high cheekbones and firm chin. Really, the only soft thing about his face is his lips. When he talks, which is rare, I can't stop staring at them. During the long nights at school, I imagined what they'd feel like—against my fingers, against my lips, against my skin.

I rub my palm over my stomach. Abs don't move me. Nothing about Calvin whatshisface moves me. When I close my eyes at night, when I dream, when I fantasize, only one person appears

There's only one man for me.

"I give up," she scowls.

It's a good thing because I made up my mind years ago. Leka brought me here because I was weak and lacked the ability to protect myself. I spent my years here at Boone strengthening my mind and my body. It's a farm, so I've learned how to use a shotgun. I've killed chickens, filleted fish, and even cut up a deer that Ms. Darnell, our science teacher, shot last winter. Every Boone girl takes self-defense classes each year. That's a mandatory class along with English, math and science.

Almost nineteen-year-old Elizabeth Moore is an entirely different person today than she was at fifteen. I might not be a queen of a country, but I'm ready to rule my own domain. It's time I proved that to Leka.

23

LEKA

"You look tense, kid," Beefer declares as we enter the safe room in the basement of Marjory's. "The boys giving you a rough time? I can knock a few bills off their paychecks."

"I'm good," I reply automatically, but truth is, I've been feeling anxious lately. I think it's because Bitsy hasn't told me what her plans are after she graduates next spring. It's six months away, but lately she's been making some noise in her texts about coming home.

Home. I haven't had a home since she left. The apartment's a vacant, noiseless tomb. Kind of like me. I'm empty without her. Those texts she sends—the ones that say she misses me and she can't wait to see me—they're like darts piercing the most vulnerable parts of my defenses. Every time I get one of those, I have to beat down the instinct to type back, YES, in all caps and bold letters. Because, fuck, yeah, I miss her, but there's no place for her here.

I take out my phone and double-check to make sure the green dot on my maps app hasn't moved. It hasn't. It's sitting solidly in the upper right corner of her dorm building, which is good since it's after ten and she should be in bed. I rub my finger over the screen.

It's been a while since I've heard from her. I'm not a good communicator. I hate texting and I hate talking on the phone even more. I try for Bitsy's sake, but each time I talk to her, it gets harder to stay away.

But that's what I need to do to protect her.

She hasn't been back here since Cesaro took over, and in those four years, she's pretty much faded from everyone's memory. Most of the crew I oversee is new or didn't have much contact with her before I shipped her off to school. Only Mary and Beefer make mention of her from time to time and mostly in passing, as if they're recalling a memory of someone who died. That's how I want it. I've taken great pains to erase her presence around here.

And while I go home every night to eat my dinner with only the hum of the refrigerator to keep me company, I survive knowing that my girl is far from harm. I do it for everyone else's good, too, because I'd have to kill anyone who looks at her wrong. We already have too much turnover on the crew as it is.

"You don't sound good. You worried because your money isn't here anymore?" Beefer reaches into the metal safe bolted to the concrete, grabs a wad of cash and shuts the door. It's payday for the boys. "Where'd you put all of it anyway?"

I hesitate, because talking about where your dirty loot is stashed with other crooks isn't a good idea, but this is Beefer. He practically raised me.

On the flip side, Beefer's been taking a small slice off the top for a while now. He'd probably argue it was a service fee. Bankers take the same kind of cut, but only guys down at the financial sector are a little more upfront about it than Beefer.

"It's somewhere safe," I say vaguely. Bitsy isn't the only thing I've moved out of reach of Cesaro.

"In your apartment? Doesn't sound very safe to me. You best bring it back here. No one's taking money from this safe. Not when they know it's your money. Who's gonna mess with you?" He pats the top of the box, using it for balance as he pushes himself upright. Beefer's put on a lot of weight in the last few years since he's been promoted. He's been eating well. No deal gets through the northeast without Beefer getting a cut. The price he had to pay for it—no, the price his daughter paid—seems to have been forgotten.

"Lots of people probably." I slide a finger over the metal butt of my gun. It doesn't get the workout it used to, but there are new dumbshits every day that want to test themselves. It never goes well for them. Greed and arrogance end up being the downfall for a lot of these wannabe gang leaders. Give someone a taste of the green and they'll lap at any dirty pool, no matter how deadly, to have another taste. And guns give them a spine that they were never born with.

"Banks? Is that where you're keeping it?" he guesses. "The Feds watch those accounts. You're going to end up wearing orange for the rest of your life if you ain't careful." Beefer lumbers over to the old metal desk that Stinky Steve lifted from some office warehouse we robbed over fifteen years ago. The guy who owned the office supply place racked up some bad debts at the horse track. He didn't have much in assets, so Steve had Beefer slice off the dude's dick as payment. Beefer used this desk as the surgery table.

"I'm careful." The banker I use to move my money around told me all about this in the beginning, in between sniffing the lines of coke I'd brought.

"You don't think I was careful with your money? Shit, boy, I kept your wad a secret from even Arturo." Beefer spits out some tobacco juice toward a cup, but half of it spatters on the desk. Clumsily, he wipes his hand across the top and then smears the mess across his patterned shirt. A deep crease cuts into his forehead. "No one you can trust more than me."

He's wrong. There's only one person I trust and she's several hundred miles away from here, tucked away in an expensive all-girls school. But I don't think Beefer's upset about a lack of fidelity here. I think it's money.

"You running short?" I ask bluntly.

"Nah, why you asking?" But his eyes are pinned on the stack of bills in front of him. He should be counting it out, making small piles that'll get tucked into envelopes and passed out.

"How much are you behind?"

"I'm not behind," he proclaims. "I'm worried about you, is all."

I swallow a sigh. If Beefer's not making his monthly tithe to Cesaro, we're going to get a visit. I don't want Cesaro around here. It's not good for morale. He terrifies the troops, constantly questioning someone's loyalty, pitting one person against another. I finally figured out that the reason he likes them "fresh," as he says, is because he gets off on fear. The more fearful the girl or boy is, the more he likes it. I'll chop off my left nut before he ever gets close to Bitsy.

I can't convince Beefer to break away from Cesaro, so the next best thing is to make sure he doesn't come around. The way to do that is to make as little noise as possible and not give him a reason to take notice.

"How much?" I've got some money to cover whatever shortage Beefer is suffering at this moment.

"It's nothing." He eyes the thick stack of bills with so much lust that it verges on pornographic. "Why don't you go upstairs and make sure the girls haven't killed each other. Shit. I don't know why those two hate each other so much. They're like two chickens in a coop that's made for one. Tell the girls I'm hungry. I don't care who cooks me a piece of meat, but I want something on the table by the time I'm done here."

I leave so Beefer can skim off the top of the wages he's supposed to pay. Upstairs, Mary and Beefer's oldest, Camella, are glaring at each other from opposite corners of the room. I know why they don't like each other. Mary's jealous of Camella's youth, and Camella fears that her future is the life Mary's leading—an aging sex worker who's reduced to sucking the cock of an obese small-time gang leader. They both have one thing in common, though—they're the happiest when everyone around them is miserable.

I give Mary a short nod before turning to Camella. "Beefer's hungry. Can you throw a steak on the griddle?"

"I'm not his fucking cook," she sneers, adjusting the strap of her black, sheer, body-con dress. When her father sees it, he's going to hit the roof. It's five and Camella's dressed for the nightclub already.

"Make your dad some food," Mary snaps.

I rub my forehead wearily.

Predictably, Camella's short fuse lights up. "You don't get to tell me what to do, you old whore," she yells.

"Whore? I'm not the one crawling around the financial district selling her pussy to the first guy who dangles a bag of coke in her face."

"At least I don't spend all my time on my knees in the hope for a few pennies."

"Pennies? My underwear, which, by the way, your daddy peels off with his teeth, costs more than your whole fucking outfit. If there's anyone on their knees, it's your old man, not me."

Camella flies across the room at Mary. I grab the younger woman and move her to one side. Whenever I get down about not having Bitsy around, all I need to do is look at these two women. This could easily be Bitsy's life. I need to remind myself anytime I have the hankering to bring her back to me.

Holding Camella back, I point a finger to Mary. "Beefer's downstairs, so I'd be careful what you say about his daughter." To Camella, I say, "Mary's higher up the ladder, so you got to give her some respect."

"Bullshit. I don't have to give her anything. She can eat my ass."

Camella turns around and flips up her skirt, waggling her thong-wearing ass in Mary's direction.

This time it's Mary who launches herself at Camella. I'm holding the two of them off when Beefer appears in the doorway.

"What in the fresh hell is going on here?"

Camella immediately sidles over to her dad. "Mary's being mean to me."

Mary calculates whether to defend herself or to try to flirt her way out of this mess. When Beefer's arm goes up to wrap around his daughter's shoulder, Mary makes the decision to play for something south of Beefer's heart.

She cocks out her hip and slams a hand on her waist. Tits forward, she winks. "We both know my skills aren't in the kitchen, babe."

Beefer eyes Mary hungrily and his arm starts to slide away.

Camella senses her father's withdrawal and tries her own play, but she can't read the room like Mary does.

"I'm not cooking," Camella declares. "I just got my nails done and I don't want to mess them up. What do you think of them, Leka?" She lays them on her chest, so the tips are pointing at her barely concealed tit. I shift my gaze over her shoulder.

"I don't know much about a girl's nails."

"What are you asking Leka for?" Beefer says in annoyance. He's finally noticed what little Camella has on. "Why aren't you wearing actual clothes, girl? Shit, you're always complaining about how you're treated like trash. Maybe you should stop dressing like you want a bed in the stable."

"This is Gucci!" she fires back.

"I don't care if it's from the Pope himself. You look like a slut. You might as well hang a *for sale* sign around your neck."

"Like you did?" she taunts.

His hand comes up so fast I almost miss it. Almost. I push Camella out of the way and grab Beefer's arm on the downstroke. He trembles beneath my grip. Beefer's carrying a lot of extra weight around the middle, but he's still strong as shit. The thing is, though, he doesn't want to fight his daughter. He's wracked with grief and guilt and this is how it plays out for his family. His daughter acts out. He hits her. She replies by wearing even skimpier clothing and doing harder drugs and worse men.

"Go out in front. The girls will get dinner ready," I say quietly.

Beefer backs down and turns on his heel, but as he's leaving he swipes his arm across a stack of stainless steel bowls, sending them crashing to the floor. He picks up a pan and whips it against the wall. Mary ducks as some plaster rains down above her head. Camella's still cowering into the corner where I pushed her.

"Go ahead and make the meal, Mary," I direct.

"I didn't sign up for this shit," Mary declares as she pulls a pan off the shelf. "When Cesaro gets here, things are gonna get straightened out."

Camella makes a noise in the back of her throat. Bringing up Cesaro's name is a dirty hit. I grab my black suit coat off the hook and toss it to Camella. "Put this on," I order.

She lets it fall to the ground. "Does my body bother you? Aren't I good enough for you?"

"Stop your whining," Mary snaps, but Camella's been triggered and she's not paying any attention to Mary anymore.

Her mind's back on the night that Cesaro took her. The night her dad gave her to a monster. And she's desperate to wipe that night out from her memory banks, taking drugs to numb her mind, taking men to replace the pain.

She tugs at her top, pulling the stretchy lace down so far her tits fall out. "What's wrong with these? They're tight and bouncy. Is it my pussy? You haven't even seen it. I take care of myself. I—"

I rub a hand over my eyes, which is the wrong action.

"Look at me!" Camella screams. "What's wrong with me? Don't like the used goods, is that it?"

"You're a disgrace," Mary sneers.

"That's enough," I order as I grab a tablecloth from the stock room and throw it around the younger girl's shoulders.

Camella tries to wriggle out of my hold, but I keep her wrapped up, hustling her out the door and into the back of one of the delivery cars that don't have handles in the rear. These cars are used to deliver things other than food.

I jerk my head toward a fairly new recruit who I know isn't going to take advantage of Beefer's daughter. She's not his type. "Mason, get over here and drive Camella home. If you so much as look at her, I'll take your eyes. She's not doing well, okay?"

Mason nods and climbs behind the steering wheel without another word. I like him—as much as I can like anyone not named Bitsy.

"Why don't you want me?" Camella pounds on the window. "I'm hot. Look at my body!"

Mason turns white.

"Go." I slam my fist on the top of the car.

At my order, he peels out of the alley, driving a wailing, demoralized girl away. I don't understand why Beefer can't see her pain. She's not mine, but her tortured eyes appear in my head when I close my eyes at night.

I'll be dead before Bitsy comes back here.

24

"Why don't you stay for one more day?" Audie suggests as I cart my suitcase down to my car. All the boxes are stacked in the back seat. I only need to grab one laundry basket upstairs and I'm set. "We'll go to a party! I wrangled an invited from Rachel Hoover. She's been seeing this guy Max Trent for like six months now. He's on the football team. I think he's a back, a quarterback or fullback or half-cup back. Something like that. It'll be fun."

We aren't into sports. The only reason we know about the runner is because the track can be seen from our third-floor lounge.

"I'm going home, Audie."

"Look at Trent's Instagram feed. He's got some hot friends." Audie waggles her phone in front of my face. Instead of the picture feed, the phone's message app is open. I spot my name.

Pulling her wrist close, I read aloud, "Liz is graduating early and has never been within spitting distance of a boy. We should rectify that."

"Oh no. That's not—" Audie twists out of my grip, but not before I snatch the device free of her grip.

I read Rachel's response. "What's the point? Liz isn't the type guys want to—eggplant emoji—on site. She's more good personality know what I mean?" I look up at Audie who's grimacing. "She used the eggplant emoji unironically and misspelled sight. I'm supposed to trust her taste in men? Also, is she calling me ugly?"

Audie snatches the phone back. "You're not supposed to read the messages," she chides, "and no, she's not calling you ugly."

I reach up and touch my wild, crinkly hair. I've a smattering of dark freckles across the bridge of my nose and along my upper cheeks. My nose flares at the bottom more than I'd like, but I tell myself that at least I don't have breathing problems like Kira who had to have surgery on her deviated septum. I touch my finger to the tip. I know I'm not the type of girl who's ever going to blow up on social media for my face or body. Guys aren't going to drop their bags and rush over to open the door like I've seen them do for Jeanette, but none of that really matters because I'm going to marry Leka.

A sense of anxiety stirs in my stomach. On the beauty scale, Leka and I are on the opposite ends. He *does* get random strangers flustered. Women are always straightening their clothes, sticking their chests out and fluffing their hair when he's around. It was annoying as hell when I was younger.

His looks haven't faded as he's gotten older. His body, as far as I can tell from the few video chats we've had, is just as fine as it's always been. His hair has darkened from blond to a chestnut gold, and his eyes are still a piercing blue. I've no doubt that there are women left panting everywhere he goes, but he's never noticed in the past. Why would that change? Why would it change just because I'm here in Vermont and he's hundreds of miles away?

"You're not ugly," Audie says, interrupting the dangerous thoughts. She pulls my hand down to my side. "Can we focus on what's important here?"

"Yes, I'd like that." I grab her and pull her in for a hug. "The important thing is that we're going to stay in touch."

Audie sags against me, finally giving in. "I'm going to miss you," she sniffles.

"I'm moving back home, not dying," I tease gently.

"I know, but I'm a crier. You know this."

I do. Audie cries during commercials. During the Olympics, we had to skip all the human interest segments because Audie kept breaking down. I think we went through five boxes of tissues during that week. I make a mental note to see if the tampon subscription box could throw in a few tissue packs.

"I know, but you're going to be okay."

"Don't let him walk all over you."

"I won't."

"Tell him if he hurts you, I'll come and kick his ass."

"I will."

We hug for a few more moments until Audie pushes me away from her. "Go on," she says through her tears. "Or you're going to hit Springfield right during rush hour."

"I love you," I tell her. "I'll text you when I arrive home."

I give her a cheery wave, hop into my car, drive five miles and then pull over to let the tears come.

I couldn't let anyone know, but I'm scared. I'm scared of leaving Boone, which has been my safe place for four years. I'm scared of the rejection I might face from Leka. I'm scared of my future, but I couldn't stay in Boone forever.

My future is with Leka. I just have to convince him of that.

I pull out my phone and send him a message.

I'm coming home.

I wipe my tears, put my car in gear, and head south.

WORN OUT AND HUNGRY, I PULL UP IN FRONT OF THE apartment building around three. An unfamiliar doorman comes over and peers through my passenger window, gesturing for me to open it.

I push the button and once his face is clear of the glass, he says, "You can't park here. This is a private residence."

"I know. I live here with Leka Moore. I'm his..." I trail off, not sure of what to call myself. I don't want to say *sister* because when the doorman sees us holding hands or kissing, I don't want him to call the cops. And I will be holding Leka's hand and kissing him in public. That's what couples do. But we're not a couple yet, so I can't exactly call myself his girlfriend. "I live here with Leka," I finally say.

"Mr. Moore lives alone," the doorman responds. "Move along or I'll call the police."

"You're going to what?" I sputter. "I'm serious. Here, look at my driver's license." I reach over and fumble for my purse.

The man barely looks at my license before handing it back. "Where's your key?"

"My key?"

"Yeah, your key. If you live here, you have a key."

I stare at him blankly because I do not have a key. Four years ago, I woke up to a frantic Leka who hustled me from my bed to the car. He'd packed my stuff and it didn't include a key to the apartment. Mrs. M has a key, though. She let herself in and out of the apartment when she came to sit with me after school and before Leka would get home.

"Mrs. M knows me. Call her."

"I don't know any Mrs. M. I'm sorry, miss. You need to leave." He steps back onto the curb and makes a show of pulling his cellphone out of his pocket. Is he really going to call the police on me?

I gape in disbelief until the sound of a siren spurs me into motion. *Fine*, I think as I jam the gear stick to drive. *I'll go, but you're going to look damn stupid when I waltz in here tonight with Leka.*

I have no choice but to go to Marjory's. It's probably where I should've gone in the first place, but I kind of hate that place ever since I saw Gerry get his throat sliced there. Not to mention that Marjory's is a symbol of all that keeps Leka and me apart. He carted me up to the Boone School for Girls and left me there because whatever he did for the people at Marjory's was too dangerous for me to be near.

And now I'm rolling up in my ten-year-old Mercedes, the car that Leka abandoned with me in Vermont. Leka will probably have it repossessed and crushed when he finds out I've come to Marjory's, but it's the afternoon. Going to a restaurant seems safer than sitting like a stalker outside the apartment where I'm fairly positive the doorman is itching to arrest me. I know Leka wouldn't approve of me cooling my heels in the park until he got done doing whatever it is he was doing.

And, frankly, this is his fault. He should've answered the text I sent nine hours ago. By some miracle, I find on-street parking a block away from Marjory's. I throw on my puffy jacket, stick my phone in my wallet and head down the street for the restaurant.

There's a tall, slender boy wearing a green apron under a wool coat at the front door of Marjory's. He gives me a once-over, eyes clocking the red goose label on the sleeve and the Dior Leka sent me a month ago, and decides I'm not some random tourist looking to use the bathroom. He pushes the door open.

I give him a weary smile in return and thank him for holding the door. Inside, I blink a few times until my eyes adjust to the light. A figure halfway across the room moves in my direction, but it's not until she's standing in front of me that I recognize Mary Shaughnessy. The last time I saw her, she had just finished slicing a friend's neck open, and while it's only been a few years, her face is wearing at least a decade's worth of time. Is that what killing a person does to you?

"Hey Mary," I say, wondering if she recognizes me. I'm different, too. I've lost a bit of my baby fat in my cheeks. I'm an inch taller. She still towers over me since I'm wearing tennis shoes and she's got on six-inch red-bottomed platforms.

"Why if it isn't young Elizabeth. Although, what does Leka call you? Bitsy, right? Only you're not so young anymore, are you?" Like the boy in the front, Mary inspects me from head to toe, but she's not evaluating whether I'm here to spend money. She's looking at me as if I'm a...threat? Leka has never liked her. I wonder if that's changed.

"Where have you been all these years?" she asks.

"School." I force a smile on my face and hide the unease that's tickling the back of my neck. Mary's the type to take advantage of every weakness, but most especially fear.

"You didn't say where."

"No." If she doesn't know, it means she's not supposed to. I don't volunteer any new information. I just keep smiling. She knows why I'm here. There's only one person I'd be waiting to see.

"Leka's not here," she says.

"I know," I lie.

"He might be a while, but that's good for us." She smiles back and threads an arm around my stiff limb. "We have a lot to catch up on. I'll introduce you around. The nice young man out front is Mason. Isn't he delicious? He started working a year ago for us. I haven't had a taste of him, but the girls in the stable say that he's very good in bed. You should try him out." She gives Mason, who is thankfully out of earshot, a little wave. Innocently, he returns it. Mary swings me around, past the few tables filled with patrons and into the back.

A lanky guy with an army buzz cut wearing a white chef's coat is bent over a pot. "This is Justin. He replaced Gerry. You remember Gerry, don't you, Bitsy?"

Despite the down coat that promised to keep me warm in thirty below temps, I'm growing chilled. "It's Liz," I inform Mary. "Everyone calls me Liz." No one is allowed to call me Bitsy. That's Leka's name for me.

"Is that right? All grown up and now you're calling the shots?" She laughs and pinches my cheek way too hard to be cute. "Anyway, Bitsy, like I said, this is Justin. Justin, honey, come over here and meet Leka's little girl. He raised her since she was a baby and she's just come home from boarding school."

Justin jerks back in surprise. This is obviously the first he's ever heard of Leka having a kid. *Don't let that bother you*, I counsel myself. This is Leka's way. He never wanted me to be around his work.

I use the opportunity to get out from under Mary's arm and move forward to offer my hand to Justin. "Call me Liz, and I'm not Leka's child. Obviously, I'm too old for that. We grew up together."

The man's brows crash together in obvious confusion, not sure who to believe. "Uh, okay. Nice to meet you, uh, Liz."

Score one for Elizabeth Moore. I make a point of not waiting for Mary to take charge again and introduce myself to the rest of the kitchen crew. The tatted sous chef with the shock of red spiked hair is Brady. He's been here for three years. The two line cooks, both of them short and round and looking a little like Porky Pig, tell me their names are Otto and Jannik. Everyone seems friendly.

Otto makes me a spiced cider and Brady fires up a pan to make me chicken alfredo. "Best you e'er had," he declares.

Mary stands off to the side, arms folded under her envious rack, carefully watching every move. Does she think I'm going to announce to everyone that she murdered the last chef? I'm not that naïve. I never was.

Jannik grabs me a stool and helps me take my jacket off.

"Never knew Leka had family," the man says as he toddles over to the back to hang the coat on one of the empty hooks that line the rear wall. "You don't look much alike."

"Isn't that the truth," Mary agrees.

The kitchen looks the same even if the people are different. There are two stainless steel tables. One is speckled with floor. A plastic container full of dough sits to the side. Along the front wall are the cooktops—one large gas-fueled one and one long flat metal surface. Underneath are the ovens. It smells good back here—warm and inviting.

"Priest never does talk much about anything. Hell, the guy could have his own stable and none of us would know," Otto replies and then shoots a guilty look in my direction as if I might tell Leka the men mentioned bad things in my presence. It makes one wonder what Leka does that inspires such a reaction. Of course, I never ponder this in Leka's presence because I know it would bother him.

"Shut up and shred those carrots," Justin orders.

The line cooks fall silent as Chef Justin turns up the music to, I suppose, mask the dirty talk the two are exchanging. *Priest?* Is that his nickname now? Better than Monkey, although, I've never heard anyone call him that.

This nickname implies a certain...celibate lifestyle which means his practice of staying away from women still exists. Delighted, I hunch over the cider, breathe in the spicy cinnamon and nutmeg scent, and hide my smile. This is all going well. Leka's not had any serious relationship while I've been gone. No one seems particularly dangerous—except for the viper in the corner. But I know what she's capable of and all I need to do is keep an eye on her.

The long day catches up with me and I blink sleepily over the mug. Driving can really wear a person out. It'd be nice if Leka could show up soon and take me home. I could shower off the grime of the drive and then sleep in my bed—alone, sadly, but I'll convince Leka to join me soon enough.

The back door opens and I jolt upright only to slump again when I see Beefer, followed by three more men I don't recognize. There's been a lot of turnover in the last four years.

"Mother Mary, is that you, Liz?" Beefer booms. "I haven't seen you since you were yay high." He gestures at his waist.

I climb off the stool. "I was at least to your chest."

"Nah. You weren't more than a babe when Leka took off with you. Come here and let me take a look at you."

Obediently, I walk over.

"You're looking good. Real good. All grown up and everything. Leka know you're here?"

Just by the way Beefer says it, I feel like he knows that Leka's in the dark and I'm a giant surprise. Guilt spirals up my spine. I should've called Leka again, but I'd been mad that he hadn't texted me back. My pettiness better not hurt Leka. I need to do better.

"It's been in the works for a while," I hedge. "I graduated early."

"I didn't know that was a thing. Congratulations. You got a job or you going to college? What's your plan?"

It feels like he's fishing. "I've got a deferred placement," I reply.

The three men I don't know leave Beefer's side to come around and crowd behind me. I move forward to avoid them but find Beefer unmoving in front of me. There's a strange glint in his eye that sends a wisp of unease down my spine. Unlike the kitchen crew, these men radiate menace. The hairs on the back of my neck stand up, and my fight or flight response is being triggered. I rise on the balls of my feet when the back door opens again.

Beefer twists to see who it is.

"Bitsy." It's Leka and he's not happy, but...he also doesn't seem surprised. "What are you doing here?"

"Surprise." I clasp my hands together and smile. "I'm done with school."

"But you, we just..." He trails off as he realizes that everyone in the room is watching us raptly.

Please, please, please, I plead silently. *Don't send me away. Not in front of everyone here.*

A thousand emotions flicker through his eyes, but in the end, he holds out his hand.

I grab my coat from the hook on the wall, yell my thanks over my shoulder and run to Leka. He folds one arm around my shoulders, keeping his right arm free. He's always done this, and I've finally realized why. It's so he can keep his gun arm free. I let him go immediately and move to the side.

"I'm parked out front. A block down the street," I say quietly.

"I know," he murmurs. He dips his head toward Beefer. "I'm gonna settle Bit at home. I'll text when I'm available." He doesn't wait for a response. He steers me past three bulky men who came in behind Beefer.

Leka gives them all a silent nod but doesn't introduce us. Instead, he hurries me through the front of the restaurant and out the door. On the sidewalk, just out of earshot of the young man who held the door open for me when I arrived, Leka asks "How long have you been planning this?"

I lift my chin. "Since the day you left me."

25

LEKA

Sheer panic. That's what's in my veins. Dread started replacing my blood a couple of hours ago when I pulled out my phone and saw that the green dot wasn't in Vermont anymore. Instead, it was on the outskirts of the city. Beefer asked me to drive upstate about four hours away to retrieve a lost shipment. I found it right away, but I had to deal with a couple stupid people who thought that they could steal from Cesaro. That took time and I didn't get an opportunity to look at my phone until I was on my way home. By the time I pulled into town, Bitsy's car was parked a block away from the restaurant.

I broke a dozen traffic laws to get to the restaurant. Fear rode me hard. Bitsy was at Marjory's. People saw her. People talked to her. I reach inside my jacket and rub the metal butt of my gun for reassurance. I need to get her back to Vermont, immediately.

"Did you get kicked out?" It's the only reason she would have come home. While I didn't go to school like she did, after nearly four years of paying tuition, I know that she's got a semester left.

I had this all planned out. Vermont and then a summer in Europe or some fancy shit like that. In the fall, she'd go to college south or west. I sent her a bunch of admissions brochures I'd picked up from a life coach who was trying to move his mother's jewelry to cover funds he'd embezzled from his firm. Thinking back, she never told me which one she was interested in. Or whether she even applied.

"No. I graduated."

"You what?" I almost trip on the sidewalk in surprise. "How? You got a semester left."

"I graduated early. Aren't you proud of me?" She opens her arms wide. Snow's starting to fall. It catches on her curls, twinkling like diamonds against a dark velvet backdrop. A few tendrils of her hair rest at the base of her neck. Her zipper is undone and above the collar of her plain striped shirt, I can see the delicate rise of her collarbone, the tender hollow of her throat.

I lose my breath as I take her in. I haven't seen her in four years and she's changed. Her round face has slimmed down. Her eyebrows are finer and her lashes longer. Her lips are plush and full—a look she comes by naturally. The puffy coat I had to stand in line to buy her is open, and underneath I can see how her leggings hug and mold to her figure. How the long-sleeve shirt hugs her upper curves. Curves I've spent years trying to forget.

Seeing her for the first time in all these years is a shock. It's a kick in the gut. It's a burn lower.

"Yeah, I'm proud of you," I manage to get out past the rock in my throat and my thickening tongue.

Everything's changed. She's older and smarter. I'm older and weaker. I wish I could blink and transform her into the little elementary girl I used to know, the one that didn't come up much farther than my hip, the one that didn't make me want things no good man should want.

I didn't plan for this, and I don't know what to do.

She starts shivering and pulls her jacket close. "It's cold out."

I give myself a mental slap. She's standing in the middle of the side-walk outside Marjory's in the middle of winter while I wrestle with my guilty conscience. I can do that shit job somewhere warmer.

"Why didn't you text me?"

"I did. Like ten hours ago. Or is it eleven?" I start to check my phone when a huge yawn cracks across her face. "I'm losing track of time."

Reluctantly, I replace my phone in the inside pocket of my leather coat. "Let's go."

She reaches for me, tucking her arm into the crook of my elbow and resting her tired head against my arm. I swallow hard and try not to let the brief contact turn me to ash, but my heart's pounding wildly and my body's feeling abnormally hot.

We walk to the car that's packed to the gills. A surge of happiness courses through me at the idea of having Bitsy home. I remind myself that this is temporary. As soon as possible, she has to leave.

"What'd you do with the college brochures?" I ask as I settle into the driver's seat.

"They're somewhere back there." She waves a casual hand over her shoulder. "I've got a lot of time to go over them now."

Okay. So she's not abandoned the idea of college. She probably graduated early to attend college earlier. She's always been smart like that. I was getting worried over nothing. She hasn't come home to stay. She's come home to pass a few days until she moves on to her next adventure—somewhere far away from Marjory's and the city...and me.

That thought leaves a bitter residue in my mouth. I swallow again, but it doesn't go away. We don't speak again until we arrive at the apartment. Bitsy is tired and I'm a mess of contradictions. If I open my mouth, I will be telling her to leave one second and begging her to stay the next.

As I pull next to the curb, Terry, the doorman, rushes over to open the car door.

When Bitsy steps out of the car, she gives him an uncharacteristically curt nod. "I told you I lived here."

Terry flushes all the way to his dyed roots. A frown creases my brow. Am I going to have to teach my doorman a painful lesson?

"What happened?" I demand.

"Sh-She didn't have proof you lived here," Terry stammers.

I turn to Bitsy. "Where was your key?"

She yawns and stretches. "I didn't have it. We left so fast and it wasn't in my things. Besides, I didn't realize I would need it. Why would I be locked out of my own home?"

Shamefaced, I give Terry another nod, this time not so curt. It's not his fault this mess up happened. It's mine. I'm off my game. I lost track of Bitsy, allowed her to spend time with people I despise, and kept her from her home. If anyone should get pistol-whipped, it's me.

"Sorry," I mutter.

She shrugs. "I'm tired. Can we get this stuff tomorrow?"

"I'll have everything delivered," Terry proclaims, eager to make up for the misunderstanding.

"That would be great." She gives him a thumbs-up.

I want to protest. Everything should stay in the car because Bitsy will be leaving soon, but the girl is too worn out for an argument. Besides, no one needs to know about our business but us.

"Okay," I give in.

I usher her over to the elevator. She slumps against me, a warm, curvy, sleepy bundle of sweetness.

A dozen inappropriate thoughts swim through my sick head of her snuggling up to me after we've worked out our frustrations of the day on each other's bodies. I bat them away. This is my Bitsy. She's my girl, not some...object. I shouldn't be having any kind of thoughts about her that involve bare flesh and beds.

When the elevator doors open on our fourth-floor apartment, I wait for Bitsy to step off. She doesn't move. Looking down, I see her eyes are closed and her bee-stung lips are parted slightly. Her breathing is deep and even. The girl's so tired, she fell asleep standing up.

I lift her to my chest. She wraps her arms around me and whispers something...something like *I love you. I'm glad to be home.*

My weak, stupid heart swells. I carry her to the apartment and manage to open the door without dropping her. Her bedroom is in the same condition as it was when she left four years ago. The white and gold mirror over her desk still has a pink crepe paper ribbon wrapped around the top. There are pictures of us stuck into the side, and on the table rests a hairbrush, notebook and pink pen.

Her pillows are plumped and her green and pink comforter is smoothed over the mattress. A guy comes to clean the apartment twice a month, but this room is off-limits. I dust things with a cloth, straighten the comforter, punch the pillows a couple of times until they look fresh from the store. No one comes in here but me.

I lay Bitsy on the bed still dressed in her leggings, boots, and puffy coat and that's how I leave her. I can't risk my hands on her bare skin. Even taking her boots off seems too intimate.

I fish the phone out of my pocket. An alert shows on the front screen.

I'm coming home, the message says. I missed it. The phone company must've screwed up. I sink down next to the bed and rest my head against the side of the mattress. Inches away are her fingers, splayed out and relaxed. I'd like nothing more than to bury my face in those fingers and drink in her warmth. In my hand, the phone buzzes. It's probably Beefer. The notification is a good reminder of why Bitsy can't stay.

I get to my feet, but my body doesn't want to move. *You should stay,* my inner voice says. *She might need you.* I force myself to leave. I can't get used to her being here. It would be too dangerous.

The weekly visits to her room, the texts, the rare video calls—that's how I survived these past four years.

It was enough then and it'll be enough in the future. It has to be.

26

BITSY

It's dark when I wake. There's barely a sound in the room other than the low hum of the furnace. When I roll over to check the time, I discover my clock is missing. I flick my eyes over to Audie's bed and see a door instead. Then I remember. I'm home. I'm really home.

With a satisfied smile, I starfish on the bed, stretching my sore limbs and muscles that were cramped from sitting in a car for eight hours. It takes the weird sound of nylon against cotton to make me realize I'm still in my coat. I prop myself up on my elbows and take stock.

I'm in my bedroom, still wearing my coat, yoga pants, long-sleeved navy and white striped Splendid T-shirt and my white Timberlands. Underneath my butt is the same white comforter with the pink and green accents. The overwrought gilt-edged mirror that I thought was the bomb when I was thirteen hangs over the matching desk. I have to get rid of that. My small carry-on suitcase rests just inside the door with my little Dior clutch perched on the top.

I vaguely remember the doorman offering to carry all my shit up from the car. That was decent of him. None of my boxes are present, but I suppose Leka didn't want to wake me. They're probably sitting outside the door.

I find my phone in the pocket of my coat. I have a few messages from Audie and one from Ms. B who writes that she hopes I made it home safely. I shoot off quick replies to both of them.

After, I toss the phone onto the empty nightstand and get up. I listen for any sounds in the apartment but hear nothing. It's nearing midnight, which could mean Leka is sleeping or he's out doing his thing for Beefer.

Or he could be at a woman's place.

I wrinkle my nose at that thought. No. Even if he did have a woman, he wouldn't go to her the first night I was home. I kick off my boots and pull the coat off, tossing it onto the bed.

It's weird that Leka didn't remove my coat and boots. Was he concerned I would feel he was taking advantage of me? I suppose that's a good thing. It shows he's a decent guy, although I already knew that.

I should shower. My clothes feel gross from the long drive, but it would be good to unpack a few things. As I reach for my suitcase, my stomach rumbles in reminder that I haven't eaten anything but fast food, and that was hours ago.

Food first, I decide. Then shower, unpack, and once I have everything in order, I can commence my seduction of Leka.

I pad down the short hall and find my love sitting at the kitchen table, hunched over a mug. A smile of delight breaks across my face. *He's here!* my heart sings. He did not go to run some terrible errand for Beefer. He is not at some woman's house, drinking her wine and climbing into her bed. He's here at *our* table, drinking coffee, and waiting for me.

His T-shirt stretches across his broad shoulders and then hangs loosely around his narrow waist. He's got a good ass, which I attribute to all the lifting he must do for Marjory's. My fingers tingle with the urge to map out the valleys and slopes of all those muscles. One day, I promise myself, one day I will have the right to crawl into his lap, wind my arms around his neck, and kiss that tender, private spot behind his ear. One day soon. I practically skip into the kitchen.

"Hello, Leka." It feels good to even say his name. "I haven't eaten much all day and I'm starving. I thought I'd make a—" I pause because I'm not sure what he's stocked his refrigerator with, but I always remember there being cheese, soup and bread in the house. "—grilled cheese. Want one?"

"No, thank you."

His response is so formal. I cast an uneasy glance in his direction. He can't still be angry that I was at Marjory's. Nothing happened there. Everyone was perfectly polite. The one guy even made me cider and the other line chef was about to get me dinner before Leka showed up.

You're imagining things, I chide internally. "I'll make two anyway. If you don't eat it, I can reheat it in the morning," I decide. In the refrigerator, I find some cheddar cheese, mozzarella, and a soft, goat cheese. The last one is so unlike Leka that I get another pang of anxiety. Is this a sign of another woman?

I hold it up. "Since when do you like goat cheese?" I ask carelessly as if the wrong answer won't send me to my bedroom in tears.

"Guy down at the market said it made good sandwiches. Lower melting point or something like. You'll like it." Leka barely flicks a gaze away from whatever he's reading.

I release my death grip on the cheese and set it on the counter, ignoring the indent marks I've made with my fingers. *It was just the guy at the market,* I tell myself. *Not another woman.*

I take a deep, reassuring breath and look around for the bread. My search skitters to a stop when my eyes land on the table. The colorful brochures and pamphlets aren't junk mail, but marketing material from colleges. Blood thuds angrily in my ears.

Leka notices my interest and taps on the top brochure labeled USC.

"I called around this evening to some people I know. They told me that there are places that will accept you early. You can be enrolled as soon as their term starts in January."

"That's not true." I'd never heard of that.

He ignores my objection and shoves the brochures forward. I step away from the counter and approach carefully, as if the brochures are snakes ready to poison me. I rifle through them. USC, Stanford, Cal Tech. "Oxford, England?"

He shrugs. "It's a good place, I hear. Good enough for royalty. Good enough for you."

I flick the brochures away. "I'm taking a gap year," I inform him, crossing my arms over my chest.

He frowns, keeping his eyes on the catalog in front of him. "What the hell is that?"

"It's where you take time off to recharge your batteries, experience the world, and then enter college with a renewed sense of purpose." It's where I am going to convince you that we belong together forever. No more separations. No more excuses.

"I thought we agreed you would go to college," he replies, still not looking at me.

This isn't how I imagined the reunion would go. I knew it was too much to hope for an immediately enthusiastic welcome, but, I figured, once the shock wore off, Leka would be thrilled. He'd been as alone as me these past four years. His heart had to be sore from missing me as mine ached from missing him. He'd at least hug me. Press a kiss to my cheek. Smile in welcome.

I didn't expect him to be pushing me out the door even before I took my coat off. I scan the apartment for the boxes. Other than the two bedrooms, there's only this kitchen and living room with a small hallway leading to the entry. None of my boxes can be seen.

A sense of foreboding creeps over me. Did he leave my boxes in the car? Did he go down and tell the doorman to only deliver the suitcase? Or worse, did the doorman bring up the boxes only to have them refused by Leka. Embarrassment burns my cheeks.

"Where's my stuff?" I blurt out.

"In your car," he replies. His eyes are on his empty mug.

"Why?" I demand. I want to stomp over there and force him to look at me as he kicks me out.

"Because you're not staying."

I knew what the answer was going to be, but it still hurts. It still makes me angry. It still burns in the pit of my stomach.

"Why are you doing this?" The question comes out plaintive, almost whiny, and I wish I could take it back.

He needs to see I'm an adult—not a child he can boss around, not a puppet he can direct. But how do I prove that when I'm sleeping in the same bed I slept in since I was ten, eating the food that he picked out, wearing the clothes that he paid for?

Abruptly, I twist around and replace the food.

"What are you doing?" He rises from his chair. "You said you were hungry."

"I'm not." My stomach grumbles in protest.

"The fu—hell, you aren't."

"I'm not eating any of your food." I jut out my chin.

His brows crash together. "What nonsense are you saying? Of course, you're going to eat. It's not my food. It's our food." He stalks over and reaches past me for the fridge handle.

I move out of the way, not wanting any contact with him because I don't want to make love to him at this moment. I want to hit him. Hard. "You just told me I can't stay here, so obviously it's not my place."

"I..." He jams a frustrated hand through his hair. I try not to notice how his muscle flexes in his biceps or how the thin T-shirt fabric stretches across his very fit pecs. I try to keep my body from clenching in response to this very fine male body in front of me. I try to keep my heart from flipping over in delight at his closeness. I try, but my nipples tighten anyway and poke insistently against my shirt.

Leka doesn't notice. "I meant you should go back to school," he continues, eyes purposefully pointed over my shoulder. "You're a kid. Kids belong in school."

"By that logic I'm an adult. I have graduated and therefore am no longer a child."

"An adult doesn't stick her tits out demanding attention. That's something a kid does."

So he does see. He sees but still insists I'm only a girl. Resentment scalds my tongue. "Mary's an adult and her tits are out there for everyone to see."

"If I wanted you to be like Mary, I wouldn't have sent you to Vermont," he replies.

"Maybe you liked Mary so much you shipped me off so you could fuck her all the time without my bothering you!"

The words fly out on the wings of embarrassment and anger, but I don't regret them because Leka roars back, "I haven't fucked anyone!"

The admission snaps my jaw shut. He's...not slept with anyone? Ever?

Before I can ask, Leka drags a large hand down his face. Defeat sits heavy on his shoulders as if this confession is more than he ever wanted to share. "You should go to bed. We'll talk about this in the morning." His eyes are fixed on some spot about five feet to the right of my shoulder.

"But—"

"Go to bed," he growls.

I don't get a chance to say another word because he doesn't wait for me to leave. Instead, he flees, leaving me in the kitchen feeling flustered and giddy.

I don't know what we were fighting over at the end, but I think I won. *No. We won,* I correct myself, because we are together.

27

LEKA

Sleep evades me. I feel like I can hear every noise in her bedroom. The swishing of her coat as she shoves it off the bed. The snap of the elastic as she pulls her leggings down and drops them on the floor. The ping of her bra clasp as she frees her breasts.

My hands curl into empty fists and the blood in my groin pounds angrily. I try to ignore my cock. It's mind over matter, I tell myself. If you don't think about the thing that excites you, eventually the erection will go away.

But when I close my eyes, all I see is her, standing out in the kitchen with her tits pointing directly in my face, begging me pertly to suck them until they're hard as erasers. The kitchen where she colored and packed school lunches and made ice-cream sundaes.

I'm a monster. I mentally lock my hands to my side. I can't touch myself—not thinking about her like this. She's my ward. I raised her. Imagining her naked, kneeling in front of me, pressing her face against my heated groin is all wrong.

I should take a spike to my brain, but then she'd be without anyone in this miserable world. I can't have that.

I need to endure this. It's because I've gone without for so long. Beefer's been after me to fuck around, and maybe that's what it's going to take to get rid of these sordid thoughts.

Beefer's answer would be for me to pick a girl from the stable. Mary would fuck me if I asked. She pretends to hate me, but she's desperate because Cesaro hasn't come through on his promise to elevate her to the main territory, which means she's stuck here sucking Beefer's dick. And I'm powerful enough at this point for her to believe it would be to her advantage to climb into my bed. I don't want that.

I don't want a prostitute. I don't want any other woman at all. Or man for that matter.

I'm coming to the realization that I'm probably going to die without having had sex because the one person I do want is the only one I can't have.

I lie like a statue until the sun breaks through the windows. I take that as a sign to leave. She'll be safe today. I'll leave her a note telling her to stay in the apartment. After a good run to sweat out my arousal and a stint at Marjory's, I'll have myself under control.

We can eat dinner, talk like two rational adults about where she's going to spend the winter vacation, and then we'll go to our separate bedrooms and fall asleep. I'll maintain this routine until she leaves.

It's a good plan.

I end up running for eight miles. It takes that long for my brain to shut off. To be safe, though, I go to Marjory's and wash myself off there with a hose. No one else is here this early in the morning. The restaurant doesn't open until eleven and the cooks don't roll in until nine or so.

But my plans for a solo morning are busted when Beefer shows up when I'm neck deep under a faucet, rinsing my hair out.

"The water line break at your apartment or something?" he asks.

"Something like that." I straighten and let the cool water run down my bare back.

Beefer eyes me speculatively while handing me a thin dishtowel. I take it gratefully and wait for the inquisition.

"You look like shit. Water busts are the fucking worst. We had one a few years back. Remember? The wife made me put her up in the fucking Plaza for a week. I swear to God, I was ready to divorce her."

I mop my face, hair and pits and toss the sopping dishtowel in the trash. There's a stash of clothes here and I trade my sweaty workout gear for a pair of jeans and a black turtleneck.

"So, Bitsy," Beefer says. "I'd kinda forgotten about her."

That was the whole point, and I'm sick that Bitsy's main source of protection has evaporated. I need to get her away from this city before any more questions are asked. Unfortunately, Beefer's curiosity has been pricked.

"She said she graduated early. Didn't know that was even a thing."

"Me either." I pull out the coffee beans and measure out enough for Beefer and me.

"We should get our girls together. Camella could stand to be around a smart girl like yours. I'm tired of her hanging around those sluts at the club."

Yeah, that's never going to happen. Camella's on a bad path and I don't want her dragging Bitsy down to hell.

"I can't decide if your girl's pretty or not. She was a homely kid, but, yesterday, there were some angles where she looked kinda good. Your girl could encourage Cammie to get some more schooling while Cammie could make her look nice."

"Bitsy's fine the way she is." More than fine. She is beautiful and any man who doesn't see that is blind. Beefer's probably trying to hide his attraction to Bitsy so I don't pluck his eyes from his skull.

"You have to say that. You're her—" He breaks off and frowns. "How was it that you were related? I forget."

Here's where I say she's my sister because as my sister, no one is touching her, just like no one would have dared lay a finger on Camella before Beefer gave her to Cesaro. But when my dumb mouth opens, I say, "We're not related."

Beefer's eyes widen in surprise. "The hell you're not. Why'd you take care of her all these years?" And then the eyes narrow. "Wait. Are you? Have you?" He doesn't finish either sentence, but I know what he's thinking. "That's not right, Leka. Not right at all."

I turn toward the coffee pot to avoid his insightful gaze and fight the heat threatening to crawl up my neck. "She's a kid, Beefer. I took her in because she had nowhere to go. If you believe I'm that kind of man, why the hell would you have worked with me all these years?"

"Right. Right. Sorry, man." He slaps me on the back, making me feel guiltier than ever. "We've all been weird fucks lately. It's the pressure from upstairs. Here's what I'm thinking. We should all go out. It'll be a good bonding time."

Bonding time means one thing. Strippers.

"We have a run tomorrow night," I remind him. We're protecting a shipment of guns moving south.

"All the more reason to do this tonight. We'll be a tighter, better unit. Who do we have driving?"

"Mason."

Beefer looks up in surprise. "That kid? Isn't he a little young for this?"

"I was younger than him when I was at the wheel."

"All right. I trust your judgment. Let's have PJ and Donny on lookout."

"What about Snow?"

"I've got a bad feeling about him."

"He'll be mad. He's been complaining about the light paychecks." And a mad crew member is a talkative, easily bought off one.

"Snow can suck my left ball. He'll get what he gets and be happy about it. Not like he has a choice. If he complains, you can treat him to a Glock special."

Meaning, shove my gun into his mouth and let him swallow the bullet. "We're going to run out of men if we do that."

Beefer snorts. "Fuck that. There's always some hungry runt willing to do anything including strangling his own mother in exchange for a few greenbacks."

I try once more for Beefer to see the light. "He'll leave then."

"Ha!" Beefer barks. "You know that no one leaves. Once you're in, you're in. Only a bullet takes you out. Either in my brain or yours." He flicks a finger in front of my face but doesn't quite make contact. He's not that dumb.

I hesitate because I promised to have dinner with Bitsy, and since I'm going to send her away soon, I deserve a little time with her.

"Look, I'll be honest," Beefer says when I don't immediately agree. "You're real closed off and I get that's just how you operate, but there's a lot of newbies in the crew and they don't understand. Some of them are starting to wonder if your loyalty belongs to the business or yourself. If you go out and spend a little time with them, all that uncertainty will clear up in a sec." He snaps his fingers. "If it was up to me, I'd pretend to care for the rest of the guys so that when we were out on a job, I wouldn't always have to be looking over my shoulder, worrying whether some friendly fire was going to plug me in the back of the head."

Beefer's always been insightful—far more insightful than me. He's giving me a warning that I should pay attention to.

"It'll have to be later," I tell him and then cast around for an excuse that doesn't involve Bitsy. "The good dancers don't work until after the dinner hour."

"Need to go home and see your girl, do you?" He pegs me perfectly. Like I said, insightful—uncomfortably so.

"She just got back," I say by way of explanation.

"Take her over to La Frais tonight. The wife loves that place. Says it makes her feel rich or shit. A fancy dinner goes a long way to settling hurt feelings."

I give him a short nod. He's closed off all my exits. Besides, Beefer might be right. Seeing other women might give me the relief I need to keep ignoring my feelings for Bitsy.

"Great. Get the word out to the crew. We'll blow off steam tonight and tomorrow the unit will be tight as a witch's pussy."

Beefer pours himself a cup of freshly brewed coffee and salutes me with the mug. "To pussy."

I hold up my mug, too. If this is what it takes to make sure that I don't fuck things up with Bitsy, then I'll be at strip bar every night until she's shipped out of here.

28

BITSY

"I thought you were bringing vermicelli salad from Pho What down the street," I whisper in Leka's ear. I had plans for us tonight that didn't include leaving the apartment. Seduction is not an easy task in public.

"This place is more popular," he replies tersely. He shifts away, as if my nearness is irritating. He's been mad since I came home, but we haven't had a minute to talk about it.

Is he still upset about the revelation of his sex life last night? He shouldn't be. I don't think any single piece of information could have made me happier. I'm *glad* he's a virgin. It's incredible, of course, that a man who looks as good as Leka has managed to live twenty-seven years without a single female jumping him, but I'm not complaining.

I want to tell him that I'm a virgin as well, but I don't know how to bring it up. Maybe I should've texted him. That way he wouldn't be embarrassed. We are in the same inexperience boat together. Although I've read enough fiction that I feel like I could show him a good time.

I clutch my arms around my waist and shiver at the image of me teaching Leka anything to do with sex. What a delicious, marvelous concept. I should tell him now. I'll whisper it in his ear and all dinner long he can be tormented by the same fantasies that are swirling through my head.

I lean forward on the tips of my toes. "I was thinking about what you said last night and—"

"Your table will be ready in a moment, Mr. Moore," interrupts a tall, slender hostess who is a dead ringer for Taylor Swift with crinkly blonde hair and deep red lips. "Would you like to be seated or wait for your guest?"

Leka jerks a thumb in my direction. "I'm with my guest."

The hostess's eyes widen in surprise.

"Oh, of course. Yes, well, I didn't see you there. As I said, it will be just a moment," she babbles and totters off. She stops by another tall, slender woman draped in black. The two look in our direction and for some reason, the two misjudge how noisy the crowd is because I can hear their whispering.

Can you believe she's with him?

No. You've got to be kidding me!

They must be related.

They look nothing alike. Maybe it's work?

It has to be. She's not attractive enough to actually be his girlfriend.

I glance at Leka to see if he's heard them, but his gaze if focused straight ahead. My newfound confidence dives to the floor. Leka may be a virgin, but it doesn't mean he's been saving himself for me. And maybe I misinterpreted it. He said he hadn't been having sex, but he didn't say ever. He could be in a dry spell.

Sadly, that makes so much more sense than him being a virgin at the age of twenty-seven. What an idiotic mistake to have almost made. I should get on my knees and thank the hostess for saving me from an embarrassment that would be impossible for me to overcome.

I force my gaze away from the whispering women and take in the dim interior of the fancy restaurant with its white tablecloths and suited wait-staff who all look good enough to have stepped off a runway. My unmanicured hands dig into the folds of my black skirt, which I bought from ASOS today off the sale rack because my entire wardrobe is leggings, track pants, T-shirts and school uniforms. I do have the *guilt gifts* as Audie calls them, but none of them are clothes unless you count the cornucopia of jackets that Leka's bought me.

But clothes wouldn't make a difference. Leka, in his decade-old black jeans and a thin black crewneck sweater, is causing people to stop and stare. I hear speculations behind me as to whether he's an actor. *Maybe theatre*, someone suggests when they can't place his face.

The hostess returns. "Your table is ready, Mr. Moore. If you'd please follow me."

Leka reaches behind him to cup my elbow. He drags me forward and then we dive into the restaurant, following her through a maze of tables and people until we arrive at a small table at the back. Leka waits until I sit down before grabbing the chair in the corner, presumably so he can stare broodingly at the crowd.

Menus are dropped in front of us and a new person appears, this time a male, to explain the specials of the day. I don't understand a tenth of what he says, so I tune him out and try to read the menu with the aid of the centerpiece candle.

"Water for me," Leka says after the waiter asks what he wants to drink. "She'll have water, too," he adds before I can request one of the fancy martinis in the front of the menu.

The waiter bows slightly and then takes off. When he's out of earshot, I lean over the giant menu. "I wanted a drink."

"You're underage," he reminds me. "Stop trying to act older. It's not a good look."

His words are like a slap in the face. This is not how I imagined the evening would go. I'd come home with, what I thought, was good news of a job on a cleaning crew at a meat processing shop. The hours were at night, but that worked well with his work, and the pay was decent. When I told him about it, he'd grown cold and abruptly ordered me to get dressed or we'd miss our reservations.

This place is so fancy, too. I don't like it. We've never eaten at a restaurant like this before. Before I left for Boone, we'd go to a little Italian café by the apartment or pick up sandwiches at the deli. Sometimes, we'd order food to be delivered. But we never came to a place that had multiple forks and spoons framing a giant white plate with gold trim.

I wonder how Leka even found this place and worse, who he brought here. Everywhere I look there are couples.

"What are you going to order?" Leka asks.

"I haven't decided yet." I can't decipher the stuff on the menu. A preparation of langoustine? Dashi gelée? Lemon-potato mousseline? Is that like a potato stuffed with mussels? A real woman would know what these things are. A real woman would have already eaten all of these things and would be able to explain in five-syllable words exactly why they're all so delicious.

I shrink down in my chair. "I'll have the special."

"Okay. Me, too." Leka snaps the menu closed.

The waiter shows up seconds later and takes our order.

"Two specials," Leka says.

"Very good. I'm sure you'll love it," the waiter replies. "The yellowtail collar is considered the best part of the hamachi."

"Yellowtail?" I echo. "Isn't that fish?"

The waiter shoots me an odd look. "Yes. Hamachi is Japanese yellow-tail. The hamachi kama is so special it is traditionally reserved for family or friends of the owner. Unlike most hamachi, this isn't raw, but caramelized under a low flame."

"I didn't know you liked fish," Leka says.

I hate fish. "I thought hamachi was grilled beef."

The waiter sniffs. "You mean hibachi."

I couldn't have sounded stupider if I'd planned it. My cheeks grow hot.

Leka takes pity on me. "Do you have beef?"

"No, we do not have beef," the waiter replies in slightly offended tone. "We serve a lamb loin and belly with chayote gratin topped with a chili-infused cranberry reduction."

Leka and I lock eyes. He rises and throws several hundred dollars on the table. "Thanks. We'll pass."

"What?" The waiter is shocked.

I spring to my feet. Leka rounds the table, brushes by the frozen waiter, and grabs my hand. We power walk past a dozen tables and arrive at the hostess stand where the two gossipy women are greeting guests.

Leka halts. "This girl? She's as beautiful and bright as the sun. Anyone who doesn't see it is blind."

The Taylor Swift lookalike blanches and tries to stammer out an apol-ogy, but Leka's already moving on. I give the girl a wave, though, just so she knows there are no hard feelings. Leka just told a room full of rich socialites and business people that I was beautiful and bright like the sun. I'm floating on air.

"Sorry," he says as we climb into his car. "I thought we could do some-thing nice since you just got home."

"It's the thought that counts." A pithy statement, but still true. I smile to myself.

"What those women said, about you not being pretty enough for me, that's all bullshit. You know that, right?"

"I don't care." Most of the time, my looks—or lack thereof—don't bother me. It's only when I get fearful of losing Leka that I start feeling insecure.

"Good." He guns the engine and we head for home. "Call for the vermicelli. Tell them to leave it with the doorman. While we're driving, you can tell me what you were doing all day."

"Don't you already know? Terry tailed me the whole time. Your day doorman isn't a very good PI."

Leka grunts. "He's a doorman. What do you expect?"

"I didn't expect to be followed around the city as I applied for jobs."

He tightens his hands around the steering wheel. "And why exactly are you applying for jobs?"

I sigh. "We already went over this. I'm going to get my own apartment—"

"You're going back to school as soon as we can arrange it," he interrupts coldly. "Until that time, you'll live in our apartment."

The joy at being called beautiful is obliterated by his terse words. "It's not *our* apartment. It's *your* apartment. If it was *ours*, you wouldn't be telling me what to do."

"Is this about you being eighteen?"

"No. This is about you seeing me as an adult. It's about you acknowledging that I'm a woman and it's okay for us to be together. It's about me sleeping in a bed we call ours instead of mine or yours. That's what this is about." My words end on a shrill note.

"That will never happen," he growls.

"Why?"

"Because it won't. End of discussion." His jaw tightens so hard it's a wonder it doesn't crack.

"I'm not done talking about it. Why are you stalking me?"

"It's called protecting you, and it's a good thing I sent him along because you left your phone at home."

"You track my phone?" I squawk, turning in my seat to glare at Leka. "For how long?" He slides a reproving look toward me that asks how dumb am I. "Since you abandoned me in Boone?" I exclaim.

"I didn't abandon you. You went to school like two hundred other girls from across the country."

"I disagree with your characterization, but can we get back to the stalking thing? Have you really kept tabs on me since you left me in Boone?"

He doesn't reply, but that's all the answer I need.

As soon as he pulls up to the curb next to the apartment, I jump out, ignoring the night doorman and passing by the food sitting on the lobby desk. I jab the elevator button. By some miracle, the elevator doors slide open and I'm able to dart inside before Leka gets to the lobby doors.

"Wait, Bitsy."

But I let the elevator doors close. I need some time alone. All this time that I was in Vermont, he was tracking my every move? And he never once came to visit me? Did he also have spies up there? Did they report to him how I cried myself to sleep for the first six months? Did they tell him how I didn't have any friends other than Audie because I felt so odd around these rich girls who grew up in big houses and took European vacations and never once went to a restaurant where someone got knifed in the throat?

It's a good thing he's not in the elevator. I might have had to go all Solange on him and beat him with one of my ugly black pumps.

He's waiting by the apartment door when I step off the elevator. His chest is heaving only slightly from having run up the four flights of stairs. It's irritating how sexy that is. I brush by him angrily into the entryway and kick off my shoes.

"You're my charge," he says, as if his actions were perfectly normal. "It's my job to keep you safe, which is a hundred times harder now that you're here instead of in Vermont."

I stick out my chin. "Well, I'm sorry you're so put out. I can defend myself. I have mace in my purse and my cell phone can call 9-1-1 just as easily as it can call you."

His brows crash together. "You think mace and a phone are going to protect you from some asshole on the street?"

"I also took self-defense courses. I'm not an idiot."

"Really? Then what if a man does this?" He moves so fast, I don't even realize he's bodied me up against the wall until I feel the flat surface pressing against my shoulder blades. "Look at you. I'm not even using my hands and I've got you pinned," he mocks.

I shift and press my knee against his leg. "I'm only letting you do this because I don't want to hurt you." I could easily shove my kneecap into his groin. He wouldn't be so smug then. I should do it—just to teach him a lesson.

"You wouldn't be able to land a finger on me, let alone get a knee even close to my dick," he retorts.

I straighten. "Wanna bet?"

I bring my knee up, and when he reaches down to block it, I slide my hand right over his groin. His breath catches. So does mine. He's hard.

And huge. In my fantasies, I didn't imagine him to be this big, but the length is larger than my unfurled hand. In that moment, my anger is replaced by something hotter, darker, and more insistent. My fingers curve around the shaft.

"What the fuck do you think you're doing?" he growls in my ear.

"I'm defending myself." I whisper. I squeeze him and his knees buckle. A hand slams above my ear. If I turned my head, I could kiss the inside of his wrist. Down low, between my legs, I can feel my blood pulsing hard and hot.

My squeeze becomes a caress. The cock under my palm twitches. The arm next to my head trembles. Leka's body is radiating an intense amount of heat and it's burning through my clothes, under my skin and igniting my bloodstream. His breath becomes ragged. This is it. This is my opportunity. This is what I've been waiting for. The door is open. The gate is up. I rise on my tiptoes to kiss the jaw I've been dying to kiss. I part my lips—

"Stop." The sound that comes out of him is tortured. "Don't do this." His words are one part angry, one part self-loathing.

It's the self-loathing bit that pushes my heels to the ground and unsticks my hand from the front of his pants. I want him to love me with his whole heart, not resent me because I made him horny.

Tears prick my eyes, but I keep my lashes down so he can't see. Is loving me so terrible? Is wanting me so wrong?

"Why?" I ask. "Why is this so wrong?"

"Because it is."

I hate that he's so defeated, as if loving me is the worst thing he could do.

"Sorry," I mumble and slide out from under him. I walk, unsteadily, to the kitchen. My palm is on fire, tattooed with the imprint of his cock. In the kitchen, I open the freezer and stick my head inside, ostensibly looking for the cookies 'n' cream ice cream, but really trying to cool off and gather my self-control.

Dimly, the sound of a phone buzzing registers. Someone has sent Leka a text. He must not like it because he curses.

"I have to go," he says.

"Of course you do." I slam the freezer door shut and turn around, leaning against the fridge.

The anguish on his face is gone. His jaw is set and his eyes are blank. It's his work look. I hate that dead expression.

"Stay here and keep your phone on you," he orders.

I know better than to ask, but I can't keep the question out of my mouth. "Where are you going?"

"Out."

And who protects you while you're out? I think.

"Is it dangerous?" I have to know.

"It's..." He pauses and averts his eyes. Leka hasn't ever lied to me—at least, not outright. He hides things, but when confronted directly, he will never lie. I learned that when he carted me off to elementary school.

"It's what?"

"Strippers. We're having a company dinner at a strip club." He shoves the phone back into his front pocket and palms the abandoned shoulder holster. "Don't leave. Please," he tacks on.

My first instinct is to tell him to go to hell, but I'm emotionally worn out. All I can muster up is a warning. "If you touch one, I'll cut your fingers off."

"I'm not touching anyone," he replies, shrugging on a jacket to hide the gun.

In a strange and sick way, the gun makes me feel marginally better. He really is going to work. You take singles if you're going to have fun, not a weapon.

He stops at the door. With one hand on the door, he turns back and finally looks me in the eye. "I'd rather stay home than go to this."

I give him a tight nod of acknowledgment. The reassurance isn't much, but I'll take it. Once he leaves, though, I decide that I'm going to do a little shopping. He's not going to be the only one tortured by jealousy tonight.

29

LEKA

S he bought a dildo. The credit card fraud alert is for a bland company called FHP. I'm about to reject the charge when I recognize Bitsy's card. As the crew piles out of the Escalade, I google the company. For Her Pleasure is a sex shop in midtown that touts itself as providing same-day delivery all hours of the day and night. The amount charged matches the "deal of the day," one six-inch version that touted itself as close to the real thing.

I clench the phone in my hand until my knuckles turn white. A dildo is better than a real dick attached to a real man, I tell myself, but that truth doesn't make me feel better. All I can see in my head is a dick-shaped object delving between Bitsy's thick thighs slick with her cream.

Can I be jealous of a rubber thing? Because I am. Because I want to reach through the computer and choke everyone who is beyond this stupid site. When I get home tonight I'm burning that piece of crap.

She must know I look at her credit card statement. I pay that bill monthly, although she hardly charges anything to it other than food, tampons, and lotion shit to pretty up her face. Not that she needs anything to make her look better. She's fucking gorgeous. It's why I sent her to an all-girls school where she'd be dick free.

"You coming, Leka?" Beefer sticks his face in the auto. "Everyone's waiting." I look up from the screen, and whatever is on my face makes Beefer take a step back. "Bad news?"

"I'm going home."

I reach for the latch to close the car door, but Beefer resists. "No way. Unless your apartment is burning down, you need to come with us. You're a live wire. If you don't blow off steam, someone's going to get hurt. And like you said earlier, we can't afford to lose manpower. Not with a run tomorrow. You don't have to stay long. Just wet the whistle, play nice with the girls, and let your boys know you've got their backs."

Outside, the crew stands impatiently stomping their feet and blowing on their hands as they wait for me to claw through the reeds of heat and jealousy that threaten to choke off all good sense. *If you don't blow off steam, someone's going to get hurt.*

He's right. I nearly broke down earlier. If she'd managed to make contact, I would've lost it. I climb out of the Escalade and join the crew on the sidewalk.

Snow, a new enforcer, greets me. "Didn't think you were getting out of the car, Priest. Not to worry. I'll protect you from those big bad strippers."

He slaps his knee as he laughs.

"I thought he had a honey stashed away and doesn't want us to find out," chirps PJ with the same floppy-bang haircut that Snow is sporting. PJ's a fairly new recruit but good with a gun. In fact, most of the crew is. There are very few guys still with us who'd worked when Stinky Steve was in charge. Cesaro cleaned house in every arm of the organization, wiping out the old guard. Everyone below me and Beefer got spared. Lucky, I guess.

"Nah, he's got a ball and chain. I feel for ya, dude. I got a sister, too, and she's always up in my business." Snow reaches out and claps me on the shoulder. The wet cigar butt of Beefer's foot soldier rubs against the fabric of my jacket. It wouldn't be hard to whip my hand up and break his wrist, but fortunately for all of us, the door opens and a bouncer gestures for us to enter. Snow moves fast enough to win a medal somewhere.

I let everyone else go first. Inside, I scan the crowd. Despite the early hour—it's only around eleven—there's a lot of testosterone in the air.

"Good to see you out with us," murmurs Donnie. He was one of Gerry's friends but managed to survive the purge. He directs his gap-toothed smile in my direction. I give him a nod of acknowledgment. Donnie's harmless but eager to please anyone. That kind of attitude will likely get him killed in the next five years. He'll be busy doing favors for everyone, not realizing he's pissing rivals off in the process.

"There are so many fucking babes here," PJ exclaims. "I'm 'bout to nut in my pants just looking around."

"I'm taking those two home." Snow points to two brunettes who look so similar that they might be sisters.

"Yeah, man. Hit it!" PJ cheers.

"Nothing better than hanging with the boys," Snow replies. "Free booze, naked chicks, and good music. Best night ever!" He punches a fistful of singles in the air and dives toward the stage.

Across the room, Beefer meets my eyes with a knowing smile. *I told you so*, his expression says.

I try to put the image of Bitsy and the rubber dick out of my head and focus on what is making every other male in the joint frenzied with excitement. But I can't summon any enthusiasm. The women gyrating on stage are doing so because they need the money, not because they're in love with shaking their bare tits in front of a bunch of half-drunk meatheads.

I take a sip of a foul-tasting whiskey and dig my shoulders into the concrete wall. Snow must have a shitty home life if this is what qualifies for the "best" of anything. The best night is sitting on your own couch, watching television, eating microwave popcorn with the sweetest girl to breathe this godforsaken air sitting next to you.

Fuck. I wish I was with Bitsy. I'm glad her strawberry shampoo is smelling up the bathroom and that there five pairs of identical white tennis shoes resting inside the front door that trip me up every time I walk in. I've missed buying dozens of containers of yogurt only to have most of them expire before she remembers we have them. I've missed her brown eyes laughing at me from across the breakfast table and her cheerful voice telling me all about how the boys are too silly and the classes are too easy and that Sister Mary Katherine needs to pluck the mole hair nesting on her cheek.

I'm tired of hurting Bitsy to keep her safe, but there are no alternatives to the path we're on. She can't stay.

I throw back the rest of my glass. I'm going to have something five times as strong as this to drown out my bad mood.

Before I can make my way to the bar for a refill, Mason, the boy I had drive Camella home, appears next to me. He sticks his hands in the pockets of his baggy jeans. "This is lit, man," he says in a tone that says he'd like to die.

"Not drinking?" I ask. Out of all the guys I work with, I probably hate Mason the least. He's quiet, does what he's told, and doesn't engage in a lot of shit talking. This scene isn't up his alley. The kid's gay, but he's not out—at least not to us. It doesn't matter to me. As long as he's loyal to Beefer, he can fuck whoever he wants. Besides, it's one less dick out there that's looking to violate Bitsy.

"I'm driving."

I wonder if he volunteered for that task. If so, he's smarter than I gave him credit for. "Good move."

"Thanks. Gotta be honest. I didn't expect you to come. Strippers and sex shows don't seem to be your thing."

"It's not," I admit.

We exchange surprised looks. I'm not usually that forthcoming. The Bitsy thing is messing with my head.

Mason breaks eye contact first. "You'd think that given who you are, you wouldn't be doing anything you didn't want to."

"You regret hooking up with us?" He's staring at the floor so I can't read his expression.

"Nah, it's just..." The kid searches for his words. "A guy should be able to do what he wants when he's in your position."

"There's only one way out of this business, Mason, and it's not by finding a new job." *Death is the only exit.* I can't get out, but I can get Bitsy out. Maybe even Mason. "You're new. If you leave now, it's possible no one would care." Cesaro might not even know of Mason's existence.

"Leave for what?" the kid replies. "If I had better options, I wouldn't have hooked up with you all in the first place."

And there it is. The reason we're all here.

"Boy! Get me another drink," Snow yells over.

Or most of us.

Mason stiffens slightly at the slur.

I give the kid a bit of free advice. "Snow once bit a guy's nose off. It was about three years ago and we were moving some prescriptions up to Canada. We'd been on the road for a couple of days—five of us in a semi-tractor trading off driving, sleeping, and guarding the cargo. It was hot in the trailer because it was July. This kid named Rob complained, and Snow said that if he didn't shut up, Snow'd give him eight inches of winter up his ass. Rob shot back that he didn't think Snow had more than one ball in his pants, and Snow, well, he leaned over and bit Rob's nose off."

Mason turns pale—or as pale as the kid can get.

"Whatcha doing?" Beefer asks, lumbering up before Mason can respond.

"Mason's getting Snow a drink."

Mason nods and hops off.

"I like that kid," Beefer comments. "He's like you, though. Doesn't like the girls."

So Beefer does know.

"Thought that may be the way you leaned," he adds.

"No."

The boss rocks back on his heels, tucking his thumbs inside the waist-band of his too-tight dress slacks. "That's right. You like 'em young."

It takes everything I have not to stiffen like Mason did.

"I like 'em private."

Beefer smirks. "Nah. I understand where you're coming from. I'm not a fan of used pussy either. Cesaro has the right idea—take the fresh ones. They're tighter and hotter. Plus, if you raise them right, they won't stray. Those used sluts will fuck any dick that waves a few bills in their direction. Look at these hoes"—he waves a hand toward the stage—"they wouldn't give Snow and PJ the time of day outside this club, but tonight they're crawling on their hands and knees."

"They are strippers," I point out mildly. This is literally their job. They're trying to earn a living in a more honest way than we are, but Beefer wouldn't want to hear that, so I keep the thought to myself.

Beefer harrumphs. "Yeah, well, if I don't get off and good, I'm burning the whole place down." He snaps his fingers, the rings on his digits clinking together at the base. Mason comes running. "Get me the two brunettes. I want to watch them eat each other out and then I want them to give me a blow job."

Mason sets off to find a manager as Beefer moves toward the VIP rooms. "Come on," Beefer tells me. "You can watch."

It's not a suggestion.

"After I get something to drink." I'm going to need a lot of booze to last the night.

30

LEKA

The low rumble of the furnace is the only sound in my apartment when I arrive home. In the entry are a pair of black boots, thin at the ankle and chunky around the heel.

I'm an adult now, I can hear her saying. *White tennis shoes aren't the only things I've grown out of.*

The plastic bag full of yogurt brushes against my leg. Perhaps her shoe choice isn't the only thing that's changed. I shelve the dairy and strip out of my stinking clothes, tossing the sweat- and alcohol-drenched items into a heap in the corner of my bedroom. I might wash them in the morning or I might stick them in the trash. I'll make up my mind later.

In the bathroom, I crank on the shower. Before I step under the water, I swallow four aspirin and stare at my sorry mug in the mirror. An exhausted, frustrated man stares back.

Beefer declared I needed a woman. He'd said that the night I took Bitsy to Vermont. He'd said that tonight after he sprayed his come all over the two girls' faces and told me it was my turn.

But no one in that club was going to get me hard. Not the one with legs a mile long or the one with the butt that was so round it looked unreal. Not the two girls who looked like sisters that entertained the crew and moved Snow to show a deep reverence I hadn't realized he was capable of. Not virgins, experienced women, burly men or slender, pretty twinks.

Sure, I get erections. Everyone does. I wake up with one, rub it out, and go on my way. The relief is the same as pissing or eating a good meal. That routine had been enough for me until Bitsy returned. Now it feels as if I'm one exposed, throbbing nerve.

I haven't felt this weak and out-of-control since that day in the dress store when pieces of Bitsy's clothing dropping to the floor one by one as she disrobed. I sat there in that chair with growing dread as my pants grew tight and my chest caved in. I couldn't get out of that place fast enough.

Later, after the blood was cleaned up from the floor of Marjory's, I chalked it up to adrenaline and my surroundings. All that soft stuff, all that lace, all those high heels. It wasn't anything that I was familiar with. That's why I felt those stirrings low in my gut. The same ones that are settling in now, making my balls tighten and my cock grow heavy.

I duck inside the shower, crank on the cold and try to freeze out those feelings. I didn't save her all those years ago to put her life in danger now. She deserves to live a normal life—one where she's not watching people get their necks sliced open or looking over her shoulder for someone to act out some dark revenge or coming home to someone who has to spend an hour in the shower scouring the blood off his hands. I scrub those hands across my face.

Bitsy deserves the world and I'm determined to give it to her.

Does her world include a man? Or do you plan for her to die alone?

I drop my forehead to the tile wall. These thoughts are gonna kill me. I shut off the water. The freezing temps aren't doing anything for me. I could be in Antarctica and my dick would still be hard if Bitsy was around. I do a half-ass job of toweling off.

My feet carry me past my bedroom to the end of the hall and stop in front of Bitsy's door. If I wasn't so tired or so lonely, I would've been able to force myself back fifteen feet and into my own room. But I can't stop myself from sinking to the floor.

Knowing she's a breath away is killing me...and bringing me to life. The last four years I've been dead inside. I've eaten, slept, killed, come home to an empty apartment and lain in my bed until the sun came up. I take a deep breath and instead of stale air, strawberry and soap and floral perfume fill my lungs. The taint of the night drains away. The water, no matter how hot, can't do that for me.

Bare assed, I sink to the floor. From here, I can see a tiny sliver of gold from the light under the microwave in the kitchen. I close my eyes and see her in front of me. She arches her back and her hard, erect nipples press against the thin fabric of her T-shirt. Her eyes are full of challenge and invitation. *Take me if you dare.*

Her tits are small but juicy. Big enough to fill a man's palm—*my* palm. She probably has dusky nipples, darker than her golden skin.

My cock turns rock hard.

Yeah. There's only one female that turns me on and it's the one I can't have. Not just because she's young, but because I raised her. I took her in. I cared for her when she was sick. I held her tiny hand while we watched cartoons and ate cereal out of the box. I bought bunny slippers for her and tied her shoes for her and *fuck*. It is wrong. This lust I have toward Bitsy is just so fucking wrong.

I order my legs to move, but my ass is glued to the floor. I've tried to erase the desire, ice out the heat, shut down my heart. It was easier when she was gone, but now that she's here, telling me that she wants me, it's too hard to shove these wicked feelings into a concrete box in the back of my head.

Maybe if I...if I just this once...I reach between my legs. My shaft is thick and hot. I close my eyes and rest my head against the wall. I force the image of the two brunettes up. They had big boobs and long, slender legs. Their waists nipped in, emphasizing two bubble butts. One was shorter than the other, her breasts tucking under the ones of the taller girl. They played a game where the short girl was rough with the taller one. She'd grabbed the girl's hair in her hand and yanked her head back so hard I thought I heard a bone crack. Snow choked on his tongue and soiled his pants at that scene.

It left me cold.

I pump my hand along my shaft and the two girls disappear, replaced by a dressing room.

Take off all your clothes.

All of them?

Yes.

The image shifts again and now she's in the kitchen, lowering herself onto the table. Her shirt rides up, revealing a thin patch of skin. Her fingernails scrape along the edge of the hem. The lace of her panties peeks above her tight black leggings.

My throat is thick. Lust lies heavy on my tongue, like a thick cream. I shift on the floor, but I can't get comfortable. The floor's too hard. Her wiry, curled hair rings her face. A nervous hand comes to rest between two small, juicy tits.

A groan escapes from me. My breathing grows ragged and fast.

Her hand drifts lower. As I watch, her fingers work their way under the waistband. Her knuckles move against the fabric as her fingers find a rhythm.

Come seeps out the top of my cock. I spread it around and jack myself a little faster, a little rougher.

Her lips part and her eyes drop from mine to catch at my waist. My balls tighten in excitement. I wish those delicate fingers were wrapped around my dick. *This is wrong*, some part of the back of my head screams at me.

It's not real, the devil whispers.

But it feels real. It feels as if she's here just steps away, lying with her hand between her splayed legs, her tongue flicking out to touch the corner of her mouth wondering what I taste like.

She'd be soft. Everywhere. And she'd taste like...I lick my lips. She'd taste like heavy cream, rich and sinful.

I sit at that table, spread her legs wider and tongue her cherry until she is screaming my name. When she's done coming all over my tongue, I slide right into that hot, slick sheath. I don't last long. Three thrusts. Maybe four. It's a blur of heat, slick skin, and friction.

The come spurts out of my cock. Seed smears on my stomach and trickles down the inside of my thigh. I'm a mess.

My sticky hand drops to my side. In my head, I've balanced my soul's ledger by reminding myself that for all the corrupt wrong I've committed, at least I saved Bitsy. If I touch her, even once, even if she's begging me, I'll have betrayed the sole purpose of my life—to protect this one precious being.

Would I have taken her in, all those years ago, if I'd known that the greatest danger in her life would be me?

I look down at my already hardening cock with a miserable realization. Yes. I would've made the same choice fourteen years ago because my life is worthless without her in it.

My chin drops to my chest. Somewhere inside of me, I must find enough self-control to send her away—even if it destroys me.

31

BITSY

When I first wake and hear the pained sound outside my door, I think he was injured. It's always been my biggest fear.

I fly to the door. Hand on the doorknob, I stop when I hear my name. I crack the door open and see him sitting on the floor. His knees re slightly bent, but it is obvious what he is doing. His face is tilted back and his eyes are closed. His lips are slightly parted and the expression he wears is half pain, half ecstasy. I drop to my knees when I hear the first guttural sound.

He never once looks in my direction. I close the door so he doesn't stop, but with the door shut, I find that the walls are both too thin and too thick. Thin enough that I can hear him groan but too thick to hear the slap of skin against skin as he sits outside my bedroom door and touches himself.

My imagination runs wild. Time and place warp as if I've fallen down the rabbit hole into some decadent fairy tale where Leka sits in front of me, hand curled around his massive dick.

His attention is pinned on me. A hungry, needy, anticipatory look is stretched across his face. I crawl over to him and brush his hand away. I use both hands to grip the shaft. It pulses in my grip. His hand comes down to tangle in my hair as I rub my cheek along the hard, throbbing length.

"Open up, girl," he commands.

I part my lips and let the knob of his penis slip inside. I lay my tongue flat and let the whole length glide down the back of my throat. His hand comes up to palm the back of my head and hold me in place as he works the long, hot length in and out of my willing mouth. My own sex clenches in need. I drop my hand between my legs because tasting him, sucking him, fucking him make me instantly wet.

The wooden floor scrapes against my knees. My breasts hang heavy between us. My mouth is full because he's big, so very big. It's difficult to take all of him in, but I try. Leka palms my face with one hand and holds the back of my neck with the other. He's groaning, whispering things like how hot I look, how he's not going to last long because he's wanted this forever. He dreams about it, he says, and every time he wakes up before he comes, but not this time. Not this time.

And then he can't talk anymore because he's too intent on shafting my mouth. I open wider, taking him all the way in, until I feel him in the back of my throat. The pressure is intense, incredible and it's building on my tongue, between my legs, in my head until it explodes with a wet *splash*.

I jerk to attention. It takes me a moment to recognize my surroundings. I'm on the floor of my bedroom with my ear pressed against the wall and my fingers between my legs. The shower has turned on for the second time tonight. And I am alone.

That he'd rather masturbate outside my door and then wash away the traces of his lust does me in. His displeasure sends me spiraling back to that night he woke me up and took me out of my home to abandon me hundreds of miles away in an unfamiliar place with unfamiliar people. I cried myself to sleep every night for six months straight after he left me in Boone. I ignored all his messages, refused all his calls, and returned all his gifts.

I finally got tired of being mad at him. My anger turned to pent-up longing. I read the messages, all of which professed his sorrow at leaving me, along with his assurance that it was all done to keep me safe. I clung to that, believing that when I was an adult and strong enough to fight for myself, I could prove that we would belong together.

I didn't think it would happen immediately. I wanted it to, but realistically we hadn't seen each other in four years. There were bound to be adjustment pains. I didn't expect him to be so resistant, so put off by his own desires.

He's so far from coming around that I think we might as well be in different countries even as we live in the same apartment. He's Russia, cold and foreign, while I'm...some small country that is trying to lap up any scrap of attention he's willing to give me.

Is this where I give up? No. That's what he wants. He's driving me away because he's afraid. His disgust isn't toward me...I don't think. It's self-loathing. He doesn't believe he has the right to want me.

I run a shaky hand through my hair. The positive is that he doesn't see me as a child anymore. I can work with that. I just need to tear down the barrier between his heart part that love and want me and his head part that says our coupling is wrong.

Easy, right? I give a sour, silent laugh. It's going to be very hard, but the prize at the end is worth it.

Commence Operation Seduction.

"LEKA, DO YOU KNOW WHERE MY BLACK LACE TEDDY IS? I JUST bought it the other day and now I can't find it anywhere!" It is, in fact, draped over the back of the living room sofa where I left it last night.

After a few moments of silence, I creep out of my bedroom to see if Leka is even in the kitchen. I thought I heard his footsteps pass by me a moment ago. Sure enough, he's sitting at the kitchen table bent over coffee.

"Um, Leka, did you hear me?"

"It's gone," he says abruptly without looking in my direction.

"What do you mean 'gone'?"

"I threw it away."

"You what?" I rush over to the garbage can. That piece of lingerie cost me $80 and I didn't even wear it once. I cut the tags off and tossed it in the living room. It landed on the sofa back where it could be easily seen by anyone coming in from the entry.

Inside the garage can I find the teddy, crumpled into a ball. I pull it out and hold it up by the straps. It's torn through the midsection with only a few pieces of lace and thread keeping it in one piece on the left side. "Um, what happened?"

"It got caught on something," Leka replies, still bent over the coffee.

Something like his fist. Is this a good sign?

"It's your money anyway," I reply. "I haven't received my first pay check yet, so I used the credit card to buy it. I didn't think you'd mind."

"You don't need shit like that," he says. He rises fast. The chair legs scrape loudly against the tiled floor. "Wear regular...stuff that doesn't get torn easily."

He can't even bring himself to use the word "panties" around me. I dip my head to hide a smile. "This is comfortable. Besides, it makes me feel sexy." I peek under my eyelashes in Leka's direction.

His hands tighten around the back of his chair. "You're working in a meat processing shop cleaning up shit. There's no need to feel...stuff there."

Ha! He can't say "sexy" either.

"The morbid surroundings are exactly why I need things like this. I have to remind myself I'm still a woman." I open the sink cabinet to toss the damaged undergarment away.

"You didn't even wear it," he snaps.

I pause, my hand half inside the trash can. "How do you know?" I ask in surprise.

There's a long, pregnant pause followed by heavy footsteps carrying Leka into his bedroom. The minute that his door slams shut, I let loose the smile that I had been hiding.

There's only one way to know that I didn't wear this and that's to give it the smell test. An erotic shiver shakes me as the image of Leka standing in the living room sniffing my underwear dances through my head.

This is progress, I tell myself. *Time to turn up the heat.*

"WHAT IN THE HELL DO YOU THINK YOU'RE DOING?" LEKA thunders.

Bent over at the waist with my booty high in the air, my upside-down view of Leka is framed between my two legs. Even from here, I can see his frustration. It fills me with a sad sort of happiness. I'm glad I can get a reaction out of him but dejected that all he's done in the past two weeks is to tell me to cover up, stop leaving my stuff around, and to go to sleep.

He likes the last order a lot as if I have a bad hangover that's causing me to act weird and if I just get in a couple naps during the day, I'll return to the meek girl that I was when he left me four years ago.

"I'm exercising. What does it look like I'm doing?" I swing my hips around, trying to mimic the half-dressed woman on screen. My actions are sluggish, though. I'm tired, but not because I've been working out for a long time. I started only minutes ago after I got the word from doorman

Terry that Leka was on his way up. I'm tired because I've gone through steps two through twenty without one physical reaction. That lack of response kills my morale like a bus hitting a pedestrian at forty miles per hour.

"You're watching a porno. That's what it looks like you're doing." He sounds unusually agitated.

"Gold star for you. It is a porno, and your immediate recognition of it makes me wonder how much you watch." The online article I'd read about seducing your man suggested watching porn with my man. I'd never be able to con Leka into that, so I combined that idea with the one about doing a sexy striptease. I thought it was a brilliant idea at the time, but, currently, faced with Leka's dumbfounded stare, I'm reconsidering.

He stomps over to the living room and snatches the remote off the television. "None. I don't watch porn. This is fucking ridiculous. If you want to work out, go to a gym."

"But there are men at the gym," I taunt. "What if one of them is overcome with lust and attacks me?"

Leka presses his full lips into a thin, angry line but doesn't have a rejoinder. There are dangers everywhere in this world and there's only one way to avoid them—by hiding. I refuse to do that.

32

LEKA

"There's still some taco meat left. Want it?" Bit leans over my shoulder, deliberately brushing her unbound tit against my arm.

It'd be so easy to reach around and pull her down on my lap. Or even better. I could clear the table with one swipe of my arm, lift her onto the empty surface, slide down whatever pair of panties she's wearing—if she's wearing any—and eat her out like she's been begging me to for the last three weeks.

I remind myself how fucking wrong that would be, bite into my tongue until I taste copper and then shake my head. "I'm full. Thanks."

But I'm not full. I'm hungry. I'm reaching the state of starvation. Every time I look at her, my tongue tingles and my fingers twitch. My dick rises to half-mast and my tiny pea brain screams at me to take her. Strip her clothes off, tie her to a bed, and fuck her every dirty, naughty way that anyone has dreamed of and a hundred new ones that people haven't even invented yet.

Days have become a torture. Nights are pure hell. I work myself hard, but I find that I can't be far from her. The invisible tether that has connected us since the day I found her reels me back. My body can walk and talk and function, but the heart of me sits in her little hands.

She putters over to the sink, pulls out the trash, making sure her ass is high in the air. I catch a glimpse of apple-green lace covering one juicy cheek. A man can only take so much before he breaks. My control is whisper thin. One wrong move and it will snap.

I drop my hands below the table and stab my palm with the fork. The pain allows the lust to recede a fraction—enough so that I don't throw the table out of the way and attack her.

I'm tired of this. I'm tired of having to exercise self-control while she peels off her underwear in the middle of a rerun of *Brooklyn Nine-Nine*. I'm tired of having to pretend I don't see the outline of her figure when she stands in front of the fireplace in a white nightgown so sheer it's a miracle it doesn't fall apart when she breathes. I'm tired of going to bed each night with my dick in my hand, furtively jacking off because if I don't get some motherfucking relief, I'm going to explode.

The hardest times are when she comes home from work at ten, tired and sore. I want to scoop her up into my lap, rub her feet and make her a midnight snack, but I can't bring myself to do anything more than give her curt nods of acknowledgment because I'm afraid that if I touch her in any way, no matter how innocent, I'm not going to be able to stop.

Above all else, the thing that drives me to the very edge are her eyes. They tell me everything. They're black when she's angry and lit from within when she's joyous. There's a glint at the corner when she's feeling good about herself and about to do something that will drive me wild. And then there are the times when her eyes are big and clear and all I see in them is my reflection—as if I make up her whole world.

How in the hot hell am I supposed to turn away from all that? It's impossible.

"When's your next shift?" I ask. It's Saturday and I'm half hopeful she has to go in so that my dick can have time to deflate, but I also hate that she works at all. I'm fucked up.

"Not until tomorrow night. I'm going to cut up some strawberries and have some ice cream with them later. Do you want any?"

An image of me spreading the cold, sweet treat all over her body makes me light-headed.

"Leka? Leka? Hey, you still with me?"

Bitsy's at the table, nudging me.

"I'm good," I croak and escape to the bedroom, hoping my enormous hard-on isn't too visible.

Bitsy mutters something that sounds very close to "you coward" as I run away.

THE LONG LINE OF BLACK SUVs FILLING THE ALLEY BEHIND Marjory's gives me ample warning that I'm not going to be happy with what I find inside the restaurant. Beefer's weepy, shivering daughter crouching under the single bulb above the back door drives home the point. This is going to be a bad night.

I knew that Cesaro was bound to show up at some point, but I'd hoped, probably uselessly, that it would be during a time that Bitsy was out of town. I don't much like the fact they're sharing the same zip code at the moment.

I pull out my phone and shoot off a quick text.

Change of plans. Will be a long night. Don't wait up.

She gets off her cleaning shift at two. I'll have to send a car for her. I don't trust cabs this late at night. Having taken care of Bitsy the best I can, I pull off my suit coat and drop it around Camella's bare shoulders. I wish she'd start wearing more than a couple of Band-Aids. It's winter and the girl has got to be cold. I can't tell whether half of the stream of air flowing from Camella's lips is condensation or smoke from her joint.

"Need a ride somewhere?" Mason should be somewhere inside. "Why don't I call Mason to take you home. Your dad's gonna be here for a while."

She shakes her head with enough force to set her large hoop earrings swinging. "No."

This is another girl who should be far away from Cesaro's clutches. I try once more. "You want some cake from Magnolia's?" Bitsy and I waited in line for like two hours the other day for the newest creation. The cake really wasn't worth it, but Bit's euphoric delight over it was.

"Don't wanna," she mumbles as she clutches the lapels of my jacket tight with one hand.

"Let me know." I tuck my phone in my back pocket and enter the stockroom to find Beefer looming over our chef.

"What's he doing here?" I demand.

The man doesn't look up from the stove as he answers. "There's a shipment of rocket launchers and AK47s being moved up to the north. A Korean group is funding this, and word on the street the Tongs are going to try to move on it. Big nationalist rivalry or some shit. Cesaro wants to make sure we don't fuck this up. It could mean more money in the future.

Don't turn it over yet." Beefer grabs Justin's arm to prevent him from touching the smoking meat. "Cesaro likes his cow dead."

I peek out the window and see Cesaro camped in the corner annoying the fuck out of the rest of the patrons with his loud voice and non-stop cigar smoke. The few patrons that are left are finishing quickly. Soon, the place will be empty of everyone but Cesaro and his four bodyguards. Three are new and one is Arturo's favorite, Sterno.

The last one is a surprise to me. Since Arturo's death, Cesaro's wiped out most of the old guard. During the previous visits, there was a different fourth—an Eastern European with a heavy accent. Laszio or something close to that.

"What happened to the Hungarian?"

"Dead. He made a move on Cesaro's daughter, so the boss cut his dick off and fed it to his dogs."

I hadn't heard that. "When'd this happen?"

"Just a few days ago. Sterno's part of Helen's guard. He's just filling in."

Helen's Arturo's widow and Cesaro's aunt by marriage.

"Did Cesaro bring any more than what's in the kitchen?"

"Four more at the hotel."

Beefer's answers are terse. His shoulders are tight and he's got a furrow in his forehead deep enough to plant a couple trees.

I make a guess as what's bothering him. "Your daughter's outside."

"I know. Goddammit." He thrusts a hand through his thinning hair and turns. "That fool girl thinks she's going to be the next Mrs. Cesaro. I tried to tell her that he's already got a wife and three kids, and while he might fuck pieces on the side, he's not going to divorce the wife. You never divorce the wife. Besides, Cammy's all used up now. She's not the marrying kind. Sooner she understands that, the happier she'll be."

Camella hasn't been happy since Cesaro raped her, but Beefer's blind to this. It's the way he copes, I guess, otherwise the guilt would drive him to either kill Cesaro or himself.

"When's the drop?"

"Two days from now."

That's not so bad. I can buy Bitsy a three-day spa retreat. She needs the pampering after all hard work she's been doing. I grab my phone and start searching. I need to get her the fuck out of town.

33

BITSY

"You should visit a friend," Leka tells me after I answer his call.

"No. I'm working." I can't believe he's still trying to get rid of me.

"It would only be for a week. I'll pay for everything." In the background, I hear someone ask for the address to the dungeon.

"Audie's with her grandmother in Connecticut. It's the only family she really loves and so I'm not going to bother her."

"Then a solo trip." He sounds desperate, which means he's close to breaking. If I leave now, he'll rebuild his defenses. I haven't put all this time and effort to have it be demolished by going away—particularly by myself. I'm tired of being alone.

"That sounds as much fun as getting an enema. No."

"Please, Bitsy, I need you to go. It's for your own safety."

I scowl at the phone. "Of course it is. It is always for my safety. What's wrong now? Mary doesn't like the way the new chef is cooking her steak? I'll stay away from Marjory's, don't worry."

"It's not Mary."

"Then what is it?"

"It's…look, can't you just go?"

"No. Either tell me what the danger is and let me weigh my own consequences or leave me alone." I can't always run away every time Leka thinks that there is a problem in our world.

"Can't you do as I ask just this one time?"

"No. Because it's never this one time. It's every time and I'm tired of it, Leka." I hang up because I don't want to hear his excuses any longer. This whole process of him avoiding me is getting tiresome. And I'm running out of ideas. None of the internet articles I've read have had any success. Really, the only thing I have left to try is to make him jealous, which is a card I've avoided playing because I didn't want to bring some innocent party into this awful struggle Leka and I are engaged in.

But what else can I do? The random lingerie around the apartment didn't work. The stripper workout was a big fail. The walking around half-nude, stretching in front of the fireplace, and rubbing my breasts against him every breakfast were also non-starters. My limited bag of tricks is empty.

I slump down in the kitchen and stare at the granite countertops, willing an idea to spring up. I pick up my phone and search *the dungeon*. The top hit is an advertisement for a new club downtown that promises a boundary blurring experience. I tap the phone against my bottom lip.

Is this the "work" that Leka is doing tonight? Is he watching cage dancers, flirting with bar hoppers, and downing expensive, silly drinks while I'm sitting in this apartment decked out in three-year-old leggings and a holey T-shirt prematurely aging?

I get up and go down to my bedroom to take an inventory of my closet. I don't really have club gear. My closet consists of my school uniforms, the ugly skirt I bought to wear to dinner with Leka at that French restaurant, a bunch of designer coats, and a handful of lingerie—still with the tags on. I push the hangers back and forth, rejecting item after item. Nothing here is going to get me past a bouncer at a hip nightclub. Unless…my hand hovers over my school uniform. When I was paging through the porn selections to find the right one to "work out to" there were several featuring the bad schoolgirl.

I unclip my plaid skirt from the hanger and hold it up to my waist. It hangs down to my knees, but if I cut the hem off at the thigh, I'd look just like those sexy schoolgirls. It takes me an hour to wrestle my hair into braids, slap on enough makeup so that I don't look like I'm actually a schoolgirl, but rather a grown-up woman playing a role. I trim off the hem of the skirt and search for a top. I come up empty. My white polos are not going to look sexy enough, no matter how much fabric I chop off.

Another thought springs into my head. I raid Leka's closet and return to my bedroom with a white button down. It's too big, but that's the whole idea. One of my unused lingerie items is a black lace see-through bra. I put that on and then shrug into Leka's shirt.

I roll up the sleeves several times and then knot the front shirttails around my belly. Knee-high white socks and the stupid black pumps complete the outfit. The full-length mirror on the back of my door says I look cheap and slutty. I love it. I cover myself up with a long puffy coat and grab a roll full of cash. I don't have a fake ID, so I'm going to have to flirt and buy my way in.

At the lobby desk, the night doorman, Pete, eyes me suspiciously. "Do you need a taxi Ms. Moore?"

"Nope. I'm going to the drugstore. I forgot I was getting my period and my bathroom looks like a crime scene. There are so many clots—"

"Okay. Just wondering. Have a nice evening," Pete says with a wave of his hand. The poor guy looks ready to throw up.

I skip out delightedly and hail a taxi a block away.

Once downtown, I shrug out of my coat, leaving it in the back of the cab. "Give it to your wife or your girlfriend. I barely wore it," I tell the surprised driver.

He nods happily and speeds away.

The Dungeon turns out to be a popular place, or so the long line of people suggests. A handful of bouncers mill about the front door behind a short velvet rope. They're checking IDs. I wonder if there's a backdoor I could slip through.

"You lost, honey?" says a voice behind me.

I swing around to see an older man—probably in his late thirties—dressed in a dark suit and a dark shirt unbuttoned one fastening too far. Around his wrist is a heavy, expensive watch. Four men spread out behind him.

"No." I wish I'd kept my coat.

The dark-haired man gives me a thorough once-over. "How old are you?"

I stiffen. "Old enough."

"Sure you are," he says quietly. "Come with me. I'll get you in." He curves an arm around my shoulder and pulls me close to his side. "What did you say your name was?"

We both know I hadn't said any such thing. Warning bells are ringing wildly in my head. "Actually, I'm waiting for my girlfriend. We're going to mass tonight."

"I can give you a holy communion," the man jokes. "It won't be round, though. It'll be long and thick."

Three of his four men laugh loud and long.

"I suggest you let me go," I tell him. "I'm not the kind of girl to play around with."

"Really?" he drawls. "Because you're playing dress up and that's exactly the kind of girl I like."

The door opens and a blast of sound hits us. "Cesaro, the VIP room is all set up—"

Leka pulls up short and his jaw drops. I want to sink into the ground. I know what he's thinking. Worse, I've played into his fears—that the city's dangers had finally gotten to me. The thing is, though, at least I'm in a public place. There are the bouncers at the door and the people in the line. If I make a scene, this guy is bound to get scared off.

"Hi Leka," I say, trying to be proactive. I move out from under the man's arms.

"What in the fuck are you doing here?"

"You two know each other?" The man, Cesaro, waves a finger between us.

"Yeah. She's going home. Aren't you?"

"Yes." This isn't the place to argue. "I'm going home."

"No. Stay. We're going to have some fun." Cesaro reaches for me again, but Leka darts forward, moving me out of the way.

"Sorry. I'll be back as soon as possible." Leka snaps his fingers. A young, pretty man hurries forward. "Mason, take Cesaro and his men to the VIP room. Get them whatever they want. You—" Leka's fingers curl into my arm. "You're coming with me."

Those are the last words he says to me until we arrive home.

"Of all the idiotic, *childish* things you could've come up with, this takes the cake!" Leka roars the moment I cross over our threshold. He must've been saving it up.

"It wouldn't have happened if you had been honest with me. Instead of giving me some vague warning about it being dangerous, you should've said that there was specifically someone you didn't want me to see!"

"I want to keep you away from that. Have you ever thought of that? That I was doing it for your own good?"

"How hard is it for you to give an explanation? That's all I needed."

"Oh really." He shakes his head in disbelief. "If I'd told you that a gang leader was in town that liked to fuck virgins, you'd have just stayed away?"

"Yes, I would have." At least, I'd like to think I had enough smarts to stay home instead of following Leka around. I have a momentary pang of doubt, which Leka sees.

"You'd have followed anyway." He's lost his anger and replaced it with that damned blank mask that he wears when he's with everyone but me.

"No." I shake my head because I can see him shutting me out, shutting his feelings down. "No." I have to stop him. "No. Stop assuming the worst. I made a mistake and so did you. We learn from this. We—"

"We go our separate ways. This..." He waves his hand between us. "Whatever this was, it's over now. It's too dangerous."

Feeling helpless, I lash out. "You think everything in your life is dangerous!"

"Because it is! That's why I sent you away. That's why I don't want you here now!"

I stumble back as if he struck me. Those words are cruel and he knows it. "That was low," I say through the hurt clogging my throat.

He stares impassively at me as if he doesn't care.

"Take it back."

He folds his arms across his chest and says nothing.

I fought before because I thought I could win, but if he can say those words with sincerity, then I don't believe I want to win. Not this fight. Not this war.

"Why did you save me if you won't let me live?"

34

LEKA

I don't know how long I stand in the kitchen after she leaves. Her last words ring in my ears.

Going into the bedroom is a huge mistake, I discover minutes later. No. Scratch that. Renting an apartment with only one bath is where I went wrong. She's so close. Her stifled cries are easy to hear even over the running water.

I lean my arm against the wall separating us and rest my head in the crook of my elbow. I try to remember all the reasons I shouldn't be in that bathroom on my knees worshiping her, but my mind draws a blank.

A moan whispers between the walls. My hands fist. This is torture, more painful, more excruciating than any punishment Beefer or I could've ever thought up.

"I can hear you breathing," she says. "I know you're there."

When did these walls become so thin?

"I want you, Leka. I want you so bad that my hands are shaking. I'm having a hard time eating and sleeping. I've tried everything that I know of to tear down that wall you have built up. I've tried everything but begging, but I'll do that. I'll do that if that's what it will take."

Her voice cracks at the end, and the iron will I've been trying to exercise melts in an instant. Shame and self-loathing make my gut churn.

The cruel, untrue words I bashed in her face careen around in my head like a bowling ball tossed by the Hulk. I've been successful in this stupid, wrong life of mine mostly because when I make a decision, I don't waver. That certainty has made me reliable. Beefer knows that when he orders something to be done, it's done and done correctly. The men in the crew I work with can depend on me to have thought out the contingencies and eventualities so that they're safe when they execute the tasks they've been given.

The decisions I made with Bitsy—to keep her and then send her away —kept her safe. All I need to do is to stay away from her until I can find her a new home.

Where she will be all alone again.

Where there is no one to dry her tears.

Where she will be with no one to love her.

I think of her tiny and afraid. I think of her sick. I think of the time seven-year old her beat up a boy older and bigger than her. I think of her mischievous smile after she smashed a bag of rotten eggs and fish to the punk-ass kid at the bus stop who'd been harassing her. I think of her awkward pre-teen years when I begged Mrs. M to help me out with the woman stuff that I barely understood myself and would've rather poked daggers in my eyes than talk to Bitsy about them.

I think of her fifteen-year old self coming out of the dressing room in that blue dress looking like a goddess had floated down from heaven to grace us mortals with her presence.

I think of her, only a few steps away, crying in the bathroom because she loves me and she's hurting and it's my fault.

I don't know what the right path is any more. It's clouded—by her tears and my longing. I don't want to let her go because…I love her. My heart formed when I found her. She created it with her trust. She nurtured it with her hope. She protected it with her love.

She asks so little in return. She asks not to be hurt again. She asks not to be abandoned again. She asks to be loved.

I swing out of my room and into the bathroom to find her sitting on the counter, legs tented over the sink and head tucked into the corner of the wall. Her face is blotchy and her eyelashes are wet from her tears.

My heart caves in. I saved her all those years ago so that she could have an ordinary life, but we never lived like regular people. I wear a jacket every day of the year, no matter how hot, because I'm almost always packing. I left her at night while I was out doing things I knew that were wrong. My justification was that the money was going toward making

Bitsy safe, but while I may have been protecting her physically, I was damaging her sweet heart.

What's really keeping me back? Is it that I fear for her safety, or is it more that I fear for mine? Is it because, like she said before, that I'm a coward? That I'm afraid she's going to wake up one day, look at all blood on my hands, see the darkness in my heart and run screaming into the arms of one of those suit-clad bankers who cheats on his wife and snorts his millions up his nose? Is that the bolt that keeps my feet rooted to the floor?

Because if it is, then *I* should be taken to the basement of Marjory's and stretched over the Butcher's table and filleted until all my stupidity is taken out of me. I am hurting her. Right now, every second that passes, her pain deepens, expands, driving out the joy and sweetness that make up my Bitsy.

I open my hands and let the crumbled remains of my resolve fall to the floor.

"I surrender."

"I don't want you to surrender. I want you to want me." She jabs a thumb against her chest, a finger catching on the tiny lace ribbon that keeps the whole nightgown from sliding down her shoulders.

I ball my hands at my sides so I don't tear the fabric off her. Digging deep, I find a few strands of composure left. Gathering them up in a mental fist, I give her one last chance to escape.

"You're not even nineteen, Bitsy. I'm old and not just in years. These hands"—I spread my fingers wide—"they're so dirty that a hundred showers won't clean them off. You deserve someone as decent and pure as you. Not this aging gangster who doesn't even know where he came from."

She scoots to the edge of the counter. The nightgown catches under her butt and pulls down to display a set of perfect tits hanging down like ripe fruit ready for the picking.

She grabs my palms and presses them to her chest. She's hot, and I can feel her pulse galloping madly under my fingers.

"Like my origin story is so perfect? Like I didn't hide under my bed while my junkie mom sold herself to strangers for drugs? Like she didn't leave me to be used by those same strangers while she was sniffing coke off the kitchen table? Like you didn't save me when you were just a kid yourself? How in the world could you imagine that there was someone better out there for me than you?"

A lump, unfamiliar and unwelcome, lodges itself in my throat. "I just want the best for you, Bit. That's all I ever wanted."

"Then let me have you, because that's what's best." She slides my hand lower, under the soft cotton, over the rise of her breast until my entire palm is engulfing her. She exhales, and the hot, pointy nub of her nipple blazes against my skin. "Take me, Leka. I'm yours. I've always been yours, just as you've always been mine. Take me." Her eyes pierce mine and a smile tilts the corner of her precious lips upward. "Take me, you coward."

"Coward, am I?" My fingers close roughly around that soft mass. A shiver wracks my body. Perhaps I am. I have never felt this alive. I've been plugged into a current so potent that I will never be able to return to the life I once led—a life of drab, colorless gray.

I scoop her up and carry her into my bedroom, settling her in the middle of my bed. The sight of her there hits me like a fist across my face. I crash to my knees beside the mattress.

Apprehensive eyes meet mine. I don't know what she sees, but the brakes are off this train and we are barreling down the track. The future is unknown, but at least we'll be together.

"Do you think I'm scared of you?" I rise to my full, intimidating height and push her backward onto the mattress. I take one leg and bend it at the knee. "You'd be right." I lean down and press a kiss against the inside of her knee. She shivers from the contact. "You scare the hell out of me."

"What are you going to do about it?"

I flip up the bottom of her nightgown to display a tiny scrap of silk and lace covering neatly trimmed dark hair. I run a finger over the center. The tip comes away wet. My cock jumps with glee. I'm not going to last.

"You're too fine for the likes of me, Bit, but you've given yourself to me and there are no take backs. This cherry's mine, for now and ever."

She shudders, and her hips gyrate in a primitive, unpracticed response. I swipe the back of my hand over my mouth. This is my fantasy come to life.

Her skin feels like silk—not the cheap kind you find sold by the bushel in Midtown on the street corners, but the fine stuff that's under glass and you can't touch unless you're dripping with diamonds and gold.

I smooth a rough, calloused hand over one golden leg, taking a slow journey from the tender skin behind the ankle bone, up her muscular calf, over the kneecap all the way to the crease at her upper thigh. My hand trembles lightly the whole way. This is art I'm touching.

What's a surprise is that I haven't rammed my dick into her yet. My entire lower body throbs like a toothache. I welcome the pain. It's the only restraint I have.

"I'm dying here," Bit moans. Her fingers, white around the knuckles, press into the mattress. Her back arches, pushing her tits high into the air. Those nubs are tight and begging for my mouth.

I want to touch her everywhere at once—the curve of her waist, the secret spot behind her ears, the sweet, wet pussy winking at me coyly as she writhes in unquenched need. My head gets light. I made her like this. It's me, not any other man in this world, but me. She's saved herself for me. She wants me.

She deserves so much more. She deserves a man uptown with clean hands and a big bank account. She deserves a house at the seashore, vacations that require passports, and a safe place to come home to every night. I can't give her any of these, but she wants me anyway.

It's humbling and intoxicating all at one time.

I bend down. She arches up. Our mouths meet and fuse. She makes a small sound, like an excited kitten who gets her first scratch along her throat. Her lips part and my tongue dives in. I've never done this before, so I take my time and savor the moment.

Pleasure drugs my blood. Everything slows down and time becomes a foreign concept. I'm not fully aware of my surroundings. Beefer and the crew could batter down the door, the stove could catch on fire, a bomb could drop outside the apartment. I'd be deaf and dumb to it all.

My existence has narrowed to this one small being beneath me. Her mouth is all I can taste. Her sighs are all I can hear. The soft, warm, welcoming body is the only thing I can feel.

I'm not aware of the sheets coming off the mattress or the chill in the air, which is the result of failing to turn up the furnace. She is my world now and I'm reveling in her.

Nails dig into my waist as she pulls me closer. "Now," she pleads.

"Not yet." I shift my cock away from her tempting pussy. I want to explore her. There's the dip at the base of the throat and the shadow in the valley between her breasts. I roll one pert nipple between my fingers and take the other one in my mouth and suck deep and hard.

Her breath comes out in ragged, uneven beats. "Now, then. I want you now."

I'm aching for it. My cock is hard and desperate, but something holds me back.

"Bit, if I do this, if *we* do this, I don't—I can't—" Never good at speaking anyway, I stumble over my words.

"Can't give me up?" She catches my hand in hers and drags me down until those ripe tits are burning brands into my chest. "Don't think you'll be able to let me go? Oh, Leka, it's the same for me. I want to hold you here, against me, skin to skin, forever. That's all I've ever wanted. There will never be another man for me. If you don't have me, then I'll lock myself away. We were both dealt terrible hands in life, but fate made up for it by bringing us together. You're going against the universe if you turn me away now. You have to take me for the sake of mankind."

The last words are a tease, but there's a glimmer of uncertainty behind her eyes—a kind of vulnerability that suggests that I could break her easily if I wanted to, and not by taking her rough or wrong, but by turning her away.

I brush my calloused thumb across one smooth, satin cheek. "I can't be responsible for the downfall of the universe."

"I know, right?"

I dip my mouth to nip at her earlobe. "I can't have you locking yourself away. That'd be a crime, too."

"I thought so."

I use one hand to lift her hips. She grinds against me, slicking my shaft and sending my arousal into overdrive. "You can't back out now."

"I don't want to."

I swallow hard and slowly, carefully, I push the broad head of my cock against her small opening. Her body parts, but there's resistance. I stop and take a deep breath, counseling myself to wait, to hold on for one more friggin' minute so I don't ruin this first time for both of us.

"More." She wriggles slightly under me. "I want more."

So do I, Bit, so do I. My dick is aching. I move a fraction deeper, her swollen tissues snug and hot around me. Bracing myself with one arm, I lean down to take her tit in my mouth again. Her response is to bite into my shoulder. I lurch forward.

She yelps but grabs me before I can withdraw. "If you don't fuck me right now, I'm going to lose it."

"I'm going slow for your benefit." I clench my jaw. "It hurts the first time."

"That's an old wives' tale. Not everyone's first time hurts."

I choke. "Bitsy, let me—"

"No."

I'm hurting her. I know it, but I can't stop. The lust has me by the throat and until it all drains out, I'm worthless. I'll make this up to her. I'm going to spend the rest of my days and all my nights making it up to her.

"I'm sorry," I whisper in her ear and thrust home for a final time.

The come floods out of me like I've split a hydrant in half. It's a lifetime's worth of seed filling her channel, leaking out between us even though the seal between her sex and my cock is so tight it could pass a lab inspection.

"I'm sorry." This time it's more of a prayer for forgiveness than an apology.

She surprises me again by wrapping her arms around me and laughing. Clinging hard, she whispers in my ear. "I love you, Leka Moore. I love you."

And I'm hard once more.

35

BITSY

"Fuck, I love you, Bit. Love you so much I wanna to tear my heart out of my body because the thought of not having you would ruin me." Leka shudders and groans under me like a thoroughbred after an exhausting race.

When he thrust inside me, it hurt. It hurt more than anything I've ever felt before, but just beyond that pain, there's a glimpse of glory, a horizon full of pleasure. I dreamed of this moment—the one where his body and mine came together in some sort of holy communion. I fantasized hearing those three words from him. Pain recedes and the joy in my heart bubbles up, spilling out between my lips.

"What're you laughing about?" Leka asks, his sweaty forehead resting on my shoulder. A braced forearm keeps his body from crushing mine.

I hug him tight, wanting to be flattened by him. "I'm happy."

"Happy? Then I must not've done my job, because I'm wrecked." He levers himself off of me and drops on his back. "I couldn't last more than a few strokes."

There's a dark tone of displeasure in his voice that pierces my cloud of happiness. I push up on an elbow and cast a confused look in his direction. "What's wrong?"

"Me." He runs a hand through his hair and then jumps off the bed. "Stay here," he orders.

In the bathroom, I hear the water turn on.

I look down between my legs and nearly shriek in shock.

He runs back in, a wet washcloth dripping from his hands. "What's wrong?"

"Nothing. Nothing." I look around for something to cover myself with. I can't let him see the mess or he might jump out the window.

"I saw it already," he admits. The bed dips down as he takes a seat. Carefully, he peels my hands away from my thighs and presses the warm cloth between my legs. "Are you hurting much?"

"No."

"You wouldn't tell me if you were, would you?" He sighs and reaches up to smooth a hand over my hair. "How bad does it hurt? I have some painkillers. The real kind, not the worthless shit you buy at the drugstore."

"Do I want to know why you have those?"

"No."

I nod. There are things he's not ever going to want to talk about. I get that and accept it. I don't need to know the details. As long as they don't affect how he feels about me, he can keep his secrets. I know he finds them shameful.

"It was more shocking than painful."

His lips thin and I can tell he's disappointed in himself. He finishes cleaning me off and goes to the bathroom to get rid of the washcloth. I take the time to pull on my nightshirt and strip the sheets.

When he comes back, I'm in the process of tugging a new, clean fitted sheet onto the bed. Silently, he goes to the opposite corner and helps me pull them tight. It's as he is bending over to grab the flat sheet that goes on top that I notice he's sporting a huge erection. It's heavy weight bobs in the air.

Lust thuds in my veins. How can I want him again?

His breath hitches. He shakes his head. "No. Get in bed, Bit."

I push my lower lip out. "Don't wanna."

"Get in bed," he orders in a harsh voice.

I can't suppress my shiver of delight. I flash back to that scene in *Secretary* when Lee's stretched across Edward's desk and how her face grows more satisfied with each slap. "What are you gonna do? Spank me?"

His eyes snap. "Don't test me, Bit."

But I want to. I want to push his limits until he loses all control again and again and again. I want him to be free with me like he's never been before or will be with anyone else.

I drop my hand to the hem of my nightgown and dip my head down coyly. "I'm scared of the dark, Leka. What if a monster comes for me? I don't know what to do. Should I run? I should I let him take me?"

A growl rumbles through the room. "Over my dead body."

"What if the monster tries to take off my nightie?" I inch the white fabric up until the valley between my legs is clearly visible. "What if he tries to touch me here?" I use my other hand to press against my throbbing clit. "I've only ever had you there."

His nostrils flare and a red, angry flush appears on the top of his high cheekbones. "And you're only ever gonna have me there."

"But what if he—"

I don't even get to finish my sentence before he's by my side, flinging me onto the mattress.

"You're my girl now, Bit. You saved yourself for me." He wrenches my legs apart. "You gave yourself to me." He lifts my hips up. "This pussy's mine now."

His mouth comes down on me like a hammer. The first lick across my seam is a shock. I didn't realize how sensitive it is down there. I didn't realize how much I'd like this. In the porn Audie and I would read online, the girls loved being eaten out, but like everything I read, I wasn't convinced it would feel as great as the writers made it out to be. It's almost too good. I try to squirm out of his grip.

He breaks and arches an eyebrow. "You want me to stop?"

"No," I cry, bereft without his magic tongue. "Don't stop."

He slaps my ass lightly. "Then don't move."

It's a struggle. His touch sends me writhing. There are nerve endings between my legs I didn't realize existed. With effort, I lean into the toe-curling pleasure, allowing the sensations to build like waves crashing against a dam, ready to batter the wall down. .

When he breaks away the next time, it's to replace his tongue with a long, rough finger. I sob into the sheet as he strokes me softly.

"That's right, Bit. That's how it's supposed to feel."

"Like I'm dying?" I choke out.

He chuckles. That damn man laughs. "Yeah, just like that." And then he slides in another finger. "You're so pretty down here. Lots of contrast. Dark and light, pinks and purples. Like an exotic flower. And this here —"he pinches my clit—"whaddya call the center?"

"A-a-stamen?" I gasp out.

"Yeah. That." He pinches it again and I almost lose consciousness.

This is nothing like the first time. This is leaving me aching and throbbing, hollow and full. I want more. Way, way more. But if I move, he'll stop, and I don't want this intense pleasure to end.

He adds a third finger and replaces his thumb with his mouth, sucking my clit hard. My toes curl as a torrent of sensation explodes, filling every nook and crevice inside of me until I'm reduced to a sobbing, shaking, emotionally spent bundle of bones. But he doesn't stop his onslaught. He flips me over on my back and drives into me.

I scream, but this time it's not in pain. This time it's glorious. This time it's all pleasure. This time I figure out why people ruin their lives just to have another taste of this kind of euphoria.

He buries his mouth in my neck as he invades my body. He's slower this time, more measured than before. I feel every luscious inch of him dragging across my enervated nerves. I tilt my hips up and match his rhythm—or try to.

He groans. "Stay still. I don't want to come yet."

Still is hard. I squirm against him. He grits his teeth and grabs the edge of the mattress while I use his body mercilessly. He's so perfectly built, with hard slabs of muscle covered by hot, velvety flesh. I want to touch him everywhere at once. I curse my small hands.

"You're killing me," he growls. "I'm not gonna last much longer."

I feel the rumble of his chest when he speaks. The arms braced beside my head *are* trembling. It's taking an enormous effort for him to allow my exploration while he's hard inside me. I can feel the rapid pulse and thrum of his heartbeat as he moves. Sweat glistens on his forehead and chest.

With wonder, I run my hands over his shoulders and down his quivering sides. I can't believe we're making love. I can't believe I'm in his arms. I can't believe any of this and yet it's my reality.

I reach up and kiss him, gentle and fleeting. "Then don't."

He spurs into action. His hands come off the mattress. One sweeps under me to palm my ass and hold me in place. The other slams down by my head. He digs his knee into the mattress and powers forward. His ragged breaths echo in the room as he thrusts into me, finding a spot that makes me catch my own breath and then working it over and over until I lose control again. He comes with me and I hang on to him as we ride those waves of ecstasy until we're both spent.

Panting, exhausted, but oh so satisfied, I slowly uncurl my legs from around his ass and my arms from his shoulders. He collapses next to me, bundling me close. We hold each other, trying to catch our breaths, trying to organize our thoughts.

I wonder if he's as blissed out as me, and because I'm weak from the sex, I just blurt out my thoughts. "Was it okay for you? No, don't answer that. I don't know why I asked."

He chuckles softly and gathers me up in his arms. "Best I've ever had."

The smirk sets me off. I summon all the paltry energy I have left and bash him with a pillow. "What's that supposed to mean? Are you bragging about all the other women you've had?"

He laughingly fends me off, which infuriates me even more. I find renewed strength and grab his pillow and fling it at his head. He wrestles it out of my hand and covers me with his heavy body. His dick is hard again, but he doesn't seem to notice. Instead, he's dragging my fingers to the edge of the sheet.

"You want me to hang onto this?" I wriggle the fabric.

"No." He pulls on it and I see now that the mattress piping has come loose.

My lips form a circle. "I did that?" I didn't even remember grabbing the edge of the mattress, but, then, there were full minutes when I was having an out-of-body experience. I could have kicked a hole in the wall and not realized it.

"No. It was me. I've never..." He pauses and rubs the heel of his hand against his temple. There's a slight flush on his cheeks. Is he...embarrassed? Is this about his virgin status? My insides liquefy at the adorableness.

"You've never had sex," I supply softly.

"You know." It's not really a question. "When I told you I hadn't fucked anyone else, you understood that to mean ever."

"I did."

"You were right."

I nod because I don't trust myself to talk. I'm far too happy about this. Unreasonably overjoyed. I almost clap, but I don't want to look like a fool. I clear my throat.

"Me either," I share, forgetting momentarily about the mess we cleaned up earlier.

The side of his mouth quirks up. "Yeah. I figured."

I finger the torn fabric and contemplate what kind of strength it takes to rip a mattress apart with your bare hands. Then, I start giggling.

"What?"

I keep laughing, my giggles turning into full-on crying guffaws.

"What?" he repeats in an annoyed tone.

"This is like when Edward bit the pillow," I manage to gasp out.

His face is blank.

I catch my breath. "Remember the sparkly vampire?" I made him watch the entire *Twilight* series when I was twelve. He covered my eyes during the tamest sex scene ever filmed. I watched it on YouTube later to see what I was missing which was nothing. Vaguely, I wonder if Leka is aware of all the sex scenes that could be watched on Youtube. I decide to protect his innocence and keep that information to myself.

"I've tried to block it out," he admits.

I burrow into his embrace. "You sat through all four movies with me. That's how I knew you loved me."

"It wasn't that bad," he demurs, but he'd say anything in this post-sex haze.

"It was terrible. Name one good scene."

He falls silent, absently rubbing a thumb down the side of my arm. It's so comforting and I'm so tired from all the sex that my eyes flutter shut. Drowsiness envelops me. When I've almost fallen asleep, I hear him say, "The baseball scene?"

I laugh tiredly and hug him close. I could never love a man as I do Leka. Who else would rack their brains to find one good scene just so I wouldn't fall asleep disappointed? No one. "Don't leave me again. I won't make it."

"I won't."

"Promise?"

"We'll be together forever."

Those words are almost better than sex. Almost. I drift into unconsciousness with a smile on my face.

A MONTH PASSES. A BLISSFUL, GLORIOUS MONTH WHERE THE only thing we fight about is who gets to make breakfast. I win most of the time because Leka surprisingly has zero self-control around me. It's as if the first time we kissed poked a hole in his emotional dam and the hours of sex has fully battered it into dust.

I try not to take advantage of his vulnerability. Audie would've demanded that I squeeze him for jewels and cars and property just in case he changes his mind later on, but the only thing I want from Leka is his love, which he is showering all over me.

"What are you doing up so early?" Leka comes up behind me and pulls the silk of my robe aside to place a warm kiss on my shoulder.

"I'm working a double shift today. Cindy, the girl who does the day shift, is taking her grandmother to the hospital to get her hip replaced."

Leka frowns. "Did you tell me this yesterday? Because I don't remember."

"No. I knew you wouldn't like it and I didn't want to spend a lot of time arguing about it, so I saved it for this morning." I lean back and give his tight jaw a kiss. The one thing that makes Leka unhappy is my job. He believes I should sit home on my butt and do nothing.

"Two shifts?" he replies stiffly.

I flip the eggs over carefully and check the butter and cream sauce. "Two shifts. It's not the end of the world."

"You're already tired after one."

"I know, but I don't mind. It's honest work and I like getting my paycheck. It's nice to be able to pay for things with the money I earned myself."

"All right," he says.

Surprised, I nearly drop the egg off the spatula. "No argument?"

He scrubs a hand through his hair, the ends sticking up in an adorably messy way. "If you like it, then I wanna be happy for you. I guess it'd get boring sitting on your ass all day."

"It would be very boring."

"You could join one of those clubs," he suggests.

I finish plating our breakfast. Leka carries the plates to the table and holds my seat for me.

"What clubs are those?"

"I dunno. Sometimes the bankers I, ah, work with talk about clubs."

I hide a smile. "I don't think these clubs are the kinds you want me hanging around. They're mostly populated by over-inflated egos who like to rack up points by seeing who can sleep with the most models or actresses or some kind of combination of the two."

Leka immediately scowls. "No clubs. Definitely no clubs."

"I am going to join a spin class. There's a gym close by work so I can go there before class and then go to work. I'm hoping I can get on the night shift so our hours mesh better."

"I don't really have hours."

"I know that, but you're generally gone at night and that way we can spend our days together instead of me skipping out on you in the middle of the afternoon."

He toys with his food a bit. "You never ask me about my work."

"I didn't think you wanted to share."

"I don't," he admits, "but couples share shit, right?"

"I suppose, but we share everything else from the bathroom to the bed." I reach over and squeeze his hand, which has formed a fist. "I don't have to know this stuff. You love me, right?"

"Yes."

"Then there's nothing more that needs to be said." There's a niggle in the back of my head, a little alarm that goes off that suggests that I'm not entirely right about this, but I ignore it because Leka loves me. That's all that matters.

36

LEKA

Cesaro is back, supposedly to oversee the shipment of some weapons through the territory, but I fear his true motive. It's been a concern of mine since I abandoned him at the club to take Bitsy home. To help me sleep at night, I'd convinced myself that he'd forgotten about her.

But he has returned for an unprecedented second visit in as many months. As Justin bends over the stove cooking Cesaro's dinner, I run my finger across the fillet knife. It's sharp enough to slice a man's throat. Mary used a knife just like this four years ago to kill Gerry. I could use it to kill another man at the very same table.

The hilt rests lightly in my palm. I'm better with a gun. Perhaps I should shoot—the kitchen door swings open. Sterno appears. "A female is here to see you, Priest."

"A female?" Beefer and Justin chorus as one.

All three men turn to me as my knees turn to water. Oh, fuck, no. It's Bitsy. I know it. The knife falls to the floor as I rush for the door, slamming it wide and nearly crushing Sterno in the process. Standing within arm's length of Cesaro's table is my gorgeous girl, her hair pulled back in a rose-colored bandana, wearing nothing more special than a pair of tight light-colored jeans and a heavy black sweater that's sliding off one shoulder to reveal the thin silk strap of her undershirt.

In the low restaurant light, that bare patch of skin looks like molten gold. Everyone wants to touch it.

"I didn't realize you knew this girl, Sterno." Cesaro's voice carries across the room.

"She helped ID your uncle's murderer," Sterno answers from behind me.

"A hero then. Come closer, girl. I can barely make you out." Cesaro waggles his fingers.

This is my worst nightmare come to life. I reach Bitsy's side in three strides and tuck her half behind my body.

"Cesaro, nice to see you. Your dinner'll be out in a sec," I say.

The corners of Cesaro's cruel mouth tip up. "Nice that you could join us, Leka. I didn't know you were working as the wait staff. Is your gun arm broken?"

"Gun arm is fine." *I could smash your face in so you could get an up-close demonstration of how well it's working.*

Cesaro laughs. "Good. Good. We wouldn't want you out there with us if you can't shoot. You've never been much good for anything besides that. Now that we've got that out of the way." He points a finger to my left side where Bitsy is holding on to one arm. "Who's this? I recognize her from the night outside the club. We were supposed to be celebrating together but she showed up in a delicious costume and you swept her away before we could get to know each other."

"She's his sister," calls Beefer, who ambles up to my side, hitching up his pants.

"They don't look nothing alike," chirps one of Cesaro's guards.

"Don't really matter to me." Beefer shrugs. He holds his hand up to his knee. "They've been together since she was a little tyke."

"Interesting." Cesaro drums his fingers against his chin. "You know what the girl said when I asked who she was?"

"No."

"'I'm Leka's.' That's what she said. I asked who she was and that was her response. That loyalty is breathtaking, my man. Breathtaking. You don't see that these days. Everyone's got their own agenda. Everyone's looking out for themselves, ain't that right, Sterno?"

"I serve the family," Sterno replies blandly.

Fuck. Is this some test for Cesaro's men? If so, we're in for an ugly time. I force myself to breathe normally, to not react, to not show how fucking terrified I am in this moment. Cesaro is a cruel man with an uncanny ability to figure out what's important to a person and take it from them. He destroyed Camella and would do the same to Bitsy. I must be careful. I can't make a mistake.

"Go and see how Cesaro's meal is coming," I order.

Bitsy bristles at the command but leaves without arguing. Everyone watches her except for me. I keep my eyes on the snake in the room.

When the door shuts behind her, Cesaro raises his lust-filled gaze to meet mine. A smirk spreads across his face.

"Your *girl* can't be more than eighteen or nineteen. That outfit she wore last month looked genuine. I've always had a thing for girl's in uniform."

I remain silent because I know what's coming. Mentally, I'm plotting out Bitsy's escape. A ticket abroad tonight, to the Far East and then to the Maldives where I bought a small property a couple of years ago when I learned Cesaro's contacts are concentrated in Western Europe. After she's gone, I'll put a bullet through his head and anyone else who might breath in Bitsy's direction. I'll spray a blood barrier down the eastern seaboard if that's what it takes.

"I didn't realize we had so much in common," he continues. "I like them young, too. How much?"

"She's not for sale."

"Everyone is. Besides, you belong to me and so she belongs to me. I could take her without compensating you, but that wouldn't be fair. I like to treat my people right."

"She's his sister," Beefer repeats. He knows that he'll lose me over this. I'm the best soldier here. There's never been a shipment lost or a job failed while I've been in charge. Cesaro might not be able to read the room, but Beefer knows that his hold on this region is nothing without me.

"Is this true, Leka? Is that girl your sister or some piece you've been grooming like a sick pedo since she was a kid?" Cesaro leans back, stretching an arm across the top of the leather banquette.

"She's my sister," I answer. Because if she's not, she's toast. She'll be passed around this gang like a cigarette, smoked until she's a stub and then crushed under someone's boot heel.

"You telling me I can't have something I want?" Cesaro asks.

It's a question I can't answer, so I don't. If I say yes, I'm challenging his authority. If I say no, it's acquiescing to his demands.

I assess the situation. I've a Glock strapped to my back with eleven bullets. I could take Cesaro. I could take his four goons here. From there, it would be up to whether Beefer would stand down or order everyone in here after me. Beefer sold out his own daughter for more power. He'd gun me down in a heartbeat.

The kitchen door creaks open. Holding my breath, I swing around, my hand on the butt of my gun, only to exhale in relief at the sight of Mason bringing out Cesaro's dinner.

"Where's the girl?" Cesaro demands.

"Ah, which one?" Mason plays dumb.

I could kiss that boy.

Cesaro screws up his face in annoyance. "Leka's girl. Where is she?"

"Oh, her? She went out back and I haven't seen her since. Did I do wrong?" The kid looks completely lost and I don't know if it's an act or sincere. It doesn't matter. Bitsy's gone. She's got good instincts and knew that she should leave.

I drop my hand to my side and give a short bow to Cesaro. "If you don't need anything more, I have to review the plan with the guys. We'll want to map out the best route and do a dry run tomorrow."

He grunts his acknowledgment and digs into his food.

I gather up Mason and push him in front of me so he's not in the line of fire. I owe this kid. I owe him big. He's too good of a person to fall in with us, but since he's here, I might as well help him along.

"You're on the crew tomorrow," I tell him when we reach the kitchen.

"Really?" His eyes grow big.

"Really."

He's bursting with excitement but manages to contain it. Another mark in his favor. The door slams open again and Beefer strolls through.

"Leka, let's talk."

I follow Beefer outside. Two of our own guys are guarding the back. With a jerk of my head, I send them inside to warm up.

I wait for Beefer to light up his cigar before asking, "What's up?"

"Why are you being a hard-ass about this? It's one night. Cesaro's real generous. He gave Camella her wheels, you know. She doesn't regret it for a second. You saw her tonight. She was back here begging for more."

I gape at Beefer. He's lied to himself so long and so often that he has a completely fucked up view of what happened to Camella. That night ruined her. She's never been the same since.

"It's not happening."

"What is it going to hurt? If it's her first time, it might hurt a little, but Cesaro's a good-looking man with a lot of experience. Women are falling all over themselves to be in his bed."

"I'll be dead before he lays a hand on Bit."

Beefer rolls his eyes. "You're building this up to be some dramatic thing when it doesn't have to be. You provide everything for her. You schooled her, put a roof over her head, clothes on her back, and what do you get in return? She does this one little thing to make sure you stay in the favored position that you are and that she continues to receive protection for as long as the business is around. If you die, she'll be taken care of. That's the benefit. That's why I encouraged Camella to do it."

I stare at him for a long moment while he smokes and avoids looking me in the eye. I guess I knew Beefer had lost it all four years ago. He made a bargain with the devil for his money and his power and his so-called favored position. There's nothing more for me to say, so I turn and leave.

37

BITSY

There's a suitcase in the hallway when I get home from work. I kick off my shoes, bypass the case, and stride into the kitchen.

"God, I'm tired. I need a drink."

"You're nineteen," Leka says from the living room.

"Thank you for letting me know. I hadn't the first clue how old I was despite having a birthday two months ago." A birthday he did not celebrate with me. I grab the beer out of the fridge and pop it open defiantly. Guilt sits like a rock in my stomach. I shouldn't have gone to Marjory's. I know this, but I was hungry—both to eat and see Leka. I'd worked two double shifts and hadn't spent a single moment with him in two days. I thought, stupidly, what was the harm.

Now I know, but there's nothing I can do about it. I pretend to be calm as I drink the beer I don't really want. "What's with the suitcase? Business trip? How long will you be gone?"

His gaze slides away, breaking the contact. That bastard. He won't even look me in the eye as he exiles me.

"You're taking a vacation." He rises and pulls something out of his back pocket.

I turn away. I don't want to see it. If I ignore the paper, the suitcase, the grim expression on his face, then I can go on living my life here with him.

As I drain the rest of the beer, a single piece of paper appears in front of me. My name is on it along with a barcode. It's a ticket of some sort.

"It's a two-week trip to Tokyo. I booked you a tour guide so you can visit all the famous ramen shops."

My fingers curl around the marble counter. The edge cuts into the skin, but all I can feel is the heat radiating from his body. Yesterday, before the nightmare at Marjory's, he took me from behind. His arm dug into my waist and the other pressed my shoulder into the mattress, punctuating each thrust with a promise that he'd love me forever.

That's the kind of memory I want. Not this one.

"I hope you enjoy it." I pull open the sink cabinet and hurl the can into the recycling bin.

"Bitsy. Listen—"

I turn on him. "Did the last month mean nothing to you? Do you only keep the promises you want to keep? You promised that you wouldn't send me away again. You swore that we'd be together forever."

His face grows pained. "This is for two weeks, Bit. It's to keep you safe."

"I'm sorry I went to Marjory's. That was a mistake, but people know I exist. I was there when Mary knifed your chef, Gerry. That scarecrow man knew me instantly. I can't be your big, bad secret, and you can't send me away every time there's the slightest scent of danger!"

"You think this is easy? You think that me sending you away is easy?"

"Yeah! I do. It's a helluva lot easier than being abandoned. I can forgive you for leaving me when I was fourteen. I was a burden then. Dead weight. But I'm not now. I can drive. I can handle a gun." I weighed the risks. I'd rather stay with Leka and take my chances with whatever's out there than be constantly sent away whenever there's danger. Life's full of danger.

"You can kill, too?" he cuts in.

"If I have to." I stare back at him, trying to appear steady despite my internal flailing.

"I didn't take you off the street all those years ago so you could grow up to kill people." His face twists up in pain that I don't want to acknowledge because I'm hurting, too. We're both dying inside at the idea of being apart, but this won't be the last time. I know I'm right. He will send me away again and again unless I take a stand.

"Are you saying it would've been better if you left me? What were my other choices? Starvation on the street? Being raped by old dirty men when I was barely old enough to pee on my own? You saved me."

"And I'm going to keep saving you or that one act all those years ago don't mean shit."

"I'm good enough to fuck, but not good enough to keep around."

He flinches at that one, but it's not enough. No weapon in my arsenal is going to move him from his position. Helplessly, I realize this. I could be the most gifted orator, come up with the best arguments, and I will still lose. He's convinced himself that there's only one solution.

My heart is cracking. It's so loud it's a wonder he can't hear it. Maybe he can and he's ignoring that, too.

It's for my own protection because I can't keep loving Leka and be abandoned in return. I barely recovered when I was fourteen. There's still an echo of that heartache that rings whenever we're separated from each other for any period of time. It's why I went to Marjory's tonight. I missed him. I was afraid and so I went to him. Now, he wants me to live with the terrible anticipation that we could be separated at any time and that kind of awful uncertainty would wreck me. I don't want to be ruined. I want to be happy. I want to be happy with *him*.

"If you do this," I say quietly because it's hard to speak through the giant rock in my throat. "If you do this, I won't come back. I forgave you once. I forgave you because it made sense when I was fourteen, but it doesn't make sense now. If you do this, we're done forever."

I lay it out there. Ultimatums aren't right, but it's not really an ultimatum. It's a promise.

He exhales. "Maybe that's for the best."

I stagger back, catching myself against the counter. So there it is. He'd rather live apart than keep me close. He must know whatever the threat is today, it isn't going away.

I don't know why, but I try once again. "There's no silver bullet that is going to make me safe forever. I could die tomorrow getting run over by a car or falling into a subway station. I could die choking on a nut or being shot by a random burglar."

And Leka knows this in his head. It's his heart that is clouded with fear. Our love will never survive if it's not strong enough to overcome his fear.

"I'm sorry," he says. "I do love you. It's why I'm doing this."

There's nothing more to say. Not that I have the strength to talk. I pick up my purse, toe my feet into the discarded tennis shoes, not even bothering to pull up the backs. I open the door and walk out. I don't want the suitcase. I don't want the passbook full of money. I don't want memories of him. I want to start a new life. One that doesn't involve a man who holds his fear closer than his love.

It's hard to see through my veil of tears, but I know this path well enough. I walk it slow, aching to hear the door open. Aching to hear my name called. Aching to be back in his arms.

But the door behind me never opens. His voice never calls out. The only sounds in the hallway are my sniffles and the chime of the elevator that has just arrived to take me away.

I cast one last long look at the front door of the apartment. It remains closed. I step into the elevator. The doors slide shut and the car begins to descend.

So...this is how it ends. I stumble to the corner and grope blindly for the railing so I don't collapse to the floor. My chest is so tight. So very, very tight. I slap my hand over my left breast and squeeze, but that pain doesn't abate. It only grows with each small chime of the elevator, with each block I get farther from the apartment building, with each smile from the hotel staff until it grows so big that it explodes and pushes me to my knees.

No one told me that heartbreak was a real, physical thing.

<hr />

AFTER CRYING MY WEIGHT IN TEARS, I DRAG MYSELF OFF THE hotel bed. In the bathroom, I wet my face with a cold cloth, straighten my silky blue blouse that got twisted around my torso, and internally debate my options. I need to get out of the city because if I don't, I'll be tempted to run back to Leka. I need a new start in a new location—somewhere far from here.

I'm going to survive this. I'm young. The wound is fresh and that's why it feels like tomorrow is too great of an obstacle to overcome. That's why I want to lie down in the tub and sink under the water and stay there until there are no more thoughts in my head and no more pain in my heart.

At the desk, I pull out the hotel stationery and start making a list. I want a place that is big enough that I can get lost if I need to and small enough that I don't feel overwhelmed.

I don't need a warm place. Spending four years in Vermont has gotten me used to the cold. I sort of like snuggling next to a fire and watching the snow blanket the earth. Everything seems fresh at that point. Like you can really start anew.

I'll need public transportation since I don't have a car and I don't have a lot of money. I don't want to use the credit cards Leka gave me. I need to cut off all access to him for my own sanity.

I pull up a map of the US on my tablet and start filtering until I arrive at Minneapolis, one of the Twin Cities. It's cold up there, but they know how to do it right with ice festivals and snow parties. There's decent public transportation and dozens of different neighborhoods. I find an apartment that's within my budget. It'll be tight and I'll need to get a job right away. I can clean homes or wait tables or both.

There are night school classes I can take to get some kind of associate's degree. Once I get a better job, I can save up and go to college to get a bachelor's degree. I intend to work in social services. I know it's a sucky job, but I want to help kids if I can.

I send in an inquiry about the apartment's availability and begin my job hunt. There are lots of low-wage jobs available but not one that pays enough to cover the bills. So, two jobs it is. For the next hour, I distract myself by filling out online applications. After the fifteenth one, my tears have dried and I'm no longer feeling sorry for myself.

Well, not much anyway.

But I'm cold. I check the thermostat, but it's broken because the tiny LED screen declares that it's a temperate 72 degrees. Not likely given the goosebumps on my arms. I grab the comforter off the bed and wrap it around me and fill out five more applications. The fifth one is for a delivery position, and for some reason that makes me think of Leka. The tears start up again.

If only I could stop wanting him. Maybe I could see a heart surgeon and he could cut out all the Leka pieces in that worthless organ. No. I'd have to take my whole heart out because there isn't a part that doesn't have Leka in it.

Feeling helpless, I drop my head to the desk. The faux leather pad covering the work surface feels sticky and gross against my tear-soaked cheek, but I'm too emotionally spent to move.

You're going to be okay, I tell myself. *It'll be okay.*

I'm going to keep saying this until I believe it.

A knock at the door interrupts my chanting. I didn't order room service and no one knows I'm here. I glance warily at the door. "Who is it?"

"It's me."

I jump to my feet. Leka? How could he find me? I just picked a random hotel. My gaze drops to my phone. *Dumb. Dumb. Dumb.* I shouldn't have turned it on. What a rookie mistake! I'd used cash to check in but didn't think to get a burner phone.

"You have the wrong room," I say. "Please leave or I'll be forced to call security."

Leka's response is to unlock the door and walk in.

"Hey!" I wave my arms as if I can magic him out of my room like some wand-wielding wizard. "Get out. You're trespassing."

Since I don't have a wand and am not a wizard, I fail.

"How mad are you?"

"I'm furious." I glare. "My rage is incandescent, and it will remain at that alarming level for a very long time."

"Okay." He leans in and kisses me. I let him because I'm angry but also very much in love and I can't turn him away. But I only allow the kiss to last a few minutes before breaking away. No amount of kissing is going to reduce my anger.

"Only time—" He interrupts me with another kiss. I try again. "Only time will make it"—kiss—"I really mean it"—kiss—"I'm serious—"

He tongues my lips apart and dives in. My righteous anger dissolves like chocolate under a flame as he tugs on the belt loops of my jeans until my body is flush against his. He parts his legs and fits me into the notch between them. The hard, stiff length of him juts against my stomach—the flimsy fabric no barrier against his desire.

My head spins and I lose track of exactly why I was mad until he releases me and then it all comes flooding back.

I push out of his arms and put a few feet between us so I can catch my breath. "You don't get to kick me out and then waltz back in like nothing happened."

"I agree. I'm sorry. I'm scared shitless of you staying, but you leaving forever is my biggest fear. If you stay, you could get hurt and that will kill me. I don't think our relationship would ever be the same."

"Of course, it wouldn't," I reply impatiently.

He frowns. "What do you mean?"

"Our relationship will change all the time. It already has, from guardian and ward to lovers. Tomorrow, maybe we will be parents. I've grown; you've grown and so our relationship changes. What doesn't change is our love. As long as we have love, we can weather all the changes. If I get hurt, then we deal with that hurt and our guilt and our pain and we move the fuck on together."

He gives me his quirky smile. "All right then, my love. We'll fight this battle together."

"Fine," I reply stiffly, but my lip quivers.

"You done being mad at me?" His voice is so tender that it sends my heart flying, and because I have zero control over my emotions, the tears start to flow.

Leka panics. "Shit. What's wrong? What did I say?" His rough hands come up to cup my cheeks, as if by force he can stem the tide.

"N-n-nothing," I blubber. "You called me *my love.*"

"I'll never say it again," he vows.

"If you don't say it every day until I die, we're going to fight." I hit him on the arm.

He doesn't flinch. I don't know if he even feels it. His biceps are like rocks. "We good?" he says, a mite impatient.

"Why?" I cock my head. "Are we going somewhere?"

"Hopefully, five feet to your left."

"Five feet to my—" I look over my shoulder and see the bed. "Oh."

"Yeah. Oh."

38

LEKA

I'm a criminal. I break the law. I kill people. I steal. I work for people who traffic in guns and drugs. But none of those misdeeds compare to the sin I'm committing now. But I can't let her go.

I've had a taste of heaven and am too damn selfish not to want a repeat.

"If I take you now. That's it. You can't leave again."

"A threat is something that I should be afraid of. I'm not afraid of you."

"You should be." I thread a finger inside the waistband of her jeans. "You should be afraid of me. Of my world."

"Leka, don't you know? I'm your world." Boldly, she steps forward and rises on her tiptoes to place a kiss on my chin. My cock pulses against her stomach.

"That's even more terrifying."

"But you've never been afraid of anything."

I wasn't before you came into my life, but that's because I didn't have anything to live for. I cup the back of her neck and tilt her head with my thumb until her eyes meet mine. "Last chance." *Last chance to escape before I tie you to me with binding so secure and tight that not even death will keep us apart.*

She leans forward and presses her cheek against my thudding heart. "I was once afraid. Back in that dark alley, running away from the bad man that wanted to hurt me. I was afraid of everything. The shadows in the apartment. The noises as the springs bounced above my head. The smells of sweat and vomit in the bathroom. But most of all I was afraid of being alone and forgotten. You drove that all away, Leka. I don't care what happens to me so long as it happens when you are with me. This world is shit. I know this. I know that there are probably lots of people out there that would say you and I are wrong, but they don't matter. Only you matter. I only want you."

I tried. I tried hard to be a good person and to send her away. I did the right thing and now...well, now, I grab the lapels of her robe and whip it open. Now it's time to claim her.

I sweep a hand under her ass and lift her. Her legs automatically wrap around my waist, her ankles locking at the notch of my lower back. As I cross the small distance to the mattress, her ass brushes the head of my straining cock. The wispy contact makes my dick ache. I clench my teeth.

Every time we have sex, I'm fighting the battle of not coming too soon. She makes me so fucking hot that just looking at her eviscerates my self-control. But I want to go slow this time. I really want to make love to her, to bring her to heights she hasn't known before, so that if there ever is a time she has to choose, her body will remember me.

Gently, I lay her onto the mattress. The white terry cloth falls to frame her perfect, beautiful body. She gestures that she wants me in her arms. I shake my head.

"No. Not yet." I pull a finger between her legs and hold it up so she can see her arousal coating the tip. "I'm need my daily ration of this." I suck the finger into my mouth, tasting her salty essence.

Her eyes widen in anticipation.

I don't make her wait. I drop to my knees and press her legs open wide —wider than she prefers, but I like to see her fully on display. Her sex is beautiful. It's soft and suckable, glistening with a need that makes me humble.

"Are you gonna stare at your food or do something about it?" she chirps, half challenge, half irritation.

I laugh. "Maybe I'll take a picture."

"Do it and I'll kill you."

"This is fucking gorgeous. It's art." I frame her pussy with my fingers, pressing my thumbs against the puckered, forbidden skin. She tries to scoot away, but I drag her back.

"Well, it's the only art you're going to see."

My fingers dig into her thighs. "I better be the only one seeing it."

"Or what?" she teases.

I'm deadly serious. "Or I'll be keeping a collection of eyeballs in a jar in the fridge." I lean forward and give her one long lick from back to front. "You're mine now. I'm the only one that gets to look at this pussy. I'm the only one that gets to touch this pussy. I'm the only one that gets to eat this pussy."

I lock my mouth over her sex, tongue her folds apart and fuck her with my fingers and teeth and tongue until the only thing that comes out of her pert mouth are screams of pleasure. She writhes below me—both wanting more and afraid of the sensations. I have to hold her down to make her take all of the ecstasy that her body and I want to give her. I hold her in place to my mouth until she unravels with a high keening scream.

And while she's hurtling down from the top of that one peak, I tear at my fastenings, pull out my heavy, soaked cock and thrust into her. She cries out again, but I show her no mercy.

I stretch her with the broad width of my cockhead. I drive forward until I'm fully seated, from tip to root.

Ragged, short pants escape between her lips.

"It's too much," she chokes. "You're too big. Holy *fuck*, you feel enormous."

It's because she's already come once. Her tissues are swollen. Her lower lips are engorged with blood. Her sheath is like a vise grip. I want to come in that instant. My legs threaten to give out.

I suck in my lower lip and bite down until the copper taste of blood fills my mouth and the haze in my head clears just enough for me to grasp a few tendrils of restraint. I draw back slow, fighting against her hold.

She moans again, her head thrashing sideways.

The motion makes her tits bounce. I can't resist the urge to bend over and suck on one hard nub and then another until she creams on my cock again.

I want to come. The orgasm sits heavy and hard at the back of my spine, a cannon ball ready to be fired. But she hasn't come enough times. She's not been pleasured enough. All my veins throb in readiness. This time is going to last. This time we're going slow.

I grit my teeth and slide out. My cock is so sensitive, I swear I could count every single nerve ending in her channel. I settle into a hard, steady rhythm of fucking while I explore her with my mouth. I find a tiny freckle under her lower lip and a small mole on the curve of her shoulder. I mold her tits together, thumbing the nipples until she begs for my mouth.

I give her that, too. I give it all to her.

"You are too good at this. You shouldn't be making me feel this good," she exclaims.

I pause in mid-stroke and lift my head from her breast. "What?"

She shakes her head. "I know this is ridiculous and entirely the wrong time to bring this up, but you are way too good at this."

A rivulet of sweat rolls down the side of my face. I brush it away so it doesn't drop onto Bitsy's face, which is tight and flushed. Her lower lip juts out. This does not make her less sexy. If anything, it makes me want to fuck her harder until that petulant look on her face is replaced with pure ecstasy. It also makes me want to drag my dick along that pouting lower lip.

"Do you want this to be a bad experience?" I ask in mild surprise.

"No. Yes. But no."

Confused, I start to withdraw.

She grabs my hips and holds me in place. "You sure you were a virgin?"

I huff out a surprised laugh. "Yeah."

"I can't believe it."

"Why not? You were."

"Because look at you." She waves a hand in my direction.

I look down and see my ordinary body. I do physical work so I don't have much extra fat. "What about it?"

"Don't you know how gorgeous you are? How people's heads literally turn when you walk by? How whole groups of people will fall silent when you walk into a room? "

I scratch the back of my neck. "Who cares?"

She sighs. "You're still so good at this. I can't believe you never had sex before."

"It's because I pay attention."

"What do you mean?"

"It means when you're hungry, I feed you. When you're angry, I give you space and hunt down reruns of *The Powerpuff Girls* to play when you're ready to come out of your room. When you're lonely, I get Audie on the phone. When you have your period coming up, I stock up on Advil and ice cream. It means that when I touch you here"—I stroke the tendon at the back of her knee—"you tense and your sex clenches. If I stroke you right"—I thrust in and out a couple of times until I find that one spot that makes her gasp out loud.

"—there," I growl evilly. "I can make you come without touching your clit if I can find that small patch of skin that makes you scream." I withdraw slow, dragging my dick over that tiny bundle of nerves that sends her into overdrive.

She hisses. Her toes curl into the sheets. I thrust into her wet, sensitive heat, pressing her thighs open, pounding her hard, showing her exactly how much I pay attention. How much I know what she wants. How desperate I am to give her everything.

I fuck her long, hard, and when we're done, I flip her over and start again. I scrape my teeth over her breastbone. I suck the vein at her wrist and the one at her neck until purple bruises appear. I spank her ass until it's red and her pussy is weeping and she's begging me to take her again, *would I fucking listen and take her again.* We fuck for hours, until the skin is raw, until the afternoon sun slips under the horizon, until the outside world and all its horrors are shut away.

We fuck until the truth of our lives crystallizes and etches itself on our souls. She loves me. I love her. That is the only thing that matters in this world.

And maybe that's why I don't sense the danger at first.

Why I didn't hear the footsteps in the hall.

Why I didn't see the masked figures until they were bursting through the door.

Why my gun was halfway across the room when I needed it the most.

39

LEKA

"You left without saying goodbye. That's real rude," Cesaro says. "And not very loyal. How am I supposed to keep all my other boys in line if you, Priest, are going to flaunt my orders at every turn?"

"I've followed all your orders."

"Except this one. This tiny little thing I ask of you and you're just ignoring me, which makes no sense because I'm in charge here. I'm king of this territory, which means every single one of you pissant subjects belongs to me. If I say I want to fuck a girl, it doesn't matter who she belongs to because ultimately, she's mine just like I own you, isn't that right, Priest?"

The lie is thick on my tongue, but I force it out. For Bitsy's sake. "That's right."

Cesaro taps his slim fingers against the table. "You're saying all the correct words, but I don't get a sense you feel it. Do you feel it, boys?" He turns to the men in the room. All but Sterno shake their heads. "See, no one feels it. If I let this go, everyone will believe that Cesaro lost his edge. I like you, Priest. You've done a good job, but you need to prove yourself to me now. It's real easy. You call your girl down here and give me an hour with her. I promise I'll deliver her back to you, safe and sound. Beefer knows. You tell him how much Camella liked how I treated her."

Beefer, who is in the middle of laying out his special tools, pauses, and we both remember what it was like that night. How Camella lay broken and bleeding on the stainless steel counter upstairs. How Beefer puked his guts out in front of me.

"Beefer," Cesaro warns.

Beefer picks up a massive pair of pliers and wipes a cloth over the sharp steel ends. For some men, just seeing the torture devices would be enough to loosen their tongues. Down here, we've had men vow to slit their own mother's throats just on the threat of pain. My stomach roils.

"Sorry, boss," Beefer says, "I was thinking about what tool would be best for the job tonight. Camella liked you real good."

Cesaro claps as if his favorite dog just did a trick for all of us. "There you go. Camella got nothing but pleasure from me, and that's what I'll deliver to your girl, too. In fact, you should thank me because there's not many men in my position who would choose her over all the other ponies in the stable."

Whatever Beefer opts to do tonight is going to hurt like a mother-fucker, but I have to keep it together because Bit's upstairs and the only way both of us are walking away from this is to endure. This pain is fleeting; the kind that Cesaro would inflict on Bit's mind would last forever.

"I've always been loyal," I tell Cesaro. "I've been part of this crew for more than fifteen years. Everything that's been asked of me, I've done. Isn't that right, Beefer?" Up until yesterday, I'd have said Beefer would back me on anything. The world's turned upside down now and I don't know who I can trust.

The man who I've worked for and with for my entire life contemplates me for a long, silent moment—likely weighing the odds of me surviving against whatever gifts Cesaro has promised. I tell him, as best I can with only eye contact, that I'll repay any punishment that he can deliver.

"Leka's been my right-hand man for a long time," Beefer finally says. "He keeps the crew in line. He's good with logistics, and the other gangs around here are scared shitless of him. It took four guys to bring him in and only because one of them got a shot off in the girl's direction. He's a valuable tool."

In sum, we can hurt him, but not too much. It's the most Beefer can give and I appreciate it.

"Let me at him, boss," growls one of Cesaro's men. I don't know his name, but he'll be wearing that scar along his cheek for a long time.

Cesaro shakes his head and clicks his tongue against the roof of his mouth. "You know how good Beefer is at his job, don't you?"

"He's the best," I agree. It's going to be a long and torturous night, but these wounds will all heal. I settle into the chair and ready myself. As long as my girl is safe, there isn't anything that these guys can do down here that will break me.

"The best? We'll see about that. Let's begin."

Beefer starts small, smashing the pinkie on my left hand with a hammer. I release a long hiss of pain and break out into a sweat.

"I don't get you." Cesaro dips his head close to mine. He's lucky I don't bite his nose off. "One night is all I want. One night and everyone goes home happy."

Like Camella? Like the other girls who work for the organization who nearly piss themselves in fear when they hear Cesaro's in town? I'll never let him touch Bit. "She's not for sale."

"You're a dumb motherfucker," Beefer mutters under his breath. "There's no point. He's going to have her anyway."

I stare steadily at both of them. Cesaro gives the signal to continue, and Beefer, with a little smirk on his lips, smashes the knuckle on the next finger. These fingers are going to be totally unusable when they heal up. He'll have to switch to the other side soon.

Usually, Beefer's calculated and businesslike, but tonight there's an anger in the way he's carrying out his task. It's resentment, I conclude. He didn't fight for Camella and he doesn't like seeing me fight. The outcome has to be the same for Bitsy as it was for his daughter or he won't be able to live with himself.

Cesaro pokes the mess of bones and blood. I nearly pass out from the pain. "I can't believe you're sacrificing yourself for some snatch, but your loyalty to her intrigues me. She must be dynamite in the sack. Is it how she sucks dick? Is her pussy laced with ecstasy? I want her even more now." He sticks out his tongue and runs it across the bottom of his lip. "I bet she tastes juicy."

I explode, the force of my anger ripping through the bindings on one arm. Cesaro jumps back, but not before I catch the front of his shirt in my hand. I drag him forward. "Don't fucking talk about her that way," I growl through clenched teeth.

He claws at my hand as I tighten the fabric in my fist, cutting off his air supply. It takes all four of Cesaro's men and Beefer to drag me back and tuck Cesaro out of reach. He jerks out of the grip of his men, dusts his hands against his pants as if a prisoner didn't just almost choke the life out of him. "Cut off his hand," he orders.

Beefer balks. He's resentful but not stupid. "He's not going to be of much use to us if we do that."

"I don't care," Cesaro explodes. He's losing it. Spittle forms at the corners of his mouth.

"Why don't you do two of his fingers?" Sterno suggests. "She's a young girl and an old deformed man isn't going to appeal to her much."

"Start with his fingers," Cesaro orders, pretending that Sterno never suggested that exact thing. "We'll see how much the girl likes him after that."

"I'm sorry, kid," Beefer says as he takes out a blade familiar as my own hand. "At least let him choose," he asks. "Cuz of all the years of loyalty."

This is a poor sort of mercy, but I'll take it. "The pinkie," I tell him. "Who needs five fingers anyway?"

They laugh like I'm a comedian at Madison Square. I nearly bite through my tongue not to make a sound as Beefer saws off the top of my digit. That pisses Cesaro off too—my continued silence.

He picks up a board and slams it against my side. I feel my ribcage cave in. The cracking echoes in my ears. He slams it again and I want to scream because the pain is excruciating.

But Bit's upstairs. She could hear me.

40

BITSY

I strain my ears for any sound from Leka, but the basement is silent as a tomb. Chilled, I pull my heavy puffer coat tighter around me. It was all I was allowed to grab when the men broke down our door and dragged the two of us out of the hotel.

It took only one man to subdue Leka. The tall, scarecrow-shaped man named Sterno held a gun to my head and ordered Leka out of the room.

"Go quietly and she will not be hurt," the man had said. Leka believed him and walked out.

That same man threw me my coat and took me down to a town car. We followed a large black Escalade to Marjory's, where I got a glimpse of Leka, hooded and restrained, being led out of the car and into the restaurant. The scarecrow directed me to the stool I'm sitting on and told me if I was patient, Leka would return to me.

Then he disappeared downstairs. That was thirteen minutes and five seconds ago.

I'd told Leka it was as easy for me to be killed by walking in the city than by someone in his business. Because he loved me, he let his guard down and now here we are, with him in the torture chamber in the basement and me up here shaking like a stupid leaf. I want to stab myself in the eye for all the stupid things I said. For not paying attention to Leka. For not heeding him.

If I had listened rather than insisting like a child that my way was the right way, he wouldn't be hurting right now. And I know he's hurting. They didn't force him downstairs to drink beers and play poker.

Two of Beefer's men guard the door. When I told Leka I could shoot, I wasn't lying, and in this moment, even though I haven't even killed a deer, I wouldn't hesitate to fire a bullet into these men to save Leka. But I don't have a gun and I'm not stupid or naïve enough to think I could take even one of them with kitchen implements. I'd probably trip and stab myself if I tried to attack with a chef's knife.

Leka's right. I can't protect us with a bottle of mace. I contemplate calling the police, but I'm sure that would doom Leka, too. I can't just sit on my ass and do nothing.

"Should I take something downstairs for the guys? They must be hungry. They've been down there for a while."

Fourteen minutes and twenty-seven seconds to be precise.

"Cesaro will call for you when he's ready," Mary says. Her voice is cold and dark.

I try not to look terrified, but I don't think I'm succeeding well because Justin, the cook who replaced Gerry, makes a sad sound in the back of his throat. "Why don't you grab me that plate over there?" he jerks his head to a stack of small white dessert plates.

"Are you really making him a chocolate cake?" I ask. This whole scene seems so macabre. Downstairs, Beefer and Cesaro and who knows who else are torturing my Leka.

Justin confirms. "Cesaro already ate. I'm making his dessert and it's not done yet. The chocolate isn't as smooth as I'd like."

"Hurry up," Mary snipes. "He likes to have his dessert before sex."

My stomach clenches. It's not Mary he's going to be boning after he's done with Leka. My best guess is that Cesaro will rape me in front of Leka. That seems to be right up his alley.

I need to take action. There are four people up here and four men in the basement plus Cesaro and Beefer. How can I take out eight people? A timer dings and Justin reaches into the oven and pulls out a small ramekin filled with chocolate cake. A plume of white spirals up from the oven. A thought strikes. I could start a fire and smoke everyone out. In the chaos, Leka will get free and we will run.

It's a risk, but it's my best option. I scan the kitchen for tools. There's olive oil sitting on the island and butter in a bowl. I just need to get those to a flame. The stove that Justin is cooking on is gas. That's my target.

I step away from the wall. In front of me, the scene blurs. I no longer see the slender, dark-haired Justin but thicker, red-haired Gerry. Mary's dress is blue instead of red. She reaches into her pocket. I blink and shoot to my feet.

"Stop!" I yell.

As one, Mary and Justin turn to look at me.

"What?" Justin asks, his hand suspended above the chocolate cake sprinkling white powder on top.

Because I know what to look for, I see Mary's fist shoot out. She opens her palm and a dust-like substance drops onto the cake. Before I can blink, her hand is back by her side. If I hadn't suspected, I would've missed this.

The image of Arturo grasping his throat with spittle forming at the sides of his mouth materializes. Mary is at his side. She accuses Gerry, but before Gerry can protest, Mary strikes. The knife slits his throat just as he is about to say something. Holy *fuck*. Mary killed Arturo all those years ago. And in his place, Cesaro rose to power.

But he didn't take Mary along with him as she thought he would. If he had, she wouldn't still be here, doling out her favors to Beefer and whomever else is willing to pay for her services. So, either out of spite or anger, Mary's going to kill Cesaro the same way she killed his uncle—by poisoning his food.

My eyes meet Mary's, who recognizes my new understanding immediately. We both move at once, but I'm younger, quicker, and closer to the basement door. I swing it open and launch myself down the stairs before the guards can stop me.

"It's Mary!" I scream. "Mary killed Arturo. Mary poisoned Arturo. Don't eat the cake. Don't eat the cake!"

"You bitch." She manages to grab a fistful of my hair and yanks me backward.

I fight through it, jerking out of her grip and racing forward.

Her breath is hot on my neck, but I reach the floor first and sprint toward the backroom door. I've never touched that door. Hell, I've never so much as walked down these stairs, but somehow I know precisely where to go.

"It's Mary," I shout as I whip open the door. "It's Mary!"

Everyone inside turns toward me. Two guards on either side of the door reach inside their jackets. Cesaro, two feet away from a table in the middle of the concrete box of a room, holds up a hand. The guards fall away, and I spot Leka sitting next to that table, his arm lying across it at a funny angle. My stomach churns.

My gaze travels from his arm to his swollen face. Patches of skin near the sides of his mouth and high on his cheekbones are already turning a sickly purple and yellow.

Two feet away from the table, Beefer's holding something metallic and menacing in his hand. The contents of my stomach threaten to spew out of my mouth and coat the floor. I press a hand against my churning stomach and order my body to get itself under control.

Like Leka who sits calmly, not an ounce of pain showing on his face.

"Do you have something to say, young Elizabeth?" Cesaro quirks an eyebrow up. "Or have you arrived to provide us a show?"

"I, um—" *Get it together, Bit,* I order myself, but it's hard to keep calm at this moment. Everywhere I look something horrible appears, whether it's the instruments on the table or the dull metallic glint of the black guns in everyone's hands but Cesaro or Leka himself sitting in that metal chair with blood pooling on the table and bruises decorating his face.

"She's just a dumb bitch." Mary appears over my shoulder. She sticks something sharp in my back. "I'll get rid of her."

"No. Please. She should stay and watch." Cesaro beckons me forward. "Your boy, Leka, didn't want you to spend time with me, so we're showing him what happens when people deny Cesaro of what's rightfully his. How do you feel about that?"

How do I feel, you sick fuck? I'd like to take the big knife on the table and stick it through your right eye! I dig my fingers into my palms. I turn toward the one man Cesaro brought that I recognize—scarecrow man. He was there the night that Arturo died. He was there when Arturo promised me the boon that I never cashed in.

"Do you remember me?" I ask.

He nods.

"Arturo owed me a boon. I'm cashing it in. Mary poisoned Arturo and killed the chef to hide the truth. She was upstairs sprinkling Cesaro's food with the same poison."

Sterno looks over my shoulder at the two men who were guarding the door at the top of the stairs. "What happened?"

The young one, Mason—I think—answers. "Mary did put something on the cake, but I thought it was sugar." He produces the plate. "I can't tell by looking at it."

Sterno takes the plate and pinches off a piece that is liberally dusted with something white. He holds it to Mary's mouth. "You first."

Mary's eyes are wide. "I-I'm allergic to chocolate," she stammers and backs away. She doesn't get far. The two guards block her escape.

"You need to address this first," Sterno informs his boss. "These two can wait."

"I'm in the middle of something," Cesaro complains. "I can't just stop now. Besides, the minute we let these two out of our sight, they'll run."

Sterno shakes his head. "Your uncle was a man of honor, but he died a disgraceful death. He still watches, waiting for his revenge. So that he can rest, you must attend to this matter."

"Wait. Hold on—" Cesaro says, but his man is out the door.

Mary tries to dart away. The older man captures her easily and drags her back into the room.

"Stop it. Let go of me. I didn't do anything," Mary cries. She tries to peel his fingers away, but it's useless.

"We're done here." Leka reaches down to his ankles and I notice for the first time that he was tied to the chair. He slices through the bindings with the knife he slid off the table. He rises slowly, holding his right arm close to his side.

"Wait. I said, wait!" Cesaro nearly stamps his foot.

"This woman killed Arturo," Sterno replies. His face is stone. "She is more important than him."

The other men murmur their agreement and it is the threat of his men turning on him that pushes Cesaro to give in. He glowers and spits out one last threat. "Just remember. Death is the only way out, Leka Moore! You can't run from me. We own you. Both of you."

"Go," Sterno orders.

We don't have to be told twice.

I TUCK AN ARM AROUND LEKA'S BACK, HELPING HIM AS MUCH as I can. He walks out slow, with each breath a labored, harsh effort.

"We can't go to a doctor, can we?"

He shakes his head. "No, but you can pick up a couple of things for me at the drugstore. We'll stop on our way home. You'll need to listen to me, carefully, okay? And do as I ask. No questions."

"Yes. I promise." I want to sob with relief and terror and guilt, but I know that would hurt Leka as much as anything, so I keep a lid on my emotions as we walk to the end of the alley. Each step is slower than the last, and I worry that he won't make it.

"Why don't you tell me what hurts so I can get the right stuff."

"What doesn't?" he jokes and then groans. "Shit. I can't laugh. Okay, so cracked ribs, some damage to my fingers. Maybe a broken femur."

I die a little inside. Some damage to his fingers? I caught a glimpse of them on the table and the last two on his right hand were mangled. "What about the stuff we can't see? Do you have any bleeding inside?"

"No."

"How do you know?"

He stops walking and spits on the ground. "See?" He gingerly toes the wet spot on the ground. "No blood. It's all good. You came down just in time."

"Right. That's me with the perfect timing," I say sarcastically. I should've started a fire earlier or called the police. Anything to have gotten him out sooner. Guilt and shame mix together to make a sickly cocktail in my stomach.

When we arrive at his car, I hold my hand out. "I'm driving."

He gives up the keys without an argument and slides into the passenger side, wincing with all the pain.

"The city roads are shit," I curse as I avoid yet another pothole.

Leka's trying to keep his pain complaints to a minimum. Sweat breaks across his forehead and his breathing is even more forced. I wish he'd just pass out.

"I'm going to stop at the Duane Reade near our apartment," I tell him.

He nods weakly and closes his eyes. The drive home is as smooth as I can make it, but I know from the occasional clenching of his jaw that this is terrible for him.

When I pull up to the grocery store, he rouses. "Get a brace for my fingers. Some antiseptic and a couple of bottles of vodka."

"I'm underage," I remind him.

He taps his elbow against the middle console. Inside, I find a wad of cash and two passports fastened with a rubber band. I pull off the rubber band and two plastic ID cards fall on my lap. The driver's licenses are from Arizona, a state I've never visited, and the last name is Reed not Moore. Mine says that I'm twenty-two. I pocket the fake ID, and despite the new fear these forms of identification stir, I manage a light-hearted quip. "I could've used this years ago. I would've been the most popular girl at Boone."

A faint smile ghosts across his face. "Popularity that you buy is fake. I had to protect you from that."

I want to scream for him to stop protecting me because if he doesn't he'll die, but this is what I begged and pleaded for, so I have no one to blame but myself. I stuff my fear and anxiety and guilt down deep. Those emotions aren't going to help me here. Leka needs a clear head and a steady hand, not angst-driven emo self-pity parties.

"So you're going to do this with one hand tied behind your back and drunk to boot. Very boss." I grab my purse.

"The liquor's for after," he says grimly.

"Got it." I'm thrilled he's thinking that far ahead and terrified that he's going out alone against Cesaro with a broken arm, cracked ribs, two mangled fingers and who knows what else.

I run out and get the stuff. It takes only a few more minutes to get to the apartment. I fish out a hundred-dollar bill from Leka's emergency stash.

"Take four more," he suggests.

"That much?"

"To be safe. Money isn't our problem."

"Right." Our problem is lack of manpower and Leka's injuries. I fold the five bills in half. I hand the stack to the parking attendant.

"We aren't here," I tell him as he raises the gate.

"Never saw you," he says after a quick count of the cash.

Leka gives a nod of approval and falls back onto his seat. I don't know how much time that buys us. A couple of days? A week? Certainly not enough for Leka to heal.

I ease him out of the car and help him over to the elevator. We take it up to our floor.

"Why'd we get the apartment at the end of the hall?" Leka huffs as we stare at the long hallway. It looks as impossible as spinning hay into gold. Leka forces one foot in front of the other while I hover behind. If he collapses, there's no way I'm getting his big, two-hundred-pound frame into the apartment myself. I silently send him waves of energy and he manages to drag himself all the way to the end.

Inside the apartment, he staggers to the living room and collapses on the sofa, leaving streaks of blood and dirt all over the gray cushions.

"There's a bottle of hydrocodone in my bathroom. Get that for me, will you?"

I'm down the hall before he finishes his request. I find quite a few prescription bottles in his cabinet: sleeping pills, anti-inflammatories, and narcotic painkillers. I scoop them all into my shirt and carry them out to the living room, dumping them on the table.

It's then I notice two black duffels on the floor. One is full of cash and the other is guns. And magazines. And bullets.

"I'll need you to splint the ring finger and bandage the pinkie, but make the bandage thin so it doesn't interfere with my grip," he orders.

I raise my eyes from the floor to his face, which is so hard it could be carved from stone. His eyes are set on the magazine he's filling. Something inside of me cracks open. "You're going back tonight? You could barely walk down the hall and you're going back tonight?"

"They won't expect it. Cesaro will go to some club and get wasted. His men will be tired. It's nighttime, so there will be fewer people who will notice me."

"Leka, please. Give yourself a night to recover. Maybe two. We'll think of something. You said money is not a problem, so let's hire some people. You can't go in there alone."

"I thought you said you could use a gun."

"I did, but to shoot pigeons and turkeys and, I don't know, the occasional deer!" My voice grows high and tinny. I can feel hysteria sweeping up and taking hold of me.

"All you have to do tonight is drive the car."

"Leka. Please." I sink to my knees. "This is madness. You are going to get yourself killed. Let's run away. Let's leave the guns, take the money and our new IDs and find some small town in the middle of nowhere. Cesaro won't find us. We'll start new lives."

He shakes his head. "No. Cesaro won't let this go. I'm known to be his man, and if I run off and Cesaro lets me go, it sets a bad precedent. He's got to kill me, and right now is the perfect time for him to strike, too, because I'm weak and injured. You said you would always listen to me, without question, if we're in danger. You going back on that?"

I bury my face in my hands as my own words come back to haunt me. I did say those things and I meant them, at the time, but like so many promises, you don't realize the consequences until you come face to face with them. "I'm not going back on my promise, but you pledged to love me forever. This is not forever. It's been barely a month."

"I'm not going to die tonight."

"How can you say that?"

"Because I have too much to live for. Now bandage me up."

It's the calmness in his voice, the utter surety of his words that gets me to battle back the abyss-eating panic. I pick up the antiseptic and the bandages and get to work, keeping all my tears and fright and anger inside. I don't even show an ounce of surprise or sadness at discovering that half of Leka's pinky is missing. That's Beefer, the Butcher's, work. Maybe I can shoot a human. If that hog was in front of me, I'd aim right for his balls.

Leka sits stoically while I tend to his wounds. I try to be careful, but every movement has to be agonizing. Finally, I'm done.

"Go get anything you want to keep. We're not coming back."

I run to the bedroom. In a backpack, I throw together some clothes and toiletries. In the corner of my bed, I spot the first bunny Leka ever gave me. It was the one he bought me that very first time we were in Macy's. I'm going to give that to our kid. I take out a shirt to make room for the stuffed animal and run outside.

He's waiting in the foyer.

"That's all you're taking?" he asks.

I shift the backpack on my shoulders. "I don't need anything but you."

He gives me a crooked smile, hefts the two bags up over his shoulders and heads out. I know better than to ask to help him.

As we drive over to Cesaro's hotel, Leka reels off the instructions. "Stay in the car. Don't come up. No matter how long I take. Promise me so I can focus all my attention on Cesaro. If I don't come out in thirty minutes, leave."

I balk at that order.

"If you don't agree, you can't come with," he says.

"I'm never leaving you," I declare fiercely, fisting my fingers around the steering wheel as if it's his life line. I'm never leaving him and I'm not letting him go. We're going to make it out together or not at all.

41

LEKA

The hotel is packed. Cesaro likes this place because there's always some young woman who is willing to trade a night with him for a boat load of cash and some lines of coke. Sterno would've never let Arturo spend a single night here because there's no way to adequately protect his boss. There are too many entrances and exits. Too many non-residents flowing in and out of the doors. Too much of everything.

Loud music is pulsating from the basement club, and pretty young things of both genders are streaming in and out of the lobby and nearby bar. There are two security guards at the front, but neither one notice me as I enter. They're too busy gawking at all the eye candy.

I bypass the elevator and head for the stairs. If I was in charge and forced to protect a body here, I'd put at least two guards in the stairwell, two outside the elevator bank and two in front of the door. Inside, there should be at least four. As far as I know, Cesaro's only brought eight men with him, but that doesn't mean he isn't borrowing some of Beefer's crew. Or that Beefer himself isn't here.

I creep up the stairs, back to the wall, gun pointed up and at the ready. When I reach the fifth-floor landing, I spy a flash of black above me. To draw out the guards, I throw a coin against the railing and duck back out of sight, pressing a hand against my aching ribs. Before I left the apartment, I was tempted to swallow half the bottle of codeine, but if I had, I wouldn't be worth shit on this job. No task has ever been so important.

I'm not fighting for the crew or for money or even for my misplaced loyalty to Beefer. I'm fighting for Bitsy's life and mine. I'm fighting for our future. That's as effective a painkiller as any pill created.

One man leans over from two floors up, dressed in black and wearing an earpiece. Bingo. Targets one and two are in sight. I take the next two flights faster. The guard who peeked over the railing is the first to go with a bullet between his eyes. The second one is dispatched a heartbeat later. I prop one up and shove him out the door.

Bullets spray his body from the guards in front of the hotel door. I drop those two and duck down to wait for the elevator crew to round the corner. It doesn't take them long. I use the last of my bullets on those two.

Adrenaline's powering me forward. I can barely feel the pain in my ribs or the throbbing in my hand. I trigger the release on the magazine. The empty cartridge falls on top of the body at my feet. I slam another in place, knock on the door, and step back. A familiar face sticks his jowls out.

Our eyes meet. His widen and his mouth forms a circle. I don't know what he would've said. Maybe he would've apologized. More likely he would've called a warning. I don't care.

"I'm sorry," I tell him and shoot him twice—once between the eyes and the next in the heart.

Beefer falls. A flood of gunshots follows. I plaster myself to the floor, using the bodies of the guards as shields. When the bullets stop, I hop to my feet and run inside. A burning sensation flares on my right outer thigh. Something whistles past my ear. I keep running. I keep shooting. I keep moving forward until there's no sound in the room but my labored breaths, Cesaro's mewls of fear, and the cries of two partygoers.

I straighten and blink the sweat and bloodlust out of my eyes. There were more than four people inside. Beefer was here along with Swan, his friend, and another of our crew. Sterno lies on the floor along with one of Cesaro's main guards.

"Go on," I tell the girls. "Leave and forget this ever happened or you won't wake up from your sleep tonight."

The two nod and stumble out, wailing like professional mourners at a funeral of a rich man. I only have a few minutes before they send security up. I don't need more than one. I switch out the now empty magazine for a new one.

"Wait. Wait. We can make a deal here. I have a lot of money. Beefer's dead. You can have his territory. Don't want to share your girl? No problem. It was just a test anyway. Just a loyalty test. I never wanted her," he babbles.

I shoot him between the legs. Tears pour out of his eyes. He wails, louder than the sirens on a fire truck. "Fuck. Motherfucker," he screams. His cups the blood pouring out between his legs. "I swear to you that I'll let you go. Call me a fucking ambulance and I'll forget this ever happened. Jesus Christ. You shot my balls off. You sick fuck. I hate you."

"Tell me you're sorry," I say, pointing the gun at his stomach. A gut wound is the worst way to die. It's slow and painful. I like that.

"I'm sorry. I'm sorry," he says over and over, like the pathetic worm he is.

"Apologize for the shitty things you said about my girl."

"Yes, I'm sorry for that, too. My God. Why did you shoot me here? Why?"

"Apologize for raping Camella."

"Who?" He shakes his head and then screams because the motion must have jarred his gonads.

"Beefer the Butcher's daughter. You raped her four years ago."

"Jesus. Who cares about that bitch?" he cries.

"Apologize for all the women and girls that you raped and ruined."

"For Christ's sake. What are you? Some white knight? You think those bitches are going to care that I've said two measly words? Let me give you some cash. You can buy all the virgins you want and put them in a special house and keep them from everyone. You can set up your own little nunnery where only you get to diddle the little girls. That's what you like, isn't it?"

I've dragged this out long enough, I decide. I don't care to hear any slander against the relationship I have with Bitsy. It's like she says, the only opinions that matter are ours.

"What I like isn't important. I'm here for one reason. As you told me, death is the only way out," I remind him.

"Not my death," he protests.

"You weren't specific," I say, and then I put a bullet in his brain and end him.

42

BITSY

"Come on. Come on," I plead with my phone. "You've been in there twenty minutes. You said that would take ten, tops."

I shake the device in frustration. I hate sitting on my ass doing nothing. It seems like all I've done for the last five years is to wait for that man. Next time—God forbid that there should be a next time—I'm going in because he shouldn't be doing this alone. Someone needs to watch his back and that's clearly my job. I'll spend every day practicing with a hand gun. I'll learn martial arts: judo, taekwondo, karate—

"Miss?"

I look up from the phone to see a patrolman knocking his baton against my car window. *Oh my God.* I let out a yelp and drop my device. It tumbles to the floor between my legs. The cop glares at me in suspicion and knocks harder.

I roll down the window immediately. "Yessir?" I'm a young woman sitting outside a hotel slash nightclub wearing sweats, a tank top and my hair's in a messy bun. It's not exactly club gear. After all my yapping to Leka to be careful and I'm the one that gets caught? I'll never see the outdoors during my twenties. He'll have me locked up tight somewhere until I can prove I'm not a hazard.

"You've been sitting here for fifteen minutes in a no loading zone."

"Um, right, well, you see..." *Think, you idiot. Think.* "I'm waiting for someone."

"Clearly. Let me see your license."

Think harder! My heart thuds hard and fast against my chest.

"It's my grandma," I say impulsively. "Her apartment's being treated for bed bugs, so my dad put her up here for the night, but she's old and has a tendency to wander around."

"It's midnight," the cop points out.

Sweat dampens my forehead. He obviously doesn't believe me because no one would put their grandma in the Bennington, a hotel that has a reputation for hosting the hippest parties in town. Grandmas go to nice, quiet hotels, not ones that have a ton of paparazzi waiting on the curb outside in hopes of catching cheating celebs in the act.

Paparazzi. That's it!

"Okay, you caught me. I'm with the GlossUp." I flash my insurance card quickly as if it's a form of press credential. "I'm trying to run down a story. I heard that Kiwi LaVante is seeing Jack Torin on the sly. If I get a pic or video of them together, I can pay my rent for like three months."

Interest flicks across the cop's face before he quickly replaces it with bored dislike. He tugs down his cap. "Doesn't matter. You can't park your car in a no loading zone. Now get going."

I open my mouth to object when the phone buzzes between my feet. It's hard to read the words, but I think it says, *lose the cop. I'm done.*

I flash the officer a smile and put the car in gear. "I'll drive around the block," I say.

"Drive around the block and keep going," he says sternly, tapping his baton against the side of my car.

I pull out into traffic slowly, avoiding a few staggering patrons. In my rearview mirror, the cop is watching me, so I don't dare stop. Leka walks to the end of the street and turns left. I can't follow because it's a one-way street with traffic slowing south. I get his plan. I drive down one block, turn left. Up on the corner, I spot him on the side of the street. He's removed his stocking cap. His hands are shoved into his jacket. I slow down, barely stopping. He climbs in the back.

My heart is galloping and my sweaty hands can barely keep a grip around the steering wheel.

"Everything okay?" The words come out high-pitched and tinny.

He gives me a lopsided smile. "Everything's okay."

I take off again and watch him in the rearview mirror as he begins to undress. The jacket goes first. He one hands his shirt, reaching over his shoulder to grab a handful of fabric and then pulling the garment up and over his head. He winces as he does this.

His whole body must ache. Even in the dim light, I can see the bruises on his face. The top of his left cheek has swelled so much that it's starting to impact his vision. The bandages on his left hand are soaked with blood. I can tell by the way he's holding his arm close to his ribcage that it hurts for him to even breathe.

He grabs the bottle of antiseptic from one of the duffles on the floor and pours it over one hand, hissing loudly as the alcohol eats away at the germs. Tears wet my eyes. I wish I could take his pain away.

"It looks worse than it is," he says, reading my mind.

"I didn't think it looked bad at all," I lie. "I've had paper cuts at school that went deeper than some of your wounds."

He huffs out a small laugh. "Tell me what forest the tree came from so I can punish it for hurting you."

"Not until you tell me the name of everyone who's ever hurt you," I parry.

The humor falls away from his face. "There's no one who's left, Bit. It's all done. You're safe now. No need to cry."

"And you?" I press because I don't give a shit about myself. "I'm not crying because I was scared I was going to be hurt. These"—I flick the moisture away—"these are for you. My tears are always for you. If you're not safe, I will always be afraid. If you're hurt, I will always be in pain. I love you, Leka. You are my life. I've never wanted money or things or other people. I've only ever wanted you."

A rough, hot hand wraps around my neck. He presses his lips to the back of my head and I find it hard to see. Too bad there aren't eye wipers that can clear away the tears.

"I love you, Bit. We're going to be fine. Keep driving. We're going to be fine."

And so I keep driving, holding on to that promise, holding on to his love until the tears dry up, the clouds clear, and the sun breaks through the morning sky. I keep going until the promise he's made from the moment he found me comes true.

"YOU'RE GETTING DARK," LEKA SAYS, RUNNING A FINGER OVER my arm.

I crack open my eyes a tiny amount. "It's the sun. It's so close. There's no sunscreen powerful enough to withstand the rays here." Especially not when you're spending most of your days lying on a cushion, drinking from a mini punch bowl out under the tropical sun. I reach out a languid arm and pat around for the bottle of sunscreen. My fingers hit the small plastic, but before I can grab it, Leka swipes it away. "Hey, I can do that," I protest.

"I know you can," he says. "But this gives me an excuse to touch you."

"I didn't know you needed one." I watch him from under the brim of my hat as he squirts a generous amount of lotion onto his palm. He's dark, too. Two years of island living has that effect. Everyone's melanin is popping and it's beautiful.

He picks up one of my bare legs and props my foot against his stomach. Against my toes, his muscled abdomen flexes as he starts to smooth the liquid over my skin. He might've lost his pale winter skin, but his body remains as hard as it's ever been.

"Was there anything in the mail?"

Before I fell asleep, Leka told me he was going to go into town to get the mail.

"A couple of DVDs. A part for that radio I'm fixing up."

I nudge him with my toes. "Anything else?"

"Were you expecting something?"

"Yes." I tap him again. "And if you opened my package, I will get my revenge."

His beautiful lips curve up. "Your Hershey's Kisses, all 64 ounces of them, are unopened in the kitchen."

"Your life is saved," I announce and lie back. I peer through my eyelashes. He's beautiful to look at, glorious to touch, and delectable to taste. With him in front of me, I forget why I so desperately needed chocolate the other night. There's nothing sweeter than him. I run my tongue across my lower lip.

He pauses mid-sweep, his fingers tightening around my right calf. "You hungry?"

We both know he's not talking about food. I smooth a hand over my burgeoning stomach. "When am I not?"

Leka glides upward to rub his cheek against the small bump. "Then we'll need to feed her."

"It's a him," I correct but pat the top of his head to lessen the sting.

Leka's wanted the baby to be a girl since the moment we discovered I was pregnant.

"Could be a her," he stubbornly insists. He rises and then helps me to my feet. I'm drowsy from the sun and from the lazy lovemaking we'd engaged in before my nap.

He pulls a yellow gauze dress peppered with bright blue flowers over my head. We laugh because my arms don't seem to be working properly and keep getting in his way. He finally gets the swath of fabric over my head and then tucks me against him.

I lean into that powerful frame of his and allow him to half carry me into the kitchen, where we find a platter of fresh fruit on the counter and the makings of sandwiches in the refrigerator, courtesy of the part-time housekeeper Leka employed when I found out I was pregnant. The man has read every article on the internet about pregnancy and is convinced that any amount of work is too much. To say that he's overprotective would be an understatement.

I let him think I'm being lazy and when he's gone, I get my stuff done. I've learned to be very efficient. I bypass the fruit and tear open the silvery bag of goodness. The foil-covered Kisses tumble out onto the counter. I unwrap one and pop it into my mouth. Leka starts assembling a sandwich big enough to feed the island.

What a perfect life this is. My child is growing in my belly. I have a huge bag of chocolate lying by my right hand and my very fine man is standing in front of me with his off-white linen pants hanging low around his hips and his red and white cotton shirt unbuttoned enough that I can see the hard slabs of muscle and the sharp V-line definition where his obliques and abs meet. I shift in my seat as my sex starts to throb. Another side effect of pregnancy is constant horniness.

"Which movie do you want to watch? *Italian Job* or *Oceans 8*?" he asks. His head is bent over his culinary masterpiece, so he doesn't see the need in my eyes.

"*Ocean's 8*, of course. Rihanna over everyone."

The corner of his mouth slides up again. "Rihanna it is."

I stick another chocolate into my mouth and watch the best movie reel on the planet—the one involving my gorgeous husband slathering mayo over his bread. It's a simple, domestic scene, but it's my dream come to life, and that is something better than Hollywood could ever conjure up.

There's only one thing I'd change and that's the setting. I rub a hand over my stomach and broach the topic that has been knocking around in my head for the last few weeks. I don't know what he'll say. He's never once shown any dissatisfaction with our current situation. Not many people would. This small patch of land in the Maldives is more beautiful in real life than any picture could convey. The water is so clear that you have to boat out for miles before the bottom disappears from sight. The fruit seems like it is always ripe. The fish are plentiful and the people around us are kind and generous.

If we get the hankering for company, there are several resorts, although they are rarely very busy and the tourists usually keep to themselves. The one thing that paradise is lacking is families. There aren't many families down here, and with a little one on the way and possibly more children to come, I keep thinking that perhaps the island isn't right for us any longer.

Paradise is wonderful for two people with no responsibilities, but now that we're going to have a family, I want to put down roots.

"I think we should go back," I tell him.

"You miss the snow?" he asks mildly and without an ounce of surprise, as if he's been on the same wavelength.

"Yes, as silly as that sounds, I do miss the snow and the pine trees and fall colors and spring rain. I want to live in a neighborhood with a patch of grass that you mow in the summer and a driveway that we have to shovel in the winter. I want to see our kids riding their bikes in a cul-de-sac while I gossip with the neighbors about whether that chorus teacher is part of a cult because she makes the kids sing weird chants."

"Then let's go." He slaps a slice of bread on a mountain of ham, turkey and Swiss and takes a bite.

"Is it still safe?" Once Cesaro died, Arturo's organization suffered one brutal overthrow after another until everyone with strength and power and connections ended up in a body bag. The people that were left standing didn't have the will to hold the gang together. From the last that we'd heard, everyone had died or left. Mary was forced to eat her poisonous cake. Mason ran off and was never heard of again. Snow and the others joined another, smaller gang who boosted cars.

"Yeah. There's nothing left. Marjory's was razed to the ground to make way for a high-rise." He takes another bite. He seems unaffected, but this is Leka. His foot could be blown off and he'd tell me it was a scratch.

"Marjory's was your home for a long time," I say. "It's okay to miss it."

He places his sandwich and reaches for a napkin, which he pats at the corners of his mouth before coming around the island to draw me against him. "I never had a home until I met you. You're my home. You and now the baby inside of you and all the other babies you'll have. Wherever you are that's where I wanna be."

EPILOGUE
ZACH

Many years later

I'm not sure why I agreed to come. The Moore household with the smiley mom and the scary dad scares the shit out of me. I'm the only one that sees the danger. Everyone else calls Mr. Moore by his first name, Leka, like he's not some predator ready to take them all down if they so much as look cross-eyed at his kids. If someone told me that there were bodies found at Tom's Quarry where Mr. Moore works, I wouldn't be surprised.

The Moore house itself makes the back of my neck itch. It's too neat and pretty. The counters are the white expensive kind that my mom sighs over when she watches cable. The kitchen cabinets are a soft gray that remind me of clouds that appear just after it rains in the summer. It smells like vanilla and cinnamon and some other warm, wonderful scent. There's an actual bowl of flowers in the middle of the kitchen table. They're round and really pink.

I hate that I like them. My mom deserves something like this. Instead, our kitchen is crushed beer cans, old cigarette butts, and sticky vinyl flooring. The only thing on our table is a bag of chips that my old man left out after binging the night before. Sometimes there are flies in the kitchen, lapping up spilled milk or melted cheese.

This place doesn't look like it's ever held a piece of garbage or hosted even one fly. Outside, my classmates are already filling the pool. I look down at my oil-stained jeans and my Tom's Quarry basketball T-shirt and know instantly I should leave.

I might go to school with all these kids. I might play on the same club basketball team—the one that Mr. Moore pretty much ordered me to join. I might even eat lunch at the same table, but none of us have a thing in common. I need to get out of here. I need to find Beckett and Kincaid, say my goodbyes, and get the hell out of here before I start melting like the Wicked Witch of the West.

A hard hand lands on my shoulder. I spin around with my fists up only to stare into the unsmiling face of the Moore siblings' father. "Sir."

"Brooks." His gaze falls to my fists, which I quickly hide behind my back. "You forget something at home?"

My good sense, the smartass side of me says. I give that voice a boot in the mouth and manage a respectable, "No, sir."

I'm certain he knows I'm on the verge of fleeing.

He squeezes my shoulder before releasing me. "Good. My kids were looking forward to you coming today."

I don't need a Moore anger translator to understand that means *disappoint my kids and I'll bury your body so far beneath the earth that your fossilized remains won't be discovered until the next millennium*. I'm big on self-preservation, but that's the very reason why I need to leave. The longer I spend in this house with Beckett, the harder it will be for me to give her up. I highly doubt that Mr. Moore wants me around his precious daughter.

I give a short nod and say, "Thank you for inviting me," and turn toward the front door only to be met with a bowl of cut watermelon.

"Oh, Zach, you came! Take this outside for me, will you?" Mrs. Moore shoves the fruit into my stomach and lets go, forcing me to take it.

Or maybe she thought I was going to grab it and didn't realize I was intending to leave. Either way, I'm left with a fruit bowl in my hands.

She waves her fingers toward the deck. "Go on now. Leka, sweetheart, could you come here and look at something? The bulb on the front porch has burned out. We should change it before it gets dark."

Mr. Moore lets his wife drag him away, but he casts a stern glare over his shoulder. *Don't fuck it up*, it says.

Uncertainly, I stand in the now empty kitchen. Does not fucking it up mean I should leave or stay? The back door slides open and a wave of kids crashes through.

"Mom! Dad! We broke the table," Beckett cries. She races across the tile floor, coming to a halt when she sees me. "Zach. Finally! I thought you weren't coming."

My heart thuds against my ribcage at her welcoming smile. She has her hair pulled back with some kind of floral bandana that would probably look ridiculous on anyone else. A see-through yellow shirt covers her arms and shoulders and falls to the top of her thighs. I try not to look at her bare legs. I try very, very hard.

"Yeah," I croak, "here."

I don't have good verbal skills around Beckett Moore. My mind goes south whenever I'm within shouting distance. *Get it together, boy. Her brother's five feet away and her dad's in the other room. Both would squash you like a bug.*

It'd take two of them to get one hand on me and by then I'd have her out the door and in my car, retorts the smartass side.

My smartass side is all brawn, no brains. "Here," I say and start to offer the bowl of fruit and get the hell out of Dodge, but my retreat is stymied again.

"What happened?" queries Mr. Moore, striding back into the kitchen.

"We broke the umbrella off the table," Beckett answers.

We all turn to see the yellow sunbrella lying forlornly on its side. One white, thin metal rod is poking up past the cover it's supposed to hold in place. I brace for an explosion. If we were home, my dad would be screaming by now.

"Thing needed to be replaced last year," Mr. Moore says. "I probably have some tape to hold it in place for now. Be right back."

He disappears out the side door. The latch barely catches before Mindy, a short-haired girl with legs like spindles, cries out. "Your dad is so hot, Beck."

"So hot. Like, if I had daddy issues, he'd be the first person I'd apply to fix them," murmurs her friend Sarah, who swings her heavy blonde hair over one shoulder to better display her huge rack.

"You do have daddy issues," Sam supplies. Sam's the starting guard on the All Star Shooters basketball team.

"Sam. Stop." Mindy slaps Sam playfully on the shoulder.

"What?" Sam protests. "She announced it when Kincaid was role playing as the psychologist in Mrs. P's society and behavioral issues class."

"He has a point," Sarah concedes. "I do have daddy issues and I'd be happy to enact my destructive behaviors all over the Moore men."

"Can we not?" Beckett replies, her dark, gorgeous eyes rolling upward to the ceiling. "He's my dad and he's married."

"Happily," Kincaid adds.

"Sorry. I'll try to contain my thirst," Mindy says, but her grin implies the opposite.

"I'm happy to offer my services," Sam offers. "I can slap an ass with the best of them." He swats the air with the flat of his hand.

Beckett shudders. My fingers tighten around the bowl, ready to crash the plastic against the side of Sam's face.

As if sensing my impending implosion, Kincaid grabs the bowl from my hands and gives it to his sister. "Let's hold off on any sex shows while we're standing in my mom's kitchen," he orders. "I'm going to take Zach up to change."

"Great. See you outside," Beckett chirps, and all thoughts of leaving dissolve like ice cream in July.

"See you outside," I echo and follow her to the deck.

A hand hauls me back. "Swim trunks," Kincaid reminds me.

My cheeks grow hot and I duck my head so Beck's brother can't read every lecherous thought I have in my head. "Yeah, lead the way."

As I'm tracking Kincaid out of the kitchen and across the dining room to the stairs, I hear someone comment, "Your parents are so chill. Mine would've had a cow and a half if we broke a table."

"Mr. Moore wouldn't hurt a flea," a guy proclaims.

I hope my friends are never out alone. They have the instincts of a dodo bird. *Chill, easygoing, laid-back* are never words I'd use to describe Kincaid's dad. Don't they see how he watches everything they do? He's mentally calculating the risk they pose and stands ready to flatten them the second he has a whiff of danger to his family.

I don't think I can come here again. He sees too much. Beckett's a lot like her old man. When we first met, she ignored my frowns, my monosyllabic answers, and my general unfriendly demeanor. She told me once it was because she could tell it was all a front and that she'd wear that same cloak of indifference if she was shuttled around to five schools in six years. She'd said it so matter-of-fact, like my hate-the-world outlook was completely normal, so I couldn't be mad.

Not that anyone could be mad at Beckett Moore for more than a second. She's sunshine personified. Every room she's in is brighter. Every song sounds better. Every piece of food tastes more delicious.

She caught me more effectively than a fisherman's net captures a tuna.

At the top of the stairs, there are three doorways. I force my feet to go left into Kincaid's room instead of to the right, which is Beck's yellow and white garden bedroom. I've caught glimpses of it before—enough that my dreams have a very solid setting of a twin bed covered in yellow and white stripes, floral stickers on the wall, and a yellow rocking chair. I've done a lot of things to Beck on that rocking chair in my dreams. Things that probably aren't legal. Things that aren't physically possible. Things that her brother standing in front of me, rooting around for an extra pair of swim trunks, would likely kill me for if he had a clue.

"These should fit." Kincaid tosses me a pair of shorts. "You can change in the bathroom or here."

"Here's good." Kincaid and his sister share a bathroom. The last time I used it, I almost got caught sniffing her shampoo. It's better I stay away from temptation. Besides, Kincaid and I are teammates. He's seen my junk before, just like I've seen his.

He crosses over to his window that overlooks the backyard and stares down at our friends, giving me a bit of privacy. It takes only seconds to strip out of my jeans, socks, and underwear. My sneakers are at the front door in a pile with everyone else's.

The borrowed swim trunks feel tight around my waist. I cross my arms around my chest, feeling awkward wearing the T-shirt to the pool but knowing that if I take it off, there'll be more questions that I don't want to answer. I should've never come, but those Moore kids are hard to turn down.

Kincaid's still at the window, smiling at something. He's a good friend and a good teammate. I like him—a lot. A sense of shame falls over me. I shouldn't be wearing this dude's swim trunks, eating food in his house, swimming in his pool when all I want to do is run down there, swing Beckett over my shoulder, and find a private place where I can defile her in a million different ways.

"Dude, I want to bone your sister," I blurt out.

"I know."

I nearly swallow my tongue. My jaw comes unhinged and it takes a moment before I can respond. "You know?"

Kincaid lazily turns around, as if I hadn't confessed the worst sin. He snorts. "I'm not blind. Everyone knows."

"When you say everyone..."

"Sarah, Mandy, Sam, Venny, Claud," Kincaid rattles off more names than I know of and ends with, "Mom and Dad."

My knees grow weak. "Your dad?" I bleat.

"My dad," the asshole confirms with a smile.

"Then why am I here?" I fling an arm out. "Why haven't you and your dad taken me to the garage and beaten me senseless with every power tool you have in there? Don't you care about your sister at all? Christ, she needs protection! She's out there alone. She—"

"Have you?" he cuts in.

"Have I what?" My chest is heaving and I'm starting to sweat like I've run a 5K.

"Have you boned her?"

"No!" I shout. "When have I had the opportunity to do that? I've got school and work at the quarry and ball. She's never alone. I don't want—I've never—I would die—" I stop, my thoughts all tumbling together and confused by Kincaid's lack of anger, his gentle questioning. What's going on here? Why am I still standing? Why don't I have a fist in my face? Why hasn't anyone thrown me out the front door and pointed a shotgun in my face, ordering me never to come back?

Kincaid's expression of mild amusement hasn't changed. "If you don't want to ruin our friendship, never want to hurt her, would die before you'd allow any harm come her way, why would I beat your ass? If I pummeled every guy who wanted to sleep with my sister, I'd be in fights every day, which I guess wouldn't be terrible, but my mom would kill me, so I can't go that route. Besides, Becks isn't my property. I don't own her. I can't tell her what she should do. Do you respect my sister?"

So much that I feel guilty even thinking impure thoughts about her. "Yes."

"And you're going to wait until she's ready?"

"Yes."

"Then, no, I'm not going to beat you, and neither is my dad. If you hurt her, then, sure, expect a visit from the two of us. If you don't wait until she's ready, I'll pound your face in until even your mom can't recognize you. After I'm done, my dad will take you apart and bury your bones in the quarry. Otherwise, we're cool."

He pushes away from the wall and walks past me, leaving me open-mouthed and dumbfounded.

At the doorway, he turns back and his easygoing expression is replaced with a hard-eyed glint. "If I ever hear you use disrespectful words toward her again, I will pull your dick up through your esophagus."

I nod, straighten the already situated swim trunks, and stumble after him.

This family...this family is wild. And amazing.

Bitsy

"He's like a wild animal," Leka huffs. "I don't like it."

I rub a hand down my husband's back to soothe him. "He reminds me of someone."

My man jerks back in surprise. "Me? I'm not anything like that kid. That kid is afraid of everything."

"Me. He reminds me of myself." I lean close and tuck my cheek against Leka's smooth cheek. He shaved when he heard the kids were bringing friends over. "I was a scared child and someone saved me."

His hand comes up to press my face closer to his. "That was me being selfish. I was tired of being alone. What reason would Beckett have for dragging this stray off the street?"

"I'd say it's because she's watched her daddy help people all of his life and wants to make him proud."

Leka places a hand on the cherry wood trim at the top of the window and leans forward to watch as Beckett stands in the middle of our small pool and tries to lure Zach Brooks into the water.

He's unsure of everything—the kids, the water, this house. Everything, that is, but Beckett. He adores her. When she's around, he stands up taller. He listens to every word that drops from her lips like she's an oracle sent to him from God above. I guess he's a little of both of us. Scared—like I was—and devoted like Leka.

Zach takes a step toward the pool, but he doesn't move fast enough for either of the Moore kids. My son pushes him in. Beckett holds up her hands to shield herself from the water and screams with laughter. Kincaid performs one of those water bombs where he tucks his large body into a ball and crashes the surface of the water. Droplets spray everyone. The backyard is full of laughter.

My cheeks hurt from smiling. Had I ever imagined my life would be so perfect? So full?

Leka sighs and pushes away from the window. "He better not hurt her," he mutters as he walks over to the sofa.

Kincaid tries to splash Beckett, and Zach somehow is able to sweep my daughter out of range and simultaneously dunk my son under the water. "He'd rather cut off his arm," I observe.

I leave the kids in peace and join Leka on the sofa. His arm comes up to cup my shoulders.

"Life is good, isn't it?" There's an undercurrent of wonderment. Even after all these years, Leka still can't believe his good fortune.

"Better than I ever imagined." I kiss his cheek. He tries very hard to present a clean-cut suburban appearance as far from his gangster past as possible. I suppose to the untrained eye, he appears a quiet, even-tempered dad of two. He has a barbecue, which he never uses, and khakis, which he's never worn, but there's an edge that's baked into him. His eyes are always watchful. His hand often strays to his side where his shoulder holster used to hang. His showers are always scorching hot. There's a go bag in every closet in the house and a panic room in the basement. But because of him, our kids have never known true fear. They've never gone to bed with an empty stomach. They've always had love.

They are blessed because of Leka. We are all so blessed. My heart swells with emotion.

"I love you," I whisper against the hard line of his jaw.

He tilts his head and gazes down at me with a searching glance. "What's this about?"

"Can't I say I love you for no reason?" I press another kiss on the underside of his chin and am rewarded with a swift intake of breath. He's surprisingly sensitive here. Sometimes I shave him, but only at night, after the kids have gone to bed because he never allows me to finish.

"You can, but in that tone?" He seems semi-scandalized. "There are kids here." He nods toward the backyard.

I wriggle onto his lap and wrap my arms around his neck. "They're old enough to take care of themselves."

A speculative light twinkles in my husband's eyes. "Are you suggesting we leave them alone?"

I trace my thumb over the edge of one of Leka's ears. He shivers. "I'm suggesting we draw the curtains and lock the door and that I do things to you that would horrify and embarrass our children should they ever find out."

As always, I don't have to ask twice.

He springs to his feet.

"Get the door," he orders.

Giddy, I do as he says. I don't make it back to the sofa. He catches me and pushes me up to the door.

"We'll have to be quick." His eyes gleam in suppressed excitement.

I grab hold of his shoulders as he hitches me up. "This is deliciously naughty. I doubt I'll last long."

He dives for my mouth, parting my lips with his own. I dig my hands into his silky hair and hold him close. We kiss with enough passion to illuminate the entire sky, as if this is our first time and our last time. In other words, we kiss as we always do, with our whole hearts full of fire and love that will burn eternally in this life and every other life because no matter what happens, we will always find each other.

#GETSACKED

BY JEN FREDERICK

Available Now

What he wants he gets...

Knox Masters is a quarterback's worst nightmare. Warrior. Champion. And...virgin. Knox knows what he wants--and he gets it. All American Football player? Check. NFL pros scouting him? Check. Now, he's set his sight on two things. The national title. And Ellie Campbell. Sure, she's the sister of his fellow teammate, but that's not going to stop him. Especially not when he's convinced Ellie is the one.

...but he's never met her before.

But Ellie isn't as sure. She's trying to start a new life and she's not interested in a relationship...with anyone. Beside it's not just her cardinal rule of never dating her brother's teammates that keeps her away, but Ellie has a dark secret that would jeopardize everything Knox is pursuing.

Knox has no intention of losing. Ellie has no intention of giving in.

ABOUT THE AUTHOR

Jen Frederick is the USA Today bestselling author of *Unspoken*, part of the Woodlands series, and *Sacked*, part of the Gridiron series. She is also the co-author of the *New York Times* Bestselling series, The Royals. She lives in the Midwest with a husband who keeps track of life's details while she's writing, a daughter who understands when Mom disappears into her office for hours at a time, and a rambunctious dog who does neither.

Drop her a line:
jenfrederick.com
jensfrederick@gmail.com